WATSON'S SAMPLER:
THE LOST CASEBOOK OF
SHERLOCK HOLMES

William F. Watson, Jr.

Watson's Sampler:
The Lost Casebook of Sherlock Holmes

Copyright © 2006 Stagecoach Press

www.stagecaochpress.com

You may contact the author at, (401) 683-1729

Cover design and layout by Will Watson

Previously published as: Watson's Sampler and The Lost Casebook of Sherlock Holmes.

Watson's Sampler:
The Lost Casebook of Sherlock Holmes

WATSON'S SAMPLER: THE LOST CASEBOOK OF SHERLOCK HOLMES

Watson's Sampler:
The Lost Casebook of Sherlock Holmes

THE MATTER OF THE CHRISTMAS GIFT

DEDICATED TO LOUISE

Watson's Sampler:
The Lost Casebook of Sherlock Holmes

INTRODUCTION

For anyone who has ever felt that truth is stranger than fiction, and has therefore fallen under the watchful eye of the skeptics; I have for you a case study, which not only adds credence to your feeling, it downright proves it. Truth, in fact, at times, is stranger than fiction, as I will show you in the next few paragraphs.

As any Sherlockian will tell you, John Watson was a longtime friend and associate of the late Sherlock Holmes. They might also mention the fact that Watson recounted some 43% of the cases, which the predominant and reclusive Sherlock Holmes solved in their many years of acquaintance. Finally, they might also relate that Watson was a gentleman of the finest sort, having wooed and wed two women of whom I am about to speak.

The first wife of John Watson was one Mary Morstan, and the story of their meeting and eventual love can be detailed by a simple reading of "A Sign of Four." It is generally regarded as true, and is stated in The Sherlock Holmes Encyclopedia that the union of Mary Morstan and John Watson was, while loving, a barren one, and I quote, "At most the marriage lasted six years, and apparently they had no children."[1]

It is on this point which I must differ. You see, it has recently come to my attention that John Watson and Mary Morstan did have a child, a daughter in fact. She was born on December 21, in the year of our Lord 1888. Premature perhaps, but born none the less. Her name was Susan and she was much adored by both John and Mary. Life was good for all of them and it undoubtedly would have stayed that way, were it not for the untimely death of Susan's mother, Mary. You see, it seems that while John Watson was a good and caring man, he was no match for the rigors of child rearing. Realizing this fact, and knowing that he could not continue his practice, his involvement with the great Holmes and raise a young lady, whose special needs he could not begin to fathom or predict, John Watson was compelled to relinquished the upbringing of his only offspring to the care of The Pingley Boarding School, one of London's finest.

Nearly ten years passed, in which time young Susan became both literate and beautiful while remaining with the nurses and teachers who brought The Pingley Boarding School such fame. But during these ten years, John Watson had met and wed a second woman of which I can recant little. In fact, if we turn to The Sherlock Holmes Encyclopedia once again, we can see another note which states "There is no data on this second marriage; we do not even know her name."[2]

---

[1] Orland Park; "The Encyclopedia of Sherlock Holmes"; Copyright 1962; Citadel Press; ppg. 189 & 190

[2] Orland Park; "The Encyclopedia of Sherlock Holmes"; Copyright 1962; Citadel Press; ppg. 189 & 190

Watson's Sampler:
The Lost Casebook of Sherlock Holmes

It is to their matrimonial home that Susan was summoned and received the most cordial and tender reception. But this cordiality was not to remain. Perhaps it was the progressive teaching she received at Pingley's or perhaps it was the independent disposition that pervades a child who has lost one parent and is then separated from the other for too long, but Susan and her new step-mother never secured a mutual covenant. There were arguments and hurt feelings and all the things that make life hard for those not bound by blood. That is why, in May of 1906, at the tender age of seventeen years, Susan took the name of Pingley (it is rumored that this name change was more to escape the glare that comes from being the daughter of a then famous author, than for any other reason) and moved lock, stock and barrel to the United States.

It was there, in a place called Newport, Rhode Island where she met and wed one Edward Mitchell "Sniper" James, in September of that same year, 1906. By September of the following year, two months before her nineteenth birthday, Susan James gave birth to Anna Louise James, my mother.

Now as coincidence or the calling forth of greatness may have it, Anna Louise James met and loved and wed one William F. Watson, of no relation to her grandfather, John.

I was born of this union, and being of a curious mind and dedicated to knowing all things "Watson," I read all of the works of my then unbeknown great grand father.

It was not until the death of my mother, in November 1998, and the ensuing rummage of her personal possessions that I uncovered the trove of notes, thoughts and recants that her mother had received from her famous father, and had passed down to her daughter, Anna Louise.

You can imagine my amazement at this find. I was beside myself as to what to do, until it struck me like a bolt from above. I will continue the work my great grand father started. I have the treasure of these documents in hand and the ability to be a scribe, not writing myself but merely rewriting the marvelous cases and baffling workings of the mind of Sherlock Holmes as described by the notes passed down to me from my great grandfather John H. Watson, M.D.

Here is the first...

THE MATTER OF
THE CHRISTMAS GIFT

From the Files of John H. Watson, M.D.
Presented By William F. Watson, Jr.

Sherlock Holmes was not fond of holidays. "Too much fiddle-faddle and not enough substance," he used to say before retiring to bed in our lodgings at Baker Street. He was most demonstrative and, as I remember it now, looking back in time, he was the most demonstrative at Christmas time.

I can remember one Christmas in particular. It was Christmas Eve to be exact. A light snow had fallen which was unusual for London at this time of year. Early winter is cold and wet, but rarely do we see any glistening from the skies until at least mid February. But, as I said, a light snow had fallen which made the streets and byways outside of 221B look as if a warm, white coat had been laid upon them. There was hustle and bustle everywhere in the city with the populous scurrying too and fro in preparation for the night of nights, Christmas Eve. Carolers stopped by shops and doorways to lend their charms to the occasion and perhaps pick up a shilling or two along the way. It was rumored that the Baker Street irregulars had quite a chorale, which patrolled this very neighborhood, but never stopped at 221B. Holmes would not have it.

I was at my perch with a mild tea and cinnamon, which Mrs. Hudson had prepared for the occasion, while Holmes busied himself at the window searching out the urchins who clambered about in the snow. His look was far away and if I might say, seemed a bit sad, as if he really wanted to be a part of all this merriment but just couldn't bring himself to it. As I recall, I almost felt sympathetic to his condition, until I reminded myself that this was a self imposed exile, which he would not relent. The mere mention of any display of joy or good cheer would no doubt bring forth a tirade of how impractical men's minds are, to be making merry while the world as we knew it went to hell in a hand basket. Holmes may have been of a singular and particular temperament about such things, but since he was never to be swayed, I had long since ceased any attempt.

I, on the other hand, was quite jovial at this time of year. Mrs. Hudson and I exchanged gifts regularly on December the 25th and to say that I was not looking forward to tomorrow's feast and the presents of woven mittens and scarves that came my way each year, would be a lie and make me unworthy of such delights. I liked Christmas and all that went with it. It was often the only time of year when strangers and kinsmen alike treated each other cordially and with the respect each living being really deserves. Holmes' opinion of this type of behavior was to proclaim that if we each deserved the treatment we gave and received at Christmas, then we should receive and give it all year long. My thoughts in that vein were that Holmes was correct as usual, but if we only saw this condition in our fellows and ourselves but once a year, it was better than never at all. "A bit of something is always better than nothing," I would remark when the subject was broached. But Holmes would only grunt in reply and then drop the whole silly matter, because to Holmes it was silly.

Still, as I saw him standing there, pipe in hand, looking so sullen on such a festive evening as this, I couldn't help but reach out to him in spirit, in hopes that he might someday join the fray and wish us all a Merry Christmas.

The evening grew old. Noises and clattering from the streets lulled until only the occasional clip-clop of a horse and carriage, from some stray lingerer at a party, passed our way. Holmes sat across from me taking long pulls on his pipe, which became smoke wreaths from his mouth in some distracted, repetitive schedule, which bespoke of his waning thoughts or memories. The fire was now a low glow in our grate and though the night was cold, its life had been busy for hours, filling the rooms with that cozy air of contentment that covers people like the quilt, which lies on feather beds. My brandy glass was empty and my cigar all but done when I bid my friend good-eve and started for my room.

"Before you go Watson, I want to thank you," he said in a quiet, uncharacteristic tone. "You stay with me each year on this cold night, although I know that you would much rather be frolicking with all the other good Christians. I want you to know that I realize your sacrifice, having to stay penned up with an old stump such as I. It seems to me that in this time of charity and merriment, it is always the least deserving who seem to take the greatest gifts, and I want you to know that your friendship has always been the greatest gift I ever received."

I must admit I was taken aback by this upheaval of what could only be labeled as emotion from my friend. I remember spilling out something like, "stop the nonsense old boy," or something of the like as I toddled off to my room quite flushed, leaving him alone with his pipe and his thoughts.

Before long I was asleep, not knowing what had become of Holmes or his curious thinking about holidays and friends.

I had slept what must have been a dreamless sleep, for it seemed that my head had just hit the pillow when I was shaken awake by the towering figure of Sherlock Holmes.

"Get up, old boy," he said with that glimmer in his eye which speaks of mysteries on the prowl, "we have company." And he was out of the room before I could even sit up.

The sitting room was a gloomy sight as the gas lamps seemed to protest their awakening at the hand of Holmes and Mrs. Hudson.

There, in the center of the room, looking very uncomfortable and perhaps even a bit ashamed, stood a burley man of middle age in rough but clean clothing. He seemed to shift his weight from one foot to the other as the new light from each lamp flickered and danced about his form. He held his hat in two massive hands, twisting it as he awaited the interview he obviously desired.

Soon the sitting room gained its familiar shape and glowed again with the warmth that only fire seems to bring to light, and so we turned our attention to our nervous guest. Holmes motioned for us all to sit, although only he and I took chairs.

Mrs. Hudson spoke first.

"This is Mr. Haggerty, gentlemen," she said, "he's our butcher from down the way," and she motioned to the wall in back of Holmes. "He's come to us with a problem that he feels only Mr. Holmes can solve, beggin' your pardon Doctor," she said with a nod to me, which I returned. "I know he would never come here at this hour, on this night, if his business were not of the utmost importance," and she followed that with, "I'd never let him in otherwise," under her breath. "I just want you both to know that this is a good and honest man, and you should both listen intently to whatever he has to say, — because whatever it is, I know he'll only speak the truth."

I had never seen Mrs. Hudson in such a state. She spoke to us with a mother's brow rather than that of a landlady. I think we both sat up straighter as she chose her words. Before she left us, she clapped her hand hard on Haggerty's back and said lowly, "go ahead John, don't be afraid of these two. Speak your mind man." Then, before turning to go, she looked both Holmes and I in the eyes, dead on, as if to end her introduction of John Haggerty with one last exclamation point. And her point was well made.

With Mrs. Hudson gone, we once again turned our attention to our new found friend, who faced us standing with his shoulders slumped a bit and with his head down, although not enough so that he could not read our faces as he spoke. His voice was strong and smooth, and came from deep inside his chest, and though it wavered slightly in his excitement, you could tell the power of the man from it.

"I am at a loss as to what to do gentlemen," he started. "I feel my home has been invaded, with such foul trickery as to send me to prison, and I don't know what I can do about it." He began to shake just a little and the thought crossed my mind that he might not be able to continue should this keep up, but as if on cue Mrs. Hudson reappeared with tea and some cakes which gave us all a moment to breath.

We got him to a chair and bade him calm himself enough that he might take some tea. The mantel clock struck four as we waited. After a few moments, as tea and quiet seemed to take its effect Holmes said, "please Mr. Haggerty, tell us everything, but in order so that we might better understand." Holmes then steepled his index fingers under his top lip, as was his custom, and hunkered down in his favorite sitting chair to pay strictest attention.

Mr. Haggerty took a minute; I think to gather his thoughts in chronological order and began again in an even tone. "Well, gentleman, if you have been following the reports of late, you probably already know that there has been a rash of thefts throughout the countryside. I say thefts rather than robberies because no one, as yet, has been 'held up,' no boodle has been found and worst of all, no suspects have been arrested. At least that's what 'The Times' says."

Holmes nodded in agreement to this.

"Now if you've read the reports, and obviously you have Mr. Holmes, you know that these crimes have always occurred while the chimney sweeps have been at work. And the chimney sweeps have been at work quite a bit lately."

"Why do you say that" Holmes broke in.

"Well, it's because of that Clement Moore fellow, across the way there in America. With his Saint Nicholas comin' down the chimney nonsense. He's got the upper crust all head up over it. From what I hears, the children are agog from hearin' that nursery rhyme of his and are ballin' their eyes out until mum and pop make preparations for his visit. Sweepin' the chimney is part of them preparations."

"Extraordinary," I said out loud. "How did you come by such knowledge as this Mr. Haggerty?"

"By conversation with my delivery man, that's how, sir."

"You have a delivery man, Mr. Haggerty," Holmes inquired at this juncture. "From what Mrs. Hudson has said over the years I thought your shop was rather small."

"It is, sir. But at this time of year demand is high with everyone, even those who can't afford it, savin' up their pennies for a Christmas goose and what not. We get right busy around the shop and I have little time to drop off meats and poultry to my regular customers up on the hill there, so I hires me a deliveryman every year. It was he, who told me about that Clement Moore fella havin' heard of him at the homes he delivers to."

"Well, it's pretty well known that the Bobbies suspect them chimney sweeps about pickin' off them knick-knacks from those wealthy folk on the hill, but they ain't never been able to pin nothin' on 'em because they ain't never found no loot."

"Well tonight I think I found some," and he nodded. "And in me own house too."

Holmes looked across at me and then slowly back to our guest. "Very interesting," he said without inflection, "Continue on if you would."

"You see Mr. Holmes, it all started when I bought this coat for my wife for Christmas. It took me since June to save the money," and his speech began to become a little hurried again. "You see my daughter, Amy, she has a condition, a condition that I fear is robbing her of one of God's most precious gifts," and he began to sniffle a little as he talked. "I mean, she's just the sweetest little thing and, and I don't understand why, why this should happen to her," and his voice trailed off as though he might break down at any minute.

"There, there," I put in, for want of something better to say, "is it as bad as all that?"

"I fear she's going blind, Doctor," he said with a tear in each of his big, strong, pained eyes.

"Blind! My word," I said. "Well, who has been treating her?"

"That's just it, Doctor, no one has been treating her. We've been saving every shilling to try to secure some help for her, but times is hard. Hard enough that my wife has gone through the last three winters without a decent coat to keep her warm. She hasn't asked for one. She hasn't complained, but we're almost to the point in our savin's where we can afford a man to look at Amy, and I thought that if I could scrape enough together to get my wife a coat for Christmas, we might break through the unhappiness that's been our lot and start anew. And then this happened."

"Well what happened, man," Holmes threw his hand out as if exasperated to get to the point.

Haggerty took a moment and a deep breath. His voice went low and at a steady pace once again. "So I buys the coat," he said. "Nothing fancy, mind you, just somethin' new, somethin' to keep my Mary warm. I wrapped it in butcher paper and set it out with the presents we bought for Amy," and his voice rose a notch, "who knows how long she'll have to enjoy them." He breathed again to gain control. "So I sets it out with the other stuff," he said.

"Well, Mr. Holmes, you know how children are at Christmas," and he seemed to brighten. "All excitement and eagerness, you know. By three-thirty this very morning Amy had us up to see what Father Christmas has brought. What treasures lie waiting in the dark, you know? We all tumbled out of bed and made our way into the parlor by the fireplace. There it was, all laid out just like me and the Mrs. had left it. A few boxes, a bag or two, ribbon and the like, and on the table by the door where I had left it yesterday morning was the package wrapped in butcher's paper."

"Excuse me, sir," Holmes interrupted again, "isn't it peculiar that your wife would leave a bundle wrapped in butchers paper by the door for an entire day? Wouldn't she think that it's the Christmas goose or something?"

"No, Mr. Holmes," Haggerty replied, "Mary would never touch it for two reasons. First, I have our Christmas goose delivered to my own home by my deliveryman every Christmas eve. You see, with all the business and hustle and bustle around my shop at this time of year, I'm afraid I'll forget the meat and be the only man in town forced to eat soup on the Lord's birthday. I always send the meat home with Roger the deliveryman. And now the second reason I know Mary would never touch the bundle is because she knows it's a present of some kind. We always wrap our presents in butcher's paper. It's one of the good things about being a butcher, plenty of meat and plenty of paper," and he almost chuckled to himself at the simple logic of it.

"But now back to what happened, if you don't mind Mr. Holmes."

Holmes fluttered his hand at the man in the off handed way he'd bid people to continue at times, and Haggerty began again.

"So the package is still where I left it, and I figures why not give it to my Mary right now, while we're all up and ready for fun. Amy had already ripped open her first thing and was playing with the rag doll we got her, making it dance and such, you know. Mary was watchin' her and it seemed the perfect picture of a London Christmas, so I stole over to the table and gathered up the bundle without either of them noticing. Well, gentlemen, you should have seen her face when I handed her the package. I don't think she's ever been more surprised. She had thought that I had gotten something else for Amy, you see. She never thought I'd go and get something just for her. And gentlemen, I want you to know, my heart nearly melted at the sight of that bright and generous face looking up at me in such wonder."

"She ripped the paper open immediately, of course, and rolled out the coat and held it up to her. Gentlemen, I felt the heart in me, which had one moment earlier been lighter than air, drop to the depths of my belly. Even in the dimness of our parlor, as Mary spun around, I could tell that this was not the coat I had purchased. This coat was of far greater value than anything I could afford."

11

"You should see it Mr. Holmes. It is made of fur; I mean the finest fur I've ever seen. And the color, why it's the deepest amber, orange and white marbled into a pattern that is truly exquisite. A coat for a Queen, it is sir, not a butcher's wife. Not that my Mary don't deserve the best, mind ya, but this coat is far too grand for any common citizen."

"So there we was, my Mary, twirllin' but slowly stoppin' as she realized what she had hold of, my Amy clappin' her hands and dancin' around with her new doll in the ignorance of innocence, and me standin' dumb struck as I realized the ramifications to come when word got out of this marvelous coat. And as we're standin' there, I also noticed this strange line on the floor. We set all lamps alight and what do we see, but a line of tiny footprints, like a child might make, going back and forth from the fire box to the table where the coat lay wrapped as it was before Mary opened it."

"What flies to my mind immediate like, is them chimney sweeps, leavin' this parcel inside my home to make me run afoul of the law. To frame me and set the Bobbies on me, should my Mary wear this garment out of doors."

"But I swear to you Mr. Holmes and to you Doctor, that I don't know where it came from, sir, or where the coat that I purchased has got off to, but I knew in a moment that somethin' was dreadfully wrong, so I came straight away to your door. I mean, do you think that this fur could be part of the boodle them blokes have been liftin' from knob hill?"

Holmes was on his feet in an instant and strode to the window. "Gather your coat and hat, Watson," he said peering out. "I want to have a look at this scene."

We were ready momentarily, but as we were leaving Holmes bade us to wait out of doors. He had forgotten his note pad in his room he said, and off he went to retrieve it.

Once outside it was clear that there had been a second round of snowfall on the city. There was no one about at this hour and I heard old Ben strike five in the far off distance as I gazed in wonder at the beauty of the blanket that cover everything in sight. The contrast of white earth and black sky was as striking as anything I had ever seen. The lack of pedestrian traffic had made it possible for the new fall to cover all traces that a throng of hearty holiday fare had trampled these thoroughfares throughout, just hours before. The gas lamps that dotted the byways threw a glistening of gold at every corner, as if crushed diamonds had been strewn about with the direct purpose of catching those rays. Here and there a light burned in the rooms and apartments that filled our neighborhood, as other enthusiasts of the day started early, so as to celebrate longer. It was as though I had never been here before, standing with my new, forlorn friend in front of my very quarters, as if no impurity should or could invade the perfection of that night. It was still and clear and crisp and fresh, as intended by the namesake of the day, I thought.

I, of course, was roused from my reverie by the practicality that is Sherlock Holmes, as he brusquely closed the door behind him and came to our side.

"No traps available tonight, I'm afraid sir," said Haggerty, "but it's not a far walk, if you don't mind."

"Not at all sir," Holmes came back, " the air will do us all good."

We started off on our march to the Haggerty's quarters, but after a few steps I noticed that Holmes had not kept pace. Turning about to check what had become of him, I saw the strangest thing. Here was Holmes, standing just outside our door, gazing about in much the same manner as I had moments before. It was as if he were seeing London for the first time I thought, as he took this moment to observe our city without the clamor it was famous for. Haggerty stopped a few steps further and turned to see what the matter might be. I waved him quiet, as I wanted to watch this unique event a bit longer. I must admit to you now, looking back on things, that I am not sure whether I was more mesmerized at Holmes having an obvious emotional moment with himself, than he was with that moment.

In due time I called out, "is everything all right, Holmes," and he snapped back to his senses and kept a brisk pace thereafter through the tangle of streets and alleyways that led to Haggerty's door.

But I must say once again that the city was a wonder that night. The storm had passed and the sky was filled with stars, which only seemed to serve as a reflection of the sparkle that was London. Even the darkest alleys looked inviting. There were no animals to be seen. No dogs or cats or noisy horses. The city was quiet and glorious, as if all occupants were locked up tight, safe and sound in their warm beds. I had never felt that way about this place before, and I dare say, I have never felt that way about it since, but that night, that march to Haggerty's, left an indelible impression and made me love this place all the more in the years to come.

Haggerty's home, like Haggerty's clothes was rough but clean and warm. Mrs. Haggerty and Amy sat up awaiting our arrival and keeping vigil over the infamous coat, which was the object of our quest. They would not sit near the thing. It lay on the very table it came from, by the door, as they sat clear across the room, watching it as if it might leap up all of a sudden and dash up the chimney, were it not guarded. Our arrival brought them to their feet, standing at attention like two soldiers awaiting orders. Holmes, as was his custom, went right to work examining the garment as soon as his foot was in the door, and I, as was my custom, made and received the necessary introductions and exchanges which are the very cornerstone of civility.

Mrs. Haggerty was a very pleasant woman, handsome in her own way. You could tell from her speech and the way that she carried herself that she was a no nonsense, hard working individual. After an apology for waking us as they had done, and the assurance that her husband could not have done anything wrong, Mrs. Haggerty set off to the kitchen to fetch tea and cookies, while I turned my attention to young Amy.

She was the most adorable little thing. She must have been about eleven at the time. Bright and straight with long blonde hair that seemed to glow, even in the dim light of the Haggerty home. There she stood holding a rag doll and smiling as if she had no idea that there was trouble in the house. "Merry Christmas", she said as I approached her, "are you a friend of my fathers?"

"Why, yes, I guess I am," I replied not knowing to what extent her understanding of the circumstances were, and not wanting to discourage her in any event. "We've come to see your mother's coat, and I would very much like to take a good look at you. You see, I'm a Doctor."

"I see," she replied, and looked off to my left for a moment in deep thought. It was apparent that this child had never seen a Doctor before, and I could almost see her mind at work wondering how to act and what to say.

"Do you think you can save my eyes," she said when she returned from her concentration.

"I don't know my child, but what I do know is this, if we are going to try to do something, the sooner we get started the better. Don't you think?"

"Yes, indeed I do," she said as if this were her opinion as well.

I don't believe I was ever so taken with a child as I was that night. She stood there straight as I examined her, looking ahead, listening to and answering every question clearly and concisely. She did not seem to feel self-conscious at all and kept to the task at hand until it was complete. The brave little soldier to the end I thought, and my heart within me yearned to be able to help her. She told me that when she first started noticing her vision change about a year prior, her first realization came when the things farthest away began to blur, especially at night. As time went on, the blurriness got closer and closer, until now she was at seven feet. She could still see forms and colors mind you, but features and lineal distinction had faded into the mass these forms became as things got worse.

Her pupils were reactant to light and she had the full range of motion needed in sight, but aside from these cursory indications that there was no muscular damage, I was at a loss to diagnose the problem.

"She will need a specialist," I told her father when my exam was complete. "I have heard of a young oculist named Sir Arthur in the Charing Cross district who I am sure would be happy to take the case. He is new at his practice, which is beneficial to us in that he will no doubt be inexpensive and available most likely. I'll get a message to him in the morning so that young Amy here," and I paused to find that the young girl had wandered over to Holmes' side, apparently to offer her assistance, "might get the attention she requires..." And my words and thoughts trailed off as I saw Miss Amy engage Sherlock Holmes in conversation.

Now it is fairly well known that Sherlock Holmes does not tolerate children very well. I don't think it's because he doesn't like them particularly, I just think that because of their tender years and lack of experience, Holmes finds them of little use, especially in any investigation. My first instinct, when I saw this moppet headed toward the master of scowls, was to hail her and bid her come back to me, but on second thought, the notion of Holmes bantering with this small but positive force interested me, so I stood back to watch the show.

"Young lady, be careful where you walk," were Holmes first words to the waif.

"I'm always careful, sir," she replied strongly, "you see, my eyes are not so good, and if I'm not careful my mother says I will tip something over."

Holmes gave her a long look, as if measuring her and then to my amazement he said, "stand here if you must," and pointed to the floor by his right side.

Amy obeyed without a word and stood there beside him with her hands joined behind her back.

Holmes immediately went back to his examination of this glorious coat, which lay before him. The first thing he did was to blow against the grain of the fur to check the plushness and strength of the hairs attached. He then examined the collar, which was white throughout, and fluffed up to where it would probably cover at least the lower portion of the ears of the wearer without having to turn it up. As the examination progressed, Holmes obviously became more and more agitated because his movement and turnings of the garment came in rapid succession. At one point he actually had the thing turned entirely inside out running his hands over the entire lining.

During this whole ordeal, young Amy stood by his side, hands clasped behind her back, mimicking his body posture perfectly. First, she bent low as Holmes checked the "fiber" of the pelt. She then stood up straight as Holmes reacted to his findings. Then she bent again at the waist while Holmes struggled with the lining. All in all it was a treat to watch, as if some pantomime were being played out before us, and both Haggerty and myself could not help but chuckle a bit at the comedy of it.

When Holmes finally had the coat right side to again, he turned to young Amy with that stern expression that I knew to be concentration, while others thought the devil himself was about to strike.

Amy, on the other hand, was not moved. Maybe it was because her near-sightedness prevented her from taking in the features of the man who towered above her, or maybe it was because she just didn't give two figs about his sour expression, but when he turned to her, she said gaily. "It sure is beautiful, isn't it Mr. Holmes? I'd bet it's warm too, but no one will let me try it on," and she took a look in her father's direction. "They say that some bad man left it here," she finished.

"And what do you say young lady," Holmes came back.

"I say father Christmas left it," she said smartly, and she stood there awaiting Holmes reply.

Perhaps it was the situation or perhaps it was what I knew Holmes would think of her last remark, but I have to say I laughed out loud despite myself.

"Father Christmas, you say," replied Holmes with one eyebrow raised. "Father Christmas", he repeated. "Quite...," and his voice drifted off in thought.

Within moments, he turned back to her and began what looked to be an intellectual exchange between two professors. I am afraid that I cannot relate what transpired between the two, for I was now busy myself extending comfort to Mr. Haggerty who was still quite apprehensive about the outcome of our little drama. My assurances amounted to a few gentle statements alluding to the fact that now that Sherlock Holmes was on the case, his fears and apprehensions might very well be washed away with the brilliant explanation that was sure to be forthcoming. We spoke for some minutes on the subject and I could see that my counsel was having a positive effect on the man, for his expression began to brighten, if only slightly. And in that time, I could still see Holmes and Amy in heavy conversation. Holmes even took a knee so that the youngster would not have to raise her head repeatedly to reply to, or ask questions. It was as warm a moment as I have ever seen the "worlds greatest consulting detective" have with another human being, let alone a child. At one point, he actually reached out and touched her hair ever so gently.

About the time that Haggerty and I had completed our remarks to each other, I saw Holmes point to the floor by his side again. Amy took her post like a good soldier as Holmes reached into his coat pocket for his glass and literally dove at the soot filled footprints leading too and from the table where the new coat lay. He scoured the floor studying every nook and cranny, digesting all the material he found into that systematic mind which seemed to pluck answers from thin air at times. By his side throughout this examination stood Amy, silently, never in the way and always peeking over his shoulder at the scene of this man scrambling about her floor.

At the end of his examination, he got to one knee again and turned to Amy with a smile. She was smiling too. There was no exchange between them except, (and though I know I am correct now, I couldn't believe my eyes then), Holmes gave the child a little wink. The type of wink you give someone you are in cahoots with. A simple little wink, which bespeaks a secret between those who know, and tells nothing but their connection to the rest of us.

Holmes got to his feet after this small give and take between them and came directly to Haggerty and myself smiling broadly.

"Take a look at that coat, Watson," he said to me. "I have never seen anything like it in all my years. Tell me what you think."

"And you, Mr. Haggerty, you have books don't you? Ledgers, schedules and the like?"

Haggerty nodded in assent.

"Good," Holmes went on, "bring them to me. I think we can wrap this business up in no time."

Haggerty scurried off to complete his task while I took the celebrated pelt in my hands and began my inspection. Mrs. Haggerty returned with tea and Christmas cookies, which she served to Holmes and her daughter as they once again had their heads together at a chair by another small table set near the wall.

My scrutiny of the coat took far less time than Holmes', perhaps because I was far too distracted by his interest in the child, or perhaps because the morning light was beginning to break in upon us, but I finished none the less and did find some irregularities that might be considered as clues.

"Holmes," I said as I approached them with the coat still in hand, "did you notice that the size and manufacturer's tags have been removed from the lining?"

"What else have you noticed Watson," he said as he turned to me with that knowing, wry smile of his.

"Well, it is quite luxurious isn't it," I replied as I brushed the fur. "Would you be familiar with the animal it may have come from?"

"No I am not, Watson. Not at all familiar, and that's not the only peculiarity with this garment. You said that the tags had been removed, but if you look more closely you will find that this bit of apparel has never had a tag sewn in. In fact, I am at a loss to find a single stitch in this coat. Look here," and he pulled out one sleeve. "You will be unable to find a seam in this lining. What's more, I cannot find a place where the lining stops and the fur begins. No boundaries. The coat itself is one continuous piece. Even the clasps seem as part of the whole, as if they belong there."

It was true. There was no attachment of any kind. This fur coat was of a singular nature, as if it was created of one piece, unique, and complete unto itself. It was baffling. I could only mutter, "extraordinary," before Holmes continued.

"And have you examined these footprints? They are also of a unique nature. As you can plainly see by the diminishing quantity of the soot tracked behind the walker as he went to and fro, they run from the fireplace to the table and back to the fireplace where they disappear. Also Watson," he continued, "if you look closely, you will note that while the footsteps are small, like a child's, they are not a child's at all but in the nature of an older person, I would say a man."

"How on earth do you determine a thing like that," I broke in.

"By the fact that it appears that continuous pressure was placed on the heel rather than the ball of the foot, my good man. It is well known that a child will always tend to walk on the ball of his foot, but as one gets older there is a tendency to place more emphasis on the heal for better support and stability. These footfalls were obviously made by someone initiating contact with the floor by using his heel first. This form of walking is much more prevalent in men than women, so it is logical to conclude that an older, albeit smaller man walked this path."

I repeated myself by exclaiming, "extraordinary," once again.

Holmes was beaming. I could tell that he was quite pleased with his findings and my lack of knowledge on any of the subjects of which he had just spoken, for he smiled broadly at everyone. He assured us that this investigation was quickly coming to a close and would be completed in time for us all to enjoy the day.

Mr. Haggerty returned with two volumes containing his ledgers and schedules and handed them over to Holmes who placed them on the floor next to the table where he sat. He never opened either of them.

"I'll be needing to borrow these for a short time to show to the authorities," he announced and Haggerty nodded in a dumbfounded way.

The sun was up now, and we could detect stirrings in the streets. Bells were chiming near and far from steeples everywhere in London, hailing forth that Christmas day had broken throughout the land. The Haggerty family and Holmes and I sat around a small table in their pantry chatting, drinking tea, eating Christmas cookies and generally celebrating the day and the investigation. Holmes was his usual obscure self about his findings, but reassured us all that we had nothing to fear and everything to gain from our night's endeavors. By 9:00 a.m. we were ready to leave, refreshed and content that all was well.

As Holmes gathered his cloak and cravat and the books that told the story only he understood, he turned to Mrs. Haggerty and explained that we should really turn the mysterious, glorious coat over to the authorities in case, in truth, it did belong to someone other than she. She agreed readily stating that, "if she did own it, she would probably keep it locked away at any rate. It's much too grand a garment for me," she said.

And Holmes replied to me so that all could hear, "you see Watson, the honest person only wants what is rightfully his, or hers in this case." And turning to Mrs. Haggerty he continued, "and that, my dear, is what is truly grand."

As we stepped through the door and out into the cold, I couldn't help but notice that Holmes once again winked that little wink at Amy, who shivered and giggled and ran back into the house.

This was indeed most peculiar of Holmes no matter what day it was and what the circumstances had been, and I thought to ask him about it, but before I could we heard Haggerty's voice calling after us in the street.

"Mr. Holmes," he said, "who then is the villain in all this?"

"The delivery man, of course," Holmes replied with a smile and a wave as we turned to march away in the snow.

Watson's Sampler:
The Lost Casebook of Sherlock Holmes

The trip to the local constabulary did not take long in the brisk winter air. Holmes stated that he preferred to walk this day and so we marched our way through the snow lined streets now filling with children and adults laughing, running, jumping, sliding in the snow and generally having a fine time.

We didn't speak much. I was in deep thought, trying to figure just how Holmes had come to his conclusion concerning the delivery man. I did not want to be forced to ask for his assistance in coming to the same decision that this was our man, but I must admit that I was at a loss as to how to follow his train of thought.

Once inside the station Holmes was ushered into an office to converse with whomever was in charge of the skeleton crew left to manage the affairs of the populace on this most joyous day. I, on the other hand, was given a seat in one of the outer offices, where I spent my time discussing the events of the night with a rather rotund, jolly little constable who informed me that he had volunteered for this duty so that other, married police officers could spend the day with their families. No sooner had I congratulated him on his selflessness than Holmes appeared heading for the door.

"Come along, Watson," he announced, " these gentlemen can take it from here. They have no further need of us," and with that we were out the door and homeward bound.

It was just ringing 10:00 a.m. as we left the station for our quarters at 221b Baker Street. The streets were now bustling with activity and traffic as the hansoms and traps carried entire families to exciting destinations unknown to the rest of us. "Merry Christmas" upon "Merry Christmas" was passed from one to another on the streets as we walked, and although I had never seen Holmes engage in such holiday exchanges before, I noticed him smiling and tipping his hat to passers-by on this occasion. It was wonderful. At one point a sleigh came whizzing by with members of the baker street irregulars hanging on the rear rail for dear life, squealing with joy while sliding on the packed snow that covered the highways and byways of London, making it look more like a faerie land than a thriving metropolis. It is fair to say that there was never such a morning as this, and as we turned our last turn toward home, I have to admit that my heart gave a little twinge, for I did not want this morning to end.

Mrs. Hudson greeted us at the door and after exchanging pleasantries and reassurances, and wishing her a Merry Christmas, up we went to the apartment that I have never failed to call home since first I slept there. It was on the stairs that I decided I had had enough of this mystery within a mystery, which Holmes continually lured me to, in nearly every case, and so I began my inquiry. "Holmes," I began, "what did it all mean? And how did you arrive at your conclusions concerning the delivery man?"

"You mean you don't know, Watson. Well, let me explain..."

But he was cut off by what he saw when he opened our door. There on the table in the center of our abode, sitting headband down and with a brand new Brier root pipe leaning against it, was what is commonly know as a deer stalkers hat. Even from the distance that is afforded from door to table, it was quite evident that these two items were of the finest quality. Holmes was speechless, which is such a rare occurrence that I made a mental note of it immediately. But I also was struck dumb by the discovery. Someone had actually been in our lodgings while we were out on our night's errand, had gotten past Mrs. Hudson and invaded our inner sanctum to leave this remarkable parcel.

The Matter of the Christmas Gift

We both stood and stared from our vantage point at the door for what must have been a minute, before Holmes stepped into our parlor with me at his heels.

"How truly amazing," he said. "Look there, Watson," and he pointed to the floor under the table. There, as we had witnessed at the Haggerty's, was a trail of soot heading to and from the table with its point of origin being the fireplace. And it was not alone. There, on the floor, was a second trail which led to my favorite lounging chair and, upon that chair was what I consider the finest walking stick ever created, with a silver hand piece and what must be an ebony shaft, although to this day I am at a loss to find someone who knows what wood is at its essence.

We approached these assembled gifts not cautiously, but quietly and slowly, for I feel we were both in awe of the pieces, and the benefactor who had gone to such great lengths to deliver these one of a kind specimens of perfection.

"Do you think these articles figure into the case at hand," I said as I hefted the stick to feel its weight and balance.

"Not at all, Watson," was Holmes reply. "Just as I know that the glorious coat we examined earlier never figured into this case, other than to draw us to the scene."

With that puzzling statement by my friend and colleague, I turned to face him and question him further, but my inquiry was ended before it began as I fairly burst forth in laughter to see the figure of Holmes, with the deer stalker hat upon his head and the Brier root pipe protruding smugly from his clenched jaw.

"I make a fine figure of a man, wouldn't you say, old boy," he said around the stem and we both laughed until tears appeared in our eyes. I must say that it was good to see this broodish, sullen, paramour of virtue so full of life and good cheer, if even for a moment. He looked ten years younger that day.

When we had composed ourselves again, Holmes continued. "You see Watson, none of these items received from our mysterious soot footed friend could have ever been an integral player in the crimes committed, or any attempt to frame the Haggertys, because of the singularity of each piece. Even our untrained eyes could see the uniqueness of these articles. No thief worth his salt would ever considered giving up booty such as this as a ruse to indicate an innocent's involvement. That would constitute a colossal waste of energy and ill gotten gains. No, no my dear fellow, it is fair to say that these pieces do not figure at all in this business, other perhaps than to gain our attention, and call us to the scene as it were, but more about that later."

"As to the crimes at hand, it may or may not surprise you to know that I have been following the developments of these robberies all along in the newspapers. I had not become entangled in the investigation because I was not invited by either the victims or the authorities, but my interest was piqued and I kept abreast of each episode in the event that I was called in. Knowing my methods, you have probably guessed already that I kept extensive notes on each occurrence, noting time, date, suspects, and etceteras. I was well aware that the chimney sweeps were the prime suspects in each incident, but I had discounted them from the first. You see, chimney sweeping always causes at least a modicum of tumult within every household, with all of the soot and dust and the necessity to move things around. Chimney sweeps are therefore always scrutinized because of the clamor and mess they make. No Watson, a chimney sweep is rarely a thief whether that is his inclination or not, for he invariably lacks opportunity."

"But the papers reported that every instance of theft coincided with the schedule of these sweeps," I interjected.

"Yes! And what does that tell us, my dear fellow?"

"Well, I don't rightly know Holmes."

"Well, all right then, if I must spell it out," Holmes continued, but good-naturedly. "If the sweeps are there at each event, and if we are going to say that their attendance indicates complicity, which logic will have us do, then what is their function in the scheme? My deductions led me to a two-fold objective for the sweeps. First, with their vantage point high above the crowd, they were the perfect lookout for their accomplice, and secondly, with that advantage they were the perfect diversion for that same accomplice. Had you followed the story of the crimes the way I had, you also would have seen that in every case the theft was of one or two valuable items and never anything more. And so the plot was clear. The chimney sweeps, noting the arrival of the perpetrator, would set up a diversion, say they would drop their brush and cause a soot cloud or something. The commotion would excite the already apprehensive household, and while everyone was distracted by it all, the perpetrator would walk in and walk out unnoticed. Any delivery person was perfect for the part with all the comings and goings this time of year. Who would ever suspect, even if they noticed that the deliveryman had been there. In every case, the missing gem or showpiece was not noticed until well after everyone had gone. But considering the circumstances, who first came to mind as suspect?"

"The sweeps," I answered.

"Precisely, my dear fellow. The careless, noisy, dirty sweeps whose hands, none the less, were always clean of any evidence of complicity."

"It was the magicians ruse, the misdirection, played to the hilt. Subtle and slick."

"When presented in order like that, Holmes, it all seems to fit nicely. But one thing still escapes me. How did you know that it was Haggerty's delivery man who fit the bill as the brigand?"

"Pilferer is the more apt description old boy. You see, Haggerty's man turned out to be his own worst enemy. He must have loved to appropriate other's goods to the point of distraction. Why else would he have picked up the package with the original coat in it, after delivering a Christmas goose to his own employer. I would venture to say that his plan must have been to leave for other parts this very day with his cut of the spoils in hand. That is why we went directly to the police this morning, with the hope that he will be seized before fleeing and a just end will be brought to this business."

And that is just what happened. The deliveryman and the chimney sweeps were caught "red handed," as the saying goes, divvying up the goods. They were carted off to jail that very Christmas day and everything they had stolen was recovered.

As for the Haggerty's and the wondrous coat which Holmes had donated to the collection of valuable items that filled the stations property room?! Well as you might have guessed, no one ever claimed the garment. It sat to the end with some of the wealthiest ladies in London examining it, but returning it to the pile. The coat was returned to the Haggertys in mint condition along with the original garment that Mr. Haggerty had purchased for his wife. Several offers were made for the glorious amber coat, which had first led us to this case, but none were accepted. The coat remains to this day locked away in waiting as part of young Amy's dowry.

And what of Miss Amy, you might be wondering. Well, as fate would have it, the reward money, which was considerable, was diverted to Haggerty by Holmes because of his key role in bringing this matter to light, and used to bring in a specialist to examine Amy's eyes. And also, as luck or fate would have it, Amy's condition was secured in remission with a slight change in diet (more fish, if I recall, for added vitamin A, which was an experimental treatment at the time, although it proved quite effective), and the continued use of corrective lenses. I'm told she is to be married soon, and both Holmes and I await the invitation that Haggerty says is forthcoming.

As for Sherlock Holmes who had begun a sullen, sorry old agnostic when it came to Christmas, he was downright jovial for the remainder of that day. He proclaimed "Merry Christmas" to Mrs. Hudson upon our return home and after a noon brunch announced that we were to take our evening repast with the Haggertys. "Young Amy has invited us and her mother has given her blessing to the plan," he said with a twinkle in his eye I had never recalled seeing before. He began to break in his new pipe that afternoon to the point where we were actually forced to open a window to let out some of the smoke. As we sat there in the comforts of 221b, curiosity got the better of me and I asked him what had transpired between he and the girl, which had brought this change.

"It was the Spirit of Christmas, Watson," he replied.

"What on earth do you mean by that, Holmes," I asked.

"That young girl," he said and he looked off fancifully for a moment. "I don't know that I have met anyone like her. Alert, polite, gentle. All the attributes possessed by the finest of us, yet it was her courage in the face of the devastation that she knew was soon to come that drew me to her. Not once, not once mind you, did she complain about her eyes during our conversation. And she knew about the coat long before I could have ever guessed."

"The coat, Holmes," I interjected, "she knew about the coat?!"

"Yes, my dear fellow, she knew. And not only did she know, she told me, in no uncertain terms, where it had come from and who the benefactor was."

"I must admit that it had never crossed my mind," he continued. "You know my methods. How many times have I said that once you have eliminated all other possibilities, whatever remains, no matter how peculiar it may seem, must be the truth."

I nodded in agreement.

"Well, when I saw that coat, that glorious coat at the Haggerty's, I must admit again that I was stumped. There was no logical reason for it being there, and as the thought of never understanding the meaning of the thing grew in me, I confess that I became angry. Not with the Haggertys, not with the villains in our little play, not with the coat, but with myself. It was then that young Amy stood beside me. We spoke a few words and then she asked what was the matter, for she could sense my agitation. When I conveyed to her the problem which vexed me so, do you know what she said," and he paused for a moment, not so much for me to answer his inquiry as it was, I think, for effect.

21

"She said, 'don't be silly Mr. Holmes. It's the Spirit of Christmas which leaves such things as these. You don't need eyes to see that.' And when I looked at her Watson, I saw the face of a girl who knew her destiny and accepted it calmly and courageously without the foreboding and terror which would befall most of the best of us. She was correct in her deduction as well, and I knew it without a doubt as if it were infused in my soul somehow. The simplicity of faith has the power to change all things, Watson," and with that he strode to the window and peered out as if he were still coming to terms with this new found truth.

After some minutes he turned to me with a smile on his lips and began again.

"As for our benefactor in the matter of the Christmas gifts we have received this day, I am not sure we will ever be visited again by our benevolent friend. Perhaps it was father Christmas who came to leave us this sign today, or perhaps it was an angel who stole into our home and left these gifts as some misdirected clue to quell the fever that overtakes my mind when I cannot explain away the purpose of things. I do not know. But what I do know is this; some divine intervention has taken place here today, and we were all drawn together for a greater good because of it. But as I say, I do not know who or what it was Watson, and for once, I am not inclined to pursue an answer. Suffice it to say that by this miracle I have been made aware of capable forces other than ourselves, involved with the downfall of evil and the preservation of all that is good. That knowledge has given me a comfort which I have not known before, and I feel that I have no one to thank for it save the being whose name graces the day."

With that we gathered our things and entered the growing throng outside, refreshed, renewed and happy, trusting in our new found faith that all would be well and that setting aside one day a year would not threaten the realm.

We feasted that evening with Mrs. Hudson in the Haggerty's abode and joined them later at Church. No Christmas day was better spent.

I have been sworn to secrecy, as Holmes put it, "to prevent the criminal element from becoming exuberant over the fact that London's greatest consulting detective might have become soft and might also consider taking one day off each year to celebrate the Savior's birth."

But every year from then, I couldn't help but notice a small cake left by the fire place and a garland or two strewn about the place on December 24th. And Holmes never mentioned that he disliked holidays again.

THE END

THE NOMADIC NOTES OF SWALES NOTCH

DEDICATED TO ORBÉRTO

Watson's Sampler:
The Lost Casebook of Sherlock Holmes

INTRODUCTION

I am able to set before you the tale of "The Nomadic Notes of Swale's Notch," as left me by my great-grand father, Dr. John H. Watson, with a clear conscience, even though it is mentioned within the narrative, that his colleague and friend Sherlock Holmes requested that this story not reach the outside world, unless certain conditions were met. With mixed feelings, I must report that those conditions have been met. Before I began to reveal the mystery, which took the greatest detective team from the comforts of their digs at 221b Baker Street and sent them to the low regions of Scotland, I journeyed there myself to confirm or refute any claim that the place and the people visited by these two so long ago were, in fact, still there, in the person of their descendants. Alas, my journey was in vain because all evidence of the community of Swale's Notch or the people who lived there has vanished, and while I am saddened to think that a culture so full of Christian attitude and design could have disappeared without a trace, I am pleased to be able to share this account of its existence and the perplexing case which led Holmes and Watson to the community known as Swale's Notch.

Watson's Sampler:
The Lost Casebook of Sherlock Holmes

THE NOMADIC NOTES OF SWALE'S NOTCH

From the Files of Dr. John H. Watson, M.D.
Presented by William F. Watson, Jr.

"In the southern region of Scotland, some midway between Lockerbie and Jedburgh, in the morning shadow of the Cheviot Hills, there lies a vale of such sweet splendor as to cause the locals to rarely speak of the bliss encountered by laying roots and taking up permanent residence there. Indeed, it seems that a jealous passion befalls the populace of Swale's Notch to the point of distraction, and this border village, with its rich farm lands and long meadows filled with heather and thistle, has escaped the demands of modern society, and bounded as it is by its larger, sister communities to the east and west, and by the rolling knolls that buttress its discovery from the south, has become both distinctive and peculiar in its demeanor and culture. One might honestly state unequivocally, that the fevered pace indicative of life elsewhere in the Realm has sped right past Swale's Notch in its mad dash to whatever destination has set it on the fast track, and this is exactly what the citizenry of that community prefers. To those who seek this meteoric velocity as the means of life, it is easy to understand why 'The Notch' is as foreign to them as the furthest country. Ah, but to those who live there; who wake each morning to the sweet, cool air that fills the vale with mist and glistens each strand of purple or blade of green, to those who watch the sunrise over the Cheviot, and spend the day glimpsing back at what it does to the earth and sky, to those people, the people of Swale's Notch, life is made for living, and they'll not be chasing their tails for want of more than they already have."

Thus spoke Mr. Fulton Buchanan who had stationed himself behind the easy chair customarily employed by our less exuberant clients as they endeavored to gain our assistance in whatever emergency compelled them to our door. Mr. Buchanan apparently could also be included in this group, although he seemed much steadier than most, who usually humbled themselves somewhat as they expounded on their plight.

As he stood there before us though, you could sense that this short, stout, hearty Scotsman with the ruddy complexion and all the trappings that have made Scotland the self sufficient, tenacious nation that it is, was not humbled at all by whatever predicament directed the action he now took. Indeed, it was clear by his manner, and the fact that he had appeared before us, that this man was about to ask for our assistance in some matter that he obviously deemed important, but in the same moment it seemed just as clear that should we quibble about assisting him on any level which he considered unfit, he would turn on his heels unperturbed and take his leave of us without regret or misgiving of any kind. In this regard he appeared to me to be of a unique and singular attitude, and I couldn't help admiring the air of certainty that his presence imparted.

I am not so sure that my friend was of the same opinion, and as we all took this moment to study each other in silence, I could see Holmes' impatience rise within him. He began to twitch ever so slightly, which almost always meant that a gesture or some verbal ejaculation was about to surface. I am also not sure whether our guest felt this tension as well, but he began again without prompt, continuing his depiction of the place as follows:

"As you must have surmised by now, I am a member of the parish which I have just described. We are simple folk of simple tastes, and I must admit that most of the members of the community I represent are unaware that I have made this journey to gain counsel in the business at hand. Fair chance it to say, that if they were conscious of my whereabouts at this moment, they would be none too happy with my choices. For you see, we are a people who cherish our privacy and way of life above all else, and to many in my society, the disclosures I am about to relate to you will bring grief, not joy, to an already grave situation."

He paused here once again to gather his thoughts for the upcoming story, as if there had been a necessity for the introduction he had just completed. With a deep breath he began again.

"My village has no need of local government or legislated laws of any kind. We follow the laws of God in our hearts and our actions, and have been very successful in this style of life for quite some time. We have neither elected officials nor a police force and neither have we had the need for one. For the most part, our populace stays within the boundaries of the parish and as I mentioned earlier, lets the world dash past unhindered. The good news for us is that a world unhindered has no call to stop and notice a quiet, pristine community such as ours, and that is just the way we want it. You see, no one who lives in Swale's Notch is there for any other reason than to enjoy the life that God has given him, at least until now."

"Three nights ago gentlemen, as most every man, woman and child of Swale's Notch attended a social gathering at the meetinghouse, the entire town was robbed of the savings stored away by its inhabitants. As meager as these means may have been, they were gone in the night, nonetheless."

"Extraordinary," I exclaimed as Holmes straightened himself and pressed his two index fingers together to rest his nose on them. This was the sign that he was now intrigued by it all and would know the end of it, if I were any judge.

"Are you saying that the local bank was robbed, sir," Holmes queried.

"Not at all, Mr. Holmes," Buchanan returned, "the money was taken from each home."

"Do you mean to tell us that everyone in the little hamlet you just described lost all their money individually, in a single evening," Holmes came back.

"Yes, I am sorry to say," was Buchanan's reply, but after a moment, he held up one finger and revised that answer. "Well," he continued, "not quite everyone, Mr. Holmes. I alone was spared the agony of near total loss of funds."

"And why is that," Holmes asked without accusation, although his words were pointed.

"I have absolutely no idea," was Buchanan's reply. "That is why I am here Mr. Holmes. Was I one with the others, who had lost all and found that I must start again, most likely I would never have come, but I am not. And the fact that I am not, holds me in question."

He paused again, thinking about what he was to say next.

"You see Mr. Holmes, it's not that my brothers in our society would ever think me guilty or accuse me of any wrong doing. They trust me implicitly, as I trust them. It is my own weakness, which brings me to you. My own pride which won't let the hint of scandal touch the name of Buchanan, even though I know that silence is enough where I live and no one suspects me. Pride is a weight we carry Mr. Holmes. A weight so heavy that it sinks us into the earth at last. Though no one thinks me accountable for this foul deed and God Himself knows of my innocence, I find that I cannot rest within myself until I am openly cleared, and shown to be blameless throughout."

"I understand your concern, Buchanan," I said to bolster the man who at this point was in obvious distress, though I could not figure why. "It is admirable of you to take these steps on behalf of your fellows. The only trouble I have with this whole matter is that I cannot, for the life of me, see the wrong or shame of it."

I could not help but notice that Holmes had been eyeing me keenly while I made this statement to Buchanan and broke in before he could respond. "With your permission sir, I would like to take a stab at explaining things to the Doctor," he asked.

Buchanan nodded and Holmes began anew. "You really must familiarize yourself with your Bible, Watson," he started with a smile. "First of all, it is quite obvious to me that Mr. Buchanan is a Christian, but perhaps not for the reasons you would first think. If we set aside all of the assumptions which leap to mind, such as the race issue and the geographic issue, both of which I need not remind you confirm absolutely nothing, we are left with the gentleman's own testimony to tell us his beliefs. Now correct me if I am mistaken, but as I remember your speech just now, three pieces of information present themselves immediately. First of all you stated that those who reside in Swale's Notch live 'by the laws of God.' I realize of course, that this statement in itself sheds no light on the conclusions I have drawn until it is linked with the other points made. Namely, the second statement, which was, I believe, that your brothers would never think you guilty or accuse you of any wrongdoing. Beside the obvious Christian reference in the use of the term 'brothers' to describe your friends and relations, the lack of accusation or thought of guilt holds strongly to Christian thought, in its purest sense. 'Judge not, lest ye be judged,' from the Gospels of Matthew and Luke, and 'Let he who is without sin, cast the first stone,' from John's Gospel are sentiments quite unique to Christian reflection. And thirdly, pride as a stumbling block, while not uncommon in many religions, is also a cornerstone of Christian thinking. Your notion that pride is a weight that ultimately sinks us, did much to convince me of your Biblical foundation. Proverbs' 'pride cometh before a fall,' is a good case in point and the 'all is vanity' sentiment of Ecclesiastes, led me to conclude that the Christian Bible is the guide in your society."

"Now tell me gentlemen, have I missed anything," and he ended as he had begun, with a smile.

"Quite good, I must say," returned Buchanan with a smile as wide as Holmes'.

"Here, here, old boy," I piped in. "I wasn't aware that I shared quarters with such a Biblical scholar," I beamed at him with raised eyebrows.

"The bed chamber before sleep has always been my 'theological study'," he beamed right back. "But now to your problem," he returned to our guest. "You have come here, which means you seek a solution, no matter what your beliefs would dictate. I should tell you here and now that I find your motives honorable and your difficulty at home fascinating. Can you imagine Watson, an entire town fleeced, all at once? We will be happy to assist you, sir"

"A curious turn of phrase, Mr. Holmes," our latest client returned with a wry smile, "being as the majority of the families of Swale's Notch are shepherds."

"Precisely why I used the term," Holmes returned mimicking the man's facial expression.

"We will need to visit your community," he continued in a "back to business" manner.

"Are you quite certain that a trip to the Notch is necessary, Mr. Holmes," Buchanan asked at this point.

"I am sorry to inform you that I *am* certain Mr. Buchanan. The lone comfort I am at liberty to give you is to tell you that the only way I think our visit will be successful, is if we conduct our inquiry incognito."

"You do not want anyone to know who you are," he returned.

"No sir, at least not at this time. We would not want to alert the culprit, and since I am already convinced that the guilty party is within the community, the only way to flush him out is with subterfuge."

"How could you think that one of our own brethren would do such a thing Mr. Holmes," Buchanan broke in, and would have continued had not Holmes raised his hand and quieted him."

"There are many reasons why our thief must be one of your fellows sir, but that will shortly come to light when we have him in hand. As for your objections to the possibility, just think for a moment. Christ had a betrayer. And although I know that conjecture reigns as to his motive, Christ was betrayed nonetheless. Now I ask you, what concrete facts do we have from the witnesses report in the official record?" Holmes eyed us both before continuing. "He was betrayed for money, gentlemen. And the value was a mere thirty pieces of silver, if memory serves. In this light, Mr. Buchanan, will you still deny the possibility that money can encourage sin, even in your hamlet?"

Mr. Buchanan left our company a few minutes later with the knowledge that we would be joining him the following day under the pretense of visiting relations from London. Holmes would take the first name of his brother and be known as Mycroft Jones, while I would take the name Thomas, and retain my surname. It would be a difficult leap to ever guess our real identities from these new monikers, especially in a community, which shuns the outside world. And thus we were now know as Mycroft Jones and Thomas Watson, nephews to Mr. Fulton Buchanan, born of his two sisters in London.

Early next morning, we boarded a train at Charing Cross Station bound for Lockerbie, Scotland. Late spring had shown itself to be all that you would expect of England. Flowers bloomed and days were either wet or bright and warm with a bounteous, yellow sun reigning over the festivities. Scenes flew by along our way and the rail ride to Lockerbie was long, but comfortable in our compartment.

Over the years I believe that I have solved the puzzle that has always been, just why we never travel with our clients to wherever their dilemmas carry us. If quizzed on this phenomenon, I would have to venture the guess that Holmes needs and uses this time to study the facts he has been privy to, to that point. And so it was in this case as well, we hastened along through the countryside, stopping at this town or that, but all the while Holmes sat in silence, filling the compartment with plumes of pipe smoke as he contemplated the situation at hand. More than once I noticed him jotting down notes and drawing formula designs on blank sheets of paper, which he had stuffed in his jacket pocket. He spoke little, mentioning now and then that he would like some tea or a fresh light of his pipe, but never mentioning his findings or theories in the investigation. I also knew better than to refer to our inquiries or ask any questions about his opinions in these matters. Holmes did not like to speak in conjectures. He gave little credence to guesses, and felt that discussion without firm knowledge was ludicrous and a distraction at best. Therefore we sat, or rather he sat, and puffed his pipe and jotted notes while I made the best of things by reading a journal, stretching my legs by wandering from car to car conversing with our fellow travelers or by searching the towns and countryside we passed for points of interest. The time did not fly, but it did move on and, before nightfall we alighted from the train at the Lockerbie station.

Buchanan had forewarned the station staff of our coming and a carriage had been prearranged for us to hire, for there was no coach service available to or from our destination. From our inquiries, made at the station, we learned that even the post was only sent around to Swale's Notch once a week, if there was any, and only picked up from there when something was delivered. All in all, there weren't too many folks in or around the station who knew the way to the Notch or seemed to care where it was. "Almost as if the place were hidden away on purpose," I thought to myself in passing. "But who would want to do that," also crossed my mind.

We found the postman at any rate, and he pointed to a small dirt road, which looked more like a trail than anything else, and told us that if we were to followed this path, we might just reach the Notch and Buchanan's house before midnight.

"Don't worry old boy," he said to me, since my face must have given away my apprehension, "nothin' to be afraid of up there, unless sheep make you nervous," and he chuckled to himself. "You'll know Buchanan's place right off. It's the only house of substance in the whole place. The entire population lives in shepherd's huts except Buchanan. He's like their leader, I guess," and he waved his hand to us as we stirred our hired horse and clattered down the way.

I must admit I love to drive a horse, although drive may be too strong a term. I prefer to think of the way I handle the animal as guiding him to my desired route. With reins in hand we set off. Holmes continued to draw fiercely on his briarwood, while I took in the sweet smells and sunset shades found only in the northern regions during spring. Pink and orange mixed with the bloom shades of violet, deep sapphire and striking whites eclipsed any artist's attempt to render the scene. And green like none other. I think I shall dub it "pristine green." A green which only shows itself in spring before contamination sets in to dull its hue with dust or soot, or all the things which end the purity that new life brings each cycle. As you can readily see by my meandering prose, I was lost in the moment, which lasted until a crisp, clear night full of stars and moon was ushered in. Good enough for me that I was lost in the moment because Holmes had been and still was extraordinarily quiet throughout the day and even now, with his unending exploration of the facts, as we knew them. I did see him take the time to study the countryside though with its rolling hills, fenced in properly to keep the sheep herds from mixing, and the glens and dales and spring fed streams which made this land as rich as any I have seen in all my travels.

"Watson, old boy, have you noticed anything along the way which might lend itself to our investigation," he commented as we crested a hill and could see window light off in the distance.

"Well, I'm really not sure," I replied, "I have seen many things on our little trip, especially before sunset, but nothing that struck me as helpful. Why? What is it? What have I missed?"

"Did you notice the sheep, Watson?"

"Well of course I noticed them, Holmes. They were there and there, and even now, there," and I gestured at the horizon and at the ewe grazing to our left, so close that it could easily be distinguished, even in the frailty of moonlight.

"It is their condition, which is the clue, Watson."

"Their condition. Do you mean because they are shorn, Holmes?"

"Yes, because they are shorn. What does that tell us, old boy?"

"Well, it tells me that it is spring, Holmes, that is what shorn sheep tells me."

"And it tells me that as well, Watson," and he smiled not unkindly, but it did show his impatience. "But what it also tells me is, that this is the only time in all the year, in which a shepherd has any real money. It is true that he may save and scrimp and practice husbandry throughout, but it is in the spring and only in the spring that he might be said to be prosperous. And then only for a time, until the monetary rigors of farm life overtake him and he is strapped once more."

"Well, yes, of course, now that you lay it before me like this, I realize it," I returned with as much conviction as I could muster.

"Our thief also realized it, Watson," he finished, as he looked over his shoulder at the wool-less ewe we had just passed.

As we drew near the window light we had seen earlier, I couldn't help but notice other lesser dots of light to both left and right of the main patch, scattered orderly around the landscape. We did not deter however from our main course because the trail, which had now taken on more of the characteristics of a country road remained steadfast toward the beacon. A few more minutes and the horse began to slow as if he were in familiar territory and knew that his journey was about to end. Apparently we had made good time for as we rounded the next bend a small manor house came into view. There were neither servants at the door nor any trappings, which would indicate opulence, and the only sign of life was the bright yellow light coming from what looked to be a sitting room on the first floor. As we pulled up, the front door swung open and out popped Mr. Buchanan with two fellows who resembled him so completely that they must have been his sons.

Buchanan delivered a greeting as soon as he saw us from the doorframe. "Mr. Holmes, Dr. Watson, do come in gentlemen. My sons Ernest and Robert will see to your horse and carriage."

Once inside, Buchanan's house reminded you of Buchanan. It had the same neat, tidy, no nonsense look about it that Buchanan had. There was a large fire burning brightly in the fireplace which I felt was much too robust for this time of year, but I also realized that it was by this fire that we were drawn to the spot and perhaps that was the intention. Mr. Buchanan had a small table set out with mutton, cheese, bread and greens in the event that we were hungry and he even had a pot of tea steeping by the fire. Without much coaxing I dove in, for I had not eaten since the luncheon served on the train. Holmes on the other hand only nibbled, even though he had not eaten all day. This was his way when a mystery presented itself. He was like a man possessed, and until he made some headway in the solution, it consumed all of his appetites save those employed in pursuit of the end. He sat there across from me, toying with the contents of his plate until both of the younger Buchanan's re-entered the house and sat by their father.

"Your sons know of our plan, I take it," Holmes began.

"Why, yes sir, they have both been briefed," was the reply. "It seemed essential that they know all, if we have any intention of carrying this thing off successfully."

"Well thought," Holmes returned. "I like your thoroughness, Buchanan. It is a style not unlike my own."

"Now I want to let it be known gentlemen," he continued to us all, "that I have not been wasting any time in studying our little problem here, and if Mr. Buchanan will be so kind as to answer a few minor questions, I think we may all turn in and begin anew tomorrow."

With this Holmes turned to our host and said, "Sir, when Dr. Watson and I spoke with the postal officer regarding directions to this place, he referred to you as the leader of this community. What, in fact, is your role here in Swales Notch?"

"Well, Mr. Holmes," Buchanan began, "I can assure you that my role is nothing so dramatic as leader, although I can see where a person might get that impression because I am one of the few people from Swales Notch who have regular contact with those outside its borders. You see, I conduct business for the community. For example, after the recent sheep shearing it was I and my two sons who brought the wool to market and ensured that a fair price was rendered for all our hard work. This responsibility has been passed down from generation to generation. I hold this house because of my duties, so that in the event that a business meeting of some type must be set here, within our borders, I, being the most likely candidate to hold such a meeting, also posses the most likely place to hold that meeting."

"What about the meeting house you spoke of," I broke in.

"The meeting house is for religious and social gatherings Doctor," one of the boys piped up, "we do not conduct business there."

"And when you are not conducting business, gentlemen," Holmes began again, "what do you do then?"

The other son fielded this question. "We also have some sheep, just as everyone does, but we haven't near so many as everyone else. We spend much of our time serving the others by visiting them regularly, to be sure their needs are met, and by making repairs for them and fetching supplies from the cities, that sort of thing, Mr. Holmes."

"Will you be making your rounds tomorrow," Holmes continued.

"Normally we would," Buchanan now answered, "but we are at your service now."

"Then you will make your rounds as scheduled," Holmes continued again, tapping and lighting his pipe, "with Dr. Watson and myself by your side."

"One more thing," asked Holmes as he lit the briarwood, "you said you were one of the few people in this village who made regular contact with the outside world. Might I ask who the others are?"

"Well there's Fergus Russell for one," Buchanan replied waving his hand in front of his face to dilute the pungency of the smoke now filling the room from Holmes' shag, "he handles the dogs."

"You mean collies," Holmes asked.

"Why yes, the collies. Very good Mr. Holmes," Buchanan returned with a twinkle in his eye. "I must admit that you surprise me with the latitude of your knowledge, sir. You are familiar with the breed then, I take it?"

"Let's just say that any breed of this caliber, no matter how fresh, would not escape my notice. I have followed its acceptance into the ranks of the working varieties with great diligence and enthusiasm. They show enormous energy and intelligence, and an attention to detail not found in any other canine. I admire the animal completely," Holmes finished much to the approval of Mr. Buchanan and his sons, if facial expression was any indication.

"Will we be seeing Mr. Russell tomorrow," Holmes asked as he drew in what was sure to be another billow from the briarwood.

"We may just," Buchanan replied, as he readied himself for an addition to the malodorous plume which was filling his home.

Holmes smiled quietly as if oblivious, but in a moment's time he rose from his seat and strolled through the front door taking the source of our discomfort with him.

For my part, I had been thinking seriously about a cigar, but reconsidered, for I had had enough of the out of doors for one day and couldn't bring myself to bear any further distress on our hosts by lighting up where I sat. After exchanging some pleasantries and an after dinner glass of apple cider, since there was no brandy or any other form of alcohol in the place, I bid them all good-evening and set out for bed, as I was more tired than I had realized and welcomed the rejuvenation which sleep brings.

What became of Holmes and his evenings meander I do not know, but as I deem him fit for any challenge, all thought for concern is but fleeting at best. And so it was, on to bed.

Mornings come early in Swales Notch and so it was to be for me, as I must have checked my fob watch three times before realizing that the stirrings within the house were intended, and that it was 5:30 a.m. I tumbled out of my bed and found my way into the hall in dressing gown and nightcap to find the house a bustle with all the Buchanan's attired in work clothing, setting about their chores as determined as you please. At the kitchen table, which was well within my view since the visitor's sleeping quarters were on the first floor, down a corridor, which began at the kitchen and passed the parlor as it headed straight to where I was standing, sat Holmes also attired in a casual workman's garb and fitting in considerably well. Granted, he was not setting about his chores, as were the others, but he was the very picture of the country squire on working holiday. He sat there watching the commotion which surrounded him, and at his feet sat a curious black and white mid-sized dog, which he stroked amicably.

Turning back to my room I saw him wave and give the "come-along" sign, but paid him no mind since I was not about to suffer the barbs which would surely ensue, should I make my mornings entrance clad as I was. Instead I merely popped into the room, dressed in attire equivalent to theirs' and met them in the kitchen for tea and a warmed cereal concoction, which was quite pleasing to the palate.

"Is this the breed of which you spoke last evening," I asked Holmes who was still attentive to the panting, happy faced creature at his feet.

"Yes Watson," he replied, "this is one of Buchanan's collies. Watch this," and he took his hand away from the dog, made a whistling sound between his teeth and we all watched as the hound stood up, walked to the door and sat to one side, looking from the handle to Holmes and back again.

"A little trick I learned," Holmes chuckled. "The Buchanan's have been teaching me the signs and whistles the dog understands. Notice how alert he is, Watson. And always ready to serve. See, also, how he sits to the side of the door so that it will not hit him should we, or some unseen force, such as a neighbor, open it without warning. That skill was not taught to the dog. It is his own intelligence, which leads him in this instance. That is the attention to detail of which I spoke last evening. This is truly an exceptional breed, Watson."

"What are they called again, Holmes," I asked.

"It is a collie, Watson. This one's name is Jake, but he is a working collie by breed. Some also call them border region collies or Scottish collies, but they are working dogs, so I prefer the working collie rendition. It tells the story."

The Buchanan's had finished their business about the house by now and had wandered outdoors on errands unknown. Just about the time I had taken the last swallow of my breakfast porridge, Ernest stuck his head in the door to say that they were ready to check the sheep, before they began rounds. Jake, who came nowhere near being hit by the swinging door, ran out, after it was open, with Holmes and I following a moment later.

The sun had just crested the rolling hills to our east as we emerged from the cozy home into the morning chill of the countryside, just waking up along the Scottish border. The day was going to be bright and warm if the present condition of things was any indication. Long shadows crossed our path as we turned and walked from house to barn and past in the direction of the fields, which surrounded everything in sight. You could see some of the other farms from our vantage point as we crested a hill along the dirt trail that we were following to the meadows where the sheep grazed. Buchanan, Holmes and I walked three abreast along this road, while Ernest and Jake moved on along ahead. Robert had stayed behind to hitch the wagon which carried the supplies and tools needed in the rounds we would make today in service to our neighbors. As we walked there, on that hill, Buchanan pointed out the singular layout of the farms and other buildings, which made up the community of Swales Notch. It seems from his description, and the confirming evidence of my own senses that very day, that the village was laid out by a circle of farms with only a few essential buildings and places of meeting being located in the center. I have tried my best to diagram it as follows:

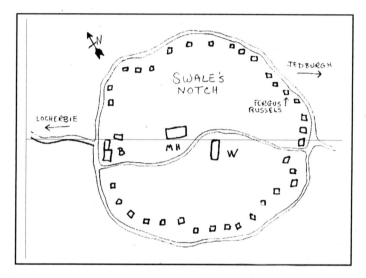

Mr. Buchanan explained to us that this design had been employed as a means of defense in time gone by and that an inner wall had once stood surrounding the inner buildings, thus creating a fortress against attack, which was nearly equidistant from each household. This outer wall had been torn down by the new residents of Swales Notch, since their fortress was God and they had never felt the pangs of fear that necessitate such drastic measures as employed by others.

"Interesting point of view," Holmes had commented when he heard Buchanan's explanation, "especially considering how little protection man has ever really been able to afford himself with all of his devices. Has there ever been a culture which remained unconquered by its own designs," he asked rhetorically.

"Exactly," Buchanan returned.

By the time this little exchange had taken place, we had reached our destination, which was where two fenced pastures met. As I have said before, the terrain was hilly in this area and though we could clearly see that we were at the point where the two were meant to intersect, there being one gate on the center fence between them; because the pastures ran over the hills and out of sight, there was no activity of any type in view in either field. I must admit that I had no idea at this point that this was the place where we were intending to go, and I would have continued walking down the path cheerily discussing the benefits of Christianity and the failings of mankind as a whole, had Ernest not stopped and opened the gate. I for one stood there looking at the others with many questions in mind as to our decision of this spot, until Ernest turned to Jake and pointing to the pasture on our left, gave a shrill high pitched whistle, which sent Jake scurrying off, through the pasture and up over the hill, out of sight.

"This is what Jake lives for," said Mr. Buchanan, beaming. "He'll be back soon."

As we all stood there waiting, each with his own method of passing the moments, Robert pulled up with the wagon ready and waiting for the next leg of our daily routine to begin. I bid him "Hello," while Holmes lit his pipe and the others leaned against the fence, marking time as we waited.

"Are these pastures large," I asked Robert, who never seemed to stop smiling for some reason.

"Why yes, Doctor," he replied, "some are quite large indeed. This one, for example," and he pointed to the pasture where Jake had just set off, "runs back fourteen acres or so and is just as wide. It is great pastureland for grazing sheep, but we need to keep them moving though."

"Why is that," I questioned.

"Because sheep love to eat, Dr. Watson. They love it so much that they don't know when to stop. They'll eat all the grass, and when they're done with that they'll eat the roots, and when they're done with that they'll eat the bark from the trees if we let them. If we left even our small herd in one pasture for more than a week, they'd eat it roots and all, and we, and they would be in a fine mess. That's why we move them every other day or so from place to place. Here they come now."

I pivoted, but all that presented itself to my eye was the same empty pasture, which I had seen before speaking with Robert. What a puzzlement, I thought, but as I looked back to ask just what he meant, I heard the slightest tinkling noise coming from the hill where Jake had disappeared minutes before. All heads turned to see the source of this sound, which was increasing, as it grew nearer. Just as flowing water hugs the ground as it cascades over whatever obstacle chances to be in its way, so the flock of sheep in unison came scurrying down the hill before us with Jake at the rear, driving them on. As the open gate came into their view, the sheep made for it with Jake shifting his position in the rear, jerking to left and right to insure that all were headed correctly and none were left behind. He herded them. He pushed them. He directed and controlled them as if they were a giant being of some sort with he their legs and brain. It was almost like watching a ballet. The athleticism and intelligence of this animal was as nothing I had ever seen. Not once did he relinquish his grasp on them until all were safely within the confines of the new pasture. Had not the gate been closed by Ernest, I believe he might have stayed there, on guard, becoming a door himself so that not a ram, lamb or ewe would cross over into the field now secured by his presence. It was an event to behold, and Jake a champion.

"I must congratulate you Ernest, on your extraordinarily talented animal," I remarked enthusiastically, "how long did it take to train him?"

"Oh, not long at all, Doctor," Ernest returned. "What you have witnessed here today is a routine accomplishment for a collie. They have not only been trained to produce the results you saw just now, they are also bred with those same results in mind. They are born with the natural instinct necessary to accomplish the tasks you have witnessed, and many more. Why, I have seen young pups herding geese, on their own, without the benefit of any training whatsoever. They are truly remarkable animals and a source of great pride within the community."

"As well they should be," I concluded as Jake reached his nose up and touched my hand for a pat.

Watson's Sampler:
The Lost Casebook of Sherlock Holmes

The ride to the first farm was short and pleasant as the sun had risen well above the horizon and things were becoming warmer and more comfortable. Holmes, Mr. Buchanan and myself sat on the bench seat of the wagon while Ernest and Robert fashioned seats for themselves out of the equipment and stores, which we would use or deliver to the farms appointed for a visit. Jake, for his part, spent most of the trip either running along the side of the wagon or jumping up into the rear bed to gain the attention of one of the boys. Hardly ever did he make a sound and, Buchanan informed me, that the best of this breed were quiet by nature.

Our first stop was at the household of Ian and Elizabeth McGregor. Our plan was a simple one. After introductions, I would engage our hosts in conversation while the Buchanan boys went about their chores, or whatever it was that motivated the visit in the first place. This we felt would give Holmes the opportunity to have a look around as discretely as possible. He would later connect with us again and join in the conversation affording him the occasion to ask questions without arousing suspicion as to our true motives for being there. We all felt that this plan created the possibility for as little harm to be done as possible, while still enabling us to investigate the scene and interrogate the victims without their knowledge.

Our arrival at the small but tidy shepherds hut went all but unnoticed except for another dog remarkably similar to our Jake who stepped out of the doorway and ran to the Buchanan's and to Jake as if they were long lost relatives just back from a sea voyage or something of that nature. He jumped up on Ernest and Robert who had hopped down from the wagon and jumped right over Jake who was already on the ground and the two dogs bounded off in play chasing each other and having a glorious time of it. The commotion this caused stirred the remaining inhabitants of the hut and before Holmes and I could alight from our perch at the head of the wagon, two people, obviously husband and wife, greeted us warmly and bid us enter their dwelling for refreshments and conversation.

All went as planned. I was introduced as Thomas Watson and Holmes was introduced as Mycroft Jones and so our charade began. Within minutes the Buchanan's had excused themselves and they and Mr. McGregor busied themselves with mending a fence in one of the pastures, which left Holmes and I with Mrs. McGregor to sip tea and chat. Holmes, in a manner only he seems to be master of, made a comment about the abode we now found ourselves in, which inclined Mrs. McGregor to offer him a look around, which she did and he accepted. And as he wandered in and out of the place inspecting everything he felt important, I tried to find some means of distracting this obliging young women so that she would not wonder as to how these visitors from London came to be so nosey. I must admit, I had pondered this predicament in my mind beforehand and had come up with what I thought was an excellent scheme. Playing the concerned relative, I asked Mrs. McGregor what possessed the people of Swales Notch, (as far as she knew my uncle included), to live the way they do.

I don't believe I'll ever forget what she told me then. As I look back, I realize that it did distract her from Holmes' rummaging around, but it also distracted me. It distracted me from the world I knew.

She said, " I think the best way to tell you why we're here and what motivates us, is to tell you the story of my husband as he told it to me. Firstly, is your father still living Mr. Watson?"

My answer to that question was, "no."

"Well, neither is my husband's. One day, when we were talking, this same question came up as to why we are doing what we do. You see, we also ask ourselves these things. Well, my husband said, when it was his turn to speak, that when he was a boy in London, and he and his family used to go to Church, his father often kissed him on the head during services. This was not such a problem when he was young, but as he grew into a young man, he said he couldn't stop the urge to cringe whenever his father kissed him. As if the other young men would think him less of a fellow because of the outward affection shown him by his father. Each week the time would come and each week his skin would grow cold from the shame he felt from his fathers caress. Now his father was not an ignorant man, and apparently guessed at his son's repulsion, for one day the kisses stopped. Years went by, as years will do, and before he knew it his father had passed from this earth, and the fellows whose opinion he held so high, had married and moved away and were long forgotten. Now it is ten years since his father died and my husband's fear is that his father may have died not knowing just how much my husband loved him, since he shunned the affection so plainly and openly given so many years ago. Now that my husband is older and wiser, he has said that he would gladly give five years of his life for the chance to embrace his father now. For once opportunity is lost, Mr. Watson, it never comes again, and for many, it is not until years go past that the finality, which comes from missed opportunity, is realized."

"Now God's love is like my father-in-law's love for his son. It is open and freely given, asking nothing in return whatsoever. It is in the morning dew. It is in the air we breathe. We here at Swales Notch have chosen to embrace God now, while there is time. And if we seem peculiar to the world outside, well, then the world is like those lads my husband thought so much of long ago; insignificant and soon forgotten. If you believe in God, Mr. Watson, show Him that you love him now, while you can, so that you won't wonder if He got the wrong message when time is running short. For I fear too many choose to shun this love, and may get that same cringe and feeling of shame from its embrace. Our question at Swales Notch is, 'whose loss is that?'"

I must admit that I was a bit floored by the sincerity of the words just spoken. Her sad round eyes seemed to peer directly through me as we sat at her rough rural kitchen table facing each other over tea. I didn't know quite what to say. She was totally correct of course, and I got the distinct impression that she pitied us all for our lack of understanding out here in the world.

Looking back on the scene, I now think that I was about to apologize when Holmes pushed through the front door after completing his inspection tour of the outside of the house.

"I can't help but notice that you have no locks on your windows Mrs. McGregor," he announced without regard for our conversation at all.

"Why, no Mr. Jones," she replied, "we have little use for locks in our community. Much of the time we let at least one of the windows swing free so that the dogs may come in and out as they please. In fact, we only latch them against storms and the like," she finished, smiling.

"But didn't my uncle just tell us last evening that you had all been robbed in the night recently?"

"Yes, that is true," she answered. "What a sad thing it was really. The poor person…"

"Poor person? I would think that the residents of Swales Notch are the ones poorer for the event."

"I'm sorry to say, that only goes to show how much you don't know, Mr. Jones. The rich man, who is poor in spirit and rues the day of loss of gold or steals to gain more, is always far poorer than the poor man who is joyous. What can ever bring that rich man joy, or what can ever remove that poor man's joy? The answer is the same for both questions, Mr. Jones. Nothing."

"We have no locks against those who take, and gladly forgive them in their ignorance, for they steal but from themselves."

"Please forgive my blunder, Mrs. McGregor," Holmes returned, "for I forget with whom I am dealing. You are a rare breed here in Swales Notch."

"More's the pity," she replied.

By this time, Buchanan and Mr. McGregor had returned from their fence mending and we were ready to move on to our next stop. After spending a few more quiet moments with this peaceful couple in which nothing more controversial than the weather was discussed, we left upon our wagon heading northeast toward the Duncan homestead, some three miles away.

"Did you learn anything new from the McGregor's," Mr. Buchanan asked as soon as we were out of sight of the house.

"I'm afraid not," replied Holmes nonchalantly. "Other than the fact that you all tend to leave your windows ajar, I found relatively nothing new from this part of our excursion."

"Do you leave your windows ajar, Mr. Buchanan," Holmes continued in the same casual vein.

"Why, no Mr. Holmes," Buchanan returned, "my windows latch from the inside. Do you find any significance in that sir?"

"Well of course my dear fellow," Holmes continued in a livelier manner, "any difference between you and your fellows is significant since your cash was not touched on the night in question. Your position in the community is significant. Your windows being latched, is significant. Your flock being smaller than the others is significant. Every difference we find which singles you out and anyone else who was not robbed within your band, is significant, and may shed light on this perplexing problem. Now tell me, who else was not robbed? I mean, although you announced that you were the only person not victimized that evening; I get the distinct feeling that others were left alone. Who were they, Mr. Buchanan?"

"Well, let me see," began Buchanan anew. "What I should have said was that I was the only one of substantial means who was left alone. That is what I meant, at any rate. But as to the others in our midst, Charles Hanson was not touched. He runs the warehouse where supplies are stored and sold to us as needed. I felt the proximity of the warehouse to the meeting house where we all were gathered, must have caused the thief or thieves to loose heart and give up that prize, as it were."

"Then there's Douglas Stuart who serves as pastor to us. He lost nothing, perhaps because he has so little in the way of worldly possessions, but mostly because he resides in the meeting house itself."

"And lastly there's old Jeffrey Smith, who is retired from the working world and tends the tiniest of all flocks yonder on that hill," and he pointed East to the greenest little hill, with a scant three trees adorning its southern side.

"From what I am told, everyone else in Swales Notch lost something to the thieves."

"And what do you mean by something," Holmes continued.

"Well, that is a bit peculiar, Mr. Holmes, because not everything was taken. Only paper money and little else was found to be missing from every site. Coins and other valuable items were not considered in these burglaries, it seems. Isn't that the oddest thing? Many of the families have much more to offer in the way of heirlooms and valuables than their money, but only money was taken."

"And only paper money," Holmes corrected.

"Yes, and not even all of that," Buchanan went on.

"What do you mean," Holmes inquired pointedly as he sat up straight as if new interest had energized him.

"You see, Mr. Holmes, country people keep their money in different ways and the people of Swales Notch have their own style of caring for their funds. For example, hardly anyone ever carries any cash with them, unless they are expressly planning to spend it that day. There is much less chance of loosing it that way, and since we are all limited in the amounts we have, losses can be devastating. Also, since we have no need of banks, most money is kept at home in a sock or bag or in a piece of pottery or something of that nature. We do not secure our money because there is no need."

"Not even now," I dropped in.

"Not even now," he returned, good-naturedly. "We will not change because of this experience, Doctor. It would defeat our way of life. Try never to be altered by evil, gentlemen, for evil does not change with your alterations, you do, and that gives evil power. Evil has no power in Swales Notch."

"It has the power to rob you," I came back, staying with the argument.

"Only of our worldly goods, Doctor, and Matthew 16:26 counters your point quite nicely I think."

Time passes rather quickly now and then with such things as good work, good study and hearty discussion as the guide. We had reached our destination before I realized it, and sat before the home of Arthur Duncan and his family of five.

"Our business with Mr. Duncan will be brief, gentlemen," Robert advised us as we stepped down from our perch once more. "We are merely delivering supplies at this stop. The Duncan's have a sick ewe and Mr. Hanson sent a remedy. I'll just pop in and drop it off if you don't mind."

"Actually I would like to meet the Duncan's if no one has objection," Holmes stated as if asking permission. "It would be the proper thing to do to introduce us as your nephews anyway, don't you think?! Common courtesy and all that," he added.

Pleasantries and introductions were exchanged, just as they were at the McGregor home. It wasn't long before we were once again left by the Buchanan's, who took the remedy they had brought out to the barn, which was really nothing more than an oversized shed, where Mr. Duncan and his oldest son Andrew were tending the sick animal.

Mrs. Duncan was a handsome looking woman in her early thirties who seemed to be doing everything in her power to make us as comfortable as she could. She insisted that we both sit down and have tea and a crumpet type cake with honey, and would not hear that we were quite sufficiently filled at our last stop. She sat there, as her two youngest children played and jumped and ran around us squealing incessantly, and asked us question after question about London with its theaters and gardens and cricket matches. She was most inquisitive and from all outward appearances seemed to be in need of a change. I was about to broach the question when Holmes broke in with one of his own.

"You will excuse me, Mrs. Duncan, but ever since my uncle told me about the unfortunate business of a few evenings ago, I cannot seem to get it out of my mind. Tell me, did you loose everything to the thieves?"

"Nearly, Mr. Jones. You see, my husband prefers paper money to coin for what he calls convenience sake. He is forever converting coins to paper at the warehouse. Since we all know that the thieves took mostly paper and since almost all of our money was inside a sock in a jar on that shelf," and she indicated a shelf in the rear of the abode, "nearly everything we had was taken. It seems we are going to have to sell off part of our flock in order to make due this year."

"What do you mean by 'mostly paper money,'" Holmes asked.

"Well, Mr. Jones, I mean that there were some coins in the bottom of the jar that were spared. We came home to find the jar shattered on the floor with the coins, which were inside the jar mingled among the shards. The few coins, which were inside the sock containing our paper money were forfeited though. Isn't it strange that a thief would go to all the trouble of stealing money only to leave some behind."

"Strange indeed," Holmes agreed, "was anything else of value taken?"

"No, sir."

"Was anything else disturbed?"

"No, sir, nothing. My goodness Mr. Jones, you are beginning to sound just like a constable," Mrs. Duncan concluded lightheartedly.

"I do beg your pardon," Holmes returned, "but you must admit the happenings at Swales Notch have been very unusual lately. When we return to London our mothers will be most interested in all that has transpired here of late."

"I understand thoroughly," Mrs. Duncan continued. "Is there anything else you'd like to know?"

"No, my dear, what you have told me is sufficient, and any further discussion would be mere conjecture at any rate."

At this last remark Mrs. Duncan stared rather curiously at Holmes to the point where I would have sworn that she was about to begin questioning him as to who we really were, had it not been at this point when her husband and the Buchanan boys came through the door laughing and carrying on.

Holmes took the lead once things had quieted a bit. "I see," he said, "that things have gone well with your sheep, if your grand entrance is any indication."

All agreed that, yes indeed, things had gone exceedingly well with the ewe and that this was a joyous occasion, but before anyone could suggest just how we were about to express our joy, Holmes broke in with a request that we be on our way to our next stop.

"I have just remembered an important business connection which must be made with London," he stated emphatically. "I am sure that I can avert calamity by sending a wire, but that means I must travel to Lockerbie this afternoon, so you can see my dilemma. How many more stops do we have uncle?"

"Three more," Buchanan replied.

"Well, I hate to hurry everyone, but we really must go."

Buchanan and I took a few minutes more to apologize for the urgency we now felt and I assured the Duncan's that we would return in the next few days, if it was at all possible, and then we took our leave.

Back in the wagon we all turned to Holmes, who, feeling our stare, began to answer our questions before anyone asked them.

"It is true that I do have to return to Lockerbie to enquire into a few matters which have presented themselves in this case. I have already learned quite a bit from the interviews conducted thus far this morning and I feel an end to this business is near. My enquiries at Lockerbie might just wrap things up as soon as I have made them," and he sat there looking back at us as if we should have already known all of this. "Now Buchanan," he broke the pause with his high handed tone, "who have we left to visit?"

Buchanan had a list, which he now consulted, looking very serious as though he were deciding who had priority.

"Do not ponder so," Holmes declared, good naturedly and with a chuckle. "I certainly want to complete your route, I just wanted to get an approximation of how long our journey will take."

"Well, I figure, if we do not dawdle," he returned, still consulting the list, "we should be finished and home by 2:00 p.m. or thereabouts."

"Splendid! That should give me time to return to Lockerbie this afternoon, which should also mean that I would be able to conclude my business early tomorrow and return before sundown. That will be perfect," and he rubbed his hands together as one does before digging into a hearty meal.

The next three stops were as casual as could be with no talk of larceny or the like. We merely visited while Buchanan and the head of one household loaded three sheep on our wagon, which we delivered to a second household along with other sundries from Hanson's warehouse.

Lastly, we looked in on Fergus Russell to tell him of a herder named Styles from the southwestern portion of the Notch who had lost a dog recently in some mishap or another. Fergus immediately fetched a dog for us to take back with us and deliver to Styles that afternoon.

"I train these animals myself," he said proudly, but added, "what training they need. Now you take this one," and he pointed to the leashed animal, which Buchanan held. "I've had this pup over to Styles' place a few times already. I always bring a dog to each of the five homesteads he may end up at. I have seven dogs here at all times, plus my own. When a herder needs one, and that's quite often since we've got thirty-five families with sheep in this area, I've got 'em trained and ready to go. Best dogs in this region, if I do say so myself."

"What an ingenious plan," I added, "trained and ready to go you say."

"Yes indeed sir, would you like to meet my trainees?"

Before I could answer, Fergus (who insisted we call him by his first name) was around the corner of his house and out of sight. Holmes and I looked at each other for a moment when we heard the clatter of a gate and all at once, around the same corner where Fergus disappeared, came seven young, happy, dog faces clambering over each other to get at me. They went right for me. I must admit, I really did not know what to do. They jumped up on me, licking my hands and sniffing me incessantly; even in those embarrassing places hounds often choose to place their nose. I laughed out loud at the thought of how humorous it must have looked. I spun around and pushed them away, but they came back straight away. Never had any member of the animal kingdom taken to me so quickly or completely and since I never felt threatened in any way, I thoroughly enjoyed the experience.

I do not know how long this most enjoyable assault on my person took place, although I don't think it could have lasted more than a minute or so, but I do know that it came to an abrupt end once Fergus reappeared on the scene. At the sight of him, every dog withdrew and sat, panting, looking between Fergus and myself.

"I am very sorry sir," he said looking quite anxious and bewildered. "They have never acted this way or taken to someone in this manner before."

"No bother," I returned, fairly giggling to myself. "That was quite an extraordinary experience. I enjoyed it thoroughly. I may have to get myself one of these little beasts," and I reached my hand down to pat the one closest to me and almost started them all up again, were it not for Fergus' control over them.

Once we were all quiet, Holmes spoke up to ask a question.

"These are fine animals Mr. Russell," he said, "and this is a fine service you provide for the families of this region. Tell me, where will you go to obtain a new hound to replace the one you are loosing? Since Thomas here," and he indicated me with an offhanded wave, "has taken to them, perhaps we will stop on our journey back to London and acquire one of these collies."

"First off, please call me Fergus, Mr. Jones. And next, let me tell you that a collie of this kind would make the most perfect pet. I purchase my animals from Mr. Reginald Mortimer of The Lockerbie Kennels," and he produced a card from the pocket of his breeches and handed it to Holmes. "They have the finest animals, and well tested too at the monthly competition which precedes an auction. I try to take in at least three a year, to keep up with the standard of the breed. But remember gentlemen that my dogs are work animals and must be of the highest caliber, whereas any collie would make a superior pet. I have studied these animals straight through the process of becoming a registered breed, and I am here to tell you that no other dog living or dead is their equal for intelligence and disposition, let alone stamina and diligence. They are perfectly suited for rural or city dwelling, work or leisure. They love children and love to play and swim and hunt. This gentlemen, is the perfect breed."

His speech was so forthright and enthusiastic that I almost applauded at its completion.

"Well," said Holmes, "you have certainly sold me. I think it will be most necessary to stop and see your Mr. Mortimer before we leave the district." And then with a step back and a look around at all of us, he continued, "and now gentlemen, if we have everything we need, I must be a spoil sport once again and remind us all that business calls, and I really must be on my way to Lockerbie this very afternoon."

To this remark we all, to a man, mumbled our disapproval, but turned to the wagon and our way home, nonetheless, waving good-bye to Fergus and shouting back how we would return, if at all possible, and other words of that nature. The ride back was quiet, with Holmes pondering, and I petting the Styles' new sheep dog, who sat in back of me with Jake and the boys. This ride home was much shorter than the hopscotch manner in which we had visited the families on our way out, because since we no longer needed to stop, we were able to cut through the center of the community, past the warehouse and the meetinghouse and straight to the rear of Buchanan's domicile.

"You really have a lovely place here," Holmes said offhandedly. "It is amazing that there is no jealousy among your neighbors."

I think that Buchanan was about to take exception to this last remark, when Holmes finished his thought with, "You are a unique group of people. Blessed by God in the way we all are blessed by God, but self blessed in your approach to life and to Him. I envy you that. Were we all so selfless, there would be no need of consulting detectives, and those of my profession could become beekeepers and live the quiet, peaceful life God must have intended for us. I envy you your world and your way, Mr. Buchanan."

"And now I must ready myself for my excursion to Lockerbie and the end of this business of your nomadic notes."

And with that Holmes hopped off the wagon and marched vigorously into the manor house, only to return moments later in new dress for business in the city. "Hitch my carriage, will you Ernest," he called out as he lit his pipe and played with the walking stick he carried at times.

No one ever really knows Sherlock Holmes. I have been his confederate and biographer for a number of years now, and I consider myself as close to the man as anyone, even his brother, but I must admit that although I know his methods and his motives, I rarely understand where his thought processes take him or why he does things the way he does.

It was obvious that Holmes did not want me to accompany him to Lockerbie, because he had left me out of the announcement. This I knew for sure. Why he did not want me along was anyone's guess, but I did not ask him, because over the years I have realized that it matters little whether I am with him or not. All would be revealed eventually anyway, and keeping my curiosity in check gave the appearance that I had the facts of the matter well in hand, and needed little or no coaxing to come to the same or similar conclusions as my friend. And so it was in times like these, when I was summarily being ignored as an assistant of any kind, I would sit there smartly, saying nothing, ignorant of any facts and carrying it off quite well, if I do say so myself.

Holmes boarded our hired carriage and clattered off toward Lockerbie before 2:15 p.m. had passed. I, on the other hand, was left behind to be charming and inquisitive and ready to pick up additional tidbits of information, in hopes of lending something to the quest for truth. I must say that in this particular instance the chore was most pleasurable. Once Holmes had gone, and we had refreshed ourselves anew with juice and cold sandwiches, we headed out once again to deliver Styles' dog to his new home.

I cannot tell you just how impressed I was with these animals. It is, of course true, that the suggestion that I would purchase one of these energetic rascals was but a ruse meant to keep the conversation lively and hide our true identities, but should I ever want for the company of a good animal, I do believe that this is the breed for me. The country life has its benefits, I thought to myself as we crossed past the meeting hall once more, and one of those benefits would be to own an animal such as this as companion, protector and friend.

Before long we were at the Styles' home, which was nestled within a grove of pines, looking quaint and romantic as any spot I've seen. Shorn sheep roamed about the place lazily and a single cow chewed away as she watched us pull up in front. Styles and his wife were in the doorway and they smiled and waved and shouted hallo as we climbed down from the wagon. Both Jake and the new sheepdog pranced right up to Lester and Emily Styles, to get their complimentary dose of pats and scraps, and all went smoothly.

Lester Styles shook my hand vigorously at our introduction, and I received a genuinely warm feeling from both he and his wife as we shuffled about making small talk and getting to know each other a little. Before long Buchanan mentioned my interest in the breed of dog we were delivering, which brought a smile and a spark of enthusiasm to our hosts.

"Would you like to see him work," Styles asked, turning to me.

"Why, yes, that would be nice," I returned.

"Okay, then, follow me." And he led the dogs and I to where his fenced areas began. "Now remember," he said, "although Sam here (the dog's new name) has been here before, we have never worked together as a team."

To this I nodded and at my nod, Styles let out a series of whistles, which brought both Jake and Sam to their feet. Styles smiled broadly and Robert sounded one shrill whistle, which turned Jake to him and sat him down again. With Sam now paying close attention, Styles swept his right arm out toward the dog with the palm of his right hand perpendicular to the ground, but out flat. He then moved this hand toward the sheep who loitered by his hut and stopped when he was pointing at them. Then with one long and one short whistle he swept his arm and hand around until he pointed to the open pen at his right. When he had finished this maneuver he balled that same right hand into a fist and brought it down into his left palm making a slapping noise with the concussion.

Without hesitation Sam ran wide around until he had cleared all of the sheep and was positioned to their rear so that the sheep were directly between he and the gate indicated by Styles. Then with a series of bluffs and parries to the right and left of the now forming flock, Sam began to move them toward the open gate. With each variance that a sheep or number of sheep would make away from the desired destination, Sam would counter with a sweeping charge which virtually always brought them back to the group and the course. I remember how I couldn't help thinking how much this dog reminded me of one of those circus performers whose act it is to place a plate on a shaft and swirl it until it balances. Once he has one balanced and spinning, he starts another and another until there are any number of plates spinning on any number of shafts, and how he then must run from one to the other to keep them from loosing their momentum and dropping to the floor. Sam was doing much the same thing with the sheep, keeping them moving in the correct direction until his act was complete. Finally, (and I say finally because of the amount of energy expended rather than the amount of time it took), finally the ewe at the head of the flock and therefore the one now closest to the open gate, crossed the line and was inside the pen. Literally as soon as she made that move, all the remainder of the flock darted into the pen as well, as if they were now sure what was required of them. Once they were inside, Styles closed the gate and all was peaceful again. Sam, for his part, once the gate was closed, sat and watched Styles for a moment, but when he could see that no further instructions were forthcoming, went back over to where Jake was and gave him a sniff in the face. They both then sat panting happily and looked at us as if they knew exceedingly more about everything than any human.

I applauded in spite of myself. "Sensational exhibition, old boy, sensational," I said to all.

"Thank you very much, Mr. Watson," Styles returned, "although the dogs deserve the credit."

"How did he know just what to do," I asked.

"Well," Buchanan broke in, " he was trained by Fergus, as were all the dogs in the district, and they are all trained the same way with the same signals. It's like speaking the same language, you see. We, as well as the dogs, all speak the same language. It's just as if we went to the colonies. We'd all get along very well there, both understanding and being understood. It's the same here; any dog can understand any master and do his bidding without any trouble. Even Jake was ready to herd that lot into the pen, had Styles indicated that it was his wish. That's why Robbie whistled up Jake's individual signal, to avoid confusion for the dog. Each dog also has an individual signal given him by his new owner, once he's been sent around by Fergus. Like you and I have individual names. Sam will have his own before the weeks out unless I miss my guess. And that's all there is to it, Mr. Watson, unless you wanted to learn the whistle language, that is?"

"Oh, no, no, that's quite all right. I'll leave the language and the herding to you, if you don't mind. My pursuits run more to academia than practicality. Better to keep one's mouth shut and be thought a fool than to open it and remove all doubt, and all that."

This last remark evoked a chuckle all around and served as the perfect segue to a discussion about opening our mouths to dinner. Without much ado we were invited to dine with the Styles family, for the mealtime hour had arrived, and after feasting on hearty country fare, spiced with flavored breads and sharp cheeses, we bid the household good evening and made our way back to the comfort of the manor house and our soft, warm beds.

Sleep came quickly and stayed late, I am afraid, do to the rigors and early hours of the day before. By the time I awoke and roused myself from the bed, sunshine had pervaded the household and the family Buchanan had, once more, marched off to right the wrongs and mend the fences of those they served. I must admit that I was not too disconcerted by their early departure, for with them gone I was afforded some time to try and make head and tail of all that had transpired thus far. I also must admit that to this point I actually had very little to go on, other than the points which Holmes had expounded in the days prior. What spurred me was the inclination in my mind that Holmes knew something, which would be obvious once spoken, but was oblivious at present. Mind you, it wasn't so much the feeling that I should be keeping up with him on the proceedings, which drove me, as it was the desire to figure it all out for myself for once. A desire, I might add, that I feel I have shared with many of my readers throughout the years. But alas, this case, as do so many, left me wanting and waiting for explanations and logical, straightforward conclusions from the mouth of one Sherlock Holmes.

My wait was not a long one, for I fear I had slept later than I normally would and found lunchtime come and gone before I had finished contemplating the mystery. Feeling restless, I was about to have a look around the manor house and barn for any signs of clues, in case our host had been less than honest with us. My eyes widened when I opened the door to find Holmes about to enter.

"You've given me quite a start, old boy," I said as he entered the house and took a quick look around.

"Very sorry, wouldn't think of startling you, Watson," he returned. "Are we alone?"

"Yes, the Buchanan's left early, I think, and have been gone all morning. They left no note, but I would imagine that if yesterday is any indication, we'll not see them for some time."

"Good," he replied with a nod and a move to the door, "come along then, we'll leave before they return," and out he went.

I am not unused to having Sherlock Holmes' spontaneity take charge of a given situation and send it this way or that at his whim, but I have never become so familiar with this particular aspect of his personality for it not to take me utterly by surprise. I followed Holmes obediently and directly to our waiting carriage, which we mounted with him taking the reins and directing our noble steed toward what I had come to think of as the center of town. We did not speak for a number of reasons, but mostly for my part because he gave all the appearances of someone in a hurry, and because I knew that if he was not revealing the purpose for this trip on his own, my prompting would, in all likelihood, produce little in the way of explanation. The horse's hooves clack-clack-clacked along as we made good time toward whatever destination Holmes had chosen. I could see his keen eye checking left and right, scanning the horizon and surrounding region to ensure that we were undetected as we sped on our errand. Once, for no reason which I could identify, we slowed to a walk before returning to the trot like speed we had been generating minutes earlier. When I asked Holmes about this later, he told me that he had noticed a wagon in the distance and had slowed in order to maintain our secrecy in the best case and, at least our anonymity in the worst. "Remember," he said to me, "that if you must move, but wish to remain unnoticed, move deliberately but slowly, and you will be less likely to attract attention, and even if you are observed, you will seem of little interest to the viewer."

Just as I was certain that Holmes was taking me all the way through the center of town and intended to exit the region on the western frontier, he made a sharp left turn, which sent us on a heading toward Fergus Russell's front door. We were there in two shakes and Holmes immediately alit from the carriage calling Russell's name as he moved for the door.

When no answer came forth from Holmes' calls, he burst through the front door and called out again, and still there was no answer.

"Watson," he shouted back to me, "do you have any money with you?"

"Why, yes," I returned, " a few pounds and a shilling or two. Why do you ask?"

Without further explanation he said, "here Watson, put them in here," and he handed me a small tin with a lid on it. "Just the paper, mind you," he added, as I fumbled through my pockets.

Within moments I had emptied the contents of my trouser pockets and separating the paper money from the assortment of objects I carried with me, I secured the notes into the tin with the lid on tight.

"Now," he continued seeing I had completed my task, "place the tin in the carriage box and close it."

Upon accomplishing this second duty, new instructions were given. "Now Watson, I want you to gather those dogs who seem so fond of you and meet me in the shed out back."

Without question, although I had many, I followed the same route which I had seen Fergus take yesterday and rounding his house, found the gate to the enclosed yard where five dogs sat wagging and awaiting my arrival.

"Hello, fellows," I said as I opened the gate and bid them follow me, which they did without hesitation, although they were not as energetic toward me as they had been the first time we met.

Holmes was already stationed inside the shed by the time I got there with my wagging, panting crew in tow.

"Whatever is this all about," I asked as I entered.

"All in good time," he returned. "We are fortunate that Fergus was not here upon our arrival, because we are now afforded these moments to attempt an experiment which, if successful, will lend light to the end of the troubles at Swales Notch."

I did not say a word, but waited and watched as Holmes surveyed the scene of dogs and humans milling about the small shed interior awaiting instructions. Holmes had closed the door behind us, but the three windows provided adequate lighting in which to see the implements and feed bins neatly arranged about the walls and dirt floor, where we stood.

Only seconds passed, but anticipation makes seconds long and at the moment I was about to begin questioning our situation and motives once again, I saw Holmes reach into his pocket and produce from it a small cylindrical object which he now brought to his lips.

Just then the door of the shed burst open and there stood Fergus, flushed and out of breath.

"What is the meaning of this," he asked. "What are you doing?"

Since I had no actual knowledge of what we were doing, I remained silent and stared at Holmes who, with the cylinder now at his mouth, began to blow vigorously.

"No," Fergus screamed, but it was too late.

Without hesitation, the dogs within the shed became agitated and began dashing about, some with their heads down to the dirt and others with their heads up, sniffing the air. My gaze went from dogs to Holmes to Fergus, for I was completely in the dark and searched for some explanation in their eyes. It was then that I noticed Fergus plunge his right hand into his pocket. My first thought was that he might be going for a weapon of some sort. With all the commotion and agitated movement going on about us in the excitement of the moment, the thought of an open weapon in such limited quarters sent an instinctual urge through me that sent me bounding to him with an uncommon agility. Before he could retrieve his hand from his pocket, I had him firmly about the wrist with both hands, rendering the object he sought there useless.

We wrestled there for a moment, until our eyes met and reason took control. Releasing him from my grasp, I nodded to him as an expression of apology and respect. His nod in return assured me that there were no hard feelings. In the hand, which now cleared the pocket's rim, was a brass cylinder similar to the one Holmes had produced earlier. He did not raise it to his lips though, as Holmes had done. He merely stood there holding it, looking past me, over my shoulder to the commotion in the corner. With order restored in my area of concentration, I now turned my attention to the sight, which had diverted him so thoroughly.

The scene was one of controlled chaos with Holmes supervising, as the dogs dug in the earth for all their might. Soil flew everywhere, but despite the fact that Holmes' shoes, trousers and greatcoat were covered in dirt, he stood his ground, cylinder in hand, awaiting what he must have known would inevitably come to pass. A minute must have passed where we all just stared silently, before Holmes once again put cylinder to lips and blew. Immediately the dogs broke off their attack on the earth and settled to their haunches wagging and waiting. It was at this point that Holmes stooped down and lifted from the cavity created by the dig, a large woolen sock, tied at the top by a woolen strand.

My mouth had dropped open, I fear. I turned to find Fergus with a look of resignation that I have rarely seen. His face was a combination of dread, sorrow, exasperation and relief, all in one. He stood there with his hands by his side staring at the stocking in Holmes' hand, as amazed as I was but obviously for different reasons. He didn't speak. He didn't move. He waited for my friend and colleague to take the lead or ask the question, which would initiate the ruin of his life. The moment passed forever. When Holmes' first words were uttered a shiver passed through the man, which almost brought me to tears. I don't believe I have ever seen anyone so ashamed and devastated.

Fortunately for him, Holmes' words were not the lashing he anticipated, but soft and kind as someone not so triumphant as understanding and empathetic.

He began this way. "We have here Watson, the nomadic notes of Swales Notch, which Mr. Russell has so ingeniously liberated from their rightful owners. I must commend you sir on your superior yet simple plan, which accomplished this step in the lonesome journey on which you were about to embark."

"Mr. Jones, you seem to have the better of me at every turn,'" he began, but a raised hand from Holmes quieted him.

"The name is Sherlock Holmes," my friend announced as a tear fell from Russell's eye. "And this is my friend and associate Dr. John Watson."

"Then I am completely undone," Russell half whispered as his shoulders rounded and his face became pale. "You are not unfamiliar to us, even here Mr. Holmes. I have read of your exploits many times over the years," and he sighed a heavy sigh before continuing. "I do not suppose that it would do much good to tell you that I couldn't go through with it."

"Fergus," Holmes interrupted, "I already know that you couldn't go through with it. I made the acquaintance of one Samuel Sisson at the trials yesterday. Mr. Mortimer put me on to him, and as soon as he heard that I knew you, he began to ask after you. The man is seeking you out, Russell. He told me that you are overdue in paying him certain funds he is owed. He says that he is a friend of yours."

"No friend of mine," Russell broke in quietly.

"Quite true, old boy," Holmes replied smiling, "and you'll be happy to know that you won't have to deal with him again."

"How, you say," Russell asked pointedly.

"Mr. Sisson and I had a long talk, Fergus, and your troubles with him are over."

"But what of the money sir?"

"The money is taken care of, and so is Sisson. What he was doing is not legal, my good man. Once I reminded him of that fact, and mentioned that my investigation showed that his wagers seemed more like embezzlement to me, he backed off quite rightly."

"But how, Mr. Holmes? Why? What happened to make this miracle come about? What should I say now? What should I do?"

"Well Fergus, first of all, when all is said and done, I feel that what we have accomplished here will be looked on by Those really in charge, as less than a miracle. As to what you should say, my suggestion is that you say absolutely nothing to anyone."

"Think it out, old boy. You will burden your fellows, if the knowledge we now hold in secret is revealed to them. You would do them a disservice my friend, because of the undo strain they might feel in the process of forgiving. Better that they remain ignorant of the facts. For I am sure that if we gave them the choice, they would choose ignorance over knowledge tied to the possibility of feeling ill-will toward anyone in any degree. The kinder road is the hard road, the road that maintains silence and seeks its peace with God."

Fergus had the look of a man not sure of what he was hearing. He did not speak, and seemed to be trying to take it all in and understand the wisdom or foolishness of what was being spoken. I also kept quiet for much the same reason. One thing was sure; to speak out against himself would do no good to Fergus or anyone else I could think of. Silence was best for him, and once I had thought it through, I could see the rest fall into place as well. Perfection is a fragile thing and must be maintained. The people of Swales Notch seemed to know this. There is a faction in religion, which believes that God, being perfect, is incapable of seeing sin. Not that it is not possible, because all is possible to God, but because He wills it so, to eliminate all possibility of coming into contact with sin at any level and thus being contaminated by that contact. Perfection therefore dictates that there be no contact with sin. Should this logic be true, then the wish to remain ignorant on the part of the populace of Swales Notch is wise indeed for it affords protection not only to the innocent, but to the guilty as well. Pure charity. I smiled to think of the simple beauty of it.

I was snapped back to reality by the voice of Sherlock Holmes who must have sensed the need to return from our reflections and become practical again, because he said, "now if you are still wondering what you should do, here is my suggestion. Give Watson and I a hand with these money pouches so that they may be returned to their rightful owners, that things might be set straight. Once this is accomplished, you may begin work on forgiving yourself. Remember that repentance is a good thing, and an action which God condones, 'for all have sinned.'

And lastly, breed your own dogs from now on. Surely you realize that your stock of animals is among the finest in all the land. Improve upon it through breeding, not buying, and you'll avoid further calamity, I promise you."

"I thank you Mr. Holmes," Russell said with his head low, "I don't know how you managed to come up with the answers as you've done, but I must say you've turned it round for me, and I promise it won't go back."

"I'll take you at your word sir," Holmes replied, then added, "but answers often lead to more questions; and so, if you have a moment, I would like to test my theories by asking a few questions myself. Will you excuse us, Watson?" And with that, I began to load the pouches into our carriage while Fergus and Holmes spoke.

When all was accomplished and everyone was satisfied, we waved good-bye to a shaken but newly steadfast Fergus Russell, and trotted off toward the manor house, taking the same route which brought us there.

My questions were numerous, as I am sure you can imagine, but I left them unasked opting rather to securing the pouches and filling a satchel with them, which Holmes must have brought for that reason.

Once back at the Buchanan's home, Holmes spent little time on anything other than packing and readying ourselves for departure. It was about 3:30 p.m. when we had completed our business at Fergus Russell's and Holmes had mentioned that if things went well, we would be dining this evening on the 8:15 p.m. train to London.

I will not bore you with the details of what happened when the Buchanan boys came home. Let it suffice to say that Holmes would give them no more information than their senses offered. It was obvious that we had indeed recovered the stolen funds, and since that was all that was intended for them to know, that was all he let them know. It took little persuasion to convince them. A reminder that in many cases ignorance is truly bliss was enough.

It was also decided that the best thing for all would be for the Buchanan's to make a clean breast of everything. First they would explain who Holmes and I were, and why we came to Swales Notch; and then they would distribute the money to the original owners, whom I was informed could identify their pouch from the others by color or design or stitch pattern. Ingenious really. The Buchanan's would be able to give no further details because they had none, and so all would be set right without guilt or honor or scandal coming into play. Sherlock Holmes could always tie a nice bow.

I could hardly wait to return the carriage and board the train. Knowing Holmes penchant for the theatrics of suspense, I had not begun my questioning, but rather took the three hours we spent behind the horse, formulating my questions and putting them in order.

We boarded the train and entered our sitting room. Just as I was about to begin my barrage, Holmes held up his hand. The porter had been standing by and Holmes ordered some cold sandwiches and tea, for neither of us had eaten, and I must admit that in the excitement of the day, I had utterly forgotten. Just as my father used to make us all sit down and have something to eat on a Christmas morning, before we could begin to open our presents, Holmes made me sit and eat before he would allow himself to be cross examined about Swales Notch.

When the time finally came, I was ready, but with my first question of, 'how did he do it,' Holmes ended the session by announcing that the best way to examine the facts was to go in order.

"Begin at the beginning, Watson, it's the only way," he said. "And the beginning of this tale starts at the dog trials at Lockerbie, where our Mr. Russell first made the acquaintance of Samuel Sisson, dog trainer and scoundrel. You see, Mr. Sisson has a bit of a reputation as a gambler, as Mortimer disclosed yesterday when I asked him who Russell's friends were at the trials."

"With this information I was then able to bluff an answer or two out of Sisson, which confirmed what I had suspected. Fergus owed more than he could pay of a gambling debt from a plan that Sisson had orchestrated in order to snare the naïve breeder. It was simple enough to turn a friendly wager into a large debt for a swindler like Sisson, and Russell's confidence in himself and his knowledge of 'his' breed didn't help. You see, Sisson could manipulate certain dogs through subterfuge and a silent dog whistle, and thus influence the outcome of certain trials. He would get Russell into a bragging war concerning pre-picked dogs, and then coax him into putting his money where his mouth was. It all started out friendly enough and Fergus would even win on occasion, but in the long run, in the course of the last year, Fergus became deeper and deeper immersed in the debt that led him finally to resort to thievery in order to once and for all get free."

"But how did you gain all of this knowledge, Holmes? Where were the clues?"

"Well, first, I must admit that I was not at all sure who was suspect and who was not. The entire population of Swale's Notch seemed so innocent that when I announced that I was going to Lockerbie on business, it was merely to inquire as to who might be in trouble financially or to see if anyone had shown up there recently with extra money. It was not until we actually arrived at Fergus Russell's home that I truly understood what had taken place on the night in question. Curiously enough, it was Fergus who gave me the final piece to the puzzle, without either of us knowing it, but more about that later."

"To answer your first question, the knowledge I received about Sisson actually came from Sisson himself. You see I caught him at his own scheme."

"After Mortimer pointed Sisson out to me as Russell's friend, I approached him as a breeder from London who had heard of this marvelous new breed. Suspecting that Sisson played more of a part in all of this than first met the eye, I let it be known that my interests in this breed were less than above board. In other words, I let it slip that my intentions were to exploit the animals for my own gain, and that ethics were not a consideration. I offered Sisson money for his assistance, which he was happy to give, and I had him. After gaining the information I needed, I revealed who I really am, and set him a warning that if ever I heard of him cheating another, I would bring the full force of the law to bear. I then paid him the money owed by Russell, and took my leave of him."

"You paid him, Holmes?"

"Yes Watson, I paid him to protect Fergus from any possible further repercussions. Basically, I protected his name. As proverbs tells us, Watson, 'a good name is more precious than gold.' My feeling is, that this mark against Fergus is not irreparable, and therefore is more easily healed if left alone. The fewer people conversant with the error, the better."

"Now, to answer the question you are about to ask, if the fault in the character of the man is unalterable, it will surface again, and since I intend to keep track of the goings on at Swales Notch from now on, I am sure I will hear of any relapse, and be swift to bring justice to bear. My opinion on the matter is, that we have heard the last of the nefarious dealings of Fergus Russell, and therefore, I'll not be the first to cast a stone at that good sinner."

"All right Holmes," I broke in. "So now I know that he did it and now I know why he did it, but what I'm still not sure of is how he did it. Could you clear that up for me?"

"By all means, Watson, by all means. So Fergus owed money and what was he to do. He had very few resources. Apparently he had squandered the funds that his neighbors had given him with which to purchase animals and actually had to beg Sisson for time in order to pay. He was in terrible straights."

"He must have realized that his only recourse was to take the money from the very neighbors who had trusted him in the first place, and then try to repay them somehow over time. Now, before we judge him too harshly Watson, we must realize just how desperate our Mr. Russell felt. He was truly out of his depth in all this, and his fear of Mr. Sisson could only have been exceeded by his fear of being found out by his peers. He feared that he would be cast from them and left on his own in a world in which one of his only contacts had just duped him. As I said, he was desperate, and that desperation lent itself to the downward spiral he was riding. In his state of mind, he could never see that his own fellows would readily forgive him and keep him from this anguish. His brush with the real world was costing him. He had seen sin and it contaminated him. My hope is that our actions here have exorcised that demon."

"So he needs money. He plans to take it from his neighbors. How can he do it unnoticed, Holmes," I asked impatiently.

"This is where we see a stroke of genius from our Mr. Russell, Watson. Answer me this. How do you commit a crime without being present at the scene of that crime?"

"Why, by having someone do it for you, Holmes. That's elementary."

"Exactly. And in Russell's case, he used his pack..."

"His pack, Holmes," I broke in trying to understand his meaning. "What pack?"

"His dogs, Watson, his pack of dogs. You see, Russell was going to commit a crime. A crime he did not want to be seen in any connection with. He had no human allies, but he did have non-human ones. He had his dogs, Watson. They are intelligent, they have keen eyes and a sensitive snout, are easily trained and above all, they are mute accomplices."

"Extraordinary," I said.

"Extraordinary indeed, Watson. Simple and effective and nearly foolproof."

"But how did they do it," I asked again.

"It was quite easy when you think of it. Do you have a five pound note in your pocket?"

"Why, yes I do," I returned.

"Good. Take it out and sniff it."

I did as I was told and then looked, once again, to Holmes for answers.

"There is nothing in all the Realm with the same scent as our paper money. It is quite distinct, you know. I have even written a small treatise on scent distinction in crime detection. Paper money is one of the points which I touch upon."

"It was a simple matter for Russell to train his dogs to hone in on paper money and seek it out when given the correct signal. He could have accomplished that stage of the scheme in days. And from the description we received of the interior of the cottages visited, I would also bet that our Mr. Russell taught the dogs to check for the scent in and around clay pots and inside woolen pouches. Getting in and out of the buildings was no great feat being as the locals kept a window unlocked for just that purpose. It was almost easier done than said."

"You would bet, Holmes? Isn't that an assumption," I asked, knowing that he hated to assume.

"Yes, I suppose I did assume, Watson. But since it had no real bearing on the investigation or the solving of this dilemma, I did not substantiate my facts by asking, and thus was left with an assumption, which I use here merely to heighten the narrative."

"And now I'll make another assumption, Watson. I will assume that I am forgiven."

And he continued on without waiting for any response from me.

"Next he had to teach the dogs to seek out the homes they would violate. Since he routinely brought each dog around to a set of five homes, the way was already clear. Each dog had its own distinct set of homes, so their paths would never cross."

"And what of those homes which were not touched," I put in at this point. "How do you explain them?"

"Funny you should ask that, Watson, because that was one of the possibilities I examined in deciphering this mystery. I asked myself why those not touched, were not touched, and this is what I came up with. Jeffrey Smith was left alone, not because he had no paper money, but because he was retired and poor, and was left out of it on purpose. You see, Russell does not bring dogs to Jeffrey Smith's. When Mr. Smith's dogs die or become too old to work his small flock, one of the older dogs in the community is retired to Mr. Smith's and the household it leaves gets a new dog. But even before I was given this information from Russell, the fact that Smith was retired led me back to the premise that the perpetrator of this act was local, and selective in his choice of victims. Why steal from someone who has little?"

"We have to remember that Russell, while desperate enough to steal, retained his conscience to the end. That is one reason why he took only paper money, so as not to leave his fellows destitute. He was well aware that, with the exception of Mr. Duncan, most of the people of Swales Notch did not care if they had paper or not, and so by taking only paper he would ensure that most were left with something. But I digress."

"Next, let us consider Mr. Hanson and Mr. Stuart. What distinguishes them from the other members of the community? One is clergy, while the other attends to the warehouse, but they neither have sheep nor dogs and that is key. Surely Stuart would not have been touched on the night in question because of the gathering held at what is substantially his home. But Hanson would be a prime target in anyone's mind because he must be a man of some means in order to maintain the warehouse, with its inventory. Buchanan's announcement that he was the only person of means in Swale's

Notch nearly set me on his track at first, but too many other factors pointed to a conclusion that Buchanan was either mistaken or forgetful in his assessment of his own and Hanson's worth. Therefore, as soon as I learned that Hanson was not robbed, it was necessary for me to set my sights on those attributes common to all those who were victimized, and the attribute or common denominator, if you will, leapt out as, sheep and dogs. All the victims had sheep and dogs."

"Then what about Buchanan himself, Holmes. He has both sheep and dogs."

"Ah, but he does something the others do not, my friend. He latches his doors and windows. And, you know, Watson, as I think of it, Hanson must also latch his doors and windows. Another relevancy. See how essential you are, Watson. But, at any rate, whether Russell sent a dog to the Buchanan home or not is inconsequential, considering the fact that the animal would be unable to gain entrance to the domicile, if it were there. My thinking is that Russell probably did send a dog to Buchanan's, and that dog came back empty."

"Very nice Holmes, very nice indeed, but what put you on to the dogs in the first place?"

"Why you did, my dear fellow," came the reply.

"I did? I did? But, how? Why? When?"

"At Mr. Russell's home the other day, of course. Really Watson, I realize that your charms exceed the bounds of mortal men, but did you actually think that the animals at Russell's loved you instantly, and for no reason?"

"Well, Holmes, I hadn't thought about it," and I hadn't.

"Well I did old fellow, and I must admit that I was quite befuddled by it all, until I realized one thing. You, old boy, were the only one carrying paper money. I hadn't brought any, the Buchanan's, by there own admission, rarely carry any, and Russell knew better. The dogs, who had been sent to track the notes down just a few nights before, must have made the connection once again when they smelled them on you, and took the bait as it were. The result was a spontaneous and positive reaction to you, which may have ended in your being knocked to the floor and the notes you held being ripped from your pocket, had not Russell come on the scene and ended the fracas."

"How fortunate for me," I said offhandedly, for while I wasn't hurt by the remarks, I never have become accustomed to Holmes' musings at my expense.

He must have noticed my less than enthusiastic posture on the matter at hand, because his manner changed somewhat and he slapped me on the back as he said, "there, there old man. Don't feel that way. Don't you realize that it is your contributions, which nearly always set things in perspective and solves these cases for me? This case is a perfect example; for there we were, distracted by the attentiveness of the dogs toward you, when I happened to notice Russell come up, see what was going on, retrieve a dog whistle from his coat pocket, and end the whole thing by sounding a silent signal to the dogs. He then sounded a normal whistle to dupe us all into thinking that everything was above board. It wasn't until then that I knew, that it was he who must have designed the whole business, and at that same moment I knew how he had triggered the offensive against the homes in question…"

"You see he could not have used verbal signals to send the dogs out on their evenings errand for two reasons; one, he might have been heard either sending or retrieving them, and two, at a future date someone, say a potential owner, might unknowingly mention the signaling word or whistle, and send any dog trained in that signal into a frenzied search for paper money. A silent signal from a dog whistle, which no one else knew of, or cared about in sheep country, was the perfect device for the job."

"This is how it went, Watson. After training the dogs to fetch paper money in woolen pouches, which themselves were almost always in clay pots, Russell trained them to go to the homes he had brought them to throughout the course of his everyday business. Each dog searching out each pouch in each house along the circuit routinely traveled by the trainer and the dog."

"Russell confessed to me, that on the night of the gathering at the meeting hall, he made sure he entered late. He did this so that no one would notice that he had brought the dogs with him and left them by the warehouse out of sight. Remember, these dogs are highly trained and will stay where they are told, especially if they are together in a group. Also remember Watson, that they are prized for being a very quiet breed of dog, not barking or whining without good cause. Once inside the meetinghouse Russell made sure that everyone was there. This accomplished two things; one, he would know if there were a dog he should not send, lest it find a victim at home when it arrived, and two, Russell knew he would be seen by almost everyone, and thus known to be a victim himself, which he did claim the next day I might add."

"Once secure that all were inside and none had remained home due to illness or any other calamity, he stepped outside, took pipe in hand and sent the silent signal to his innocent gang of thieves. Off they took, and within a few hours all were back at home with ill-gotten gains. Russell made sure he was the second person to leave the festivities, which assured him that he would be home and the money would be covered in the hole he had already dug in his shed, before the first alarm went out. Ingenious, wouldn't you say old boy?"

"Extraordinary," is what I did say, but after a moment of reflection a new question came to mind. Turning to Holmes, who was all smiles, I asked, "tell me, how did you know the signal, Holmes? When we went to Russell's today, you made the dogs go for the money once again. How did you know what signal to use?"

"Actually, that part of it was simple enough, Watson. You see, since there were just the secret signals to deal with, because all of the other signals were open and known to everyone, I only had to understand what those secret signals must say. For instance, one must say to the dogs, 'make your circuit to the five homes you will visit,' and the other must say, 'hunt out the pouches.' The only other signal would be one that ends the sortie because of emergency or detection. Being that this particular signal would be offered during extreme circumstances, it is necessary that it be the shortest signal, and common to all. Therefore one short blast would suffice as the recall signal to the dogs. The only other signal common to all dogs would be 'hunt out the pouches,' therefore two blasts would be the logical conclusion for that signal. After that, each dog probably had his own set of blasts which sent him on his route to the homes but, of course, it was not necessary for me to learn that set of blasts to bring about the result I sought at Russell's today."

"Amazing bit of deduction Holmes," I concluded as we sped along toward our city.

Watson's Sampler:
The Lost Casebook of Sherlock Holmes

Once back in the comforts of 221B, Holmes forbade me ever to publish the tale of 'The Nomadic Notes of Swales Notch' as long as that fair community remained in existence. His motives in this instance were clear to me before they were spoken.

Never in all of our travels had we found a group of people so truly Christian in their approach to life as we had in Swale's Notch. Not that there were not chinks in the armor they sported, but that they remained steadfast to their belief and attempt to continue as chaste as possible, despite the tugs of everyday life on this small planet. I must admit, we both found them remarkable and refreshing, fighting the good fight quietly, and asking no more than to be left to themselves. Many a holiday we spent in their company in the years that followed, and I am happy to report that we were never forced to regret our decision regarding Fergus Russell and the friendly people of Swale's Notch.

THE END

THE OCCURRENCE AT VARGAS CASTLE

FOR WILL, WHO GAVE ME THE IDEA.

Watson's Sampler:
The Lost Casebook of Sherlock Holmes

INTRODUCTION

Confession, it has been said, is good and healthy for the soul. You can imagine my comfort in realizing this, after recognizing the fact that I had inadvertently lied while writing one of my former introductions.

You, as a reader and therefore a participant in the newly published exploits of that genius with the spy-glass, Mr. Sherlock Holmes, will surely understand the embarrassment of admitting a failure which proceeded from the unparalleled enthusiasm I felt when I discovered the treasure my mother had unintentionally kept in storage all these years. I speak, of course, of the notes and papers left by my great grand father, Dr. John H. Watson, which chronicled and described many of the "lost" cases of his friend and colleague. My error was innocent enough, for in the final analysis I feel that you will realize that I merely "jumped the gun" in announcing that my grand mother received these notes after John Watson's demise. As you will see, and as I became aware after reading the entirety of the accounts in storage, quite a different chain of events took place, which resulted in these papers reaching America and finally my hands.

But why reveal the truth too soon, when as always, the fun is in the reading. Let it suffice to say that I apologize for my inaccuracy, and wish you all the best as you investigate "The Occurrence at Vargas Castle."

Watson's Sampler:
The Lost Casebook of Sherlock Holmes

THE OCCURRENCE
AT VARGAS CASTLE

From the Files of Dr. John H. Watson, M.D.
Presented by William F. Watson, Jr.

I have been reminded of late by doing no more than rereading my own accounts of the exploits of one Mr. Sherlock Holmes of Baker Street, that I in fact described myself as a lazy chap to the aforementioned Mr. Holmes on the very first day we met. In those days that may have been true. The difficulty, which faces me now, is that I am no longer living in those days.

Perhaps there is a condition, which rises out of the spirit, when faced with the life or death situations created either for, or by a man of action and intelligence such as Sherlock Holmes, or perhaps it is a conditioned response which grows within someone dealing with such situations over the years, but for anyone who has led a robust life and spent his days in pursuit of adventures and mystery, to find himself idle in the bondage of retirement, leaves one in the least, ill at ease, and in the most, devastated for lack of stimulation. This, then, may be referred to as an apt description of my situation as I marked time in southern Scotland, making the best of things, while secretly praying for activity. It is true that I had notes too numerous to number, and that there were investigations to be chronicled, but to be honest, without the thrill of the chase to increase my vitality, the thought of setting down escapades gone by, left me cold and unable to do them justice.

Often, in the days that followed this voluntary cessation, which left me wanting, my mind would revisit my dear friend and colleague, whose aversion to inactivity was legendary. How was he coping? I set my sights on obtaining that answer during my next appointed weekend with him at his Sussex estate overlooking the channel. Three weeks it would be until I made my journey south to England, and time passed slowly, but at least there would be purpose to my next visit and that brought new life to my routine.

As credit to my leisure lifestyle, Scotland in summer is a glorious place, filled with color and scents, reminiscent and comparable to only the finest gardens in London. Also, as a physician in good standing throughout Britain and the continent, I was afforded the opportunity to pursue a limited career treating private patients who might seek my service. For a portion of the time this kept me busy and out of the house, which was of inestimable value to my health and well-being. I had not want nor need of anything, and even now, after all that has happened, I feel my face go flush to think of the audacity required to complain as I did, even if it were only to myself. Like a racehorse set out too soon to stud, I was eager for the bit and danger of the run. I ached for excitement, and while I did not blame Holmes, who had surely done his part in securing the Realm against villainy, I could not keep myself from looking back with a feeling that we should never have quit our quest to defeat crime at every turn. The realization that Holmes did not necessarily hold with my opinion thus stated, did not aid in easing the melancholy mist, which seemed to dance along with me, mockingly, bringing me lower still.

From these few words, perhaps you may understand the exhilaration I felt when, before the appointed day, I received a summons from Holmes requesting my immediate attendance at his home to hear of some strange new problem, from some strange new client, calling us from our rest.

The telegram, which arrived by courier from Lockerbie, read as follows:

WATSON OLD FELLOW (STOP) TO MEET WITH CLIENT AT MY
HOME ON SATURDAY JULY 5 TO DISCUSS POSSIBLE CASE
FOR US (STOP) MAY BE OF SOME INTEREST TO YOU
(STOP) DO COME (STOP)
S.H.

Excitement welled within me as I spent the next two days modifying my schedule to secure the time needed for travel and perhaps more. With all my lamenting about the idle life, I should state that in this condition, it is much easier to change one's calendar than it was when Holmes would summon me from my regular practice. With a push here and a pull there and an early visit to my few private patients, I was ready in no time to take an extended leave, if needs be. Packing was of little consequence, since I kept a trunk at the ready for just such an event. It was the simplest matter to add my revolver to the stores I had laid aside, and I was ready to embark on what I hoped would be a diversion which would set my equilibrium aright for years to come.

By July 3rd I had secured passage from Lockerbie to Sussex, arriving an entire day early in order to make no mistake in time or place. In my haste, I had failed to wire Holmes informing him of my acceptance of his invitation, and therefore was amazed to find him standing on the platform when the train pulled in.

"Holmes," I sputtered, "how on earth did you know... Why are you here?"

The features, the hair and the style of a man often betray his age to those who notice him, and while these frailties of stature have not touched Holmes in the same manner they would to the sedate, friends and colleagues are often able to detect variations which the casual observer might overlook. And so it was with Sherlock Holmes, for I could see where time had left its mark though others may have glanced past. But not when he smiled. As with most people I have known or seen, like an eraser removes chalk from a board, smiles can wipe years from the face of those who wear them. This is how it was with Holmes as he stood there smiling broadly with that familiar twinkle in his eye, which bespoke the wicked joy he experienced whenever his mental superiority showed itself.

"It was the simplest of conclusions, old boy," he said with a chuckle, "but it is your face which is amusing."

He threw his arm around my shoulder, we collected my luggage and entered a carriage Holmes had secured for our ride from the station. Once comfortable, he continued his discourse, "Watson, I do not know if you would concur, but I would venture to lay claim to being the one person who knows you better than all others."

"I would say that is probably true, Holmes," I returned.

"That, my friend, is why I was standing on that platform when you arrived today. I knew that you were just itching to get back into the fray. Each time you would visit me, I noticed an increased listlessness. A searching, wandering atmosphere pervaded you, accented by a pent up energy, which I realize you tried to conceal but were unable, at least to me. And I have two admissions to make. First is, that I may have recognized your lethargy because I am tormented with the same malady. Ever since the business of the Lion's Mane, I have had an increasing desire to begin anew. There is work to be done Watson!"

"Hoorah," I exclaimed involuntarily.

"Hoorah, indeed," Holmes returned in his usual controlled fashion.

"Also, Watson," he continued, "I have to admit that I came to the station today on mere speculation. It was necessary for me to be in this sector to arrange our passage, and with the aid of the train schedule I keep and the knowledge that the only arrival from Lockerbie Station would be at three o'clock today, I manipulated my timetable accordingly, and voila, another baffling deduction simply explained."

"Ever the showman, Holmes," I said with a chuckle. "The entertainment value alone is worth the price paid."

It was a short trip to the country home of my dearest friend. We chatted throughout the ride catching up on those things which had kept us busy while we were apart. Of course Holmes had his bees, which interested him so. And, of course there was that Lion's Mane business, which, much to my enjoyment, admittedly took longer to write than to solve. For my part there were my patients and their ills to discuss, but both of us readily acknowledged that the leisure life left much to be desired, and that activity is the key to both mental and physical health.

Once within the comforts of Holmes' townhouse, I had the presence of mind to realize that there had been mention of "securing passage" during our discussion, so I brought it up at this juncture.

"Holmes, you mentioned that the reason you were in town this afternoon was partially to make travel arrangements. Might I ask, to where."

"Watson, old boy, if things work out as I feel they will, you are going to be a very happy man indeed, but let us not put the cart before the horse, shall we. We still have an interview to conduct tomorrow and the outcome of that interview has everything to do with my excursion this afternoon. Here is the message I received from our new client. Let us see what we are able to deduce from it."

Holmes then handed me an envelope bearing his name and address. Within it were two sheets of paper containing a hand written note. It read as follows:

Watson's Sampler:
The Lost Casebook of Sherlock Holmes

Dear Mr. Holmes,

Please forgive the abruptness of this letter, but I find the situation at hand, while it is of great interest to me, is a serious dilemma for my friends Jeffrey and Priscilla Ainsley. It concerns the strange occurrences at Vargas Castle.

I find that my travels will take me near your Sussex home on or about July 5, and would greatly appreciate meeting you there on that date, when I will relate to you all the particulars.

Until Then,

Sir Arthur

I completed the reading in a moment and handed the pages back to Holmes.

"Do you know these people," I asked.

"I am only familiar with Sir Arthur in regards to Miss Amy Haggerty, as you'll remember," he replied, "although we have never met."

"I also have never met the fellow, Holmes," I put in. "I referred Miss Amy to him, nothing more."

"Well," Holmes continued, "I took the liberty of researching the old boy, and I have found that he is really quite an interesting fellow. As you know, he is a physician like yourself, Watson, and a writer. He has written a few historical pieces, and has dabbled in mysteries and the sensational. He lectures extensively on spiritualism of all things, and that is the extent of my knowledge. But what can we derive from the note itself, Watson? What do you see?"

"Well, he's certainly not long winded, is he Holmes," I ventured.

"No, indeed not," he replied, "and yet I feel there are things we can glean from this little message. First, as you say, he is direct and to the point, assuming, correctly I might add, that I will be available and interested in his assignment. He is also forceful, leaving no return address, and therefore no means by which I might bow out of this meeting gracefully. Like myself, he does not like to give too much information prematurely, but, he has given enough to whet our appetites and, he has also given us a small mystery to keep us busy while we wait on him."

"What might that be, Holmes," I asked.

"Why, who or what is Vargas Castle, of course."

"Ah, yes, I see that now," I returned.

"But what Sir Arthur didn't realize is, that I already know who and what Vargas Castle is, and that is why today, I began preliminary arrangements for our passage."

"But where are we going Holmes," I asked impatiently.

"Well, if you must know, unless I miss my guess, we may soon find ourselves on our way to the United States of America."

"The United States, Holmes," I exclaimed. "How on earth did you divine that from the few words on these pages?"

The Occurrence at Vargas Castle

"Quite simply, dear fellow, because the United States is where Vargas Castle is situated. You do not think that our new client would have us investigate those 'strange occurrences,' as he puts it, without having us on hand at the location where they occur. The United States is where he shall send us."

I sat there for a moment contemplating Holmes' last announcement. Once again he made perfect sense and so, to not let on that I could not have come to the same conclusion, had I been privy to all the facts, I let his statement stand without further discussion and moved on to the next topic.

"What of Vargas Castle, Holmes? I'm afraid I'm not familiar with it. Enlighten me," I said in an off-handed manner.

"Vargas Castle, Watson! Really, you must keep up with the daily papers you know. It was some years ago. Carlos Vargas was a man of many talents, but none worthwhile. Bulgarian, I believe, and a gypsy. He was a tower of a man, if the reports are true, powerful and cunning. It was reported that he either duped his victims or outright embezzled fortunes from those who fell captive to his evil charms. He was said to be a magician of some renown with ties to the netherworld, using his powers to summon up the dead for examination by family and friends. Very mysterious indeed, and very successful, until one day he and his family pulled up roots and disappeared from the continent. Speculation had it that the legal authorities may have been closing in on him just as he departed, but no official announcement to that effect was ever furnished for public scrutiny. It is my opinion that Vargas merely found himself at the end of his design and moved into the next phase."

"He was next heard of about one year later residing in a castle of all things, in New England. Since he no longer concerned Europe and was now the property and problem of the colonies, no further report of him or his family has reached my eyes, until this note arrived last week. There you have it Watson, in a nut shell, all I know of Vargas and Vargas Castle."

"Now Holmes," I said, feeling rather clever, " we both know that that is not the full extent of your knowledge regarding this fellow and his whereabouts."

"Why Watson, whatever do you mean," Holmes returned coyly, with that wry smile which told me he was pleased.

"You have been preparing passage. That tells me you know where exactly the castle is located, and yet you left the information out of your narrative. You wouldn't be attempting to conceal something from me would you?"

"Bravo, Watson," Holmes said, and he slapped me on the back. "You saw right through my plot to veil you from the truth. That was excellent, and I would fully confess and tell all, were it not that my intention is to surprise you when our guest arrives. Unless you are able to figure things out for yourself," he added.

By this time Holmes' housekeeper had prepared a sumptuous dinner of roast beef, boiled potatoes and greens, and bread pudding. Throughout the meal and during brandy and cigars, I attempted to use Holmes' methods to determine where our forthcoming destination was. It was New England for sure, but where in New England? I was at a loss. I replayed our conversation repeatedly in my head, trying to eek out the clues, which would lead me forward, but to no avail. Each time, after what seemed like promising progress, I had to admit that I was out of my depth. I tried to put it out of my head in hopes that a fresh start in the morning might wipe away the clouds and let the solution be seen clearly.

We spent the remainder of the evening reading and chatting about old times and old cases, and I quizzed Holmes on a few points I needed cleared up regarding previously solved mysteries. The evening drew on, and I was about to say my goodnights and head on up to bed when Holmes smiled broadly and asked, "so what have you come to, old boy. Where are we bound, come the sixth?"

I was irritated to say the least. I had not had time to think things through and Holmes knew it. He was being smug and highhanded as usual, and at my expense as usual, and he knew it. I'm afraid I glared at him a bit as I searched my mind for an answer. I would give anything to best him at his little game, but I was blank. I couldn't think. I had no idea where we were going, but I vowed to give a try and guess. Taking one last survey of the places I knew in New England, I hit on the one city that I actually wanted to see. I looked Holmes dead in the face and with an air of stubborn pride stated, "Rhode Island. I think that we are leaving for Rhode Island in New England in the colonies. More than that, I think we are headed for Newport, Rhode Island, where my daughter resides."

I have never before nor since seen the look, which set itself upon Holmes face. Dumbfounded is the only word which I feel fully describes it. There was a mixture of shock, suspicion and joy all together dancing across those features, which rarely showed any emotion. I am sure that the look on my face was just as curious as I stared back in anticipation of what was to follow. A long moment passed in which neither of us spoke. It was as if we were under a spell, until Holmes leapt up, slapped me on the back again and exclaimed, "bravo once again, old boy. You've really outdone yourself this time. How on earth did you come to this conclusion?"

I sat there amazed. For those who have read my accounts in the past, an understanding of the emotions that I experienced in these few blissful moments may be evident, but could never be sensed as I sensed them. I had been correct, not once but twice in the same day. The fact that one time was a mere guess had absolutely nothing to do with it. I had been correct, and that was all that mattered. I could not let this chance be passed without parading the triumph, which I felt, for at least a moment. I gained control of myself and hoped that my facial expressions had not given away my secret, and with as nonchalant an expression as I could muster, said, "all in good time, Holmes. All in good time," and I picked myself up and walked from the room to my bed.

Morning broke to find Holmes at his bees while I basked in my newfound glory. Although starting with the conclusion and working in reverse had not helped to clear the mystery before me, and I therefore still did not know why or how I should have determined that Newport, Rhode Island would be our place of destination, the knowledge that I had mentioned the correct answer kept me happy and contented throughout, and I replayed the events of last evening repeatedly in my mind to bolster my confidence and delight.

One thing had crossed my mind though. If we were heading for the colonies, there were certain items I needed to retrieve from my abode in Scotland. A plan formed. I would first hear from our guest today, and then, once timetables were established, I would try to find a way to dash home and recover the articles before we sailed. With a newfound feeling of security and anticipation, I joined Holmes outside in the rear of his house while breakfast was being prepared.

"Have we any idea as to what time to expect our visitor," I asked as Holmes fussed about the man-made hives he used to house his insects.

"It shall neither be too early nor too late, if I make my guess," he returned without taking time to think. "Our man states that he will find himself 'close by' on this date and that suggests he is not here exactly and will not be here long. I therefore deduce that we must give him time to come to us and then time to get to wherever it is which brings him 'close'. My conclusion is that he will be here by, but not before luncheon and leave before tea. Time itself will test if I am correct."

We breakfasted on eggs and sweet bread, taking our time and lingering over tea. Holmes did not enquire again as to how I came to my conclusions about Newport, and I looked upon this as a mark of respect.

By late morning Holmes was back at his bees and I sat in the parlor, jotting down notes, which would later become this record. The noon bell came and went without a sign of our awaited guest. Since the parlor was in the front of the house, it commanded a view of the road and long drive, which wove its way to Holmes' door. I could not help but peer out every now and then to try and get a glimpse of Sir Arthur's carriage coming up the way. Moments grew to minutes and I was about to call an end to my spying and join Holmes once again in the yard, when my eyes caught hold of a singular contraption heading up the dirt road at a rapid pace. Within seconds, I was able to identify the apparatus as a tricycle rumbling along, and now turning into Holmes' drive. The man at the pedals was large and ruddy, with a full moustache. He was wearing short pants, such as a sportsman wears, and the rate at which he came toward the entrance to the house showed me that not only was he accustomed to such speed, he enjoyed it.

Before I could turn to call Holmes, he was by my side.

"That's our man," he said deliberately, as he said all things, "let's welcome him in."

We walked to the door and opened it to find the man himself already dismounted from his vehicle and brushing the dust from his clothes.

"Sir Arthur," Holmes said as he approached our guest with an outstretched hand, "welcome to my humble home." After a brisk shake and a smile from Sir Arthur he continued, "may I introduce my colleague and friend Dr. John H. Watson," at which point he took my hand and shook it, and with a strong, low voice said, "A pleasure sir. I have heard of you and read your accounts with great interest."

I thanked him for his compliment and we retreated to the parlor for the interview he desired.

"May we offer you some refreshment," Holmes asked, as I took note of how retirement had softened his politic.

"Something cool to drink might be nice," returned our friend who now patted his brow with his handkerchief to remove the beads of perspiration, which had formed there.

"I see you fancy the tricycle," I said before we sat.

"I enjoy the exercise," he returned. "My wife and I often ride tricycles, and so, when I can, I use them to keep in shape. Today was the perfect opportunity."

By now, Holmes housekeeper had returned with lemonade in tall glasses, which she distributed to each of us. I was never partial to fruit drinks myself, but Sir Arthur didn't set his down until the glass was drained.

"Very good," he said in a pleasant manner, smiling all the while, "very good indeed."

"May I offer you more," Holmes asked.

"No, no that should suffice," he replied.

"Well, good," Holmes continued, "since we have such little time let us get down to business."

I could see that Sir Arthur also desired to attend the business at hand for he began to raise himself in his chair, as if to begin to speak, but Holmes beat him to it and started talking immediately.

"Since the trains are obviously running on time, I fear we have but a two hour period before you must depart."

"Why, that is true," sputtered Sir Arthur, "but how could you know…"

"We really don't have time for this," Holmes returned, "but, if I must, I should tell you that I know quite a few things. For instance, I know that you came here directly from the train station, and that since you are lecturing this evening, you must leave soon."

"But how could you know these things, Mr. Holmes? Who could have told you?"

"Well, in a sense, you did, Sir Arthur," Holmes said with a wry smile. "Let me explain."

"First, the tricycle you are riding is a station rental, which can be easily determined from the insignia and the condition of the vehicle. Second, since the only train to arrive in the past ninety minutes was the 11:45 from Manchester, and since the trains are never early, but sometimes late, you must have been on the 11:45, and it must have been on time for you to be here now."

"The ink smudges on your hand indicate that you were writing something while in transit and, since it is so terribly inconvenient and messy to put anything on paper while bouncing around on our trains, I must infer that you were jotting down notes for an upcoming lecture. A lecture you must give soon, or why bother to go to all the trouble?"

"Also, since only two trains depart this afternoon destined for a metropolis of any substance, and since the both leave between 3:00 and 4:00, you must be ticketed for one of them and thus your stay with us is a short one."

"Magnificent, Mr. Holmes. Correct on every front."

"Oh, but there's more," Holmes continued. "My friend and I have come to another conclusion on our own, which may hasten things along."

"Now Carlos Vargas is a scoundrel, whose reputation precedes him, and we therefore have knowledge of him and his castle. Since it is obvious where you are sending us, I have taken the liberty of making preliminary arrangement to depart for the United States in two days time, so as to arrive in New England by the 14th of the month."

Sir Arthur blinked, and his mouth was still open from when he was speaking moments ago. Since Holmes had finished his remarks the air was still and in a moment

The Occurrence at Vargas Castle

more Sir Arthur caught himself in this comical pose, and after clearing his throat, began to speak.

"I, ahem, see that Vargas is not the only one who merits his reputation. I do desire that you make the trip to the U.S. to undertake a research project I will happily fund."

"What type of research might it be," Holmes asked.

"Research into the paranormal," he returned. "Let us call it a debunking project, if you will."

"Whatever do you mean, sir," I piped in.

"If I might," Holmes broke in, and Sir Arthur nodded. "Given my knowledge of our Mr. Vargas, although it is limited, I would say that there is an attempt being made to defraud someone, using the supernatural as an accomplice. The debunking referred to would be our attempt to disprove the supernatural illusion which, once gone, will reveal the mischief and eliminate the fraud."

"Very close, Mr. Holmes," our friend applauded, "very close, but the fact is that Vargas has been deceased for some time and the castle is in new hands. Jeffrey and Priscilla Ainsley are friends of mine who purchased Vargas Castle from the Vargas family soon after Carlos' death. It seems, without the old man about the place, the family fell on hard times and were forced to sell in order to escape bankruptcy. Jeffrey and Priscilla got the place for a song and settled in to begin the family they had saved and planned for, for nearly ten years. All was seemingly going well, and I anticipated big things from the lucky couple, until I received a communiqué from them just one week ago which described the most peculiar occurrences in and about the castle."

Holmes moved to the edge of his seat and sat with his elbows on his knees and his index fingers steepled beneath his nose, in a manner I had grown accustomed to through the years. Sir Arthur sat up too, as his eyes widened and he began to tell his tale. I even found myself shifting around in my chair, for as he wove his story you almost instinctually felt that you should be tense in the event that there was need to move quickly to protect yourself from the account he presented. It went this way:

"It seems that from the time that Jeffrey and Priscilla Ainsley took possession of Vargas Castle, things began to change. Newport, Rhode Island in the spring and summer of the year is a veritable paradise, filled with warm, gently scented breezes and floral colors reminiscent of Paris in like season. As testament to this fact, thousands flock to the southern coast of Rhode Island yearly, to taste the salt sea in the air and bask in the luxury of what has become the playground of the rich in America. Vargas Castle is therefore not the only significant residence on the Island of Aquidneck, which comprises much of Newport County. In fact, Bellevue and Ocean avenues are famous for the many estates, which dot their path and house some of the wealthiest and finest families in the colonies. It was therefore not only economically, but politically correct for the Ainsleys to procure the castle when they did, for they were gaining acceptance in the better social circles and the purchase was being viewed as a noble act by those who could be called 'polite society.' I should mention here that on the advise of this 'polite society' the Ainsley's procured this property sight unseen, which, it seems, has proven to be a major blunder.

Carlos Vargas and his family had immigrated to America with a cash trove incomparable to anything they could have possibly earned in Europe. Investigations were begun immediately, but to no avail. The Americans had nothing to go on, being as Vargas had apparently received this treasure, (for it seems, there were jewels as well as silver), while in Europe, and without complaints from the continent, they had nowhere to look. All enquiries were finally closed due to the lack of any evidence of substance, and the community tolerated the situation with as much composure as possible. Vargas, who had purchased a large stone castle just off Ocean Avenue, lived in seclusion, being shunned in the higher social circles, while the elite of Newport went on about their business as if the gypsies did not exist.

Things continued this way for some time, until Carlos came to a hasty end, plummeting to his death from one of the parapets on the ocean side of the structure. There were questions, of course, but once again there was no evidence of foul play and the whole thing had to be dropped.

The Vargas family soon fell on hard times. The money dried up and with bills mounting, for they had completed extensive renovations to the structure, the family found itself nearly destitute in their luxurious accommodations. With collectors nipping at their heels, they were forced to sell the estate for a fraction of its worth in order to get out from under. Jeffrey and Priscilla were the fortunate bargain hunters whose dreams came true when they found that they had the opportunity to pick up the property for a song, as long as they struck while the iron was hot. They took possession within a fortnight and proudly owned their castle.

They secured the services of a butler, cook and housekeeper, but even before they could settle in, trouble began:

Noises could be heard throughout the house and from all quarters except those occupied by the Ainsleys or their staff. Each time an investigation was struck up by the occupants, nothing was discovered when the area in question was entered. If you were on the first floor, there would be thumping in the basement. If you were in one room, there would be a scream issued forth from across the hall. When you would get to the area in question, no sign of any disturbance would be visible. Movement at any time within the premises could be cut off by the loss of any means of illumination, but each time the authorities were summoned the place reverted to a normal condition and led the establishment to wonder at the normalcy of the occupants rather than the house itself. But as always, as soon as the officials left, the nightmare began anew.

Shadows also seem to move. You might catch a glimpse of motion with your peripheral vision only to turn in that direction to find whatever was there, gone. The electricity worked sporadically, and lights go on and off throughout the house whenever they please. And things move, gentlemen.

There are thirty-five rooms on three floors in Vargas Castle, plus the basement, and things move in that house. Not that you can see them, but an entire room's furnishings can become rearranged without anyone having been in that room. At first the Ainsleys found one or two things out of place and put it off to the housekeeper misplacing cleaned items, but then entire pieces of furniture began winding up across the room and in disarray with other pieces, so that it was quite clear that no one in their right mind was decorating things so.

And then there is the master bedroom, which is unlivable for Jeffery and Priscilla. It is continually cold in that room as if it were a crypt. That is how their wire described the room; as if it were a crypt. They have been unable to inhabit that room since they moved into the house.

Lastly, the housekeeper said that she saw a figure in the third floor hall one evening. It was a large figure dressed in a dark robe, which moved across the hall from one room to the other. She said it seemed to float, although its feet were very close to the floor, almost like a glide of some sort. Long hair covered the head so that at first it seemed as though the figure wore a hood. She remarked that there was no way to distinguish features, although the specter seemed to be bathed in a glowing blue light as it moved, which set it off from the darkened hall. You can imagine the agitation and surprise this caused within the housekeeper, who set up such a stir that within minutes the entirety of the occupants was at her side. A thorough examination of both rooms brought no results, and the shaken maid had to be sat with the entire night to quell her hysteria."

"You can see, Mr. Holmes, that the situation is becoming intolerable for the Ainsleys, and they have requested that I come to their aid with my knowledge of the supernatural. The problem is that I am hardly convinced that we are dealing in the area of the paranormal here, and business interests would delay any extended trip on my part at this time. That is why I have contacted you."

"I need your investigative powers to examine the situation and the physical arena, so that a proper comment may be made as to your opinion on the matter. If the supernatural is at work here, so shall I be; but if the cause is found to be of human design and intent, what better man to come to the rescue than Sherlock Holmes."

"Excellent story and speech," Holmes said with a glance at me. "I have questions, of course."

"I will do my best," was the reply.

"First, I must mention how inconvenient it is that you have already accepted this request on our behalf. It really puts any plans for subterfuge in serious jeopardy."

"How in the world did you know that," Sir Arthur stumbled.

"Tut, tut," returned Holmes with a wave of his hand, "your style, your demeanor, quite simple really."

"Well, it is true," replied Sir Arthur in a less than exuberant tone, "that I did mention that you would be there in my stead for the reasons I have already stated. I did not however, for an instant realize that you might take offense."

"There is no offense taken," said Holmes. "I really don't think secrecy would have been a serious consideration at any rate, but I do like to keep all options open."

"Of course, we will accept your proposal. As I said, I have already arranged for our transport to America for the day after tomorrow."

"But isn't there a ship sailing on the morrow for New York City," Arthur asked.

"Yes," replied Holmes, "but the day after tomorrow there is a smaller, working vessel departing for New Bedford in the Massachusetts colony. It carries fewer passengers and accommodations are less luxuriant with few frills, but it makes excellent time crossing the pond, I am told, and our arrival time in Newport may just improve. It will also afford my colleague time to rescue certain documents from his home in Scotland before we depart."

"Good work Holmes," I interjected, not wanting to go into long discussions on how he determined my desire before I mentioned it.

With our consultation nearly at an end, Holmes asked a few more questions pertaining to times and places and dates. We informed Sir Arthur that it just so happened that my daughter resided in Newport, and that we would be staying with her for at least part of the time.

Holmes then left us to ponder the assignment before Sir Arthur found that it was time to go, so that if there were more questions, he would have opportunity to ask them.

Arthur and I, for our part, took the remaining minutes to discuss upcoming and continuing literary projects, that being our common ground. We got along famously from the start, he being as adventurous a spirit as I fancied myself. We decided that day, that collaboration was the way for us, and set down dates and places to meet with that intent, once this business in America was at an end.

Watson's Sampler:
The Lost Casebook of Sherlock Holmes

Before long Holmes reappeared declaring that all preparations were satisfactory in his mind, and we adjourned to refreshments before Sir Arthur mounted his three wheeled steed once more, and peddled off toward the trains.

"What do you think, Holmes," I asked, as we watched him turn left out of the drive to the street beyond.

"I think that this problem is going to prove to be most interesting indeed, and dangerous too. Do not forget your pistol on this trip, Watson. I fear we may need it before we're through," and his look was grave indeed.

"Now you had better prepare to leave on the evening train if you intend to pack and be back here by nightfall tomorrow. No time for dawdling, you know. Time is of the essence and to miss our connection here, might mean death to an innocent in America."

I took him at his word and left that very afternoon for home. Railroad travel in Great Britain has been the subject of many a debate and the butt of jokes throughout the kingdom, but in defense of this tried and true means of transportation, I must make comment that on the date in question I found that rail travel was not only convenient and timely, but downright comfortable. Perhaps it was my condition, which may have been taxed by my previous jaunt south just a day before, or perhaps it was the exhaustion which may be experienced in the face of excitement, but it was necessary for the conductor to rouse me at Lockerbie Station, or I am afraid I may have slept right through my stop.

The night was clear and mild, and the air was sweet with summer. I hired a trap to transport me to my home, and left clear instructions that I was to be collected next morning in time to make the early train at 10:00 a.m. This done, I spent the remainder of the evening hours gathering notes and journals from former investigations and remembrances which, at this time, cannot be recounted to the public for various reasons, and loaded them into my large travel trunk along with a few extra clothes in readiness for our extended journey. I also took time to jot down the text of a wire, which would precede us to America and warn my daughter, Susan, of our forthcoming arrival on her shores and our wish to stay with her, if that was convenient.

With all accomplished by mid-night, I found myself once again asleep soundly with the dreams of tomorrow's adventure keeping me company.

Perhaps it is the feeling of security one receives when he knows that his services are required for the good of others, or perhaps it is the anticipation of activity following such an extended period of idleness, but to say that I awoke refreshed and energetic the next morning might very well be construed as understatement. You might say that I was veritably raring to go as I organized my belongings on my portico and awaited the station coach to arrive. The young man at the reins was the same fellow who had left me off the night before, but I am afraid he did not expect the vitality I showed when he was one quarter of an hour late. Before he was able to dismount his rig and lend a hand, I had already hoisted my cargo onto the top of the coach and prepared to enter the belly of the thing. "My word," I heard him say as he hopped down from his perch, only to have to scale the vehicle again to regain his seat and get us started.

"On, on, my good man," I shouted, as I tapped my stick on the roof of the coach, half in jest. The young driver must have read both halves of my comment though, for he made the horses lurch the coach forward, and kept up a steady, quickened pace straight through to the station. Once there, I took note of how quickly he jumped down and flung the door open before I could reach the latch handle, and how quickly and efficiently he removed my luggage from the roof and deposited it on the platform. It was as if he were showing me his best with a competitive edge to it. I appreciated that, and showed him with a smile and a hefty tip.

"Thank ya, govna'," he returned in all seriousness as I passed him and entered the station. He was a good lad.

At this point it would only tend to draw things out to relate the activities of the next week to you. Let it suffice to say that Holmes and I made our connection with the steamer bound for America, and that the Atlantic crossing went smooth with Holmes solving a neat little mystery which I will dub "The Purser's Glove" when I put it before you in years to come. We arrived in New Bedford, Massachusetts on July 13, which is exactly the same day that Arthur's suggested vessel berthed in New York City. We had, in fact, gained a day while in route and probably gained another because of the proximity of the New Bedford port to our destination. We had landed in the morning and would be in our beds at my daughter's by nightfall. The trip from New York would, most assuredly, take two days. Holmes' plan, as usual, was a success.

A fifteen-mile carriage ride and a short ferry trip across what is known as Narragansett Bay, which, I was informed, is named after a native tribe of the region, and we were in Portsmouth, Rhode Island on the Isle of Aquidneck. Now Aquidneck is an island of approximately fifteen miles long and five miles wide at its widest point. It runs north to south and is home to three communities. Portsmouth is the northernmost town and therefore closest to Massachusetts, which borders Rhode Island on its north and east. Middletown fills the midsection of the island, with Newport being the only true city, comprising the southern third of the district. I found out from our coachman that the state itself is named Rhode Island because this particular island within its borders resembles the Greek Isle of Rhodes. At least that's what the mapmakers claim.

As I said, we landed on the shores of Portsmouth and began another carriage ride south until we reached the city of Newport by mid afternoon.

What can I say about America, which has not already been said? What first struck me about the place was its size. We passed from New Bedford to Newport through broad rural roads some four carriages wide, with large farms and quaint villages dotting the way. There was talk of a manufacturing community known as Fall River just to our west, but we skirted it in order to avoid any traffic and undo delay. It was warm and clear throughout, and you could smell the sea during our entire trip. Construction appeared whenever two or three roads intersected and you could tell from that, that this was not only a young country, but also a restless one, bulging at the seams before it even had seams. The people were restless too. Strong, healthy, working types who weren't afraid to be forthright and friendly, all with the same confident manner which made them successful and, from my point of view, quite likeable. America was a place where you knew where you stood, and if there were any question, all you'd need to do is ask.

As we neared Newport, the rural look of the countryside became more congested with large homes, which were not attached to farms. Traffic increased, and the occasional motorcar passed, momentarily startling the horses who nonetheless continued their gate once they recognized the cause of their disturbance, as they would recognize a fly. Once we crossed the line at "one mile corner" and entered Newport proper, the homes became smaller, although they still took much more space than that which is familiar in the Realm, and both walking and riding traffic became heavier.

My daughter's home lay in that section of the city known as "the point," holding an address on Bridge Street. Since the coach in which we rode deposited everyone at a central square known as "the parade," we found it necessary to hire a trap to transport us to Bridge Street. While we rode the mile or so to my daughter's home, Holmes asked the driver if he had heard of Vargas Castle, and what he thought.

"I don't go there by choice," he replied, "unless there's a need. I ain't afraid, mind you, but it's always dark out there with all that fog. It's always cold, too. Even on a nice day like today." And he thought a moment, "I used to fish nearby, off Ledge Road where that castle is, but no one goes there now. It's always foggy out there. Can't see your hand in front of your face. You know what I mean?"

"Yes, I do," Holmes replied. "And what of the owners? What do you think of them?"

"Nothin', sir," he came back a bit stiffly. "Don't know nothin' about no rich folks. They come and go, and we rarely see 'em. You'd think they were Royalty or somethin' the way they act. But who cares? And who needs 'em anyway? Most of 'em only stay the summer." And he broke off again, thinking, as his horse tapped out a slow rhythm walking up the cobble -stoned roads to my daughter's house.

"But wait a minute," he started up again. "There was some talk about somethin' goin' on out there recently. Somebody dyin' or somehtin'. And ghosts too," he said with a renewed gleam in his eye. "Yeah, ghosts. That's why the place is always shrouded in fog, they say. It's them ghosts and such."

You could see from the driver's face that he was having fun with this. Newcomers from Britain interested in local legends and the like.

"You boys gonna need a ride out there while you're in town," he asked.

"Yes, we will," Holmes replied, "and as early as this very evening. Will you be able to collect us at about 7 p.m.?"

"Yes, sir, I can," the driver answered. "Lucky for you that you picked my cab today," he continued. "I'm the only one who'll go out there after dark, you know."

"Really," I put in with a questioning tone.

"Yes, indeed," he returned emphatically, with a nod. "They're all afraid," and he waved his hand to signify everyone else, apparently.

He completed his gesture just in time to pull up reins in front of a neat, little white cottage with a yard full of a variety of flowers. I had but a moment to take this all in before my daughter stepped out onto the front porch and into the sunlight. I cannot recall when I have seen anything so beautiful in all my life. The very picture of her mother in all her splendor, and I felt as if my heart would burst within me at the sight of her. If it is true that we never really know the things which mean the most to us until we no longer have them, it is also eminently true that once regained, appreciation abounds to a greater level than could ever be conceived before. My eyes burst forth with tears as I ran to my Susan, and she in turn to me. Our embrace was such that neither of us released the other for minutes. To speak the truth, I would have to say that I do not know how long we would have kept up this way were it not for the coaxing of Holmes and Susan's husband, Edward for us to break the clinch. But break it we did, and shook hands all around, and met Edward, and he, Holmes, and we moved our things into the house and wiped our eyes, and beamed as only a father and daughter can.

Should I live to be one thousand years old, I shan't forget that day. We talked and talked about everything from boarding schools, to trips across the ocean, to finding true love, to becoming a parent; Susan was with child and had been for six months or so.

Edward, for his part, seemed a fine young man with the eye of the devil in him. He'd laugh at the drop of a hat and told endless stories about the lads he worked with and for at his numerous jobs. It seemed he was a sort of "Jack of all trades," which to me seemed a bit cavalier for a soon to be father, but even as we sat there talking and telling stories, I began to trust his honesty and forthright manner. He proved to be a fine father, and husband to my Susan, and I never found need to regret any of the choices she made.

While we chatted and caught up on old family matters, Holmes busied himself unpacking and making ready for the night's adventure. He had been quite solemn throughout the day, even while questioning those we spoke to in our travel. His outward appearance was grave indeed and more than once during the hours before dinner, I saw him sit outside to test the air and light his pipe. He seemed concerned and impatient, and were I not having one of my best days, I might have joined him in his gray mood. But I knew Holmes, and I knew that if he felt things were really at an impasse for those we'd come to help, no joyous reunion would have kept him from their side. With that knowledge in mind, I reveled with my family until dinner had passed.

Abruptly at 7 p.m. Holmes stood up, donned his hounds tooth jacket and made for the door.

"Are you coming, Watson," he called back over his shoulder as I dawdled over my tea.

"Yes, Holmes, I am coming," I returned with a look and smile at my children.

"We really must go out there tonight," I explained. "The family may be in some danger, according to Holmes. Now don't wait up for us. You'll soon get used to the fact that we come and go at any and all times," and I stopped to finish the thought. "You'll also get used to the fact that you do not have to worry after us, we're…"

"Come along, Watson," Holmes called back quite sternly before I could finish.

I winked at Susan, who was well aware of Holmes methods, and our unique relationship, and out the door I went. I could hear her giggle as I descended the stairs of her porch and smiled to myself in the knowledge that years and miles had not severed the connection we had. It would be the last smile I had that night.

Phillips, the trap driver, or cab as they refer to it in the colonies, was waiting at the curb. The evening was warm and the sun was still up, yet Phillips had chosen an enclosed coach unlike the open-air carriage we had arrived in earlier.

"Why such a dreary carriage on such a lovely evening," I asked as I entered the rear compartment after Holmes.

"You'll see," was all the explanation I received.

We topped the street and turned right onto a cobble-stoned road heading for what appeared to be the center of the city. Buildings became larger and more formidable with businesses on the bottom floor and offices of various necessity and importance on the upper floors. We clopped along at an even pace with Holmes fidgeting a bit while I tried to take in the sites. At one point I noticed a street sign with a familiar name and tapping Holmes on the shoulder I said, "look Holmes a street named after our river Thames (Temz)."

To which Phillips replied, "that's Thames, (Thaamz), sir."

"Thames, (Thaamz)," I replied, "that's preposterous."

"That's how it's pronounced, sir; Thames (Thaamz)."

"That is not how it is pronounced," I demanded. "It is pronounced Thames (Temz)."

"Not around here, it ain't," he alleged. "Around here we call it Thames (Thaamz)."

Holmes shifted in his seat. I could tell by his uneasy manner that our discussion was beginning to irritate and unsettle him. I also knew that Holmes could not give two hoots what we called this street as long as we got on and off of it as quickly as possible and gained our destination soon.

I, on the other hand, was not prepared to abandon my argument so readily. I took a moment to prepare my final counter attack to the assault already attempted on the mother tongue, took a deep breath, and asked as calmly as I could, "what language are we speaking now, my good man?"

"English, of course, sir," he returned, after a second or two.

"Correct," I replied, and then asked, "and where did English originate?"

"Why, England, of course," he returned again, after another pause.

"Well, in England, my good man, the mighty river that your little street is named after, is pronounced Thames (Temz)." And I sat back, quite pleased with my accomplished logic and wit.

"Not around here it ain't," I heard him say under his breath as we turned left, up a hill, past "the parade" where he had picked us up earlier.

Perhaps it is the composition of the soil, or perhaps it is the lack of moisture in this part of the world during summer, but dust abounds in America and it wasn't long before we were brushing ourselves off regularly while we ascended the hill. We made our way past numerous other vehicles, also kicking up clouds of dust, and also passed a Synagogue and The Seventh Day Adventist Church. Phillips relayed to us that these two structures along with many others in this city were real life symbols of the Religious Freedom on which this colony was established back in the sixteen hundreds. I added that my daughter had told me that it was this sense of fair play, which had drawn her to this area in the first place.

The Occurrence at Vargas Castle

You could tell by his manner, and the descriptions of the buildings he pointed out, and the people who built them, that Mr. Phillips had driven this route many times with visitors from home and abroad. You could also tell by his manner that he was quite proud of his little city and the people who worked and lived there. He seemed to enjoy telling his tales as much as I enjoyed hearing them. I even noticed Holmes look about as he spoke. There was no alteration in the horse's gate during his dissertation, which led us to the realization that our time was being spent efficiently, and thus there were no complaints.

We mounted the hill directly and continued down Bellevue Avenue, world renowned for its mansions and the celebrities who lived there. Many a luxurious coach passed us, with teams of matched horses stepping out together, synchronized in their every move. Uniformed drivers held the
reins while brightly colored gowns and trim tailored suits adorned the passengers who took in the evening air as they rode.

I couldn't help but notice that the dust was not nearly so high once we made the grade, so to speak, and attained the "Avenue." It was quite apparent that water wagons had been employed to keep the plumes at manageable levels, so those gowns and suits were not soiled during the promenade. It was all very civilized and proper, and I, for one, rather enjoyed the spectacle of the people and carriages and mansions that we passed, even though those homes were set back from the road, behind walls and gates and fences of the most formidable style.

Motorcars were also more frequent on this road as you would imagine they would be. They darted here and there, scaring the horses where they could and generally making a noisy nuisance of themselves. Young people mostly, favored the motorcars, while we of wiser years preferred the tried and true. Horses did not break down or get flat tires or leave you stranded as a general rule. Motorcars on the other hand were capable of all of these failings in a single night. Foolishness guides youth, especially in America.

Bellevue Avenue is a rather long road with gentle curves and bends along the way, which nonetheless maintains the appearance that you are traveling straight, north to south. It is dotted evenly with a mixture of electric and gas street lamps on both sides, which we found, when lit, gave a lovely, ordered, symmetric look to the district. On the evening in question, here described, the sun had not yet set and while it was nearly half-seven before we began to see and feel the change, the sun had at least an hour left to traverse the sky, and its heat would surely linger all night.

That is why it became increasingly noticeable as we passed home after home, that the further south we moved, or should I say the closer we advanced toward Ledge Road, the cooler and darker it became. In no time at all, it seemed that we had left bright, sunny Newport and entered a cold, dark, clammy atmosphere reminiscent of the Scottish moors on a late October eve. Few carriages passed us in either direction as we traveled on. Lights could be seen in the homes and mansions nearby as fuzzy, yellow, glowing balls, where none had been necessary or even thought of just moments before. A heavy mist had also made its presence known by blotting out the warm summer evening sun and rolling around us like a cold, wet blanket, minimizing both senses of sight and sound. The horses also seemed to feel the foreboding that humans know when swift and unexpected change occurs, for their canter diminished to a walk, which required Phillips to stir them up repeatedly in an attempt to make good time.

Holmes was sharp to the task, and sniffed the air as his eyes darted to and fro, as if in search of smoke, or whatever unnatural event had caused this change.

Phillips, himself was quiet at once and stared here and there as if mesmerized, although this was surely not an unusual sight for him since he lived here on the island.

All was still. All was silent. The only sound was that of our team who had once again slowed to a walk without the driver's recognition as we turned the final turn before encountering Ledge Road itself. I, in an attempt to observe everything, phenomenon and human reaction, had myself become lost in the moment and had fixed my eyes on the dull glow of the lamp post on which the sign that marked our way was attached. As it grew nearer and the letters began to come into view, I strained to see the name, as if hypnotized on the fixture by some extraneous power. As letters became words, and meaning to those words danced through my mind, I turned to Holmes to speak, only to be jolted by his voice announcing the very words I had intended to say.

"Ledge Road," he stated sharply, and he pointed to the sign.

All manner of life, human and equine, started at the announcement as we all, in unison, jumped a bit.

Ledge Road lay to our left, and ran quickly out of sight into the gloom that had become our evening. The haze was thick and dark and still, as if we had turned and entered what seemed more of an abyss that a flat street running to the sea. Ledge Road is what is known in America as a "dead end," which means that it has no outlet and thus you must turn about in order to leave, once entered. This particular dead end existed because the Atlantic Ocean, with its craggy sentinels of stone guarding land from sea and sea from land, blocked the way. We turned the corner and began our descent down the road. There, to our left, looming up out of the night was Vargas Castle. As dark as the street and the mist and the early nightfall had become, Vargas Castle was darker still. It was also obvious that while summer had blessed the land about with lush vegetation and colorful flowers, the grounds adjacent to where we were, showed stunted growth and even dead patches due to lack of sun and warmth. Everything seemed damp and dreary. Lights flashed on and off at the castle in random order, displaying no schedule or evidence of humanity moving from one room to the next. All was quiet. All was still. No wind blew. No bird fluttered by. No sign of life dared show its face save our team of adventurers, marching boldly, though dare I say slowly along. All had fallen silent once again as we peered through the gloom to catch glimpses of flickering lights to try to make sense of.

One thing stood true and constant. Though the edifice rose at least three stories high throughout, the first floor, south end, remained lit constantly amidst the sensational barrage of flashes, to which our eyes were subject. The darkness of the structure against the darkness of the sky still could not hide the five towers, which commanded the castle and the view toward sea and land, in better days.

We entered the gates, Philips driving his team on until he reined up in front of the entrance to the courtyard at the apex of the circular drive. No wind blew. No ocean roared. All was perfectly still, as if in anticipation of what was to come. As if some sinister force was watching us arrive, measuring us against an unknown scale, to weigh our defenses should the weapons raised against us be unleashed. Dread filled my heart, as I thought these thoughts, standing before Vargas Castle.

Holmes, on the other hand was all business. "We are here," he announced as if this fact were unknown to anyone but he. "Let us knock up these fine people and get to work." He jumped down from the coach and began to march straight way toward the door leading to the first floor area which was continually bathed in light. "Come along, Watson," he said as he went his way gazing about at the castle with a curious eye rather than anything resembling awe.

I, being mindful not to disturb the peace which dead quiet brings, stepped lightly from the cart, and followed at a distance. Once I realized that I was lagging behind, I decided to step it up until I caught sight of Philips standing at his bench above the horses, looking from Holmes to me and back again. I stopped and beckoned him down, bidding him join us for both our peace of minds. He jumped down readily next to me, and securing the horses to their iron while I waited, we both walked up to the entrance Holmes had already gained.

The door swung open to find a handsome, older gentleman commanding it, who bid us enter with a bow.

"Good evening, gentlemen," he said as we walked past him into the lightly furnished anteroom. "Mr. and Mrs. Ainsley will be with you momentarily," he continued and he led us through to a larger sitting room with sizeable leather chairs, lamp tables, and books on all walls in the manner of a small personal library. He then excused himself to fetch his master, leaving us a moment alone. Holmes, of course, went straight to work examining this room with the utmost care.

"You will notice that the lights in this and the adjacent rooms seem to be in perfect working order," he announced, as he scrutinized the bookcases. "Odd, don't you think, that there should be such chaos in the system elsewhere."

I was about to comment on his remark when the far door opened and the Ainsleys were ushered in by their man.

"Jeffrey and Priscilla Ainsley," he announced before disappearing momentarily, only to return with a tray of refreshments.

"Do sit down gentlemen," encouraged Mrs. Ainsley, who was a handsome, graceful, young lady with kindness showing through her outward features. "Have some tea and cookies," she continued. "You are the gentlemen of whom Sir Arthur wired us, are you not?"

"We are," I answered. "How astute of you to recognize us…"

"Not at all," she cut in. "No one ever comes here socially. For you to call at all means that you were either summoned or sent. Since we've not beckoned you forward, someone else must have, and since you have completed your mission to arrive at our doorstep, you must have been forewarned. Only Sir Arthur's adventurous friends fit that bill. Mr. Holmes and Dr. Watson, I take it."

"Very good young lady," Holmes piped in. "A fine little bit of elementary deduction. I'm impressed. Sherlock Holmes, at your service. This is my friend and colleague Dr. John H. Watson," and we both bowed slightly. "And this is our cabman, Mr. Phillips, who did not want to be left alone outside."

"Who could blame him," returned our hostess with a warm smile, as she walked to Philips and shook his hand with her right, while her left hand patted his right shoulder understandingly.

Turning back to us she continued, "this is my husband Jeffrey, the master of the house, and, I believe you have already met Godfrey, his man servant."

Godfrey bowed at his introduction, while Jeffrey stepped up and shook Holmes hand, then mine, and then Philips' in turn. "Gentlemen," Jeffrey said, "welcome to my home. Many strange things have happened and are even now happening in this house. Our hope is that you might bring an end, or at least some answer to all of this."

"That is also our desire," Holmes returned as he sat in a large leather chair to our host's right. At his lead we all sat and made ourselves comfortable. "I would like to begin our investigation immediately, if that meets with your approval?"

"Most assuredly it does," returned Jeffrey.

"Good," said Holmes. "I would like to begin by asking a few questions. Firstly, is this everyone who resides at this address?"

"No, Mr. Holmes," Mrs. Ainsley offered, "there are also the housekeeper and the cook."

"May we have them in then?"

"Of course," Jeffrey returned. "Godfrey," he said, turning to the standing manservant who bowed slightly and took his leave.

"How long has this plague been upon you," Holmes began again.

"We have lived here for three months, and have had troubles from the beginning," Jeffrey answered. "It began with the noises."

"Noises," I asked.

"Yes, Doctor, noises. Thumping noises, which seemed to be coming from the cellar. They were rhythmic, you know? Boom – boom – boom, that sort of thing. They started nearly immediately, but we have never been able to locate their source or the reasons for them."

"Have you searched," Holmes joined in.

"Yes, but we have never been able to get very far. There is constant interference, such as the lights..."

"Yes, the lights," interrupted Holmes, "but you can always get around that inconvenience with torches or candles or something, can you not?"

"We have tried that," continued Jeffrey, "but something always seems to happen, like the candles blowing out when there is not a trace of draft in the house, or we get distracted by noises elsewhere, or someone sees something or feels something, and all is lost to preoccupation. Include that with the fact that no one is sure what we are looking for, or if we really want to find whatever it is, and you can see how this all might get the best of a person."

"I do see," returned Holmes, looking quite serious, "but I also see where there must be a solution to this problem, if you ever intend to reside within these walls. We really must have a search."

By this time Godfrey had returned with the housekeeper and the cook, and upon their entrance into the room Holmes turned his attention to them.

The Occurrence at Vargas Castle

"Come in, come in ladies. Do have a seat while I fill you in on what has transpired thus far." They both looked from Holmes to their master who made a gesture which reassured them, for they both took places side by each on a love seat by the front wall.

"My name is Sherlock Holmes and this is my friend Dr. John Watson. We have come here from London, England, to put an end to the mysterious happenings, which have occurred in this abode as of late. Tonight we are going on a little excursion to find out what has been going on in the cellar, and we need everyone to join in."

"I'd rather not," spoke up the housekeeper, whose adventure on the third floor had been told to us by Sir Arthur. "I am employed here, but that is the extent of my investment. I see no need to take things further, and I do not intend to put myself in danger to improve the condition of others; beggin' your pardon ma'am."

Mrs. Ainsley smiled and nodded understandingly.

"My dear woman," Holmes returned, "I wouldn't think of putting you in danger. Our need, this evening, is to have everyone together in order not to be distracted, or put off the chase by concern for those not accounted for. As I read things so far, the intention of whomever is causing this chaos is to keep you fine people cooped up in this area of the house, and not let you find out what is really going on. It's quite ingenious really. It is obvious that they have made this floor, at this end of the building, a safe haven as it were, and thus have had the run of the remainder of the dwelling while you remain here. If we, as a whole, search the house without interruption, we may well find what these scoundrels are up to and, in effect, put an end to it."

Holmes speech did seem to have an effect on the entire company. It was apparent that spirits were raised and confidence was gained by his self-assured manner. I noticed Godfrey nod a couple of times while he spoke and the housekeeper, whose name we learned was Alice, seemed to improve in attitude as she watched the faces of the others, apparently realizing that she may be alone in her demand to be left out of things.

Holmes, on the other hand, had not finished with his barrage on her misgivings and continued before anyone could speak.

"Young lady," he said, taking the housekeepers hand, "anyone who knows me will tell you that I am not accustomed to failure, and that I do not intend to fail now. But in order to accomplish what Dr. Watson and I have set before us, we will need complete cooperation. Now it is evident that you are a brave person, in that you spoke up just now, although I'm sure you felt that we were all in agreement as to the best course. I admire that strength, and if I might suggest that you redirect it to the task at hand, I am positive that you will feel the better for it once the job is done."

There was a moment of silence while she studied him. Had he not chosen detection as his line, I have always felt that Holmes would have made a great orator on any number of subjects. As the moment passed there was almost a palpable feeling that he had not only convinced our Miss Alice to go along, but also anyone else who may have had a silent objection at this point. As Alice's face brightened, Holmes released her hand but stepped closer to her and whispered, "I would wish for you to stay close to me as we go. Along with directions, I may be in need of an honest opinion down there, and I believe I can trust you for that."

With nods all around and the feeling you get from a group when you realize that you are all of one mind, we began the preparation for our excursion into the bowels of a house which seemed determined to keep us out. Jeffrey sent Godfrey for candles and torches, but Holmes specifically asked for lanterns, in order to avoid drafts and the chance of loosing light due to puffs of wind.

I checked my coat pocket to find my Webly as it should be, loaded and at the ready, should its services be required.

As for the others, I noticed Philips retrieve a poker from the fireside and test it for strength and balance by shaking it and holding it up like a sword, Godfrey recovered a kindling log from the same area, which made a formidable club, and the cook, who was a rotund, strong looking young woman, eyed the six-inch blade of a butchers knife she must have slipped into her apron pocket when she was called away from her stove. We were a fine lot making ready for our descent into the unknown. Holmes suggested that we walk single file, one after the other, with he in the lead, followed by Alice, then Godfrey, then the Ainsleys with Priscilla ahead of Jeffrey, then Sophie, the cook, then Philips and finally I would take up the rear guard. We were to be in physical contact with the person ahead of us at all times by means of employing our off hand to grasp the belt or the apron or the back of the blouse of the person who went before us. This way we formed a chain from which we could send up the alarm, should any link be broken. Once ready and set, Holmes swung open the door at the north side of the room where we were, to reveal the sporadically flashing hall we would have to traverse in order to gain entrance to the rest of Vargas Castle.

The scene, which lay before us, was one of utter confusion. The hall measured a good one hundred feet in length with doorways leading to rooms and other hallways on either side. While the hall itself was in sheer darkness, flashes of light emanated from those doorways just described in random fashion and interval. One moment everything was black, then one light would light, then another, then all lights in all doorways would flash on and then all would be blackness again. There was neither rhyme nor reason to it.

The hallway was decorated in a gothic motif, which merely lent to the eeriness of the sight. Sconces in the figures of gargoyles adorned the walls, harkening back to the days when candles were all there were to hold off the night. Large heavy pictures and tapestries hung from dark papered walls which caught and buried the flashes of light under their awkward gloom.

We started off slowly, each playing his part by taking hold of the person in front. Holmes held his lantern high and ahead so that a maximum of lighting could occur. He chose his steps carefully, and tiptoed along gazing always forward as we made our way down the corridor. As I took up the rear, I was afforded a somewhat clear view of everyone ahead of me, and could not help but notice Sophie with her free hand attempting to light a candle as she passed one of the sconces. Each time the candle sparked to life, it would immediately extinguish as if blown out by some unseen and unfelt, ill wind. It was a very tense and uncertain situation. No one spoke as we crept along at a snails pace. I could see Holmes from my vantage point giving and receiving hand signals from Alice as we went. With the disruption of the strobe effect, it was difficult to make out what message they were trying to convey to each other, but as time passed, it seemed to me that Alice was motioning toward the end of the hall, at which point she seemed to be saying we should turn left. Just as this information was settling itself into my consciousness there was a loud scream from the center of the line. We all jumped and froze in our tracks at the ear shattering sound, which cut the air. There, as the lights flashed on and off around us stood Sophie, pointing into the open darkness of a doorless room with both her hands. She shook all over as she attempted to speak to those nearest, while they, in turn, attempted to console and aid her.

"What is it," shouted Holmes from the front of the line.

"Sophie has seen something," returned Mr. Ainsley as he put his arm around her shoulders pulling her close, in an attempt to hear what she was trying to say.

"Is she alright," Holmes continued?

"Yes, she's okay," Ainsley shouted back, "but she has seen a face in the darkness."

"Is the face still there," returned Holmes?

"No, it vanished between flashes."

"Then let's press on," Holmes answered.

"But Mr. Holmes…"

"No buts, Mr. Ainsley," Holmes' reply was stern. "If Sophie is not injured, and the apparition is gone, I suggest that we keep moving. Distraction seems to be the greatest ally of those controlling these events. We may defeat them by being both vigilant and true to our course. That means completing our task and gaining the cellar without delay. We need to move on now, people."

And with that he began to step off toward the end of the hall with many of us scrambling to regain our handhold on the person in front of us. No one spoke again as we moved further still down the hall, lights flashing and floor creaking. Sophie had recovered herself although she now held onto Mr. Ainsley's free hand with both of hers and kept her head down so as not to catch a glimpse of any unwanted sights. Things were going fairly well considering our position and situation, until the noise began.

A low hollow "Boom" rang out from below us as we reached the halfway point of the hall. It may not have been the noise that was so frightening, as it was the reverberation through the house, which we all felt. It started slowly enough, and when it started, we stopped. "Boom," it went, away off at first. Then "Boom" again, a bit closer. Then "Boom" closer still. And "Boom," you could feel it in your shoes, and "Boom," your legs were involved, and "Boom," you felt it in your stomach, then "Boom," you felt it in your heart, then "Boom," "Boom," "Boom," louder, stronger, faster, stronger, "Boom," "BOOM," "BOOM," "BOOM!!!"————————silence!

Although we were not moving, and although we did not move, I would wager that with the exception of Holmes, every person in that hall leapt within themselves at the advent of such shear and utter silence. We were shaken to our bones, to put it mildly, and we were frozen to the spot. Only Holmes moved. And I could see from my vantage point that he was exceedingly busy feeling the walls and furniture about him for any available evidence, which might be rendered to his sharp mind.

Moment to moment we came back to our senses. I saw the Ainsleys begin to move about, touching each other to see if they were okay. Murmuring could be heard from the others, and soon everyone was looking about, as if we were a line of people waiting for a train to arrive.

"If we're all okay, let's move on," Holmes announced as he started off again without waiting for an answer.

The lights continued to flash furtively as we all, once again, began to walk cautiously toward the far end and the cellar stairs.

Watson's Sampler:
The Lost Casebook of Sherlock Holmes

It is truly amazing, the number of images which leap to mind at a time like this. While fear was an emotion prevalent within me, it was subdued somewhat by thoughts of my Susan and our reunion, just short hours before. Although I was well aware that we were scant miles apart, at this moment she seemed further from me than when the Atlantic separated us. In fact, the scene was so strange and so alien to my senses, the idea that we had left earth and were now playing out our parts in some distant universe did not seem out of the question, and I struggled to keep my imagination in check as the continuing strobe effect seemed to entrance me.

We were nearing the end of the hall. I could make out Holmes as he moved forward to turn to the left and begin what appeared to be his descent down a large stairwell. We were all moving very slowly. Holmes' lantern afforded us little light, and since it had been the only lantern in the house, most of stared after his light or let the strobe effect aid our sight since all our torches and candles had been extinguished long ago by some unknown force. We inched along. We were doing fairly well. My head was clearing. It was quiet. We were going to be all right.

Then it happened. As if by cue, all the lights went out. Holmes had just disappeared around the corner so that most of us did not have the advantage of his lantern, and the lights went out. They all just went out. We were nearly in utter blackness. Once again we stopped, trying to adjust to the dark and get our bearings. My mind raced. Holmes would be back around the corner in a moment and we would, at least, be able to use his dim beacon to navigate. We waited for what seemed to be an eternity, and then there was a scream!

I felt Philips' belt give a strong tug and, for a moment, I was being carried along, down the hall, toward where Holmes had turned the corner. It didn't take long. At the sound of the scream Holmes had wheeled around and started back toward me with his lantern. We met near the middle of the line about three quarters of the way down the hall. Our line had dissolved into a group, milling about. "He's gone," cried Sophie.

We gathered at the spot where Godfrey had stood in line just moments before. Priscilla Ainsley protested that the belt that encircled Godfrey's waist which she had held onto, had been ripped from her grasp so quickly that she had no time to determine why or how it happened, or where Godfrey might have gotten off. Further investigation showed that Alice's apron string, which Godfrey held as he walked, had torn away at the seam, leaving only the front still attached to the now much shaken housekeeper.

"Where has he gone, Mr. Holmes," she said as Holmes dove to the floor with his lantern, and began feeling the surface with his hand and tapping and scratching as he went along.

"He's disappeared," Philips started. "Disappeared into thin air. Taken by the spirits, that's what."

"Nonsense," I put in, though I didn't know why.

"Nonsense, indeed," Holmes returned.

The hall began flashing again, furiously, and the low booming also started, only further off, it seemed. Holmes had not yet completed his examination when I noticed Philips and Sophie preparing to break ranks and start for the door where we had entered.

"Holmes," I said in a way that would alert my friend to the problem without causing too much attention.

"Right," he returned without looking up. "Shall we continue on?"

"Continue on," Mrs. Ainsley shot back quite disturbed. "Mr. Holmes, Godfrey is missing!"

"Precisely," Holmes replied in a matter of fact way. "And since we are able to do him no good standing about here, I suggest that we carry on as before, and see what comes of it."

"But Mr. Holmes, what about the authorities," she continued, "shouldn't we at least alert someone?"

"I am alert, Mrs. Ainsley, and that will have to do for now."

Holmes started down the hall again with the rest of us in tow, although Mrs. Ainsley and Alice kept looking back at where Godfrey had disappeared. The flashing continued as we rounded the corner and began our descent down the stairs. The booming resumed as well, but it was far off and did not increase as it had before.

Holmes once again held his lantern high for us, for as we began our descent, the stairway was pitch black being that there were no rooms on either side of the stair, and therefore no lights flashed on and off here. We moved along slowly, one step at a time to ensure that no one fell, and to keep track of each other along the way. You could see past Holmes light, to the bottom of the stairwell, which seemed to empty out into a room on the left, where another light sporadically blinked. As I look back, I can recall the eerie feeling within the pit of my stomach, acting as a warning not to continue. The booming had increased somewhat and then died again suddenly, leaving a stark silence to the proceedings, which reminded me of the stillness, which overtakes the land before the onset of the most violent storms.

We took another step.

I could see Holmes turn to check each one's position.

Another step further.

The descent was going well. Three more steps and Holmes would be at the bottom. Did something flash past on the landing at the last flicker? I couldn't say for sure although everyone, including Holmes, froze in their tracks momentarily.

Another step.

The light in the cellar went completely black.

One-step more.

Holmes was at the landing, peering into the darkness of the wide expanse of cellar, while he awaited us all. We gathered at the landing. Once Holmes was there, we had hurried our steps to join him.

The dark was all encompassing. I don't believe any of us could see five feet in front of himself. The floor was made of dirt, and there was a musty smell, as if there were a drainage problem in foul weather.

Holmes did not miss a beat, continuing into the blackness as soon as we had gathered. The cellar seemed as if it were one vast open space with support pillars of brick spread throughout, evenly separated. We formed ourselves into a line again, but this time we walked abreast of each other, with Holmes in the center so that each individual would get full advantage of his dim beacon. (I should remind the reader that throughout this portion of the ordeal, a slight breeze blew, rendering any candle or unprotected lamp useless.) The going was slow once again, due to the continued darkness and the occasional pillar.

I could only estimate how deep we were into this man-made cavern. Aside from the breeze, the place was deathly still. No sound, save those echoes we were making, could be heard. No sight, save Holmes' lantern and those closest to it, could be seen. We inched along, hearts filled with the trepidation that something else was down here.

There was a sound. Off to the left, a scratching. We peered into the black, but could see nothing. The sound stopped. No, there it was again. Scratching, I think, or shuffling, as if someone were dragging his feet as he walked on the dirt. It stopped. It started. It was far off, but getting closer. We couldn't see. Even Holmes was transfixed in his place, beacon held high, staring into nothingness. Would it come into view? Would it all of a sudden be upon us in the night, in the dark? What was it? The noise got louder. It was just over there. Just out of sight.

There was a frightful yell and a dull thud, as if a body had been dropped to the ground. Everyone started and then froze. Before we could recover, I heard Holmes' voice cry out, "over here!"

We shuffled after Holmes' light as he ran toward the noise. We were in single file once again, and none less happy of it than myself, for taking up the rear. We sped along. Holmes took the lead like a man possessed, seemingly indifferent to those in need of his beam.

As we went our way I had the strangest sensation that I was not alone. Not that I was not with the party at hand, but that there was another, aside from us, nearby. Without time or illumination to look around, I passed it off as fear and continued on.

It wasn't long before my fear was realized. No sooner did I hear Holmes cry out, "Over hear, I've found him," than I felt two very small, but very powerful hands grasp my right hand and pull. The unexpected jolt set me spinning. I was turned completely around. I was facing back to where we had come. I could see the doorway with the reflected flashes from the lights above. My hand was released, and there, just ahead of me, between the flashes and myself something passed in and out of view. It was small, and fast, and alive. I could not make it out, and it was in and out of my sight so quickly that I had no idea what it could be, but it had been there. Holding my hand.

My first urge was to follow it. I even took a few steps before I realized just how lost I could get down here. I checked to take a bearing on the flashing doorway, and even as I looked at it, it went dark. The flashing stopped. All was blackness.

My breathing became rapid. I could feel it in my chest. A little tinge of panic leapt into my throat. I spun around to search out Holmes and his light, but it and he had vanished. I turned back. Where was I? Which way was out? I took a few steps forward, but realized I had no idea which way I was going. And that thing was out there. I turned to the direction, which felt most like the way towards Holmes. I took two steps before something brushed my pant leg. My heart was pounding. One more step and I cried out, "Holmes."

My heart nearly burst within me when I heard my dearest friend return my call.

"Over here, old boy," he said, and I saw his beam of light shine through as the other members of our party stepped back from whatever they had been so closely observing.

I nearly broke into a run at the sight of them. I may have taken five steps or so before my feet went out from under me. It was as if the floor had been removed. I landed face down, once again immersed in utter darkness. Before I could right myself my friends had arrived. Never have I been so happy to see anyone at all. I sat up to find that I was in a hole some three feet deep. Further inspection revealed it to be rectangular in shape, resembling a shallow grave.

"What is this Holmes," I stammered as I stood up and climbed out of the man made depression.

"It is what I suspected, Watson," he returned. "Let's get Godfrey back upstairs and I'll explain."

"Godfrey," I exclaimed. "You've found him?"

"Yes, Watson," Holmes continued, "he was over there in much the same condition as you found yourself I'm afraid."

We made our way back to the stairway from which we had come. Magically the lights began to flash again almost immediately upon our decision to leave.

We made our way back to the sitting room without further incident. Holmes led the way and we moved swiftly now that we were sure of our way and our goal. Once back at our original starting point, we gave Godfrey a brandy to steady him. He was shaken but unhurt. Once Godfrey had been tended to, we all took a brandy, servants as well as masters, and we sat down to discuss Holmes' findings. Sure enough we had all been there, but only Holmes had drawn any conclusions from the adventure just completed.

"What did you make of it, Holmes," I asked, prompting him to begin his explanation. It was clear that we all awaited any light to be shed on these latest experiences.

"It seems simple to me," he began. "This evening we have witnessed an attempt, by persons unknown, to keep us from looking into the cellar and seeing what we saw."

"But what did we see Mr. Holmes, other than holes dug in a dirt floor?"

"Precisely, Miss Alice," Holmes returned to the young lady who posed the question. "Holes, where someone has been searching for something."

"But what could be worth searching for in this house," Mrs. Ainsley put in, picking up on the conversation.

"Treasure, I think," replied Holmes.

"Treasure," Jeff Ainsley came back. "But what…"

"Yes, treasure, Mr. Ainsley," Holmes broke in. "But I feel I have already said too much. Let it suffice to say that my opinion is, that everyone's safety may now be in jeopardy, now that our adversaries know we are onto them."

"Just one moment, Mr. Holmes," Sophia started. "What about Godfrey and what happened to him?"

"Just a ploy, my dear," Holmes returned, "Just a ploy."

"Deduction tells me that Godfrey was both taken and then left alone because we continued on our journey to the basement. He was spirited away by use of a trap door and then left unmolested because we continued on our way. Had we stopped our search and returned to the sitting room as our inhospitable hosts in this show had hoped, I am certain that Godfrey would have been in greater danger, and been drugged or worse, before being deposited elsewhere in the house. Our efforts kept them off him, thus securing his rescue."

"This is true," Godfrey chimed in. "After falling in what seemed to be a tube, which deposited me near where you found me, I was set upon by unseen hands, which were attempting to subdue me. I am afraid they may have succeeded, but suddenly they released me and left me to fend for myself in the dark. I had only wandered about for a few minutes before falling into the hole where you found me."

"Yes, it was a daring attempt at distraction, but desperate people do daring things," Holmes continued. "That is why it is imperative that no one place themselves in any danger while I am gone."

"Gone? Gone where," Mrs. Ainsley asked.

"Watson, I would like you to stay here as protection for these fine people while I am away," Holmes said to me, before turning his attention back to Mrs. Ainsley. "My dear," he continued, directing his remarks to Mrs. Ainsley, "I am going to discover who is behind these phenomena, and how we shall bring them to justice. Since it seems relatively impossible to lay hands on these culprits within these walls, I must go elsewhere to find the means with which to bring them down."

"But who, Mr. Holmes," asked Philips, who had found his tongue since taking the brandy.

"I have my own ideas on that point, which I will share with you once I am certain of their validity."

And that is how we left things. We spent the remainder of the evening and night at Vargas Castle, sleeping on the chairs in the sitting room, while the live-in servants and owners took to their beds. Philips left for home, and although we had to escort him to the road, he assured us that he would return in the morning to collect Holmes for his secret mission. Philips also assured me that he would drop by Susan's home with a note I had written, explaining as much as I knew and could let her know. All would go as planned. I would be staying on, while Holmes investigated elsewhere. The Ainsleys and their servants would also be staying on at the castle, until we arrived at an end. Everything was set in place.

When morning came, Holmes departed leaving strict instructions for we who remained, not to venture into other areas of the castle unless it was imperative, and even then, we were not to venture forth alone. He left, reassuring us that he would have his answers soon, and that all would be well again in no time.

Once he was gone, there was little left for us to do but wait. The rules were simple. By virtue of my close acquaintance with Sherlock Holmes, I was unofficially in charge. In this supervisory capacity, I determined that teamwork was the safest approach to any problem which might arise while we inhabited the safety zone, which was the southern wing of the structure.

The morning went slowly, but remained incident free. There were noises throughout the building, but not of a very frightening nature, and as I learned from the other tenants, random noise was not out of the ordinary in Vargas Castle. I settled down in the sitting room with my notes to organize while the others went about their business of cleaning and cooking and fetching and supervising. No sun shown. No birds sang. It was gray and dull and dreary. In other words, everything was normal for Vargas Castle.

I am afraid that a man like myself, when presented with a lack of stimulation, may become less than alert during long periods of solitude and inactivity. So it must have been on this day, which dragged on so tediously, that I found myself deserting my notes early, to try to gain some perspective by parading around the exterior of the premises for exercise. I instructed those who remained inside, to conduct their business in twos or threes while I was gone, and to never be out of eyesight of each other. Assured that my orders would be followed to the letter, I set out on my little journey.

There are many different forms of fog which I have encountered in my travels. In actuality, and as many will attest, being a citizen of London, England itself, is a worthy credential to the bearer's expertise in "fog" experience. For example, there is mist, which is light and airy, and even pleasant as it winds its way through hill and dale and rises to the sun of an evening or a morning, heralding the brightest day or the clearest night. There is a morning fog, which is thick but patchy, leaving clear and navigable areas until it lifts with the sun. There is evening fog, which holds the land in its grasp until night has come and darkness is ushered in. There is a cold, winter fog, and a soaking fog, an oily fog and a blanket fog, which seems to cover everything, muffling sound and sight with its heavy stillness. There are many fogs which roam the earth and blot out light and dark, leaving the illusion of brilliance at dusk or dead of night at day, but I have yet to experience another fog like that which hung about Vargas Castle.

There was absolutely nothing appealing about it. It did not move and it was gray. What light did penetrate its opaque was dulled to inconsistency, and subdued into tricking the traveler with its shadows and hidden forms. It was as if it was alive, but without any warmth, which life brings to those fortunate enough to posses it. It was cold and hard and uncomfortable, reaching inside your clothing to touch the skin and send shivers throughout. It muffled sound, and then released it, as if to lure you away to unknown parts where it would wall you in and loose your way, hiding not only what you sought, but your return as well.

Into this inhospitable realm I stepped, as I left the castle walls to search its grounds. The muted roar of the ocean could be heard to my left hand, or was it my right. I checked the earth beneath my feet for clues, since nothing else showed itself clearly, given that I was encompassed so thoroughly the moment I strode outside. But earth itself gives little evidence, save the trodden path, to which I stayed.

I determined to keep the castle at my left throughout my journey, as its looming form was distinguishable, even in this haze. As long as the castle was to my left, I would be safe, continually having a point of reference and a safe haven to which I could retreat, should the necessity arise.

As I mentioned, I checked the ground beneath my feet and found no clues to indicate in which direction the ocean lay. I formulated a plan to take ten steps before checking my position against the position of the castle, in view, to my left. I set off, pacing ten steps before checking my progress versus the castle. Ten more steps and all was well. Ten more with no problem. Ten more... There was a noise to my right.

Nothing overpowering, but a definite crackling sound, as if someone or something was passing a few yards away.

"Hallo," I said to no reply.

I checked the castle. Its form stood black against the gray of the fog. Ten steps; no wait! The crackling occurred again. It began when I stepped off and stopped when I stopped.

"Hallo," I said once again, with the same result.

I took three steps and then stopped. I heard the whoosh of something sliding to a halt, just over there. My anger kindled, for I knew I was being shadowed, but for what purpose. I took ten more steps and checked the castle. There was the edifice, standing to my left as it should, and there was the sound, trailing off to my right, beckoning me to follow. Trees with low-slung branches blocked my way, but the movement was sure, and I was well aware that had not the cloud about me been so thick, I would certainly have the ability to spy my adversary as it stood awaiting my next response.

I took two steps. It took two. I took three more. It took three. Patience was wearing thin.

"Hallo," I shouted, as my anger showed in my voice. "Who is it?"

I took two more steps and lunged to my right. There was a rustle of trees and leaves and branches as my quarry fled. I had taken my walking stick with me from the castle and using it to block by face from any branches lurking in the mist, I was making good time. At one point, it was apparent that as I reached a spot, that spot was just recovering from the disturbance left by those I chased, but I had not caught a glimpse of them yet. My breathing began to get heavier, and fearing that I would tire soon, I took a chance. With my right hand, the hand which carried the cane, I struck out. I knew that I was close to my target and felt that if I could strike it, perhaps I could upset it enough to overtake it.

I swung the stick and sure enough, the end hit something solid but moving. I swung again and it was gone.

I stopped to check for sound. There was none. All was quiet and dim. What to do now, I thought to myself, as I stood alone in this damp, dull place. I glanced over my shoulder to see if the castle was still in view. It was not, but I was hardly surprised. Spinning directly to my right, with the castle to my left, and initiating a pursuit, which would obviously take me some distance, would also, obviously take me out of eyeshot of the castle, and I knew that before I took the plunge. The trick now, was to retrace my footsteps back to the point of origin, and regain my proximity to the building and its reassurance that I was not lost.

I made my way a few paces in the encompassing darkness, which seemed to close in ever nearer. So thick was the mist that I fear that someone plagued with a claustrophobic temperament might have become unhinged by the very lack of personal space afforded him in this gloom. It closed in on all sides to the point where securing the knowledge of ones own watch took some doing. I moved ahead a few more paces in the direction I felt was correct, but nothing looked familiar. As I reviewed our race in the mists, I could not recall making any turns or sways in any direction, other than directly away from my position as compared to the castle. This meant that continuing in the direction I had now chosen would most assuredly lead me directly back to the starting point. This logic made me bolder and I marched ahead ten paces or more before checking. There, just off center to my right, stood the towers and walls familiar to me. A wave of relief flowed over me at their sight, and although they seemed to be swaying somewhat, I was sure that I had returned safely, and that no nature's trick of eyes and land, locked clouds could disconnect reality from logic. But not wanting to become too overconfident in my, or nature's abilities, I made for the structure straightaway.

Since visibility was decidedly poor, I realized that I must be extremely close to the formation before me, in order to see it at all. It therefore should only have taken me a few steps to be at the base of the outer walls. But after taking these few steps, I realized that I could no longer see the building. A queer sensation swept over me as I strained my eyes to see, but could only make out a grove of trees, stretching before me. I carefully retraced my steps. Turning back, I looked up, and there was Vargas Castle looming up. I set off again, tripping now and again over the underbrush, for I kept my eyes fixed on the target to eliminate any chance of mistake. Within five steps, the apparition, which was the wall, dissolved into what was actually the grove of trees I had just come from. Their shape, against the gray, had deceived my eyes into thinking they were something they weren't.

My heart sank.

In the desperation of the moment, I ran back to the grove in the false hope that I was yet still wrong. I was not, and what was worse was the overwhelming emptiness which one feels when they know they are lost.

My bearings had obviously been misled. I must have turned to the left or right while in pursuit of my phantom, not realizing the movement in the heat of the chase. I decided to start off again taking a different tack, slightly left, in the event that I had only made a minor miscalculation. I also altered my strategy. I would now walk continually in the direction I had chosen, knowing that I would eventually encounter something familiar, such as a road or a neighboring home or the sea, all of whom would renew my bearing and set me straight again.

I set off, but I had hardly walked ten paces when that familiar click, which told me that my phantom friend had returned, echoed through the underbrush to my right.

Vowing not to be distracted or lured away from my present course, I carried on, forward, noting the noise but paying it no heed. I must have traveled but a moment when the click began anew. There was no path, and conditions had worsened to the point where I was reaching out with stick in hand to guide myself, much as a blind person feels his way.

Click, click, click, off to my right. It seemed to be drawing nearer.

Click, click, click. Unconsciously I looked off to the right as I walked, peering into the opaque to try and catch a glimpse. I could see nothing.

Click! Click! Click!

My eyes darted, scanning the white while I moved steadily forward. Not altering my track, but keeping watch on my flank to assure that no surprise attack would occur from being unwary. My heart was beating rapidly, I must admit.

Click! Click! Click!

"Who could it be," I thought as I moved ever further down my imaginary line to destinations unknown.

Click! Click! CRACK!

The loudness of the sound spun my head a bit, it seemed so close. As I took one more step, I felt my stick free up from ground or brush or limb, as if it were being held in mid air, without the obstacles familiar until now. I turned my head back rather casually to find the source of this newfound freedom, only to find myself walking off the edge of a precipice some forty feet above the waiting arms of rock and sea below.

With one foot already over the rim, arms and stick before me, and momentum pushing on, I could not help but fall. My stick flew from my hand in the wild spasm, which encompassed me. I was about to die. Arms flailed, and the foot, which was extended, zipped back quickly clicking the heel of its stationary partner on the brink. I was now extended over the abyss in a forty-five degree condition, which surely meant my doom, and in the split second before my plummet, when your mind realizes that all is lost, I hung motionless, connected to earth by two hapless anchors, who would be deserting there posts as soon as gravity took command.

To describe what happened next would fall on deaf ears, save those who have experienced similar circumstance. The moments encapsulating the throws of death seem endless, as if time itself has been suspended in order that the victim of the action or reaction might immerse himself in the agony of the experience. So it was with me as I began my fall. But strange as it may seem, when logic fails, and will gives up, the natural instinct to survive remains, guided by Providence or life's own spirit. Without the conscious awareness of what I was doing or why, I spun my body one hundred and eighty degrees, which turned me to the unnatural attitude of falling back first from the cliff. My feet were still against the earth with my heels still touching ground, as I reeled backwards. I must have been perpendicular to the cliff, with my arms extended to both sides, before my right hand touched something hard. Instinctively, I grabbed hold.

There are trees which grow outward, dangling precariously over most chasms, which almost seem to be daring gravity to claim them. They perch themselves, as if to show their strength against the odds that one-day they will spill over to join what lies below. It was the outstretched branch of one of these brave sentinels which touched my hand and saved my life. For a moment I hung again in mid fall, straight out, feet resting on earth while arms and hands held tightly to my link with life. Before I could decide on my next move, my feet slid from the rim and sent me swinging out over the coastline, clinging to the flexing bows of my champion. The tree was strong. An oak, I think. Its limb creaked under my weight, but never gave any indication of breaking. On the way back in, I saw a chance and took it, dropping from the limb to a rock, jutting from the face of the cliff.

There I sat, for some time, regaining my composure.

Sherlock Holmes meanwhile, unbeknown to me, had been making strides in other quarters. He was, in fact, at that moment, leaving Newport's City Hall with a list, which would lead him throughout the city, and had I but known of the progress he was making, I might have felt easier about my own situation. For here I was atop a perch, still thirty feet above the sea, and ten feet below where I had just been.

Which way should I go?

Both directions held obvious danger, and neither held solutions. I still was and would be lost, no matter the choice. After taking a moment to weigh the pros and cons of both decisions, one fact became clear, and that fact decided the issue. My walking stick, perhaps my most cherished possession, lay on the rocks below. I knew that it would never survive the tides cycle and would be forever lost, unless retrieved directly. My course was clear.

Sliding to the edge of the boulder where I sat, I noticed a hand and foot hold to my left. One characteristic of jagged cliff faces is, that while they are deadly to those who strike them in a fall, they are friendly to those who climb. I made my way with relative ease to my treasured cane. It showed no damage of any type, which amazed me only slightly, since I was aware of its origin.[3]

Now at the base of the cliff, a new plan formed. I would merely follow the shoreline to the next road or house, and thus affect my escape from my malicious shadow, who, in all probability, waited above.

From my vantage point on the shore, it was clear to see that I had crossed the outer boundary of the gray blanket, which lay outstretched over Vargas Castle and the estate, for as I gazed toward the horizon a beautiful day unfolded before me with sailing craft large and small bobbing about lazily on the ocean. The air was clear, the sea blue, and the sun as bright as ever I have seen it. It was in all, the perfect summers day and I had to look back to the top of the cliff face to remind myself of the wall of mist, which shrouded that place.

In light of my newfound ability to actually see where I was going, I made excellent time as I hopped from boulder to boulder, until the cliff sloped away and became almost level with the shore, revealing a road and my link to civilization.

It has always amazed me how quickly one can be separated from the genteel world man has grown accustomed to, and be swept into an alien, foreboding realm where one is no longer the master but the victim of the whims and desires of other forces. Upon reflection now, it amazes me equally, how one is able to throw off those shackles of fear and trepidation once he is united with familiar surroundings. So it was with me. Pacing down that avenue back to the reality of which I was accustomed, I regained some of the former confidence, which makes us all a bit brazen with our environs and gives us the swaggard's air rather than the modesty which comes to the fore when we enter uncharted waters.

It was a beautiful day, with birds singing in the trees as a gentle breeze, originating from the ocean, cooled the surroundings and fluttered the green leaves. As I came closer to what was Ocean Avenue, I met other strollers who directed me back to the castle, after offering me refreshment in the form of cool, pure spring water, which bubbled up from what was known as "Spouting Rock." I don't believe I can recall ever having tasted a more pristine liquid in all my life. With the exception of our present predicament and the dangers it presented, America was certainly proving to be as wondrous and beautiful as I had always heard, and in my heart, I prayed for the time when we were through with this dirty business and able to enjoy these settings and its inhabitants.

---

[3] See "The Matter of the Christmas Gift."

Watson's Sampler:
The Lost Casebook of Sherlock Holmes

By the time I had finished with "Spouting Rock," the sun had long passed center and the day was on the wane. I turned my steps toward home, picking up the pace slightly, as I knew my tardiness would cause concern.

I reached Vargas Castle in less that an hour, finding it as gloomy as ever, all traces of summer being left at the corner of Ledge Road. My spirits did brighten when I beheld Philip's coach by the front door, as I advanced up the drive. I entered the anteroom unannounced to the sound of a commotion in the sitting room, which we had employed as the staging area for last evening excursions. In I went to find everyone there, save Holmes, engaged in a great deal of turmoil and jabbering, with nothing being accomplished. Once their eyes rested on me, I was set upon by the entire group.

"Oh, Dr. Watson," started Alice, the housekeeper, "Mr. Holmes has gone off on his own in the house."

"We warned him," continued Sophie, "but he said, 'never mind' and forbade us from following him."

"There is danger in there, as you well know, Doctor," chimed in Jeff Ainsley.

"I tried to stop him, Sir," added Philips, "but he is head strong, you know."

"Well, I wouldn't worry too much, people," I began, trying to set a calm tone. "Mr. Holmes always knows what he is about," and I emphasized "always." "I'll just have a look 'round to be sure everything is all right."

After weak attempts to dissuade me, and an insistence on my part that they all stay put, I set off to find Holmes. In the discussions, which had arisen once I announced my intent to locate Holmes, I learned that he was heading for the east tower where Carlos Vargas met his end. Mrs. Ainsley gave me the exact set of instructions she had given Holmes, and assured me that if I followed them to the letter, our paths were sure to cross.

I began my journey down the same corridor we had traversed the evening before, and although it remained dark and flashing, I found that without the hysteria of the others about me, I made good time, walking briskly to the end of the hall. We had turned left and descended last evening, but today I was instructed to turn right and ascend to the upper floors of the building. The staircase was wider going up than the one we had used last evening and was lined on the left side with paintings of previous owners, I assume. My right flank however, faced into an open sitting room with only two walls. I felt it strange that I had not noticed this open space during last night's escapade, but waved it off as a trick of the senses.

When I reached the second level, I was forced by condition of a wall, to turn right. The hall, which lay before my was lined on the left hand with doorways to other rooms, while the right hand featured a banister, converting this entire hallway into a balcony overlooking the rooms below, which oddly enough were separated by walls but had no ceilings. Although my only light was the strobe effect produced by the flashings, I still could see the fine furnishings and hanging tapestries, which made this place a show spot in days gone by.

I continued on to the end where once again I was forced to turn, right this time, in order to ascend another, smaller staircase to floor three. This flight was not so ornate, but still betrayed the quiet elegance of oaken fixtures, with the solid, sturdy confidence they lend to any structure.

The Occurrence at Vargas Castle

Floor three then became a long wide hallway, with doors on either side, leading to what could only be construed as bedrooms. Unlike its predecessors, this hall was dimly lit by gas lamps, which must have been struck 'on' by Holmes, and did not have the usual nuisance of sputtering electric lights to contend with. I proceeded slowly down this aisle, for the altered environs lent themselves to a generalized foreboding, which succeeded in holding me back. The calm and quiet of the place must have disrupted my senses, for while this hall was bathed in weak light, I found it harder to see and distinguish the objects and features which occupied the place.

I tried to move steadily forward to the end, which seemed to be some thirty yards or so away. Nothing unusual happened as I passed the first pair of doors, which spanned me on either side. But as I passed the second set, my peripheral vision told me that they seemed to be opening, as I went by. Vowing not to let fear govern my movements, I spun to my right to catch a glimpse of who or what might be manipulating the portal. Naught but a black hole met my eye as I peered into the inviting room with its peaceful hostility, both frightening and enticing me at the same time. Immediately I decided not to take this bait, remembering the pattern, which was becoming more evident with each hour spent at Vargas Castle. To enter into this game would be unproductive at best, not to mention dangerous. Once again I determined to stay the course and continue my search for Holmes, but no sooner had I chosen this, than a slam was heard further down the hall, as if a door had been closed. I turned my head in time to see a figure at the far end of the passage. It was tall and gaunt, and from where I stood, it seemed the perfect figure of Holmes leaving one room and heading for another.

"Holmes," I called out, but neither to left or right did the figure look as it made its way directly across the corridor to the opposite door. I quickened my pace and called, "Holmes," again, but my cry had the same effect as the previous attempt, for the figure glided to and through the opened door. I gained the spot in a moment's time to find the entry now closed and the hall quiet once again. I tried the knob, which turned easily in my hand and the door swung open in front of me. There was a loud creaking from the hinges as it opened. The room was dark, and I call it dark because while it was not black within, it did remain hard to see, although there was a strange, almost bluish glow apparent. No lights were lit, and as my eyes grew accustomed to this new illumination, I swiftly became aware that this was not a room like any other. A chill breeze blew from within, which effected my hair and my temperament, as I felt a pang of fear run through me. Involuntarily I shivered as I stepped inside to search for Holmes. The room was bare, except for furniture draped in sheets for protection. The walls were dotted with pictures of indistinguishable panoramas and there were also unlit gas lamps. There was a sweet, stale smell in the air, but worse than this, the room was empty of any human form. Bewildered, I took another step. No exit doors, no closets, no escape of any kind. Where had Holmes gone?

A step to the left. There was a covered chair next to the door, which I noted as I passed. A step more, and I had cleared the doorway. Almost immediately I heard the creaking once again. The door was closing. I had half expected this, for some reason. I whirled, and kicking out, I struck the chair with my foot, toppling it over just in time to catch the door before it slammed shut, trapping me inside. My heart was pounding within me. From my position, it was clear to see that the space behind the door was empty. No one had attempted to push it closed. My heart sank at the prospect of an evil force willing this door closed to trap me within. I sank further as I heard a faint cracking from the chair, whose strength must be waning against the power of that evil. Without a moments thought, I leapt through the opening created by the failing chair. No sooner had I regained the corridor then the chair gave way under the weight and splintered into submission. The door slammed shut with a thunderous clap. I stood there, momentarily stunned by what had happened.

When I regained my senses, I tried the door to see if it would yield. It was like pushing against a boulder, and that fact set well with me. I never wanted to see that room again, anyway.

The towers of Vargas Castle were large and tall and circular. They were set apart from the house proper by thick walls. A circular stairway hugged the inside of these walls spiraling upward, or downward considering your point of view. There were landing entrances at each floor of the structure, with the remaining seventy feet or so arcing to the parapet. There were windows, or should I say rectangular portals without glass, in various places along the towers, above the final floor, which afforded light to the entire tube.

I gained entrance to the east tower on the third floor landing, and ascended the stairs carefully. No inner rail protected you from falling to the center, should you be unfortunate enough to move too close to the edge. The stairway was not difficult though, and I mounted to the top with ease. It was there that I found Holmes, dangling over the edge, glass in hand, examining the outer wall.

"Holmes," I said quietly, not wanting to startle him in his precarious position.

"This is ingenious, Watson," he said without looking up. "The length to which the villain will go at times is truly mind boggling."

He stood up smiling. "How have you been, dear fellow," he said amicably. "You look as if you've seen a ghost."

Not knowing what to reply to this statement, I simply stood there staring.

He continued as though he had not really been looking for an answer. "The household seems to be intact. Everyone well and none the worse for wear. I'd say you've done an admirable job here."

"Holmes, I...," I began, but he cut me off.

"Tut, tut, old boy. I can see that modesty is about to pervade, as it always does with you. We'll talk in a moment. First, let me show you this insidious device," and he moved over to where I was standing.

"I have made good use of my time in Newport, checking both police reports and building permits to form some theories as to what took place while Vargas and his family held residence here. For instance, I was made aware that it was not Carlos but his brother Josef, who signed every building permit, and that he ordered all of the materials needed to complete the reconstruction. He was also quite an accomplished carpenter and mason in his own right, if the accounts presented by the local tradesmen are accurate. It was he, in fact, who totally restored this rampart, adding a few of his own touches to the design. If I might demonstrate."

Holmes looked around the circular floor of the parapet, at the large stones left there from the remodeling. Selecting an average sized stone, of maybe fifty pounds or so, he laid it on the low level of the battlement. Then, striding over to where I stood at the entrance of the parapet, he began feeling the wall, pushing on the smaller stones embedded there. Within a minute, his hand had found its mark and a small, smooth stone about waist high, clicked in about one inch. Immediately a small section of the battlements shifted outward, tipping floor and wall, so that the rock, which Holmes had placed on the lower wall fell the length of the tower, striking the other rocks below. As I stood, staring, mouth open in wonder, the section righted itself and clicked back into place, hidden once again from the unsuspecting eye. Holmes clapped his hands together once and crossed the parapet to the spot.

"Be careful, Holmes," I said instinctively, but he waved his hand and continued.

"It is perfectly safe now, Watson," he returned off-handedly. "Unless you touch that trigger."

I glanced at the stone he had pressed as I joined him by the wall. Looking over, we could see the rock below, chipped where it had struck the cliff face, exactly where they had found Vargas' body.

"Josef murdered Carlos," he said in his first serious tone since we met. "I'm sure of that now. He created this device. He lured him up here on some pretext, perhaps to see his finished handiwork, and he sent him to his death by use of it. Most ingenious..."

"But, why Holmes? And how did you know," I asked, astounded once again.

"Quite simple really, dear fellow, once the facts are known. For instance, as soon as I became aware, from the records that Josef had signed for all the work to be done, I directed my inquiries to the contractors assigned to the project. What I learned from these tradesmen was that Josef had insisted on completing the work on this tower himself. The very tower, from which Carlos had fallen. I found that coincidence a bit more than I could accept. Police records were of little help, except to give location and direction of the fall, and so I felt a further examination of this area was in order. It was in examining this outer wall that I discovered the murder weapon, so to speak. You see, Josef was not as careful to conceal the seam of his teeter-totter on the outside wall. To anyone looking up there would merely appear to be a crack in the cement, if they could see anything at all. The seams on the deck here are much closer together, and since this apparatus was designed to be used only once, I'm positive Josef felt sure that his camouflage would be effective. Which it was until today, I might add. He may even have had designs on securing it to prevent any accidental mishaps, once the heat was off. But that was before he realized that the family would be destitute without good ol' Carlos."

"And what of Carlos, Holmes? What happened to the money and the family?"

"Rumor has it, in the tradesmen's world, that he hid all the money from the family, perhaps in this very house. For now Watson, that line of thinking has proven to coincide with the facts I have ascertained."

"Such as," I questioned.

"Such as the fact that within weeks of Carlos' death, this house was put on the auction block by a family who could ill afford to manage it any longer. A family, which was going great guns and improving upon the property right up until that untimely death, I might add."

"And, there is the fact that a tradesman not connected with those whom Josef hired, and not hired by Josef, was nonetheless hired by Carlos himself, and worked within these walls while the other teams completed the renovations. His name is Eugene Banks, and I have visited his office and seen the work orders, which although they were not specific, do indicate that construction was done on the premises, and were signed by Carlos."

"And what does Mr. Banks have to say for himself," I inquired.

"That's just it, Watson. Mr. Banks has been on extended holiday since the contract with Carlos Vargas ended. No one seems to know where he has got to or when he will return, although his crew has orders to continue to work on other projects in his absence."

"And did not this crew know what they had built or repaired at the castle," I continued.

"No Watson, they didn't. Uncharacteristically, Banks had completed the Vargas Castle project alone, shunning any attempts by his men to help him in any way."

His eyes gleamed as he spoke, like a dog who has picked up the scent, just before he takes after his quarry.

"Where do we go from here, Holmes?"

"Back to your daughter's home, Watson. But there are a few things I need to say to this household first."

We made our way back along the same path I had taken to find Holmes.

As we descended the tower stairs, Holmes pointed out the counter weight employed by Josef to snap his trap back into place once used.

It seems that he had balanced the platform impeccably, so that once released, even the slightest weight would tip it out as I had seen, but once that weight had fallen off, the counterweight would snap it back into place.

"Ingenious," I exclaimed, unaware that I was echoing Holmes very words.

We traveled back along the same route I had come, and although the flashing lights continued to be a hindrance, we were not molested along the way. I did chance a look in the direction of the room I had almost been locked in, only to find the door slightly ajar, with that strange, blue glow emanating from within. The sight altered my steps and I stopped. My first thought was to inform Holmes of the situation, but he had walked on ahead, distracted by his own thoughts. As I turned to call to him, I heard the creak as the door slowly and gently clicked closed. With a shiver I continued on, just as happy not to have to try that door again.

Once we regained the comfort and security of the sitting rooms, Holmes informed our small band of residents that new evidence had come to light, which must be investigated further. He would need my assistance. We should have an answer within a few days. And, while he felt that they were in no immediate danger, wandering throughout the house remained unwise.

"This is a very interesting home you have purchased," he said turning to the Ainsleys. "From what I have seen of the renovation work plans, I would say that there are quite a few surprises left within these walls. I look forward to sharing them with you upon our return."

With Philips at the reins, we left Vargas Castle and began the four-mile trip back to Newport center. It took but moments for the weather to clear into a bright, warm summers day, once we left the grounds of the estate. My spirits immediately brightened. The thought of being away from that dismal, unpredictable place, mingled with the excitement of being reunited with my daughter, gave me a feeling of well being which challenged the day for its warmth. I removed my outer jacket and sat back in the carriage, sighing deeply, content to let the world roll by.

Holmes, on the other hand, was already into the next phase of the investigation. He had charts and graphs and plans and newspapers in Philips' carriage that he was scouring. He never spoke throughout the ride to Susan's, and when we got there, he gathered his things and stepped from the carriage without a word to either Philips or myself.

I turned to Philips to offer some parting comments and pay the man for his trouble, but he held up his hand, explaining that we were not separating just yet. Holmes had retained him for the remainder of our stay in the States. He would be at our service, remaining outside, at the curb, in front of my daughter's home, should anyone be in need of his services.

With a smile and a slight bow to our newfound friend and employee, I rejoined Holmes and my family, indoors. After salutations and hugs all around, I decided that a new set of clothes were in order, but when I turned to climb the stairs I exclaimed, "What's this," rather loudly at the sight of Holmes.

He was in the dining room, which had now been transformed into what could only be termed a cross between a library and a laboratory. Holmes was busy reading and bustling about, from paper to paper; deciphering whatever clues they held, in the jumble, which was his technique. I must admit, for one who could see order in the greatest chaos, he could not keep order in his life. His systems were like his cases, imperceptible to anyone but himself. I joined him after a few moments with my daughter, so that I might catch up.

By the time I entered the dining room, Holmes had spread any number of newspapers over the table, on top of beakers, burners and tools of the trade, which lay there discarded after momentary usefulness had ended. He was searching the agony columns, as he had dubbed them many years before, looking for whatever his fancy had set out front.

"Look here," he said as he opened "The Boston Herald" and laid it next to "The Providence Journal" and "The Newport Daily News."

"These are yesterdays papers," he continued. "What do you make of them?"

I scanned the open pages until my eyes fell on the tradesman's section, where workmen advertised their abilities and prices. There, in the center, in bold letters read:

```
ALL IS FINISHED. WILL BE IN NEED OF YOUR
ASSISTANCE ONCE AGAIN. REPLY TOMORROW...

          — CARLOS.
```

The same ad appeared in both "The Providence Journal" and "The Boston Herald," but was conspicuously missing from "The Daily News."

"What have we here," I said. "Carlos sending messages from the grave?"

"Rather Josef than Carlos, unless I miss my guess," Holmes replied gleefully. "You see Watson, he has called the man in. And if Josef is not mistaken, we shall have a reply tonight."

"Have the papers arrived yet," he called to my daughter, who had come in from the piazza.

"I have sent your Mr. Philips for them," she replied politely, as she stepped through to the kitchen. "He should return with them shortly."

"Ah, perfect," returned Holmes to no one in particular, "now we are getting somewhere."

"Might I clear up a few matters," I inquired.

"Of course, old boy," returned Holmes, as he began to fidget with the assembled goods on the table.

"First of all, how did you know," I asked.

"I didn't, old boy, until I saw this solicitation in the paper this afternoon. I had Philips pick up back issues of all these papers while I made my rounds this morning, and it was not until I had read them all through, that I made this discovery, in last evenings paper of all things."

"But how did you come up with Josef as the author of this message?"

"My thinking is this way; we have someone, my guess is Josef, who is playing the odds with this message. As you can see, he has only solicited those papers which probably did not cover the news of Carlos death. He is therefore hopeful that our Mr. Banks is within a radius close enough to see the ad, but far enough away to not know that the author of that message is someone other than his benefactor, Carlos. And while our message writer may have used other methods to try and contact Mr. Banks, we have stumbled onto this one, which gives us the opportunity to see it through, and perhaps snare a criminal."

"Then what is our next move," I asked.

"We'll await today's papers to see if there is a reply. If there is, we'll follow the instructions given, which will surely help us close in on our quarry. If there is no reply, I intend to locate the person who placed this ad by visiting each publisher until I get the information needed to trace the man."

We spent the remainder of the day awaiting the evening news journals to arrive. He may have dawdled, or the delivery may have been late, but it grew increasingly clear, as the day wore on, that Susan's announcement that Philips would return shortly was erroneous. As you might guess, I had little trouble with Philips' tardiness because it afforded me time to visit with my family. It wasn't long before we decided to stroll through Susan's section of the city, an area known as "the point."

I must admit that America is beautiful and grand in its youth. We walked to a street named for the first American President. A Street, which paralleled the shoreline facing

Narragansett Bay. Numerous houses stationed quite close together lined both sides of all the thoroughfares, save the waterside of Washington Street. The regularity of the place and the economical use of space reminded me of the Surrey District, and were it not for the size of the dwellings, which were much larger than our own, you could almost imagine that you were in England.

Before long we arrived at a grassy park with benches, known as "The Battery." "The Battery" was set above an area known as "The Blue Rocks," where children played while their parents sat on the benches and scanned the activity on land and sea. Dark blue water rolled gently in and out around this place while sailing and steam craft of every description navigated amidst the numerous islands, which dotted the bay. We spent a wonderful afternoon together on "the point," and to this day I cannot remember when I have felt more loved. By dinnertime we had moseyed our way back to Susan's home, content with each other and the lives we had made for ourselves. And, by the time we reached her street, I had vowed to stay, at least until the baby was born.

The sight of Philips' carriage stationed in front of my daughter's home, with its horses pawing the ground in distracted boredom, signaled the fact that he and the papers had been there for some time. No one in our little band of three quickened their pace to see what trinkets of knowledge could have been purchased at three cents apiece at the local stand. We were much more interested in continuing in each other's company for as long as possible. The thought has even crossed my mind, looking back, that we could well have passed the house and continued on for another hour or so, had not Holmes darted out of the front door, paper in hand, pointing to the discovery, which was sure to direct our interests for the foreseeable future.

"Watson. Everyone. Look at this," he said waving the paper.

We went in, checked the "Agonies," and sure enough, there it was, the apparent reply to the previous notice in yesterday's Herald. It read as follows:

```
CARLOS,
RECEIVED NOTICE. RETURNING TOMORROW. WILL MEET
WITH MAN WHO WAITE'S FOR ME AT 9:00 PM.

                    — E.B.
```

"Do you notice anything unusual about this message," Holmes said with a wry smile and a sideways glance at Susan.

"If you mean that our Mr. Banks cannot spell the word 'waits,' then of course I do," I returned.

"Exactly," he exclaimed right back at me. "This is our clue, Watson. This misspelled word has all the earmarks of a secret message between the two men. Prearranged perhaps. Perhaps this is just one possibility of numerous, readymade signals, each pointing to a different outcome. Our job now is to figure the answer from this clue."

"Do not bother yourselves, gentlemen," Susan announced with a giggle and a wink at Edward. "It's too simple to pursue, and if you were residents of this district, you would readily know the answer."

Watson's Sampler:
The Lost Casebook of Sherlock Holmes

"Aha," cried Holmes, "I thought that this signal would hold no mystery for the populace. Enlighten us as to the meaning within the words, my dear."

"It's quite simple really, as Susan says," piped in Edward. "You see, I've been there many time in my travels around this town. There is a Waite's Wharf off Thames Street about two miles from this very spot."

"Waite's Wharf," Holmes laughed, "of course, the perfect place for a clandestine meeting. How ingenious."

With our mystery of where and when we would meet the elusive Mr. Banks and the even more elusive Josef Vargas now solved, and noting that we had more than twenty-four hours to wait, we all soon sat down, including Philips, to a scrumptious dinner of roasted beef and potatoes prepared by Susan and Edward. Like everything else in America, the dinner table was a bounteous place filled with every extravagance. Any manner of spice was represented. Sauces, made of apple and cranberry were passed. Rich, dark gravy and butter adorned the meat and potatoes. Fresh fruit, fresh vegetables, fresh milk, tea and coffee, water and lemonade, all were available to us at this one sitting. The table Susan had set was a feast for the eyes as well as the palate, with its many colors and designs. The aroma of the entire house was breathtaking, and I couldn't help but feel proud that my little girl had braved the wilderness, as many in England viewed America, and discovered this paradise.

We ate and talked and laughed and told stories and generally acted like a large family. As unusual as it may seem, and much to his liking I might add, Holmes was not the center of attraction in this place. Rarely have I seen him so relaxed and open, in a silent way, as he laughed at jokes and passed potatoes without the rigors of constant scrutiny, which followed him on the continent.

Both Edward and Philips were full of wonderful stories of Newport and Jamestown, its sister island, and the evening was a thoroughly enjoyable event. You'd think we were Royalty to gaze at the abundance laid before us, but as Susan assured me, even the most modest of households in America set a full table. God's blessings seemed limitless there.

Our evening wound down with brandy and cigars seasoned with sea tales and mysteries from the men, while Susan ooo'd and ahh'd to our deepest satisfaction.

There is nothing in the entire world like the feeling of family to send one to bed contented and filled with life's glory. I slept well that night, as I never slept before.

Next morning was business as usual. Holmes was up and out early with instructions left for me that I should first take the drawings from the dining room table, and bring them to the castle. They are self-explanatory the note explained. "When you get there, lay them out before the Ainsleys and their servants, and go over them in detail. Do not venture throughout the residence as yet though, but familiarize yourself with the plans, as they may be exceedingly important in the near future."

I was also instructed to inform the Ainsleys that there was every chance that this matter might be cleared up this very evening, and not to be surprised if we made an appearance quite late at their premises. The promise, as always, was that all would be explained in the end, and that none should worry.

The Occurrence at Vargas Castle

I was further left instructions to rendezvous with Holmes at Waites' Wharf at about eight o'clock that evening, where we would hopefully meet our Mr. Banks and Josef Vargas.

With time on my hands and merely one errand to accomplish all day, I spent a leisurely morning about the house, following Susan with her gardening and grocery chores. We talked and planned and shared our dreams and visions, and during that time, I invited her to accompany me to the castle after luncheon, to which she readily agreed.

"There is another matter of some importance, which not only concerns you and I, but many other persons, and I must discuss it with you, my dear," I said as we finished our noontime tea and sandwiches.

"What is it, father," she inquired with the earnest, good will I had known in her mother.

"It has to do with my stories, dear," I continued. "As you know, I have written quite a few accounts of the exploits of my friend, Holmes. The trouble is, that not all of the depictions of the many characters we have encountered have been flattering. The problem that presents itself then, is that while these characters may be less than perfect, many of them, or the situations they got themselves into, were or still are in the public eye. It has therefore been necessary for me, in many cases, to keep the lid on, so to speak, and not publish those dealings of a more volatile and illustrious nature, which we, from time to time, have become immersed."

"I am asking you to keep the notes and writings I have compiled in these more sensitive areas, so that they do not fall into unscrupulous hands, and become fodder for the tabloids."

"But father, what shall I do with them," she asked hesitantly. "I have no need of this sort of information."

"No, no my dear, of course not," I explained, "but the day may come, when such matters as these may need to come to light, or be able to be told without causing harm or embarrassment to anyone. In those instances, it has always been my feeling that the public has the right to know just what has happened in the past, as a point of historical reference, if nothing else."

"It is to this end that I entrust these files to you. There have been many attempts to steal them from me in the past, and I am afraid that there may be even more attempts in the future. But, if you have them here, in America, no one will find them. Perhaps, some day, you may even be able to sell them, when the time is right. They will bring a pretty penny, you know, and I'd like to think of them as the inheritance you deserve, and the education your child will need in this ever-expanding world of ours."

It was this logic which swayed her, and so, without further ado, we transferred the files I had carted across the ocean, into her attic for safe keeping. There I knew they would remain unmolested, and yet available, should time or circumstance prevail upon my daughter to publish them.

This feat accomplished, we set out with Philips, who had returned to us at Holmes request, and embarked on our small trek to Vargas Castle.

The sun shown brightly and temperatures rose as we made our way along the entirety of Thames Street this time, not climbing the hill to Bellevue Avenue as we had in the past.

Watson's Sampler:
The Lost Casebook of Sherlock Holmes

The horse's hooves beat out a gentle rhythm on the cobblestones as we rode leisurely through the business district of Newport, noting the points of economic interest along the way. Susan pointed to Waite's Wharf as we clattered by, so I would have an idea of the layout of the place before we met our quarry that evening.

At some point, Thames Street became Carroll Avenue, which finally emptied into Ocean Avenue. Ocean Avenue ran east and west, and passed Ledge Road from the opposite direction than the Bellevue Avenue route we had taken two days before. We therefore traveled east on Ocean Avenue turning right at Ledge Road after entering the gloom encompassing the entire area where the castle sat.

Once again, we found it almost as dark as night amidst the fog and overcast encircling the stone structure. Once again, we felt the trepidation, which accompanied our every visit to this place, and although I knew that I was bringing new information which would shed light on this dreariness and add a sense of logic to the chaos surrounding the occurrences there, a feeling of foreboding filled my being and sapped the joy from the day as soon as we made the turn. There was something more than logic here, something that defied the explanations available, something more than truth, and other than reality. When you stood there, at the gates to Vargas Castle, it was palpable. It set the hairs on the back of your neck on end, and you knew, that you did not know everything.

I noticed Susan glance at me repeatedly as she and Philips and I made our way from the carriage to the door. I smiled back at her, taking her hand and whispering that everything was all right, and that we were in no danger. After knocking, Godfrey ushered us into the sitting room we had occupied two evenings before.

"Please gather everyone, Godfrey," I requested as I spread out the large sheets containing the plans drawn up to direct the renovation recently completed.

When all were present and introductions were made, we began to study the plans. What we found was more of a map than a blueprint. There, before us, in hard outline, was the floor plan of the building we occupied, with dotted irregular lines which, when studied separately, (for Holmes had made an overlay of these irregularities on rice paper), showed what appeared to be another house within the real house. Every wall, it seemed, was shadowed by another wall some two to three feet opposite, leaving enough room between them for a person to walk throughout the house undetected. There were steps opposite stairs, and passages linking doors with crawlspaces, which enabled a person to crawl under a doorframe. There were false ceilings on every floor, which were easily concealed due to the fact that the original ceilings were so high. All of these factors combined to enable all of this to exist, without a hint of the changes for anyone who was not familiar with the original structure. The entire company was amazed that this labyrinth existed within inches of every wall, without any of us being aware of it.

"My word," I heard Mrs. Ainsley exclaim under her breath as we studied the design.

"This certainly explains a great deal," Mr. Ainsley returned, as he and Godfrey glanced at each other and then back to the sheets.

All were nodding and commenting on how they could now see where the noises and the movements and the mysterious appearances and disappearances could have been staged for anyone's benefit, if those who knew the maze wanted to dissuade someone from searching the premises.

"How many Vargas's were there," I asked, as I realized that many of my companions might be coming to the same conclusions as I.

"There were seven in all, sir," Jeffrey replied. "Carlos and Josef, of whom we are familiar; Lucia, Carlos' and Josef's sister; Victor, Lucia's husband, who, while not a Vargas himself, must be counted in the clan; Simone and Eduardo, the niece and nephew; and Alexandre, Lucia's son of only eight years old."

"They all resided here," I inquired.

"Yes, the whole family," returned Jeffrey. "Carlos was the leader, controlling the purse strings, if you will, and the rest followed. Carlos paid for everything it seems, not trusting any of the others with the money."

"And that is how he kept control," I added.

"So it would seem, sir," said Jeffrey.

We spent the remaining time studying the layout of the house, pointing out how to get from here to there within the walls. We even checked an entrance, which was marked clearly on the plans and found that it did indeed exist in the closet of the very room we were in. We did not explore the passage we found however, noting Holmes' stern warning that although we were making progress, we were not out of the woods or danger just yet.

Comfort comes slowly in a place like Vargas Castle, and for me, an outsider, every moment in and around those stones was filled with a nervous agitation I had never experienced before. Even with the knowledge recently received that indicated a human hand in the affairs transpiring before us, I was hard pressed to keep a hopeful attitude and not relent to the nagging feeling that something more sinister was at play here, hanging over the structure like the mists which rose but never waned through day and night. The uneasy feeling that someone or something was lurking, not only within the walls, but also within the very atmosphere of the place, set my heart rate a touch higher and kept my mind guessing constantly as to causes and affects. The imbalance between logic and emotion which kept me instinctively on alert, touched me more deeply this day, considering the proximity of my child to this ill-wind I felt in my bones. I must admit to my own forgetfulness on the matter, or I should never have suggested that she accompany me on that afternoon. For nary had we dwelt within that edifice for thirty minutes, than I realized that this was no place for anyone in her condition, and feared for her and the child within her, should she somehow stray too close to the evil dwelling here. The very thought of the chance of such an encounter, shot waves of dread through me, that some permanent wound might befall them should they get to near. By the time we had discovered the passage entrance in the closet, I had decided it was time to go, and although Susan seemed to be getting along famously with all concerned, I insisted we depart without further ado.

I picked up the pace of my footsteps and the others fell in line as we made our way to the carriage without looking back. It was as if it was chasing us away. I have never felt a sensation such as that before or since, and I am quite sure it was not a shared feeling because both Susan and Philips looked at each other and back at me quizzically throughout. I made up the excuse that I must be on time to meet Holmes in order to put them at their ease, but I am positive they did not fall for that story. We left without another word on the matter though, and so, I felt no remorse at being less than truthful, as long as my mission to remove Susan from that evil place was a success.

No sooner had we entered the carriage and made the turn onto Ocean Avenue than the overcast broke clear and the sun shown brightly around about. And as the mists broke, so did the spell cast over my mood. Another pleasant ride down Bellevue Avenue awaited us, and we talked and laughed and came alive as if we had awakened from a disturbed sleep to find life back to normal. I could see it in their expressions; Susan's and Philips', although I was just as aware that they had not realized the change.

Once home, dinner came and went without any mention of the day's events. The daily news had arrived by courier, and so I spent a leisurely time reading the headlines, while I awaited the appointed hour. When that hour came, Philips returned and we set off for Waite's Wharf.

I arrived at our prearranged meeting place early as Holmes had suggested and found him there, waiting for me.

Bright day had turned into gray evening, and although the sun was not scheduled to set for at least half an hour, it was quite dark enough for the gas lamps to be lit as I strode up to a thoughtful Holmes, puffing lightly on his briarwood.

"You have your revolver," he said without making eye contact.

"Yes Holmes," I returned patting my jacket pocket with my hand.

"Good," he said drawing on his pipe. "We may need it before this night is through," and he paused to watch a sailor make his way to one of the outer docks. "I must admit a certain uneasiness about this whole affair," he continued. "Today I spent my time seeking out the Vargas clan to ask a few questions. The answers I received were not as I expected."

"How so Holmes," I put in, for lack of another means by which to prompt him. I realize that we were older and wiser, and as familiar as an old married couple, but in all my years and dealings with the man, I had never heard him openly admit to having any expectations about a case, let alone being inaccurate as to those expectations.

"I had gotten wind of their whereabouts from one of the contractors I interviewed," he went on, "and checked on that lead. What I found was a modest cottage inhabited by the five remaining Vargas's, save Josef and Carlos, of course. The tale they told me was most unusual indeed." He drew on his pipe again. "I mean they readily admitted to skulking about the house and frightening the devil out of the occupants. They were searching for treasure, you see; Carlos' treasure, to be exact. It was rightfully theirs, they felt, being as Carlos had committed suicide."

"Suicide, Holmes," I broke in.

"More about that in a moment, Watson," he returned, "be patient."

"They are very reticent in admitting any guilt in this matter, since in their opinion, it is they who have been wronged and not those they have terrified for these many months. Our conversation proceeded back and forth in this vein for some time. They repeatedly proclaimed their innocence, while I attempted to point out their inappropriate and illegal behavior, despite their contention to the rights to any money within or without the walls. They would not agree under any circumstances, and we remained at odds until I insisted that they cease their searching and interference in the lives of the Ainsleys under threat of law."

"At that point there was a marked difference in their countenance and disposition, Watson," Holmes said in a now hushed voice. "They all drew nearer to me, Watson," he continued, "and Lucia, who was acting as their spokesman, gave a sideways glance around, as if some other, unseen party might be listening. It was quite unnerving."

"Then she started to explain that they had not been to the house in weeks. They are all too frightened to return. It seems that while they were in the walls searching for treasure and interfering with the others' lives, someone, or something as they put it, was interfering with them"

"There were constant whispers within the walls. Numerous times throughout the uninhabited portion of the house, they would burst forth into a room, sure to surprise whoever was whispering, only to find that room vacant."

"There was constant tapping, as if someone were checking for studs from the outer wall, but once again, upon close examination of the area, no physical cause could be found."

"Watson, you would have been amazed at the change in demeanor which crept over the Vargas's as they continued their story. With each new chapter they became more drawn and pale, as if they were reliving the fear, which unsettled them so in that house. At one point the child began to cry, and had to be removed from the room by his father, so that his mother might continue."

"They told me that soon they had found it necessary to have a meeting among themselves, at which they vowed to stay the course no matter what lay ahead of them, and keep searching no matter what the cost."

"The next day their resolve was shaken to its foundation when Lucia's son, the same child who had started crying, became separated from the group within the house. The parents, and indeed the entire clan were frantic searching for him. They told me that they could hear his voice, far off, calling their names and crying. Once, when panic was at its greatest, they had decided to abandon their quest, surrender to the Ainsleys and beg for help in finding the boy. It was when they were about to open one of the portals and disclose themselves, that Alexandre found the boy down a short, dead end corridor within the labyrinth devised during the renovation. The boy was facing the far wall, Watson, sobbing but unhurt. He offered this wild tale of being lured away from the group by this small monkey, which tipped its hat and ran away, as if it wanted to play. The boy followed, became disoriented and utterly lost. By the time the family had recovered him, he had become completely unnerved, stating that he had felt unseen hands caressing his head while he was frozen in fear, and continual indistinguishable whispers where spoken to him throughout the ordeal. He also swore that it was not he who cried out to the family, although they are just as adamant about the fact that they heard his sobs and his voice."

"What do you make of it all, Holmes," I asked seeing that this fantastic tale was nearing an end.

"I don't rightly know, Watson," he replied, looking off in thought. "Could there be a second group within those walls, I wonder?"

113

"Or could it be more of a spiritual manifestation," I ventured.

"Watson, there are no such things as ghosts," he replied with a wave of his hand. "The explanation lies within the house itself. We'll search it out after our unannounced rendezvous with Josef."

Darkness had stolen in on us as we spoke at Waite's Wharf. You could hear the gentle lapping of the ocean against the anchor poles as the tide increased to crown. Gas lamps were lit in the shops and on the streets, which made up this busy community, and all was in readiness for a rousing good evening in what was known as the downtown district. A distant roll of thunder could be heard to the west as one of the occasional storms, which passed by Newport from that direction, prepared to make its appearance.

We waited and watched for a sign that either Josef or Mr. Banks were among those in attendance at Waite's Wharf that evening. People strolled to and fro, walking up and down this and the adjacent docks, looking at the boats and the water, dreamily. All in all it was a nice, quiet, summer's evening, without a hint of trouble, except for a flash and a crash as the storm approached. Local constables had been stationed discretely about the area at Holmes request, being that a full warrant had been obtained for Josef's arrest, should he appear.

At the next lightening flash, the stack from a small steam powered craft could be seen puffing, not far from shore, for while the weather threatened, the atmosphere in and around the wharf district was clear and dry as yet, and calm like the pedestrians. The next flash, for they were beginning to arrive almost on top of one another, showed the small craft moving slowly, at harbor speed, but ever nearer to its destination. With the next flash, the docks began to clear as the air bristled with the charged excitement of nature's production. People did not hustle away, but you could see a deliberate motion as they all, as if on cue, began to move off toward shelter, to wait out the impending torrent. The next flash made folks jump, and the flash, which followed close at its heels, gave notice that rain was near.

All the while the little boat drew closer to the near abandoned dock on which we stood.

"Come along, Watson," Holmes said as he also made his way toward one of the shops which dotted the shore along the wharves, "we do not want to appear conspicuous."

We had hardly cleared the wooden planks and turned our attention to the first well lit storefront, when a dark figure of well over six feet tall, passed us in the direction of the dock we had just quit. His step was purposeful and he trod in a determined manner, directly toward that point where the small craft we had been watching was likely to end. In fact, the next flash and the one which followed thereafter, showed this to be the case. The boat was now but a few yards from docking as the long figure of Josef Vargas waited impatiently.

The rope was tossed, and tossed to Josef, in fact, since he was the most likely candidate, being the solitary figure on the dock. He quickly threw it around a cleat stationed there, securing the line, and ending the ride. One of the crew jumped off to secure the bowline, and a plank was laid from deck to dock in anticipation of departing passengers.

The Occurrence at Vargas Castle

From our vantage point we could see a small number of people making their way from inside the vessel to the gangway. As they passed Josef, who had stationed himself at the landing, he inspected each one casually. He did not hinder nor molest any departing passenger. It seemed that his target was not aboard.

It was about this time, as the impatient constables began moving closer, that we saw Josef turn with a start and fix his eyes upon a movement within the boat.

There he was, a small man in what appeared to be a bowler hat, darting fitfully around the cabin area. His movements indicated that he was hesitant to leave the boat, and apparently quite agitated about the fact that he had been seen.

I watched him scurry about, until I felt Holmes touch my shoulder as he passed me in route to the scene. Josef had also begun to pace back and forth along the dock almost mirroring the little man, who must have been Banks.

Without notice or provocation, for I am sure Vargas had not detected our movement, he leapt aboard the boat, trapping Banks within the cabin.

As we moved steadily closer, I could see the altercation taking place at the doorway as the little man attempted to sidestep Josef and leave the place. Muffled voices could be heard during the exchange. The smaller man demanded that he be let pass.

We were almost to the boat when I saw a member of the crew attempting to intercede on his passenger's behalf. It was then that the gun appeared in Josef's hand and everyone stopped. The crewman backed away, but Banks persisted. We could hear him protest, seemingly enraged by the show of force. He would not give into threats of violence, and most certainly would not discuss his and Carlos' agreement with anyone. His vocal output increased with his agitation to the point where overhearing their exchange from anywhere in the dock area was as easy as pie.

"I bid you good-day sir," I heard him say, as he once again attempted to pass through the doorway. To me, it seemed the appearance of a witness in the form of the crewman outweighed the dangers of the gun for Banks.

Josef now pushed Mr. Banks back into the cabin, holding the pistol in an even more threatening manner. Excitement grew, and Holmes, who had reached the gangplank, took but his first step when Banks lunged toward Josef, and the report from the pistol was heard.

Josef swung around to flee, before Banks hit the deck. His eyes were wide with fear and anger as they darted here and there, revealing the indecision in his mind. It was fairly obvious that he had had no prior intention of harming Banks, but expediency and fear had got the better of him, and now, as the tradesman lay mortally wounded on the deck of the steamer, Joseph was taken by panic to flee the scene for his life.

He took one step, and we were spied upon the gangway. Without hesitation he aimed at Holmes to fire. With the dexterity of a cat, Holmes flung himself back onto the dock, slipping gracefully behind an anchor pole, out of harms way.

The police were moving in, guns drawn and at the ready.

Josef looked bewildered for but a moment before gathering his wits. With a look of resignation that demanded notice, he turned his attention to the crewman and ordered him to cast off the tie secured to the aft cleat. As the crewman went about his chore, Joseph waved the pistol he held, from Holmes to the approaching officers and back again, keeping them at bay till the task was accomplished.

Watson's Sampler:
The Lost Casebook of Sherlock Holmes

The engine had been left at idle as the passengers departed, and this served to eliminate any delay. Lightening flashed as Josef deftly shot the bow line, which both froze his pursuers in their tracks and released the vessel from its mooring.

The small boat drifted off slowly at first, moving sideways, away from the pier, far enough so that the gangway tumbled off the side and into the bay with a splash. It took a few moments for the crewman to get the steam up, gain control, and start the little ship on its getaway voyage. Josef stood behind the crewman with the gun pointed at his back. He glanced furtively from his captive worker to our group on the dock, who could naught but stand there helpless, watching the proceedings. Away they headed, and the thought shot through me that all was lost. But, before they made their final swing out into open water, we saw the crewman gesture to Josef, who swung around as if expecting to be attacked from the rear. No sooner had he moved, than the sailor took two quick steps to his right and leapt over the rail, diving into the black waters below.

Lightening flashed again, as Josef found himself alone on the small steam ship, left to master the controls himself, so that he might gain speed and steer a course out into the bay. I almost felt sorry for him, watching him struggle to gain command of the boat and the situation, until the knowledge that here was a thief and a murderer brought me back to my senses.

Aware now that Josef was definitely alone on the boat, the constable to my right raised his already drawn pistol and fired two shots into the air. Within moments, it was apparent that this was a prearranged signal. For not a minute transpired before a police launch rounded the outer pier and struck a course to intercept the hapless Josef.

Seeing this new angle of pursuit, Josef came about and made for the next dock down from us, some two hundred yards away. Without any consideration for the safety of others in the harbor, or for those who still remained on the dock watching this strange performance unfold, he made straight for it. Only at the last moment, when the little craft seemed to be at top speed and about to crash into the wooden structure did Joseph veer his course and miss the span, springing from the boat to the dock as soon as he was able. The now unmanned craft continued on striking two vacant, moored vessels before coming to rest at the shoreline.

Holmes, for his part, wasted no time in taking up the chase, seeing that Josef would soon be on land again. He was moving fast and well ahead of me, as he made his way across the built up shore, which connected the docks by the shops.

The police launch, upon determining that they would be late in making the dock landing, slowed and picked up the quick witted crewman, who had escaped harm's way with his nimble dive into bay waters. And, last but not least, the police detachment assigned to making the arrest on shore, took up the pursuit moments after myself, making them late, but not far behind.

Josef took to his heels immediately, sprinting down the dock and through the wharf area with Holmes in pursuit. They dashed in and out and around onlookers who had ventured out to see the commotion, which began at the firing of Josef's revolver. Lightening flashed and the first sprinkles of rain hit our faces as Josef rounded the corner and took his flight to Thames Street

I would like to state, at this point, that had it not been for the circumstances of the event, it is my opinion that an arranged foot race between Sherlock Holmes and Josef

The Occurrence at Vargas Castle

Vargas could easily have garnered more than passing interest within the sporting public. Although Josef had gained the advantage through starting distance and the added surge which comes upon a person running for his life, Holmes was his equal, step for step, and neither gained nor lost ground throughout the run. They were uncanny; dodging or leaping over obstacles, shifting speeds as conditions dictated, and taking advantage of every opportunity which presented itself. If Josef passed a barrel or a pile of boxes or a bale, he would topple them into Holmes' path, and Holmes, in turn, would dodge or hurdle them to maintain his stride for stride pace.

Again, Josef stopped and aimed his pistol at Holmes, but instead of stopping, Holmes cried out, "apprehend that man," which only served to send him on his way again with renewed efforts to increase the distance between them. This is how it went for some minutes, with neither pursuer or pursued gaining or loosing an edge, until Josef spied what he felt was his salvation. There, on Thames Street, stood an unattended carriage. Without a moment lost, Josef sprang into the seat, released the brake, took the reins in hand and whipped up the horse. He was off in a shot as lightening once again lit up the sky, which thundered back its disapproval at the disturbance. Both Holmes and I stopped dead in our tracks at this turn of events, not knowing where to turn, until I noticed a delivery wagon about half way up on the next street over.

"Holmes," I yelled as I pointed to the wagon, but before we were able to make for it, who should arrive but Philips with his carriage. Off he jumped shouting, "take this Mr. Holmes. I'll wait here for the police… Less weight makes for more speed."

"Watson," Holmes cried as he took the whip from Philips and climbed aboard, whipping up the gelding without ever sitting down. I was only given opportunity enough to grab onto the boot and rest my foot on the rear iron before we sped off after Josef with the rattle and clanking of metal covered wheels on cobblestones ringing in our ears.

Down Thames Street we raced with the wind in our hair and a now steady rain in our faces. Josef had a commanding lead at this point although he was still in sight, and despite the rain, the sparks that flew as steel touched stone told us that he was not sparing his horse in the effort.

Along we went. Once, I attempted to raise myself to fire my revolver, but cobblestones make for rough pavement and as I jostled around, the possibility of striking someone other than Josef became evident and ended the attempt. This same restriction apparently had little effect on our adversary, who apparently, fearing that we might overtake him, (for we were gaining), fired several rounds in our direction as we clambered down the road. This maneuver was effective in slowing our progress, as Holmes reined in our horse out of fear for the innocents looking on.

It seemed that we had been stymied, (at least that was my opinion), until Holmes pulled hard to the left, directing our steed to turn up a side street.

"What is this now, Holmes," I yelled as he whipped up again, sending us into a new gallop toward the hilltop.

"Where will he go, Watson? Think," he returned with that excited, knowing smile on his lips.

My expression must have given away my befuddlement because, before I could make a reply he exclaimed, looking back in my direction as he rallied our animal, "the castle, of course. That is where he will feel safe. He knows the secrets of the place, and could not possibly reckon that we are wise to him. He'll run to the castle, forthwith. I am sure of it."

We traveled on, not sure if Josef had continued straight down Thames Street, or had turned, as we had, up some side road and was, even now, mounting the hill to Bellevue Avenue

As minutes passed and the realization that we would be traveling at least another mile or so sunk in, Holmes let the horse slow to save its energy, which also afforded me time and opportunity to scramble over the boot to the passenger seats. We climbed the hill without further sight of Josef or his wagon, and turned onto the gas lamp lined Bellevue Avenue at a walk.

The storm, which had pelted us with rain moments before, now sent a murky drizzle our way. Stray flashes and low rolling booms only served to show that while the storm had subsided, it had not passed. We moved slowly along the nearly deserted avenue, past mansion upon mansion, neither hurrying nor slowing. We had not seen hide nor hair of Josef all this while, and had it not been for the confidence I hold in Holmes' judgment, I might have called for a halt to the proceedings. But there was no halt, and as we moved at a walk down the road, I reflected on our many years together, and the escapades it had been my good fortune to play a part in. Life has been good to me. It has left me little time for tedium or routine, for it seems to have always been, that if left to my own devices, I fell into a schedule lacking the excitement and adventure derived from an association with someone displaying the energy of Sherlock Holmes. I am appreciative of that association, which has always stimulated the soul and awakened those areas of mind and body which weary when left exposed to the mundane.

"Crack," went the thunder, as a fierce bolt flashed simultaneously, sending me hopping back to reality. The storm had returned to us with a vengeance. Rain pelted down, as wave upon wave of flashes and crashes suddenly shook the very ground beneath our wheels. Visibility was at a minimum as the heavens opened, drenching us and everything else for miles. The gas lamps, which had illuminated our way with their quaint golden glow, had become phantom dots of yellow against the blackness of the background. The street became bare in an instant, for what scarce traffic there had been, scurried off to shelter, like rats from a light. We alone remained on the thoroughfare, plodding our way forward through the wind and rain and fiery skies, which caused our noble steed to jump and start repeatedly.

Then, all at once, it was still. The thunder stopped, the lightening ceased, even the rain let up quickly, so that only a soft mist enshrouded us. It was like being in a train, which suddenly stops for no apparent reason, leaving passengers and crew alike staring one to the other, waiting for word. So sudden had the quiet come that the horse had halted inadvertently, as if awaiting some command from the unseen force which controlled the night. Holmes himself looked around, testing the air with his senses before stirring the horse mildly with the reins. I, as well, was curious as to this condition, breathing lightly to the point of nearly holding my breath in anticipation of what might come.

My wait was short lived, for even as I trained my eyes, attempting to focus in on a particular street lamp, which seemed ill equipped to stand against this blackness, a burst of electricity so great as to light the community, sprang upon us. It lasted for nearly a complete second. The horse reared, screaming. The instantaneous clash of thunder rocked and dazed me as if a cannon had been discharged in our midst.

I swung around, my eyes searching for Holmes who was once again standing at the ready, arm raised with the whip in hand to take the measure of our animal.

And there, up ahead, pulling out at the closest side road, with horse in the same reared manner, was the cause of Holmes' agitation.

Josef Vargas glared back at us in the lightning's blaze just as malicious and fierce as the storm itself. The anger portrayed in that face will live with me forever. His lip was curled in what could only be described as a cross between a snarl and a sardonic smile. His eyes flared bright against the sunken blackness which surrounded them, and we could see him utter a curse, drowned in the drone of thunder.

He was very close now, due, I'm sure, to resting his horse once he saw no pursuit. He was startled and afraid at our sudden appearance before him, for his expression betrayed his cowardice, which we readily recognized before his steed sprang into action, carrying itself, the wagon and Josef down the avenue at a gallop.

We were after him in a moment, and as time and trees flew past, we could see him ahead, hard pressed to the task of winning this unruly race. We were making better time on this level ground, and gaining steadily as we went along, for in the luck of the draw, Philips carriage was of lesser size and weight than the one which Josef had stolen. Holmes stood as before at the reins, coaxing as much energy as he could from Philip's beast, and it was clear that we were overtaking our opponent at every step.

It was also obvious that Josef was well aware of our progress, for with curse upon curse he wheeled around, firing his revolver repeatedly, which sent sparks and wood chips flying from the coach in every direction. Holmes kept up the pressure as I drew and fired back returning volley for volley as we sped along. I truly believe that we could have kept up this way for some time before our horses collapsed, had not Josef leveled his pistol at the head of our own animal. Holmes caught the maneuver just in time to rein up to a sideways halt, as the lead left the barrel and embedded itself in the wall of the foot well, where he stood.

We stayed there still and silent as Josef flew away, down the street amid the lightening and the crashing from above. You could see his image grow smaller and smaller with each lightning's glare, as he never let up on his horse again. Soon he was out of sight around some far turn, and it was then that Holmes resumed our pursuit at a canter, not wanting to get as close as before, but also not wanting Josef to gain too much time at the destination we knew he sought.

If ever there was a darkness come upon a land which fights the light so utterly as to nearly extinguish all attempts at illumination, the darkness of that night, in that place called Vargas Castle was it. You could not see your hand before you. It was as a thing alive, that darkness. Like an amoeba, surrounding and absorbing light, until naught but the slimmest glow presented itself. You could feel the fear and trepidation in our animal as we crept along, turning the corner from Ocean Avenue to Ledge Road at a snails pace. And while it was an all-encompassing darkness, it was not a peaceful, quiet condition by any means, for as the storm had subsided on land, it must have raged on out at sea. You could hear the wind howl as it mounted the cliffs and flew past us overhead, and you could almost feel the power of the sea crashing against those same cliffs, like a caged animal attempting a violent escape.

Neither Holmes nor I had spoken since our run in with Josef, but as we entered the grounds surrounding the castle, I felt compelled to note that we had not passed Josef's stolen carriage along the way.

"He must have entered through another passage," Holmes returned.

"Another passage," I asked.

"Yes, Watson, a secret, escape passage. Every home in this area has one or two. The wealthy were afraid of capture by criminals or warriors, and so most of them had escape tunnels dug in order to outwit them, should their houses fall. Surely Carlos and his people were aware of these tunnels, because as the plans we studied showed, they did not have any new escape tunnels dug. They must have incorporated the old ones into their remodeling plans."

"And the Ainsleys," I inquired.

"I doubt they are aware of the passageways," he returned, "but I'm sure they'll discover them once their infestation problem is cleared up."

By this time we had entered the courtyard in front of the castle. The rain had ceased, but that all to familiar thick mist had replaced it, making the darkness even more impenetrable. A crow could be heard cawing in the distance as we alit the carriage. The castle was black indeed, and hardly noticeable in this night, except for the glowing windows of the occupied area. Holmes wasted no time in approaching the door to gain entrance. The knocker struck, Godfrey answered the door and ushered us into the hall.

"Is everyone accounted for," Holmes asked at once.

"Yes Sir, I believe so," Godfrey returned, looking mildly puzzled.

"Good," Holmes said, "let's have everyone assembled in the sitting room at once."

Before long we were all awaiting instructions like a school class, with Holmes standing before us as teacher, pointing to passageways as they appeared on the unrolled plans and explaining the circumstances which had taken us this far.

"Watson and I will be heading into the maze to apprehend Josef," he said. "I don't know what has become of the local police department, but someone should be sent to fetch them while we are gone."

"I'll go," said Sophie, raising her hand like a proper student. "Godfrey can take me."

"And what about me," piped up Priscilla Ainsley. "I would very much like to accompany you and Dr. Watson, if I might. After all, this is my home, and it's about time that I became more familiar with it."

Holmes tried to show that reason would suggest that the danger was too great, but it was apparent that this tact would not dissuade either Ainsley.

This settled, we made immediate preparations to begin. Lanterns were struck because the remainder of the house had gone black just before we had arrived, and thus, we could now not even be afforded the luxury of flashing lights as we searched. Alice had volunteered to stay behind, in the sitting room, to greet the police, or anyone else who might call. I checked that my Webley was loaded, Holmes had his glass and all was at the ready.

Our gear set, we entered the labyrinth within the walls, with Holmes in the lead, Priscilla Ainsley following, her husband Jeffrey next, and I taking up the rear. There was nary a sound for the first fifteen minutes that we searched. We discovered right readily that along the outer walls of every passage, at ten-foot intervals or so, small candles stood like diminutive soldiers, guarding the way. Once revealed, we proceeded to light each one found, so that if necessity arose, we could make a hasty retreat to the place where we had entered the passages, without the danger of becoming lost or misdirected in our route.

The passageways were dark and bleak and barren indeed, being narrow at times and then widening out to a five-foot width in places. They were often low and clumsy, as well as being filled with webs and dust throughout. The air was stale, without a hint of a breeze, and you could tell that these little halls had been created in haste, to be employed sparingly.

Had I made a guess, I would have said that we were making good time, though I had little to go on. As yet, we had seen nothing resembling Josef Vargas or evidence that he had passed our way at all. We continued on the central hall, neither turning left or right, although the opportunity presented itself often, and my judgment told me that we must be nearing the outer wall at the west end. Our lanterns shown brightly against the utter blackness of the corridor, and even the candles, which we lit as we passed, (for I turned to check them often), stood out strong, to light the footway back should we need them.

Things went well for the next few minutes as we followed Holmes lead, although we had still not come to the end of the passage. I brushed my waistcoat pocket often in remembrance, and to gain the secure feeling I received each time I touched the revolver stationed there. Should Josef show himself and resist our attempts to seize him, I was confident that with this pistol and Holmes by my side, he could be readily subdued and taken into custody.

The first "boom" started way off below us. It was faint, but there was no doubt that it was that same, low booming we had heard the first night.

We all froze, momentarily.

"Could it be the Vargas Family, Holmes," I whispered.

"Very doubtful, Watson," he returned. "They all swore to me that they would remain at home this evening," and his voice trailed off in thought. "The fear in their eyes leads me to believe they were telling the truth. Another curiosity, Watson, they also disavowed any knowledge of how that sound was produced," he continued reflectively.

As before, the second "boom" was louder and closer than its predecessor, and followed at its heels was a third and a forth, even more pronounced. We were not moving now, but waiting. Waiting to see where it would go. Would it come our way? Would we yet catch a glimpse of the origin of such force? And was that force as harmful as it sounded? The looks on our faces bespoke all of these questions as each repetition grew in intensity and force, until the floor was reverberating with the power of the sound. It was as if it were within the house, within the room, within the walls, and now, without a doubt, heading straight for us.

Watson's Sampler:
The Lost Casebook of Sherlock Holmes

With our retreat illuminated, but our advance in darkness, we all stood there peering into the blackness of the hall before us, bracing against the onslaught of whoever or whatever created this disturbance. Were we to be the target of this thing with such gigantic steps as to shake the house as it moved toward us? What could cause such thunderous tones as these? Our questions were answered, at least in part, in a fraction of a second as we all to a person realized that this sound, this thunder, this reverberation, was not progressing at us from the front, but from the rear. At that same moment, we spun to see the first candle, way off down the hall, blow out, as if some enormous force, with deadly quick speed, had snuffed it dead before us. Without a chance to react, the second light lost its glow and then the third.

Faster and stronger the force came as we saw the forth and fifth flames blotted from our view. Almost simultaneously the sixth and seventh went out and then the eighth. By this time the booming sound was ear shattering as it beat out its quickened, ominous rhythm. I braced myself for the worst. Glancing back, toward Holmes and the Ainsleys, you could see the shock and surprise in their faces. Never before or since have I seen Holmes' eyes as wide as on that night. By the time I regained myself and turned to check the progress of the originator of this dread, it was on us, hitting us with the power of a blast of wind as from a hurricane. It was a cold and clammy blast. A blast which seemed to go through you as much as around you, as though it were inside you as much as you were inside it.

I am sure we all lost our feet, although I can only speak for myself, since that same force totally obliterated any remaining light, and sent me crashing back to the point where I may have lost consciousness momentarily.

What I can say definitely is, that when I did recover my senses, I was in complete and utter blackness, and could neither see nor hear anything. All was still. The noise was gone. The force was gone. All was quiet, as if in anticipation of anther round. I took an internal inventory of my faculties to find that everything seemed in good working order. All that was left to do was to locate my companions and reassess our plan.

"Holmes," was the first word to escape me, to no answer, as I sat there in the stillness.

"Holmes," I repeated with the same result.

Slowly I turned and gained my feet. The area in which I stood was completely black and as I fumbled through my pockets, the realization sunk home that while my revolver was still in its place, all other articles of lesser weight had been scattered to the winds by the force, which had toppled us. No matches to strike a lantern or a candle if I found one, and no extra ammunition, should its necessity arise.

"Holmes," I whispered in the darkness. "Mrs. Ainsley?"

No answer.

I reached out and found the wall. Taking ten paces in the direction I assumed we had walked, I found no one. This seemed very odd to me, for while I knew that we must all have been thrown about a bit, I also knew that we should be in close proximity to each other.

Or had I been unconscious longer than I thought? Would that explain my present circumstance? No, it would not. Surely, had they awakened before me, they would have searched as I was now doing.

"Holmes," I said with greater force, feeling uneasy for the first time.

No answer.

I bent down and checked the wall for candles.

Nothing.

Then, to my left, back the way I had come, a little noise began. A rapid tick, tick, tick, moved off, away from me. It sounded as if a rat were scurrying across a tile floor. Tick, tick, tick, tick, tick, tick.

I shivered reflexively at the thought before taking a deep breath, setting my resolve and taking after the sound.

Tick, tick, tick, tick, tick, it went on ahead of me as I followed, feeling my way along the corridor wall. Were it a rat, perhaps it would inadvertently lead me to an exit from our maze.

Tick, tick, tick, tick, tick, it seemed to be gaining distance although I kept on, picking up speed as much as possible under the physical and mental constraints, which were imposed upon me by my situation and the uncertainty I had as to whether I really wanted to apprehend this quarry.

Tick, tick, tick, tick, tick, it seemed to be just ahead now. I reached out with my left hand while keeping hold of my pistol with my right.

Tick, tick, tick, tick, tick.

I groped in the darkness in an attempt to touch this noisy prey.

Tick, tick, tick, tick, tick.

Silence.---

It was deafening. I reached out slowly to find only dead air. I took two steps forward, toward the place where the final sound emanated but nothing stirred. I banged about, bouncing off the walls which were nearest and flailed around in the darkness, hoping to set the thing to its heels and begin the chase anew, but it was all to no avail. I was alone in there. And to this day, I am not sure whether I felt worse from the knowledge that I was, in fact, alone, or from the emptiness that that knowledge imparted to my soul.

What was true was evident. I had been tricked once more by that elusive charlatan who seemed to receive joy in others discomfort and confusion.

"Not this again," I thought. "Hadn't I learned anything during my other encounters in and around Vargas Castle?"

I had been lured away, and now "who knew" where I was within the structure.

My first thought was to try to retrace my steps back to my original position, but upon further reflection this seemed pointless. In this all encompassing darkness, one place seemed as good as the next, until I could gain an opportunity to find an exit, or a companion, or a light. My decision was thus set. I would continue on the same course until an acceptable outcome was met.

So off I started, feeling my way along, trying to stay on what I gathered was the main corridor, in hopes of discovering my friends or an outlet. The way was slow, but I attempted to maintain a steady pace, straining and peering into the black, trying to make out any glimmer that would indicate a route to escape.

As my hand moved out along the wall ahead of me it dipped inside what was obviously the corner of another intersecting passage. I was used to this by now, for there had been many such corners in my search, though I had not deterred from my path before now, and had no intention of altering that pattern. I would cross the open space created by this intersection, and begin anew where the wall took up again on the opposite side.

All was going as planned, but as I glanced down the new passage, something caught my eye. A flicker, or was it a glimmer, or maybe a beam? No matter what, one thing was sure, there in the darkness, was a glow. It was something warm and gave off illumination, which was in direct opposition to the utter helplessness that total darkness brings. It was a light, that was for sure, and I made for it with all due haste.

It was the weakest little source of illumination. A crack perhaps, or a hole about shoulder high in the wall, ten paces or so from where I stood, which seemed to just appear there, and was even now fading and brightening as I watched it. I realized, of course, that I was abandoning my plan to stay the course and remain on the main corridor, but the urge which drew me, became so uncontrollable that I could not resist. It was as if a blind man had been given the opportunity to see again, and this blind man for one, would not let that chance pass by.

I was there in a moment to find that the source of the illumination was from the hall just outside the room, which was skirted by the corridor in which I stood. There were two holes in the wall of "my" corridor, which must have also been in the wall of that room. The eyes, of some portrait, was my first guess.

It is amazing how in pitch and utter darkness, the slightest glow enters the senses and holds complete command. I stared through at the room below, becoming more accustomed with every second, and searching out the origin of that radiance. As my head cleared and my pupils dilated correctly, so that the shadows took form and form took meaning, it was clear that the source of the light was indeed coming from the outer hall, and that it was moving toward the open, double-doored outlet of this room from left to right.

Slowly it came, to the point where one might think that it had stopped somewhere in its progress, were it not for the obvious motion of the expansive beam it cast about the walls and doorway. The movements were deliberate though, as if someone were searching the area as well as finding their way with the light.

I stood there motionless, not knowing what to expect as the beam and its master drew closer and closer toward the opened portal to the perch from where I spied. Minutes may have passed before my first glimpse of the foot and leg of my mysterious lamp lighter. Sure enough, his tread was measured and in no hurry as he moved from side to side, and up and down, examining every inch, like a ferret in search of mischief. And then, without warning, he popped his head into the doorway of the very room from whose wall I gained my view. The room was flooded with light from his outstretched lamp, and I jumped within myself as he revealed his identity for the first time.

You can imagine my alarm and surprise to realize that this ferret was none other than the king of ferrets, Sherlock Holmes. He held his lantern straight out, bathing the chamber with light while illuminating his pointed, stoic features quite well, and readily recognizable.

He never actually entered the room, which surprised me as well. One quick sweep around with light and eye, seemed to be sufficient for his curiosity, and sent him moving past the door on tip-toe, in a stealthful, steady gate, designed not to attract attention.

I, on the other hand, was frantic. He had left me no time to react. He was both in and out of the room before I could signal him. With both fists, I began to pound the wall, which separated me from the chamber I overlooked. Holmes did not return. Looking back, I can see that the wall must have been made of brick or some other masonry component and must have been relatively thick, for although I beat my mitts raw against it, there must not have been a sound heard on the other side.

"Holmes," I cried as I rapped the wall again, without effect.

And then, after he was well out of sight and I could see the fading light on the outer walls, I remembered my revolver, which had held my attention so fervently until that moment. Reaching down to my pocket, I found it still there, waiting. Quickly as I could, I drew it forth. With my eyes pressed against the portal to the fading light, I pressed back the hammer and brought the pistol up, pointing it away from me and the wall, in preparation of firing.

But even as the hammer fell and the deafening explosion rang forth, a singular event occurred. There, within the darkening room below me, two figures began to loom up, out of the shadows. One was exceedingly larger than the other, and as it grew, it was clear that it was quite larger than any human I had ever known. Draped across it was an enormous cape, which stood out, even in this fading light, because of how utterly black it was. As if it absorbed light and swallowed it, making this cape and this figure, darker than black.

The second figure was hooded and foreboding in its own right, even though it was diminutive in comparison to the first. It led the way, as the two emerged and floated more than strode, toward the open door. It was clear that these two were intent on following Holmes to no good purpose, and my only relief to the anguish I felt, was that they both stopped their motion at the sound of my revolver's discharge.

There was a moment where no one moved. I could tell by the extent of the blast created by the gun in the corridor, that little if any effect was noticed outside the room where the figures stood. In fact, it seemed clear, that while these two shadows had heard something, even they were not altogether sure where the detonation had originated. As I stated, neither of them moved immediately, but rather stood there, transfixed if you will, assessing their senses for clues.

And there, in recognition or remembrance, the smaller figure began to turn. In the failing light I could make out its hood in silhouette, moving from flat on top to pointed, which meant that this figure was now looking directly away from me, or directly toward me, and I, from my position above them on the wall, with the light dimming by the second, could not tell which way it was.

Now, for my description to be accurate and effective, it must be known that this small figure was well below the level at which I was standing. Without really noticing the incline in the dark, I must have ascended a good three feet from where the floor lay of the room I was observing. Without really knowing, I would have to say that a fair guess would give the height of the ceiling of the room I observed, to be about twelve feet high. As I have stated, my assumption was and still is, that the portals from which I peered, probably corresponded to the eyes of a figure in a portrait, presumably hanging in the chamber. The eyes of that portrait must have been nine feet from the floor below. Thus, the only explanation within logic, is that the corridor on which I stood was between three to four feet above the chamber floor.

At any rate, I have told you this so that you might follow the events I am about to describe. Whether you are able to understand these events is beyond me.

For as I stated, the smaller hooded figure was either looking directly at the portrait I stood behind, or it was looking directly away. In that moment, in that light, I could not tell.

I stood there peering at it. Trying to make some feature clear in my mind. Trying to recognize something in its form, which would hint at its

pose. Hoping against hope, that I had attracted its attention, and thus distracted it from Holmes. I could not be sure from my vantage point.

Then, without warning, it flashed up to where I stood, gazing out. We were eye to eye in an instant. How it managed that feat, I have yet to learn, but there it was, staring that horrible stare at me.

At first its eyes were all I could see. Terrible, black, hallow eyes, so dark in hue that you could not distinguish between pupil and iris. They were like holes. Bottomless pits as the ones you'd imagine descended to hell itself. They did not move, nor was there a flicker of life noticeable within them. They simply stared. Not squinting, not flinching, just staring, long and hard, as a porcelain doll's might stare at you, were it set correctly.

We stayed this way for what must have been a minute, my heart pounding out the seconds.

And then in a strange turn, the figure began to float back away from me. It was then that its features were clear and I could take in the hideousness, which presented itself before me. It was ghastly. Straight off, I noticed that while the light had all but vanished, a pale, greenish glow was visible about the creature's face. It was a feeble aura, which made visible close up, what had escaped me below.

There, before me, floated man or woman, I could not tell. It had a large bulbous nose, which curved and twisted its way between the eyes already described. Its features were distended and inappropriately proportioned to the point where they could possibly be considered humorous, were they not so horrid. Its mouth was large and twisted in such a way as to produce a look which can only be described as being somewhere between a smile and a snarl. Its teeth, within that smile, were cracked and broken, and as I watched it there, its top lip twitched even further in a wavelike motion, not in an attempt to form words, but more like an involuntary, convulsive action, driven by deep, inner hatred.

And then, as I said, there were those eyes. Empty, featureless, unmoving and black. Not eyes at all, but covered pits. The only thing that moved and gave the impression that what I was watching had even a spark, as it hung the in space, was that top lip. Were it not for that, I might have been able to fool myself into believing that this thing was no more than a mannequin, suspended from the ceiling. But the lip told me it lived, and that knowledge chilled me to the bone.

I watched it for a few moments more, transfixed by the surreal scene playing out before me. It virtually lolled in mid air, caped and cloaked, with nothing distinguishable save that glowing, cadaverous face with the twitching lip, though it did bob up and down like a buoy on a calm sea.

The Occurrence at Vargas Castle

As the moments dragged past and my mind regained itself, I realized that I had lost track of the larger figure within the room. Once this awareness sunk in, I blinked hard in a "snap out of it" sort of way, shifting my gaze so as to attempt to catch a glimpse of the giant below.

As if he recognized my plan and motive, my floating friend began to move backward at that very moment. And then, like a shot, he came at me, mouth opened wide, showing row upon row of teeth, just as cracked and horrid as the first. He hit the outer wall with such force that although, (as I have stated), it must have been quite thick and secure, I felt and heard the blow from where I stood. It was as if he were trying to break through the wall and swallow me whole.

Well, of course, my reaction was instantaneous. I leapt back with such energy that I struck the opposite wall of the corridor where I stood, cracking it with my left shoulder, leaving it and myself weakened from the exercise.

Recovery came quickly being as the excitement raised my adrenalin level, and I was back at my perch in a second. To my dismay, I found my antagonist and his compatriot, gone. My mind reeled. I peered this way and that from my meager vantage point, but know matter where I looked or how I positioned myself to see better, it was clear that the room below me was now empty. They had "vanished into thin air," as the saying goes, which probably meant that once again they were after Holmes.

I realized immediately that I had to work fast if I was to be any help at all. When my shoulder had hit the wall, not only had I heard a "crack," but I had also felt it give. Perhaps I could affect my escape from this corridor through that wall, in time to intervene on Holmes behalf. Without wasting precious seconds, I dashed myself against the wall again. It gave again. I kicked out with my foot, landing it flat against the weakened structure. It gave a bit more. I repeated this maneuver again and again, and before I knew it, a hole was produced which grew with my efforts into a breach through which my body could pass.

The new room was as dark as the other and apparently the vantage point from where I had stood within the wall was just as high, for once I squeezed through the opening, I fell three or four feet to the carpeted floor below. I could see nothing, and must admit to knocking things about as I struggled to stand erect. Once situated, I began to walk, and after a few encounters, which left tables and chairs eschew, if not completely overturned, I found a door leading to the hall. I burst through to more blackness, and as I squinted this way and that to catch any brightness, my efforts were rewarded as I spied a faint shadow of a glow reflected on a wall, way off to my right.

"It must be Holmes," I thought as I scurried after it, crashing here and there into objects along the way.

By the time I reached the point where I had seen the reflection, it had disappeared, but as I turned my head again, there it was, dancing on another wall, not so far away. Off I sped in that direction, keeping better watch as the light faded before me. As I closed on my objective, it was becoming easier to distinguish objects and walls as the brightness increased, so that when I came to a corner where the source of that illumination had turned, I did not slow, but took the turn at full trot. He was just up ahead. Just out of earshot, but I knew that within a moment, I could call to him and we would be reunited.

"Slam, bang and thud!" I had run completely into someone as I made the bend. Recovery was swift, and as we both labored to our feet, I heard a familiar voice say, "hallo, sir. Dr. Watson, is that you?" It was none other than Jeff Ainsley.

"Yes indeed it is, Jeffrey," I said cheerily in order to quell any alarm our collision may have caused him. "Rather fortunate bumping into you like this. Where is your light?"

"We lost them in the hallway when we were struck down," Mrs. Ainsley returned.

"Mrs. Ainsley! Good show," I added. "Can't see a thing, you know."

"Nor can we," they both returned.

"Any idea where Holmes has got off to?"

"We thought we were following him," they chimed back. "Do you see the glow up ahead? We think that's him."

"I think so too. Let's have a look, shall we?"

With that we took off after Holmes. We couldn't be sure that it was his light, which we now followed, but it mattered little. Whoever it was, was about to meet us, whether they liked it or not.

Around the bend and a few more steps and there he was with lantern held high. It was Holmes, taking care to examine everything as he made his way through the halls.

"Holmes," I said, gasping a little for breath. "Where have you been? I've been searching everywhere for you."

Holmes, for his part, seemed unflustered. "Well, there you are old boy, and the Ainsleys as well. This is a stroke of luck then."

Holmes then went on to relay to us what had happened to him when we were separated by the force.

"I was pushed to the side into what must have been a trap door or something of that nature, for I fell and slid some feet before coming to rest in a hallway outside the corridors. All was in darkness, but as good fortune would have it, I had held fast to my lantern. Once relit, I began to search."

"Priscilla and I also found ourselves in the outer hallways after being pushed along," Jeffrey cut in, "but we saw no sign of you or your lantern, Mr. Holmes."

"And for good reason," Holmes returned, "you weren't supposed to see me. I am quite certain we were deliberately split up."

"Deliberately, Holmes," I blurted, "but how and why? Josef surely couldn't..."

"Correct Watson," Holmes cut in, "Josef had no part in this. In fact, he probably still has no idea that we are in the house searching for him."

Before Holmes could begin another sentence, we heard the most horrific, blood-curdling scream, which I for one, have ever heard. It made my blood run cold, and I could tell by the desperate expression on the faces of our hosts that I was not alone in my feelings. We all stopped and looked about, but with only Holmes lantern to cut the night, we were hard pressed to see anything. The scream ended as swiftly as it had begun, but it seemed to echo on throughout the dwelling as if it was visiting every room as a warning of what was to come.

Once the reverberations came to an end, stillness reigned within the building. It was almost palpable in the moment it held us, as if all manner of life and time had been suspended with we four as the only spectators to the event.

Then, just as I began to question my very senses, the "booming" began once again. It was loud, and distinctive, beating out a constant, rapid rhythm, but not as before. It was close already this time, almost upon us from the beginning.

Reflexively, the Ainsleys and I began to move around in an agitated manner, like corralled horses with a predator near. We had but a small area to cover because no one wanted to venture further than the lantern light extended. Holmes, alone remained steadfast and composed throughout.

"People," he said forcefully, in a manner which commanded our attention above the clamor. "I think that we should stand back, against the wall, and let it pass this time."

I must admit, it took a few moments for this directive to sink in. When a human, or any being for that matter, is in a defensive manner, the call for composure never comes easy. I could see the others bristle, as did I, but with Holmes already backing to the wall, it wasn't long before we all imitated his good sense and awaited the rush of noise and energy, which hastened toward us.

It wouldn't be long. The "booming" had increased in intensity to the same decibel level it was during our last attack. We looked at each other and then into the dark to try and catch a glimpse of this thing as it passed us by.

Then, without warning, there was a moment when the "booming" stopped and the stillness reigned anew, and it was in that moment that we heard a high, almost screaming, panting noise. It was only half human, a combination of shear panic and insane frustration, as if someone were breathing between clenched teeth, unaware or uncaring if anyone could hear or see them. The panting got closer now, and then there was a tripping sound and a table fell over down the hall and around the corner.

None of us moved, as if we were the audience in some strange play, calling for our participation.

With the sound of the table came a small, shrill shriek, and then more panting, but lighter in tone, as if the source of this noise was now trying not to be detected.

On it came, and as the light touched its features, it was easy to tell that the origin of all this confusion was none other than Josef Vargas. But as soon as he stumbled into the ring of light cast by Holmes lamp, you could also see that this was not the same man we had pursued scant hours before. His face was scratched and bleeding in places where he must have stuck objects in his flight. He visibly shook within himself as if some violent inner fear had now manifested itself into a living, breathing embodiment. His long hair was wild and unkempt where he had fallen and bumped into things, and pushed back by the wind created while running from us and whatever followed him now. And there were shocking, white streaks throughout. Long, white strands, perhaps one-half inch in width, laced through the jet- black hair I had seen on his head earlier.

His eyes were wide and crazed with fear, darting here and there, looking, but not seeing. As he came into our view, we came into his. He was breathing heavily, making an audible "he, he, he," noise through his open mouth as he went. He even stopped to look at us and seemed to show a glimmer of recognition, though he couldn't speak and didn't stay. I did notice a change in his breathing and the pitch of the noise he made as he stared blankly at us all, but he was off again before any sense could be made of things. We could hear him stumble and trip repeatedly after he left the illumination of Holmes lantern, and heard him shriek yet again in pain on one more occasion.

I, for one, was all for taking after him and shaking him back to his senses, if that's what it took to save him, but when I made an attempt to leave, Holmes stretched out his arm in protest and pushed me back against the wall, where I stayed flat without more coaxing.

The "booming" began again. It was just around the corner and down the hall, just where Josef had come. The sound was thunderous and moving toward us quickly now, as if it had stopped to get its bearings or listen for a movement, like the feint of a cat, that it has lost the mouse, only to pounce moments later.

"Boom, boom, boom," it came, only inches from us now. "Boom, boom, boom." I saw Mrs. Ainsley block her eyes, a maneuver which seemed quite logical under the circumstances. "BOOM, BOOM, BOOM."

It was before us.

Black it was, and huge. So dark and all consuming that it even had an effect on the light produced by Holmes' lamp, encroaching upon it and dulling it to a low glow. But that dim light could not hide the evil of it.

It stopped before us. Perhaps the light had caught its attention. It stood there for a moment staring into the darkness where Josef had just run. When it stopped, the "booming" stopped as well, and we could once again hear Josef scurrying off in his panicked romp. As I said, it stood there looking after Josef for a second. But then, as if curiosity took hold of it, it turned slowly in our direction and began to examine these intruders on its plan.

It was a man's face we saw as it turned. A hideous, distorted face so filled with hatred and anger, that a shot went through us all and we jumped at the mere sight of him. An audible growl, low and menacing could be heard as it stood and checked us, one by one, as if to warn us not to take any action whatsoever. It seemed to be breathing heavily, although no breath could be detected, as it grew and shrunk in size, standing there.

As I said, it gave us a look, which virtually froze us to the spot. Its face was contorted with obvious rage. And then its top lip undulated and waved momentarily in that curious expression that shot my beleaguered mind back to the face that stared me down earlier, as I peered after Holmes through the wall down the hall. It was that same face for a moment, as if that small floating creature, which nearly paralyzed me with fear, had actually been an individual manifestation of the evil present before me now. And as I stood there, mouth agape, the indication of that remembrance must have been evident, for it stopped its study of Mrs. Ainsley, and redirected its gaze back to me. At that moment, I must say, I feared for my life as our eyes met and the hint of intent flickered from within the beast. With nowhere to escape, I resolved quickly to act on my own if needs be and strike out at this dark menace, when another curious thing happened. Without notice the creature rather casually shifted its gaze to Sherlock Holmes, for only Holmes seemed to be studying it back, and that exercise was obviously not lost on our dark featured friend, for it, as well, began to spend its time eyeing Holmes. This strange duel between Holmes and the creature lasted but a moment, and I remember, at that moment, how amazed I was that anyone, even Sherlock Holmes, could be so rapt in his observations that he would loose sight of any fear of the thing he studied. This is pure analysis, I thought.

The Occurrence at Vargas Castle

Without notice, as if it were satisfied with its findings, the thing turned away nonchalantly, and faced the trail of its quarry. Although no visible steps could be perceived, and although it appeared to be floating or gliding along rather than walking, it began to move, and as it began to move, the "booming" began as well. It did not look back at us. It did not waver in its direction. It simply moved off, out of what little light was left, out into the darkness where we could not see.

"Carlos Vargas," I heard Holmes say after a moment, and before I could react, he followed with, "come along Watson," and we were after them. Yes, without another consideration, we were after them, chasing pursuer and pursued through Vargas Castle. Holmes was in the lead with his lantern, while we followed close behind using his light, which was considerably brighter now, to guide the way.

Through the hallways we went. Upstairs, turning left and right, ever following the sound, which stayed just ahead of us. We never stopped to get our bearings; we simply kept on. Whether it was because of the lack of illumination, or perhaps the speed with which we traveled, I cannot say, but the time had long come and gone when I knew where I was within the house. Nothing at all was familiar, not that there was much to see, but even what could be seen went unrecognized. Were I left on the spot, I would have been lost, and I dare say that that condition was representative of us all, even the Ainsleys. We were moving through uncharted waters. Through doors, down what could only be considered back stairs, up more hallways and around corners, never seeing a window or a source of light other than Holmes small beacon before us. When this parade came to an end, we found ourselves at the base of a tower, the very tower where I had met Holmes the day before. It was the first time that I had recognized the surroundings since our present trek began.

The commotion was now above us on the stair. You could clearly hear footsteps clicking along the stone between the deafening booms, which followed close behind. We began to scale the stair, and soon realized that the storm, which at one moment had passed out to sea, had now returned with a vengeance, sending sparks of lightening flashing continually. Being as this tower, with the spiraled stair was apparently the first area we had come to in some time with windows, we had little idea until now as to what was transpiring out of doors. Rain was pelting down and the lightening sent shards glaring across the death black, rolling sky, one after another. When we reached the first window, I darted a look out to see the ocean crashing against the cliffs with great force, sending salt water high in the sky, so that it appeared to be raining in both directions, up and down. A gale was roaring, so much so that it actually contended with the terrible "booming" for our attention.

From the constant flashing, as we looked up through the spiral, we could see poor Josef, clambering up the stairs, tripping, crawling, running as fast as he could, squealing and shrieking as the black form rose up within the center after him.

Never before nor since have I seen such a fantastic image. The combination of sounds, which accompanied the scene were just as incredible. Thunder crashed continuously it seemed for even in those seconds when there was no natural roar a growl, the repetitive "Boom," which liked to fill the house, emanated from our dark friend. We stood in awe on the stair, watching as Josef fled, while his pursuer rose lazily with him, spinning slowly in conjunction with his position on the steps, so that he always faced his prey.

131

As Josef neared the top, he became visibly more agitated, attempting to stop his climb, and at one point trying to descend the stair. Upon that attempt, the specter before him shot across to block him with such force as to actually effect the stonework of the tower, making it bow outward, dropping dust and fragments of mortar on the flight. Josef's reaction to this was to give what could only be described as a hysterical laugh and a jump, which almost sent him plunging from his perch through the hollow center of the tower. He regained himself though and once again began his frenzied ascent to the gallery, where he was apparently being herded.

But, by the next landing in the stair, Josef had found his gun. Why he had not drawn it forth before this, I haven't a clue, but he had it now, and without warning, discharged two rounds at his antagonist.

At the point in which he pulled his trigger, Holmes, the Ainsleys and I were in full pursuit once again, and had been mounting the stair two at a time. Even Mrs. Ainsley had kept up quite well, and I remember thinking to myself how spry she was, just before the shot was fired.

When Josef fired that first shot, we all halted and turned toward the report. The bullet must have passed completely through the black figure, for there was no evidence to the contrary, and the repeated ricochets revealed that its progress had not been initially hindered by obstruction of any sort. When the second shot rang out, we retreated, knowing well the danger of spent lead in full flight, bouncing precariously between the walls of this cylinder. If Josef continued to fire, the chances of innocent bystanders escaping the inevitable were slim indeed. A third shot split the air and began its careening descent, nearly striking Holmes as it sped through his coat sleeve, embedding itself in the wall close by. For better or for worse, this was Josef's last bullet. We could hear the clicking as he frantically squeezed the trigger repeatedly with no effect. Another shrill laugh left his lips, and as we turned to resume our pursuit, we looked up to see Josef far above us, standing on the edge of the highest landing. His hair was in wild disarray, with the door behind him opened wide to the elements, letting the gale do its worst. His arms were spread out on both sides of him and he held the empty gun in his right hand. Although we were three floors below him, you could see his eyes, wide with fear, showing the whites completely around in his frantic stare at his black nemesis. Fear, apparently, had also affected many of his other features, the most outstanding of which was his mouth, drawn up into a hideous smile. As we stood there gaping, it was evident that Josef Vargas' mind had snapped. He was no longer rational, laughing in the face of this monster, and now flapping his arms, up and down, like some flightless bird attempting to become airborne.

In one final attempt at freedom, we saw Josef hurl his firearm dead at the menacing figure before him. It passed through harmlessly, leaving our sight for just a moment before reappearing through the back of the phantom. It landed noisily on a lower level of the stairs above us, where it lay harmless. With catastrophe realized, Josef let out one last cackle, and fled through the open door, out onto the parapet. The black figure followed.

As for our part in all this, we picked up our pace immediately, attempting to gain the opened door and the parapet before any further calamity could befall Josef. We scurried along as he had, keeping well to the outer wall to eliminate any chance of tripping and falling through the center.

We had reached the second to the last landing when we heard the scream. A more scorching, searing scream I have never heard. It started from above our heads and quickly flew past our ears, and was below us. I leapt to the window and peered out.

There was Josef, falling from the tower. Eyes and mouth opened wide, arms and legs flailing, hair completely white as snow. He dropped to the spot where his brother had died such a short time before. But for Josef, death would not come from the rocks, for as the sea churned, and the gale blew, and the ocean crashed against the cliffs at the base of the tower, the water seemed to rise up to meet him before he was dashed against the stone. It looked to me as if it almost came to shield him and cushion his blow. He was falling, back first, when it met him, and as he gazed back, horrified at his fate, it engulfed him and brought him down.

At that moment the thought flashed through my mind that there might be a glimmer of hope, and he could escape this ghastly death. That by some miracle, he would survive the fall and not cheat the hangman, but this was not to be. For in the next second, as the next wave came crashing up, there was Josef again, flung high anew, still clawing at the air, as the sea tossed him back at us and against the tower. At the end of his second fall, there was nothing but rock to meet him for the ocean receded quickly. His lifeless form lay there on those rocks for a moment, until he was covered by the next swell, and carried off. We never saw Josef Vargas again.

We stared at the spot where he had been for only a moment before we were jolted back to reality by the sound of the phantom returning to the inner tower. We turned to meet his gaze as he floated through the doorway toward us. The hatred and anger, which filled his eyes from the first, flashed anew as he saw us waiting there, and that low growl filled the tower as a fearful reminder of the power at work here. We were frozen to the spot, unable to flee, but not wanting to stand against this thing.

No one said a word, and for a moment it seemed that we would stand there forever, locked in space and time, staring at pure rage. It was then that Holmes stepped forward. As if to meet him, the apparition moved forward as well, with the intensity of its snarl welling up to a vicious, fevered pitch.

"Your work here is through, Carlos Vargas," Holmes shouted, as the specter reared up in rage, hissing like a wild animal. "You have no power here," Holmes continued. "Be gone! And leave this house and these good people in peace," he commanded.

Another long moment passed in which the two seemed to size each other up. Neither made a sound during the time, but, all at once, Carlos Vargas, or what once was Carlos Vargas, began to grow in size. As if it were a balloon expanding, it began to swell, and as it swelled, it floated higher above the landing where Holmes stood. When it was so large as to fill the inner tower, its mouth opened wide revealing rows of teeth, such as a shark might have. With mouth agape, it bellowed forth a mournful cry, which filled the air and shook the walls. And then, in one swift move, it plunged headlong at Holmes, mouth opened as to swallow him whole.

Holmes did not flinch, standing his ground, defiant to the end.

Carlos Vargas mouth passed over Holmes from head to toe, diving quickly and covering him completely. We never lost sight of him. He never moved. He passed through Vargas, or should I say Vargas passed over him and continued through the floor, and like his brother, was never to be seen again.

Within minutes electricity began to return to the house. Lights flickered and then illuminated throughout the halls and rooms, and within the tower where the final scenes of the Vargas brother's tragedy had just played out. The Ainsleys and I, stunned by what had transpired, attempted to gather ourselves, while Holmes remained motionless, pondering silently.

As it always seems, I was the first to speak.

"Holmes," I said in hushed tones, not wanting to startle anyone, "are you quite alright?"

He did not move or speak, but stood there with his right elbow resting in his left palm, while his right hand supported his chin in such a way that his long index finger ran beside his nose to his right eye. Aside from his lack of mobility, he looked the perfect picture of health.

"Holmes," I repeated.

"One moment please, Watson," he replied.

His voice told me that he was in good shape. He was studying the situation. I turned my attention to the Ainsleys.

The Ainsleys were fine, although they were a bit shaken, which was to be expected.

"Watson," Holmes said after a minute or so.

I turned to see his smiling face looking back at me from the opened door at the top of the stairs.

"The weather seems to have cleared considerably. I think it's going to be a fine evening." And with a look at the Ainsleys, he continued, "Shall we join the others?"

By the time we had returned to what, until now, had served as the living quarters, electrical power had been completely restored to the building, and you could see the opulence of the place. Now, lighted chandeliers from high ceilings revealed the magnificent furnishings below. Each room seemed adorned with a culture and design all its own. Whether it were a music room, with piano and harp displayed, or the African room with its trophy heads on the wall and furniture covered with pelts of leopard and zebra, or the gothic style with heavy drapes and tapestries, every space was fashioned with impeccable taste.

The Ainsleys were quite pleased with it all, now that they could take a moment to look around unimpeded.

"This is the first time in some time, when I have really been able to see our purchase unencumbered," Mrs. Ainsley said happily.

"You may be surprised even further," Holmes returned. "I think I may have eyed a few pieces in those rooms, which might prove to be quite valuable in their own right. They are probably the variety of pieces that the Vargas family would have looked right past, without recognizing their merit. I would suggest a full inventory by a brokerage house at your first convenience."

"That we will do," returned Jeff Ainsley, grinning noticeably.

The Occurrence at Vargas Castle

The police had arrived by the time we returned to the sitting room, which was bustling with activity. Philips, who had hitched a ride with the constables, was chatting with Godfrey, and everyone was peeking through doors at the now, well-lit halls and rooms.

Holmes kept his interview with the police surprisingly brief, never mentioning the specter of Carlos Vargas, and simply stating that Josef had apparently fallen from the tower after being pursued throughout the halls by our group, a victim of his own insidious device, perhaps. While the Ainsleys and I were obviously unaware of his motives, we did not contradict Holmes' statements or elaborate further.

With the police well satisfied, and their time now occupied hunting up a corpse, and with the Ainsleys anxious to begin the survey of their new digs, Holmes, Philips and I bid them all adieu and set off for home.

The evening was now bright and clear, even on Ledge Road. The lamps were all lit along Bellevue Avenue, and while the horses "clopped" along at their slow rhythm, both Holmes and I sat back to enjoy this new found peace and quiet. Even Philips, with his excitable nature, seemed content to pass a few calm moments reflecting, as we made our way past storybook homes and Manors on this graceful street which went on for miles adorned as it was.

At nearly midnight, our feet touched the boards of my daughter's portico. She was waiting up, as I expected, and bid Phillips inside to sample some tea and cookies prior to his leaving us. This invitation he heartily accepted, and it wasn't long before we all were sitting around the dining room table, chatting and joking once again like one big, happy family.

Of course, the inevitable is always due, and it didn't take long once the cookies were gone. Holmes had just lit his first pipe when the questions began. Phillips led off.

"Mr. Holmes," he said, "what really happened out there tonight?"

"Why, whatever do you mean, Philips," Holmes replied slyly. "You were there to hear the official interpretation I gave to the local law enforcement, weren't you?"

"I heard it Mr. Holmes, but I ain't buyin' it. There was more that happened than you said. I knew that right off, and so would them Coppers if they hadn't been in such an all fired hurry to find ol' Josef. Now you tell me an' everyone here; what really went on?"

"Very perceptive of you," Holmes returned. "I didn't think coachmen were of such an intuitive nature here in the colonies. Astute tendencies should be rewarded whenever possible. I will tell you the story."

With these words spoken, we all settled in, as Holmes gaze fell from one of us to the other. He lit his pipe again, smiled politely and began.

"As Watson will tell you, my methods are precise and scientific, and not given to speculation or imagination. I deal in facts and facts alone, without variance. He might also mention that conclusions are drawn from these facts and not tampered with in any sense. This is why I have always lived by the tenet that once all unnecessary evidence is stripped away, what remains must be true however eccentric it may seem. Knowing these truths may help you understand the upcoming narrative and keep you from asking avoidable questions before I have concluded."

"To begin with, I knew that we were dealing with the human element and not the supernatural from the first."

"But Holmes," I ventured.

"Watson," he cut me off. "Pray let me continue without interruption."

"Very well, Holmes," I relented. "Every story does have its own author."

"Thank you," he returned.

"Now, as I was saying, I knew we were dealing with the human element from the first. Appearances may have suggested otherwise, but appearances are not evidence. Evidence is substantial and will stand to the test."

"Electricity, where it worked and where it didn't; that was evidence. Holes dug in the basement, not shown on any refurbishing plans; that was evidence. The supernatural does not dig holes. The reconstruction itself was evidence. The sabotaged parapet was evidence and the accounts of the witnesses, whether hostile or otherwise, were all to be considered as evidence, and that evidence led to human intervention in the lives and household of the Ainsleys, not supernatural prowling."

"Then what of the spectral visage we encountered," I put in at this pause, "what of its power?"

"On this aspect of the affair, dear friend, I must admit to being taken completely unawares. With no point of reference prior to these very proceedings, no chronicled and proven encounters studied, and no scientific credence given to any claims, I was completely at a loss. Add that to the fact that this specter had relatively little to do with the events which transpired before this evening, with the possible exception of some window dressing and those awful noises we heard, and you will better understand why, while I may now acknowledge that there are forces which we do not fully understand, I will not credit those forces with much power."

"How can you say that, Holmes, in light of what happened to poor Josef?"

"Two things, Watson," he continued. "First of all, 'poor Josef' as you put it, had it coming to him. He was a scoundrel of the worst sort, and though it may seem extreme, he deserved what he got. Secondly, I am of the opinion that much of what happened to him in the end, was of his own doing. To put it succinctly, he scared himself to death. To be sure, he had some help from our nighttime friend, but in the end it was fear and guilt which threw him over."

We all sat back upon hearing this short speech and explanation of how Holmes had seen the events of the evening in the light of his own logical deduction. While he filled his pipe anew and lit it again, I recounted the events as they happened, so that those seated at the table, who had not had the pleasure of the chase, might know exactly what transpired at Vargas Castle. When I was nearly through, and about to get to the part where Holmes began to order the ghost about, I stopped to see if Holmes might like the chance to explain that little maneuver himself. As I knew he would, he verily jumped at the chance.

"When all unnecessary evidence has been stripped away, what you are left with must be true, no matter how eccentric. I realize that I am repeating myself, but this point cannot be made too clear, and there is more to this tenet, which goes like this; when what you are left with is so eccentric that you have never dealt with its likes before, fall back on what you do know."

"Remember this, all of you, it may come in handy some day. Evil has very little power over the 'just man.' And what power it does have, must be furnish. This is what I knew when I faced the beast. Like the legend of the vampire, that he must be invited into a home before he can reek havoc there, evil only gains power through the fear and ignorance of its host, or victim, as the host is commonly seen. Without fear and ignorance, evil has no victory, for it is only victorious when it is permitted to be."

"Easy enough, then, to explain my little exchange with the creature on the stair. He no longer held any sway over those remaining. He no longer had permission to be there and I told him so. He was forced to leave."

"True enough, until the end, his attempt was to intimidate, but without intimidation he was powerless, and subject rather than ruler. Ordering him was a simple matter of standing fast and mouthing the words. 'Get thee behind me, Satan,' if you will."

"There is no mystery in that."

At this Phillips applauded. "Bravo, Mr. Holmes," he said, "bravo!"

I followed with a resounding, "here, here," of my own. At this we ended our discussion of the happenings of these strange, last few days, and relaxed into idle conversation for the remainder of the evening, until Phillips left for his own home an hour or so later, and we all toddled off to bed.

The occurrences at Vargas Castle had been explained as being a human phenomenon, with exceptions, and we wired Sir Arthur to that effect the next day. Little did we know that he was already in Rhode Island on that very day and appeared at my daughters home that evening. We were thus able to explain matters to him personally. He was not at all pleased that our ghost had left his earthly bounds for a more restful eternity, but after due course, and an investigation of his own, he did acknowledge the necessity of it. He spent a week with the Ainsleys, during which time we consulted each other for story ideas and medical chitchat, and I am confident that he returned to England a wiser, if not more contented man. We have kept in touch since then, and I must acknowledge that aside from Holmes, he is the most interesting man I have ever met.

I had announced that I did not intend on leaving America until my grandson or daughter was born, and to my surprise, Holmes announced that he would stay as well.

We took rooms by the Armory, on Clarke Street near "The Parade" and spent nearly a year in the "city by the sea," as it was known.

My daughter gave birth to a healthy baby girl, whom she named Anna Louise. We all became very close during our stay in Newport, Rhode Island and I am undyingly grateful to whatever Power arranged our lives in such a way to make that trip possible.

As for the Ainsleys; they became the center of society with their "haunted mansion" and all the wonderful stories and rumors that surrounded the place. They entertained often and increased their circle of friends enormously with the publicity received from our adventure. As I write these notes in my sitting room, overlooking the busy American streets, I enjoy yet another invitation to dine and speak at the Ainsleys home this weekend. Holmes does not attend these affairs, being far too cerebral for such things. He spends a good deal of his time studying his surroundings and the state of affairs in these United States. I think he is quite taken with the colonies.

I should not end this narrative without mentioning that within days of concluding our business at Vargas Castle, Holmes, who was still studying the details of the case and the reconstruction plans, made a startling discovery. About half way up the wall, in the room that proved to be the very room I was led to and almost trapped in by that vision I had mistaken for Holmes, and also the very room where Alice had seen her apparition; at any rate, about half way up the wall, was a small door which was hidden by a portrait of a straight-laced, young lady of fashion. Within that wall, behind that door, lay a treasure of precious stones and jewelry, including a crown and scepter. Investigations easily proved that this treasure was, in actuality, the crown jewels of Bulgaria. The fact that the press had not reported their theft was understandable, with the state of that government precarious at best. It had been determined by those in charge, that the mere hint of such a scandal could send that regime into chaos. The press was therefore not informed.

The jewels were returned, of course, through the British Office of Foreign Affairs. Holmes brother, Mycroft, oversaw the transfer. Both Holmes and the Ainsleys declined all offers of reward. "Justice is its own reward," I heard them say.

I have left the notes of this adventure, along with any other tale of a sensational or sensitive nature, in my daughter's safe keeping. Should a time come when the details of these accounts could be disclosed without causing harm or alarm, I have given her permission to publish. I leave them to her good judgment.

I have also left, with my daughter, the notes of the other cases, which Holmes and I became entangled while in America. We learned a great deal while in "the colonies," and some of our finest hours were spent there, but no case, either before or since, was so strange and uncanny as the occurrences at Vargas Castle.

THE END

THE PHANTOM OF FAREWELL STREET

FOR MARGARET, THE LOVE OF MY LIFE.

Watson's Sampler:
The Lost Casebook of Sherlock Holmes

INTRODUCTION

Newport, Rhode Island, once the capitol of one of the original thirteen colonies, of which we British still choose to call "the colonies," has many distinctions. Not the least of these is having a thoroughfare which runs from the "top" of the city, nearly to the country, bordered on both sides by the cemeteries of that community, and known and named, Farewell Street.

My granddaughter, Anna Louise James, arrived at the prescribed time upon this earth in September of the year of our Lord nineteen-hundred and seven, in the "City by the Sea," as Newport was known in those days. And although Sherlock Holmes and I had officially retired from our crime detecting careers in England and the continent, we had chance to find ourselves in that "City by the Sea," in those very same days, as a result of being retained to look into the occurrences in and around Vargas Castle within that community. This affair had come to a close most equitably in our client's favor, (an account of which I have left with my daughter), and thus afforded Holmes and I the luxury of idling away the days until my granddaughter should arrive.

Ah, and what a bundle of sugar she is. Well worth the wait, I must say. Born on a Sunday, seven pounds, four ounces, blue eyes and as beautiful as her mother. I ventured to suggest that she must take after me, to which Holmes disagreed most strenuously, noting many significant clues to the contrary. All in all, it was a joyous occasion with Holmes and I swearing to stay at least until Christmas and perhaps beyond, according to the weather.

It was at this time and under these circumstances that we were called in on a case so dire as to compel me to set it to paper while yet in the colonies.

Watson's Sampler:
The Lost Casebook of Sherlock Holmes

THE PHANTOM OF FAREWELL STREET

From the Files of John H. Watson, M.D.
Presented By William F. Watson, Jr.

As I stated, it was late September, three days after the birth. Holmes and I sat in our rooms at Clarke Street idling away the time until I could once again visit my little Anna.

There was a rap on the door. Before I could lower last evening's "Daily News," and rise to receive our guest, Holmes shouted, "enter," from his place by the window.

The door swung open to reveal two constables from the local police, one of which had his hat in his hand.

"Excuse us, sir," the hatless one said. "Sorry to interrupt you gentlemen this morning, but I've got a favor to ask of Mr. Holmes, if that's alright."

"Of course, gentlemen, come in," Holmes returned with his casual flair. "I would offer you some refreshment, but your demeanor suggests that we will be vacating these premises directly, unless I miss my guess."

"What'd he say," the hatted officer asked.

"He said he knows we're leaving here and don't have time to snack and chat," returned his partner.

"Now, Mr. Holmes," he continued, turning to my companion, "how could you know such a thing before we've even spoken?"

"Well," Holmes brightened, "I not only surmise that we are leaving, I am able to determine much more, if you will allow…"

"Indeed we would," he returned with a smile, a hint of a British accent and a glance at his partner.

"Very well then," Holmes began afresh. "Let us begin at the beginning. You knocked, I said 'enter,' the door swung open, but you did not enter."

"One of you removed his hat to speak, as a common courtesy I presume, but the other did not remove his hat, indicating that he will be needing it where it is rather soon."

They both smiled.

"This is my friend and colleague, Dr. John H. Watson, (and he nodded in my direction), and were he giving the dissertation, I am sure that he would remark that we are, in all likelihood, headed for the local cemetery to view the body of some unfortunate victim of foul play."

"Really, Holmes," I blurted out. "Where did I get that information?"

"Watson, from these gentlemen, of course," he returned. "Surely you noticed their trousers and shoes. They are wet with morning dew. The amount and freshness of the moisture tells us much. First, it tells us that these gentlemen have walked a good distance in high grass this morning. Where is there a large enough area with high grass, within the city, where these gentlemen could have collected this much fluid? The graveyard, of course! It is the only place I know of, that is expansive to the point where workers cannot keep up with their trimming demands and close enough to our position here, so that evaporation could not take place. Grass in a municipal park or even a private lawn would surely be kept at a proper length, which could not touch the cuffs as this moisture obviously did. And, since quantity of liquid shows distance, you are left with no other choice than the public cemetery, less than a mile from these very rooms."

"And the victim," The lead officer asked, smiling broadly now. "What tells you of him?"

"Your knee, sir," Holmes returned. "Your knee, which is soaked through, indicates that you not only walked in the high grass, you knelt there as well, and for some time. What else could induce such behavior than someone in trouble? You surely did not kneel in such a fashion to say, retrieve a coin, now did you. Also, and as I have mentioned before, you arrived here still soaked through, which indicates great haste on your part, once again leading to the conclusion that there is a victim at hand needing some attention. Since he is not with you, he must be incapable of movement. Your obvious rush in coming here is indicative of the seriousness that you, or should I say your supervisors, have placed upon this incident."

"My supervisor," the first officer repeated, straightening a little.

"Yes, your supervisor, sir," Holmes responded. "You see, you have hastened here for a reason. My conclusion is, that along with the information I have already provided, your supervisor ordered you to hurry. You, on the other hand, seem to understand that the sense of emergency indicated by your supervisor is unwarranted, and thus you have let me babble on these few minutes. From this I have further concluded that our victim has expired and you realize that there is no need for overt alacrity on our part."

By this time, the smiles had turned to gapes on the faces of our constables.

Holmes' smile, by contrast, broadened as their countenance fell, until at last he remarked. "May I assume, by your expressions, that my assessment is correct?"

"Right at every turn," the hall bound officer came back distractedly.

"Well," I chimed in, reaching for my hat and stick, "we probably shouldn't dawdle any longer."

"Right then," officer one came back, donning his own hat as if he had come to his senses once more.

Off we went. Although it had been cool in the early morning hours before the sun rose, it was now mild and clear. The officers had a motorized police vehicle with a driver awaiting us, and while it was sufficient for this trip, to my taste, it was not as comfortable as a hansom. The speed in which the driver went along might also have leant weight to this conclusion, as he must have taken his superiors at their word and wasted no time in getting us to our destination.

It was near half-past-seven in the morning, but the streets were already bustling with people anxious to start the day. We made our way through the city center for about three-quarters of a mile to where the cemetery was located. Turning right into the main thoroughfare of the burial ground, we could see a group of uniformed men standing about, just off the pathway, moving toward and then away from two gentlemen kneeling by a gravestone, which hid what they were examining. As we alit our transport, one of the kneelers stood and turned our way. We approached and he stepped directly to Holmes, hand extended.

"Mr. Sherlock Holmes, I presume," he said with a broad smile. A huge man he was, whose hand encompassed Holmes' so thoroughly that I lost sight of it in the exchange.

"My name is Peterson," he continued, "from the homicide squad. We knew that you were in town, sir, and thought you might be interested in what we've found here. I'll tell you the truth, sir, I've never seen anything like it."

We made our way to the point where the body lay. It was perpendicular to the road, with its feet closest to us. He lay on his back, arms at angles at his sides with his hands and fingers extended and bent as if they were claws. They were frozen in this manner and held rigid although rigor had not yet totally set in. And although he lay on his back, his torso was twisted to the left, as if he were trying to turn away from the sky only to have the planet hinder him.

At this point, we moved closer around the gravestones, which framed him on either side, until his face was revealed. It was only from this view that you could begin to estimate the trauma that must have rocked his constitution. His mouth was drawn up, as if in some horrendous smile, with all teeth revealed by the lengths to which his skin was stretched back across his face. The silent scream of pain and terror written on that face was so palpable that you could almost hear it still. His nostrils flared wide and his eyes, opened and bulging, told a tale of such horrifying reality, that you knew, without further examination, that his heart had stopped in mid-beat, and that he had died, not from any physical wound, but from fear, which must have welled up instantly and exploded on his features in the manner we now observed. To freeze a man's face and body in such a state would be impossible to comprehend without the first-hand, corporal evidence, which we had that morning.

"Has anyone touched the body," Holmes asked as he went to work.

"No, sir," Peterson replied, "we found him just as he is, once the alarm was raised."

"And who raised that alarm?"

"A fisherman, Mr. Holmes, passing through the cemetery on his way to the docks. It seems a barking dog attracted him to the spot. He came to us as soon as he saw this."

"Are you sure of that," asked Holmes.

"Yes, sir, quite. He was frazzled, you could tell. The sight of this man's face frightened him thoroughly. With all the talk of the phantom..."

"The phantom," I broke in.

"Yes Watson," Holmes replied. "You've read about him in the local papers. I know you have. The dark figure of a man that flies about the graveyard at night!?"

"Oh, yes," I replied. "Now I remember. An amazing bit of local fluff. I passed it off."

"Yes," he returned. "Well, I found it an interesting read, but there was no mention of any trouble or harm done, so I passed it off as well. Local legend and all of that. And although I realize that there is always a note of truth to these things, without foul play or invitation, (and he glanced at Peterson), I was hesitant to look into it. Passed it off, like I said. Wouldn't want to step on any Colonial toes," and he glanced at Peterson again.

"Well, now you have both, foul play and an invitation," Peterson answered. "We'd be honored to have some help, sir, and never too proud to ask for it. We here in the colonies," and he smiled, "are concerned with justice, not pomposity."

"Thank you. It will, as well, be an honor to serve," and Holmes clicked his heels together as he spoke. "Now tell me everything you have so far."

"Well, as we said, he was found here this morning by a local who heard a dog barking and came to investigate why. We arrived on the scene as soon as we were summoned, and found the old boy as you see him. No one seems to know him and we've had nearly all the men on duty take a look. He has no identification on his person and no distinguishing marks that we can see, although we haven't moved him or removed any clothing. Our line of thinking has it that he was chased into and through the cemetery by the person or persons who stole his possessions, and that his heart gave out from the run."

"How do you explain the look on his face then," Holmes dropped in, before they could continue.

"The throws of the death spasm," Peterson half asked.

"I do not think so," Holmes returned. "My experience tells me that a failing heart from exertion would not give us a look of horror so extreme as to contort the facial extremities to the limits such as we have here. I think Dr. Watson will bear me out when I suggest that only the severest shock to the mental system could produce these results."

I nodded slowly. It was true. The man must have been frightened, literally to death. As we stared at him, it became evident that he didn't even look like a man any longer. He looked more like a caricature than a human being. I will never forget that face with its eyes wide and bulging, as if some inward pressure was forcing them outward against the skull. What was so horrid as to kill a man who looked upon it? I shuddered again.

Holmes, on the other hand, did not miss a beat. Without hesitation, he launched back into his dissertation of the facts, as he knew them to be.

"Gentlemen," he continued, "I would also like to suggest that this person was lured rather than chased into the cemetery."

"How would you know that," Peterson asked with a slight edge.

"Well," Holmes began in a softer tone; "you will notice that he is on his back with gravestones bordering either side, the proximity of which would not allow our friend to roll over. He must therefore have fallen on his back, probably from a standing position. A running man, dying of heart failure would have fallen face first, wouldn't you think officer?"

"Yeah, I suppose you're right," Peterson agreed.

"There is more, if you will allow," Holmes continued.

"Of course, Mr. Holmes," Peterson returned. "That is why we asked you here."

"Very well. Our friend here is European, and British if the cut and style of his clothes is any indication. He was recently on Italian soil before arriving in America. He has not been in your country for much time at all, and while he was lured to this spot by promise or command, he did not remain here for very long before he met his end."

With this, he stepped back and turned to Peterson whose expression had fallen a bit at these pronouncements.

"If you will allow me to manipulate the body, I may be able to expand upon these conclusions," Holmes continued rather flatly.

"Hey Peterson," one of our earlier escorts said as he moved up beside the officer in charge. "This is the fun part. Ask him how he knows this stuff."

Peterson turned to observe his underling as he spoke, but then turned back to Holmes who did not wait for an invitation before resuming his dissertation on the facts perceived.

"His clothing is British, I mentioned that, except for the hat which is Italian by the label and new enough to be yet unblemished with perspiration on the band. Summer in Italy as in America, is a warm season. Had he been in either place for any length of time, the residue of his brow would be evident."

Holmes, once again, turned toward the deceased and then back to Peterson, who did the same, back and forth to Holmes.

Peterson spoke. "And his time spent at this spot, Mr. Holmes? How did you come to that conclusion?"

"Have you noticed his hands, officer?"

"His hands, Mr. Holmes? His hands? Do you mean to tell me that his hands led you there?"

"Yes, my friend, his hands led me there. Look at his hands, sir."

We all looked.

"What is obvious?"

We all remained mute.

"He is obviously a smoker of cigarettes. See his fingertips, especially the first two fingers and thumb of his right hand. They are brown from holding cigarettes. Many cigarettes I might add from the color of them. As you can see, there is a container within his breast pocket. A container of cigarettes, unless I miss my guess. And yet, gentlemen, there are no remnants of cigarettes about the body on the ground. Anyone who smokes and especially a habitual smoker of the degree of our friend here, would not stand about, even for a short time in such a place as this without lighting up. I suggest, gentlemen, that this man was set upon soon after arriving at this spot."

I nodded, as did the others. It all fell into place so easily once explained, that I could find no reason why the pieces of the puzzle which I now possessed, had not been with me all along. As has always been and yet I fail to appreciate, I stood there, as all did, awed by the simple logic of Sherlock Holmes.

Holmes, of course, paid us all no mind and began a thorough examination of the area surrounding the corpse, spreading out at least twenty feet in every direction. No one questioned him further, and he did not offer up any new tidbits to be devoured by we hungry onlookers.

In due course the coroner arrived to remove the victim, and although Holmes shot a disparaging glance in his direction, he did not hinder the duty.

"Are you satisfied, Mr. Holmes," Peterson asked before the body was lifted to the wagon.

"Satisfied? No," Holmes replied. "Not satisfied until all questions are answered, sir. And there are quite a few. Quite a few, indeed."

"But may the body be removed, Mr. Holmes," Peterson followed.

"Yes, yes," was the reply, with a dismissing wave of the hand. "You won't let me keep it here all day, and without a proper laboratory, little more can be established by the physical presence."

"There are many peculiarities here, Peterson," he continued.

"Might I inquire as to what, sir?"

"Motive, for one!"

"Motive, sir. Wouldn't it be robbery? His purse is gone, and dressed as finely as he is would surely indicate that he had a wallet, wouldn't it?"

"Indeed it would, Officer Peterson, but there are other considerations."

At this pronouncement, Holmes stopped and looked around. The day had begun with great promise, but early clouds were moving in from the west and the threat of showers now loomed. After sniffing the air like a bloodhound on the scent, Holmes turned once more to the officer and asked him up to tea at our rooms. He accepted readily and, with the aid of our motorized vehicle, we found ourselves back at Clarke Street in no time at all.

At the risk of sounding snobbish, I must admit that tea in America lacks the ceremonial status it enjoys on the Continent. To the Americans tea is a drink to be consumed, and lacks all of the social implications afforded it by so many other cultures. As a living, breathing example of this claim, I present Officer Peterson, a man of rank in the Police Department of what should be considered one of the most financially and culturally affluent cities on this country's eastern shore.

With Holmes ordering our refreshment in lieu of breakfast from our perplexed looking landlady, we had no sooner doffed our light coat and hat before we were presented with a tray from the kitchen complete with steeping pot, cups, lumps and a few prepared breads for munching. I personally poured and served the tea to my friend and Officer Peterson, who immediately downed the contents while standing at the serving table. He had completed this transaction with all the formality of a charging rhinoceros, and as I sat to stir my own mixture of special leaves and water, I looked up to see him standing there, impatient.

"Gentlemen," he exclaimed, "if we might get started. I am a busy man and if Mr. Holmes has further information, I will be happy to listen, but I am afraid that I am unable to dawdle over tea and crumpets today."

In a word, I was flabbergasted. I believe I began to blubber something about ill-mannered people and the Crown before Holmes raised his hand to silence my outburst.

The Phantom of Farewell Street

"Watson, we must remember that all customs are not observed in all places. We are guests in the country after all. I am sure our friend Peterson here has absolutely no idea as to what a 'formal tea' is."

I heard Peterson utter, "a what," in the background as Holmes spoke those words to me. I must admit that it hadn't occurred to me that a civilized nation, such as America, would not have its entire citizenship schooled in the proper manner for conducting a "formal tea," but as I now saw the glazed expression upon poor Peterson's face and remembered similar blank stares from the housekeeper and others, to whom we had mentioned "tea" in a reverential manner, I realized that I may have been hasty in my assumption about this matter. In fact, I might just owe the whole country an apology. But realizing the futility of any attempt in that direction, I opted for Officer Peterson, in his official capacity, to represent his nation in this instance, and apologized to him. And he, being the diplomat needed in representing a civilized nation on the brink of calamity, accepted the apology with grace and dignity, thus avoiding an international incident in a teapot, if I may be so bold. We, therefore, all had a laugh and got back to work.

Holmes spoke.

"Peterson," he began, "it is my opinion that motive is of the utmost importance in this instance and here is my reasoning. If robbery were the game here, I am afraid that the perpetrator would be considered a poor player. Yes, sure enough, the victim's purse is missing, but that seems to be the extent of the stolen items. Surely, you must have noticed the diamond on the gentlemen's left hand and the pocket watch with gold chain so obviously left in full sight. No thief worth his salt would dare leave his prey so clad."

"My contention is, therefore, that the architect of this crime removed the purse in an attempt to hide the identity of this individual rather than for personal gain. It is therefore also my contention that the victim's identity is key in locating the guilty party. Also I find…"

There was a knock at our door.

"Who could that be," I remarked off-handedly as I rose to answer.

"It's probably for me, sir," I heard Peterson say in the background as I reached for the handle. Glancing back, I saw him rise and straighten in the event that it was, indeed for him.

The handle firmly held and turned, I opened the door inward. The next sight my eyes beheld was queer indeed. For standing before me, dressed entirely in black, was a person whose gender I could not distinguish. To be sure, it had all of the outward appearances of a man standing erect, over six feet tall, thin, flat breasted and wearing pants. Where the question came in was in its great cloak, which stretched its full length to the floor. It was velvet, black, heavy and hooded. There was nothing distinctly feminine about the cloak, other than its wrap around feature and, that since it was nearly closed in the front; it gave the impression of a gown. The hat and veil were the only truly feminine articles worn. The hat was black and wide brimmed, worn square to the head with a black veil cascading down, completely circling the brim, closed in front and tied tightly around the neck at the collar level. It was a mourner's veil.

I must admit that I was dumbstruck, and stood there silent for an extended moment, as did our guest. It must have begun to get tense for it was the fidgeting

151

behind me, which stirred me from my funk and I glanced back to see Officer Peterson lean left to get a glimpse of our visitor. It was at this point that the man in black, (I could tell from his voice) spoke in a low, even, almost controlled tone.

"May I speak to Mr. Holmes," he said, ending with what I can only describe as a high, pitched, involuntary giggle, which was quickly snuffed out as he regained control of himself. I turned back to face him and enquire after his business when I noticed him lean slightly to his right, mirroring Peterson's movement of a moment before. Whether he recognized the face or the uniform, I do not know, but what I do know is that although I could not see his eyes, when those eyes caught sight of the police inspector in our rooms, there was a start within him, which shook him throughout. This reaction was so immediate and so violent, that involuntarily I spun to face the cause of his obvious distress. What I saw when I turned was nothing more than a quizzical look on the large policeman's face. And before I could turn back to face our stranger at the door, I heard his footfalls as he scampered down the hall to the exit at the far end. Without hesitation I took after him, although to this day I cannot tell you why. As a dog will chase almost anything that runs from it, I took after this man, and although I am disheartened at having to refer to myself in the same vein as a hound, there I was in hot pursuit, down the hall, down the stairs and out onto Clarke Street.

Nimble he was, and quick as a bug. He was out to the street well ahead of me, and although it was a short distance, I fear he nearly halved my time in getting there. Now while I admit that I am not the most athletic of figures, and that my age may also have taken some small toll, I am neither handicapped nor considered slow among my peers, and yet, as I have stated, he was down the stair and out of the door well ahead of me.

When I reached the street, the first appearance was that the man had vanished into thin air. He simply was not there. The street did have a few people walking about, and as I flashed my gaze to and fro in an attempt at noticing any movement that might be his, I did observe our motor carriage with driver at the ready and a hired brougham at the curb about to depart, but the tall mourner whom I pursued so vigorously was nowhere to be seen.

It was then, as I scanned the scene, that my eyes met those of a young gentleman and his lady on the opposite side of the street from me. They seemed to be studying me intently, and when our eyes did finally meet, there was that spark of acknowledgement that only happens between strangers who momentarily share a common cause. They had seen my quarry, I knew it. He must have calmed himself before entering the street to the extent that it seemed no one had noticed him, not even the officer assigned to drive Peterson about. Had it been his motion or unusual garb, I do not know, but something had caught the eye of this passing couple and once they saw me thrashing about, they surmised that I was in pursuit of the man.

I gave them a questioning look and threw up my hands as if to say, "where?" They, in return, obviously reading my sign language, both turned at once and pointed to the brougham just one moment before it passed between us and blocked our view of each other. That was all it took. I flew after the coach on foot as it picked up speed and headed for the first corner at Mary Street.

The Phantom of Farewell Street

Holmes and Peterson had entered the street as well by this time, for I could hear Peterson's gruff voice cry out to the driver as they sprinted in the opposite direction in an attempt to take up the chase in the motorized carriage.

Once again I must admit to being not as fast on my feet as I once was and I also must admit, (although it pains me), to being not as quick witted as I might fancy myself, for as I sped along in pursuit of what effortlessly gained distance, it occurred to me that I should have hailed the motor car myself and saved myself the embarrassment of being defeated so thoroughly. This realization flashed through my mind in a second and I was, in fact, about to slow my steps and wait for Holmes and Peterson, when I noticed that, up ahead, on Mary Street, where our quarry must turn in order to make good his escape, was a horse and wagon stalled at the crossroad. It seems that a merchant's wagon had dropped a barrel full of apples as it made its way up the hill. The driver had left his charge and was attempting to refill the barrel and return it to its place in the rear of the wagon. The whole ordeal had completely blocked the corner and even as I first noticed the commotion, I also noticed that the brougham was slowing to a stop. With renewed effort, I began to run again.

My complete attention now lay on the driver of the brougham. He was in the suit and manner of a paid cabman. His cab was black which, in America, was not always the case, but was customary to the upper echelon, and certainly befit our mark, who looked so much the part of the mourner.

As I steadied my gaze on the driver, and drew closer to the carriage, I was confident that this cabman, once stopped, was going to step down and assist the merchant, who was still scrambling about with his wares and his woes. The fellow even stood up as he reined in his steed before the blockade. But my heart fell when I saw him sit again and reach out for his whip, with me so close to catching my prey. It seems that passers-by on the street, both walking and riding had stopped to lend a hand to the hapless merchant. Americans, I find, are generous in that and many other ways. This time I feared, their generosity had foiled my attempts at learning the identity of our caller and his motivation for flight at the appearance of the constable. But my remorse only lasted a second for, even as he raise his whip, I could see that I had drawn near enough to gain my prize still, if I sprinted but a few more paces. The coachman whipped up his steed. Whether he realized what was transpiring behind him in an attempt to terminate his fare or not, I am not sure. What I was sure of was, that the horse carriage lurched forward just as I reached for the handle of the door to gain entrance to the passenger compartment.

Anticipation is the thing through which many battles are won, and it was because of just such anticipation that I sprang forth toward handle and sideboard and snatched victory that day, gaining close proximity to the quarry, which I sought from the first.

With my feet steady on the sideboard, my right hand on the handle and left hand on the rear bar, we took the corner briskly and headed down Mary Street toward Thames Street. I checked myself to be sure that my position on the carriage would not hinder my ability to perform my next maneuver. It was at that moment that I began to realize just how unsure of myself I was. After all, I had absolutely no idea who it was I was pursuing in this fashion. The only truth I knew was that I was chasing a caller who had fled at the sight of a policeman. With no other information, other than the peculiarity of his attire, what was the motivation that sent me scurrying after him in such a manner? I must admit that at that moment, at that place, I had no idea. Perhaps it was instinct which sent me forth, I do not know.

I chanced a glance back to see if Holmes and Peterson were following in the motorcar. What I saw as we rounded the corner, was Holmes on foot, in full stride, but well behind, while Peterson and the driver stood by the car looking frustrated and perplexed for some reason. I don't think I'll ever get used to motorized carriages. They let you down too often.

But, back to the situation at hand. I was not about to let anyone down. I had come this far. Holmes and Peterson obviously felt that this pursuit was worthy of the effort, if their behavior was any indication, and I was on the brink of discovery. There was no good, clear reason not to continue. My doubts and anguish set aside, I plunged forth and with a twist of my right hand, the handle was pulled down, the latch clicked and the door swung free.

What met my gaze as I moved to enter the carriage I shall never forget should I live to be two hundred years. There before me, reaching out to gain control of the handle I had just turned, split seconds too late to prevent my entrance, was a man. Whether it was the lurching of the horse or the motion of the carriage or the commotion on the street, his hat and veil had fallen from him, and even as his right hand reached for the door handle, his left groped the floor for his covering. Our eyes met at once. Pale blue they were. The palest blue I've ever seen for eyes, and piercing, as if he could reach down into a man's soul and pluck the essence from him. And his skin, the color of his skin, or what passed for epidermis, was more striking than his eyes. Amber it was in color; a deep reddish, orange, drawn back thinly over the skeletal presence beneath. Dark blue streaks played across that surface, as though the vessels had woven their paths externally for lack of space, having no recourse within to complete their task and channel used blood back to the pump without showing themselves. His eyes were large and protruding despite the fact that they seemed sunken into that hellish skull.

When he saw me, his mouth flew open in a surprised expression that, while apparently not intended, still took on the aspects of a snarl with malformed, discolored teeth showing through drawn back, wrinkled, skinless lips. He had no ears or nose to speak of, with mere protuberances of flesh, surrounding open holes to mark their place. His hair had been burnt or blown away, with only tufts surviving here and there as a reminder that once upon a time, features must have adorned this ravished glare.

When the door had flung open he gave a start and let out such an unearthly moan that I was stopped without entering at the sight and sound of him. We stared a stare at each other, which while it seemed an eternity, must have only been a moment. In a word, I was awestruck. With that strange combination of fascination and horror, which befalls one caught in momentary shock, I could not and did not move. I believe I might have stayed there staring indefinitely, had he not lunged forth and made a grab for the now open door. The carriage was dark inside, for all of the curtains had been drawn shut to avoid any notice, so that when he did move forward, hands and arms first and then that face in panicked surprise, lipless mouth agape, teeth dark and broken, skin russet and shiny, bursting forth into the light, into view, I stumbled back in spite of myself, leaving my perch and falling from the sideboard to the street below.

The Phantom of Farewell Street

In a jumble of hooves and wheels and dust and dirt, the carriage, transporting the strangest looking man I have ever seen, clambered off down Mary Street and around the corner at Thames.

I got up, with the help of a pair of passing pedestrians, and began dusting myself off as Holmes caught up to us.

"Watson, are you quite alright old man," Holmes started.

"Yes, yes I am, I think," I returned as I moved and checked my limbs. "It was a nasty fall, but no harm done."

"Well then, who was that person?" he continued.

"I'll tell you the truth," I said, a bit out of breath, "I haven't the foggiest idea. He has the most ghastly disfigurement of anyone I have ever seen though."

It was at that moment that Officer Peterson pulled up next to us in his mechanical contraption, which he and the driver had finally got going.

"Shall we get after them?" he said with a quizzical look at me.

"I think not," Holmes broke in. "The bird has flown, without benefit of introduction I fear. It is a lost cause," and his gaze drifted off, as if in thought. "Watson has also had a rough encounter with the curbside. I think we have had enough adventure for one morning."

"But weren't you interested," Peterson began until Holmes cut him off.

"Not in the slightest," he said. "If the episode had merit, it is merely postponed, at no further harm to any party. But, Officer Peterson, don't for a moment let us hinder you, or keep you from your duty, if you feel duty does call in this instance."

Peterson took a moment to look down Mary Street. There was no sign of carriage, driver or quarry.

"Well, I guess you're right, then. Are you okay Doctor?"

"Yes, I am actually." I was still dusting myself off. "No harm done," I said again.

"Then I think that I shall get back to work, gentlemen. We still have a murder on our hands, don't we? Will you be able to make it back from here?"

"Of course," I returned sharply, not knowing his inference.

"Good," he came back lightly enough. "But Doctor," he continued, "perhaps you should rest up some. You look a little pale."

Off he went in his motor-carriage, and as we walked back to our rooms, I asked Holmes why he had left Peterson ignorant of my encounter with the coach passenger.

"What purpose would it have served," he returned. "Except perhaps to setting the good Constable off, chasing after this fellow before we've had an opportunity at an interview. Besides, old boy, I did not lie. I am quite sure we have not seen the last of this person. Anyone who would go to such lengths of peril and disguise to appoint themselves to us will not desist over this slight setback."

Once back in our rooms we did not speak of the incident again. Holmes went directly to work on some scribbling and newspaper reading while I attended my minor injuries and freshened up. We heard from no one for the remainder of the day.

The next day was more of the same. I spent some time with my daughter and her family while Holmes visited the local library on a research project he had begun, involving the calendar of events which shaped and directed life in this small community. The local news had carried an article and a picture of the victim of foul play, whom we had seen in the cemetery the day before. They were forced to use the morgue photograph of the man, I'm afraid, with the explanation that they were still interested in his identity and origin.

To be honest, the photograph in print was not of the highest quality and did not do justice to the man but, for those of us who had seen him first hand, it was easy to recognize and remember the look of sheer horror, which apparently could not be removed from his features by the experts at the morgue.

It was also obvious that the authorities were stumped in this matter, and while every comment or quote offered up by the investigators only skirted the issue and made light of any inquiries in the general direction, the paper came right out and mentioned the Phantom and his possible connection to the incident, but not without a disclaimer.

"There is no Phantom," claimed one correspondent. "We have investigated the reports of this ghost, flying through the graveyard at night, and have determined that these reports are thoroughly unfounded. It has been written off to hysteria by The Force."

"What do you make of all this, Holmes," I asked once we again settled into our rooms at Clarke Street.

"I make very little of it," he replied. "They offer absolutely nothing in the way of explanation, and have made no headway at all, it seems. I spoke with Peterson myself today and he brought nothing new to the table. They are disregarding any information offered about this 'Phantom' fellow and remain entirely ignorant as to the identity of our victim. In fact, and although I did not confide my thoughts to Peterson, I find this entire investigation as ridiculous as this headline."

With that, Holmes flipped his copy of the local sheets in my direction so that it lay in front of me on the table. There, across the face of page one read, "DEAD MAN FOUND IN LOCAL CEMETERY."

I chuckled to myself, but to Holmes it was most serious.

"What are we to do then," I asked after a moment.

"We will do what we always do, Watson. We will take matters into our own hands."

The evening found us strolling through "The Parade" toward the burial ground where we had viewed the body of the dead man.

"The authorities are taking this Phantom business much too lightly," Holmes remarked as we walked along. "There is nearly always something of value in reports such as these. People rarely claim to see things which aren't really there, hysteria not withstanding."

"Then you feel this Phantom fellow played a part in the man's death, Holmes?"

"We cannot be sure of that, Watson, but he may know something that would be helpful, since he haunts the area."

"Do you think he is dangerous Holmes?"

"That possibility is ever present. To be sure, he is stealthy and secretive, for the authorities get no wind of him. Yet it is also apparent he has no fear of or regard for the public, being observed by so many."

"And what of this flying business, Holmes. Could there be any truth to that?"

"You might be surprised to find that I think there is something to those reports, Watson. If you remember correctly, there were no signs of another presence near or around the body when we saw it. Despite Peterson's protestations to the opposite, I do believe that his officers had contaminated the scene before we arrived, but their clumsiness was easily recognized and once observed, easily distinguished from other, more subtle signs of attention to the area. I found no such signs about the body. If the Phantom was about that night, he did not touch ground."

"Furthermore, the accounts that I read in the papers prior to the death, when police were investigating the sightings with some vigor, all denoted the fact that no physical signs of the Phantom could be produced by the witnesses or the police. He must fly, Watson. How else does he get around?" And he, in turn, chuckled to himself at that.

By this time we were nearing Farewell Street and the graveyard where most people had claimed to have witnessed the nightly excursions of our mysterious friend. Newport City's northern most graveyard was the longest of the four, which held the distinction of framing Farewell Street, and despite its size, was generally occupied by the year of 1907. A rather large, stone Chapel dominated the north-center of the yard with bell tower and slate roof replete with gargoyle drain spouts adorning the edifice. This Chapel area also held the distinction of having ground maintenance of the highest quality, as if the, "good, first impression's" theory of style, was policy here. There were grave markers of every size and shape about the field, all lined up in efficient manner, so that not an inch of ground remained vacant or unclaimed by a family. But, do not let my description give the impression that there was no beauty or design to the place, for while there were many areas where row upon row of markers were utilized, there were also any number of patterns laid out by the architect of its original plan. There were circular, family plots in places, bordered by walls or hedges or lined with small trees. There were rectangular and even triangular plots, employing all manner of headstones from a simple nameplate to the ornate in marble and granite with cherubs and Angels and Cathedral like structures. There were crypts throughout the yard, dark and dreary, locked against the thieves and vandals famous everywhere for their disregard for the sanctity of the grave and its contents. But strangely enough, Holmes had remarked while we walked, the incidents of vandalism in this area had shrunk with the advent of the Phantom.

"It's as if he patrols the place," Holmes said as we turned to walk up the small road which wound its way around and through the cemetery, "a lone vigilante against those who might harm his domain."

"Very poetic, Holmes," I came back, "but on what do you base your premise? Have there been reports that he has somehow molested an evil doer about his nightly chores?"

"No, Watson. But what is more important is the lack of complaints about such mischief. What sinners would complain to the authorities that they could not complete their sin? None, Watson, none."

"It is the fact that there have been no complaints of mischief and no signs of it within these iron fences, which leads me to my conclusion. Someone is protecting this area and doing quite a nice job of it, unless I miss my guess."

I walked along in silence after that. Sherlock Holmes has a way about him that is often times unpleasant, to say the least. More than once he has taken a word or a comment that I have spoken, off handedly, and launched into such a minor tirade, that the accomplishment that lasts is to affect complete and utter silence from me. And, while I realize that his genius lies in his ability to find order in chaos, and to extricate fact from minutia, I am forever taken back when he turns his microscope on me, dissecting my every comment, as if I were part of the populace rather than a consultant. To my mind, talk is cheap, and the free exchange of ideas, no matter how ridiculous they might seem when first spoken, is one of the fundamental building blocks of logical discovery. I have voiced this opinion to Holmes on numerous occasions, and while he does agree, often times he does not remember that he agrees, and at these times, (with the present being an excellent example), he infuriates me no end with his callous and barbed remarks. As I mentioned before, the present was an excellent example and while we strode further into the yard, I turned my attention to the night rather than the discourse.

The utter stillness of the place struck me once our chatter ended. We had walked in on a gravel drive with the sound of our footfalls being the only noticeable noise, save that which emitted from our mouths. Our mouths now being shut, the crunching under foot was noticeable to be sure and we instinctively moved off of the road to the side grass to gain stealth. The night was dark indeed for a cloud cover had formed with few gaps available for catching sight of a twinkling star or the generous moon, which hid behind this screen. In relative terms, there was no sound now. No clattering of hooves, for with all the reports of the recent happenings at this place, no one drove by the cemetery at night. No rustling of the trees, for the night was as still as the monuments to death, which dwelt there. And I realized as I marveled at the gloom of the field, that there was no sound from the animals and insects, which surely must inhabit this park. It was as if a storm was about to strike, and I halted my progress for the sheer power of it.

A glance across the way at Holmes, for we were walking on either side of the drive, showed that he also hesitated to observe this phenomenon of quiet. He, in turn looked at me, gesturing with his hand, palm down, that I should stay where I stood. He then gestured to the field before us, indicating that a good look around was in order. With a nod to him, I began to survey the area, taking in what I could in this poor light. It was as if the night had closed in upon us. From our vantage point, which was yet, indeed, nowhere near the center of the cemetery, we could see no houses, no street lamps, no sign that there was life anywhere, other than the two of us. It was almost as if we were on another planet, or an island, far out to sea, with vegetation, but little else. At the risk of sounding trite, I must say that the place was indeed spooky. My gaze swept around until it, once again, rested on Holmes, who was looking off to his right, so that we were both now looking in the same direction. I could see that Holmes had his head tilted slightly to one side as he stared. With this peculiar positioning, I soon realized that while he was staring, he was also listening intently to something. I, for myself, had heard nothing, and determined to break our own silence to ask him what he was about, when I, as well, heard a sound.

It was a low, rustling noise coming from our right side. It was the sound that a kite might make or better still, a flag, which is beaten by the wind. The dilemma in my mind, which I have alluded to before, is that there was no wind, on that occasion, to stir up a flag or a kite. And the sound was low, barely audible, as if far off and in another part of town. I shivered in spite of myself.

The sound, which came and went twice while I listened, emanated from my right, as I mentioned, so that is where I turned my attention. I could see nothing at first. All was black and still. There were gravestones, of course, which diminished in their visibility within thirty to thirty-five feet of me. Also, as I mentioned, the night was dark, with no stars or moon available for weak illumination because of cloud cover. I stared as deep as I could, but could spy no movement in the gloom. Even the sound, which had entered my consciousness a moment before, had vanished like stars in the daytime, or this night, for that matter. All was quiet once again, in a moment, and while I felt that all too familiar tingle of anticipation, all evidence that something out of the ordinary was about to occur had dissolved like the honey in my tea. Now I turned my focus back to Holmes, expecting to find him perplexed as well, but as so often happens, I was mistaken. For there he was on one knee, peering into the darkness intently. And as if he could feel my stare, he pointed off into the night, directing me to what held his interest so keenly.

I must admit it took a moment. It seems clear to me now, that when we look off into the distance, trying to focus on objects unknown, that we almost naturally extend our attention first to those things at eye level. This, of course, is what I did, and is, also my excuse for not picking up the object of my search immediately. In fact, it may have been the return of the low, rustling sound which inevitably drew me to the sight. For there, to my right, risen high above, was a figure, or a movement of something which seemed to flit from here to there. It had to be thirty yards from us, moving and stopping and popping up and down in a most unusual manner. At first I thought it some strange bird which danced before us, but in a moments time it was obvious that no mere bird could make such motions, as it slowly, then swiftly, moved off to our left.

Holmes was on his feet and moving in a flash.

"Go 'round to its back," he whisper-shouted to me while making a semi-circular motion with his right hand indicating the path he wished me to take. "I'll go to his front and drive him to you," he said as he turned and sped off to the left and into the night.

I regained myself in seconds and took off to my right in the direction indicated by Holmes. But as I looked up, I must admit, I had lost sight of the apparition we were attempting to apprehend. Nonetheless, I went my way blindly, trusting in Holmes plan while hoping not to fail him. Along I went, not staying to the road but passing off into the field, moving from gravestone to wall to sepulcher to tree, making a wide loop to my right and then back toward the left, hoping that my path remained true to what Holmes had in mind, and that I would not wander too far this way or that, and miss my appointment with the creature.

Watson's Sampler:
The Lost Casebook of Sherlock Holmes

I had lost sight of Holmes immediately upon setting off, and as I came around to make my first jut to the left, I stopped to gain perspective and bearing. Neither Holmes nor the quarry I sought was in sight. The blackness that encompassed me was deep indeed, and the all-present stillness of the night only served to enhance the feeling that I was now completely and utterly alone. A shot of panic went through me as I stood there by a tree, peering into the black of the place. No sound issued forth. No glimpse of movement or hint of life broke through to my senses. Where was Holmes? You would think that I could at least hear him moving toward the creature, or toward me for that matter, since we were, in fact, attempting to make a circle by our movement.

Nothing.

I was almost afraid to step forward, in fear that my attention to myself might distract me from any forthcoming sensual information. What if Holmes was in trouble? What if he had been set upon by that malevolence we were chasing?

I could stand it no longer. There was still no motion nor sound emitting from the black. My mind raced, and in that race, a decision was made. I would cry out to Holmes. He could not be so far as to not hear my cry and could therefore answer to say that he was safe. No answer would mean foul play and I would charge toward the area where he must be and extricate him.

I made ready my cry and was about to sing out when the strangest noise met my ear. It was half a cackle, half a laugh, shrill and high-pitched. It came from above, I think, or was it to my rear? Neither direction mattered as it turned out, because before I could cock my head either up or back, I was struck a heavy blow and my consciousness became as black as the night surrounding me.

The details of what happened in the next few minutes are unknown to me. All I do know is that when I regained my senses, I was both bound head and foot, and gagged, and apparently slung over someone's shoulder. Of course, to say that I was completely lucid at that moment would be a lie, but I could feel the movement, and while I could not see the ground through the blur, I did get the feeling that I was above my statured norm. I was not able to study this phenomenon for long though, for nearly to the moment that I blinked myself clear again, we stopped abruptly, which included a short drop, and I was lowered rather gently to the turf.

With bonds and gag in place, my struggles were in vain although I did attempt to right myself and face my abductor. For his part, it was obvious in a moment that he had observed my movement, for as I sat up, his hand came to rest on my shoulder, and in a rather raspy, high pitched voice, he whispered in my ear, "be not afraid Mr. Holmes, but I must speak with you in private."

It may surprise the reader when I state that I was not shaken by this case of mistaken identity. This was not the first time someone confused me for he, or he for me for that matter. And, while I was not used to the blunder, it was not unfamiliar to me. My problem, in this particular instance, was in my inability to correct the error. With hands tied and mouth covered, I could only produce a mumble and thus, my efforts in that direction did little to dissuade my captor.

My other problem was that I had little idea of where I was, and although I was relatively sure that I had not left the cemetery, my focus had not returned to the point where I could distinguish my surroundings with the clarity I usually enjoyed.

Furthermore, as my mind cleared, through the throbbing in my temples, my thoughts flew to the real Holmes.

Had he been attacked prior to me?

Was he, even now, lying unconscious or mortally wounded at the hand of the very person who wished to communicate with him?

What course of action could I take which would improve both our conditions?

I renewed my efforts at my bindings. My assailant had moved off as soon as he had spoken, and so, in my solitude, I had time to work on the ropes. Struggle as I may, they would not give an inch and actually seemed to tighten somewhat as I moved. With no relief in sight, I decided to save my energy and try to determine where I was.

I had been lying and now sitting, on a professionally, manicured lawn, which was my first indication that I remained within within the general proximity of the Chapel. When first I had begun to contort myself into a sitting position, my mysterious and now absent captor had assisted me into a position where my back rested against what felt like a stone column or wall, which I naturally assumed was a headstone. A quick survey of my surroundings revealed that I was, in fact, still in the graveyard, and as my eyes again became accustomed to the gloom and the lack of light, I could make out other gravestones in the distance. They seemed too far away though. They were neither in the stately rows nor close proximity I had noted a short time before. These looked distant, across a road, before they again took up their silent vigil, like soldiers at attention in the night. This was not correct. The gap was too great between myself and the first headstone for me to be merely in the next plot. I twisted to see what I was, in fact, leaning against. What I found was that my assailant had carried me for quite some length, so that I now sat with my back against the Chapel, situated in the north-center of the yard. This meant that I was at least three hundred feet from where I had been attacked, and even further from where I had intended to rendezvous with Holmes. My only comfort was, that with this new logistical information, I could better make my escape and find Holmes, once the bindings were loosed. I again, renewed my efforts at the coils and again, found them to feel as if they were tightening rather than loosening. As I have stated, I was bound both hand and foot, my hands being secured behind my back, and my efforts had been in twisting my wrists both left and right in an attempt to make some progress against the ropes. These efforts were in vain. But then the thought struck me to try the loop at my feet. After all, I was alone, and if my legs were free, it would be easy enough to make a run for it. I turned and fell so that I was lying on my side, and then bending my knees and arching my back, I found that I could reach the ties at my feet. I could not see what I was doing, but I realized that I would have to feel my way before I even started. The ropes were of the finest sort, not coarse or damaging, but smooth and slick, sliding neatly and tightly with each tug at the knots, which were small but exceedingly strong. I must admit that the exertion required in the undertaking began to get the better of me, for I am not as young as I once was and the evening's events had extended my stamina. In fact, I was about to resign myself to failure and give in entirely, when my fumbling hands ran across a single strand jutting into space beyond the knot.

"Well isn't this interesting," I thought as I gave the little line a pull.

Immediately I felt a loosening of the line. A slight kick assured me that my feet were free. Now all that was required was to get to my knees and stand. I rolled to my left and lay flat on my stomach; the idea being to draw up my knees beneath me, kneel and then stand. But as I lay there, about to attempt the maneuver, a rustling sound came from my right.

My abductor had returned. I tried to kneel, but he was on me in a flash, throwing a dark blanket of some sort about my entire body.

"There, there, Mr. Holmes," he said quietly and calmly, but with the eeriest, little giggle, "can't have you seen by your friends, can we. This will all be over soon and we can have a talk."

It was then that he began to wrap me up and lift me off the ground as if I were a doll. His strength was phenomenal and his movement, catlike. I was snatched up, rather than picked up.

It was also at this moment that I heard Holmes voice ring out.

"Watson…Watson," he yelled. "Where are you?"

He was loud enough for me to realize that while near; he could probably not yet see us in the night, and especially in our camouflaged condition.

I felt a tension mount within my captor. We were moving now, and more rapidly than I wound have deemed possible, even considering this fellow's unique abilities and yet, as I said, I could feel the tension mount within him as Holmes sang out again, "Watson – Watson!"

The fact that to this man, Holmes was calling the wrong name, seemed to have no effect on dissuading him from his purpose, for with renewed effort, he began to move even faster.

My agitated mind also began to race at this point and the first pangs of actual fear and panic pierced my consciousness as I wondered what this man might be capable of, once he learned that I was, in fact, not the person he sought. Moreover, my panic increased within the next moment.

As I look back upon the incident, my mind reels at the power with which God has endowed the most common of beings. For here I was, bound, gagged and blinded by the covering thrown about me, carried and moving quickly along, and yet, totally aware of the change in my condition when it went from a horizontal movement to a vertical one. It is true. For, all at once, I knew that I was being carried aloft through some strange horrific miracle. It was also true that our progress had slowed greatly, and that our movement was now sporadic, but that movement was in a heavenward direction, there was no mistaking that.

I began to struggle at once. My feet were free, but the way in which I was being carried, made the movement of my legs near to impossible, for they were held tight by his arm as he carried me over his shoulder like a sack. My hands, on the other hand, were unencumbered, save for the ropes, which held my wrists. I fumbled with my fingers, trying to reach my bonds. No matter how I twisted and turned them though, I could not make my fingers reach my wrists. I was doomed and running out of choices. The panic, which had welled in my chest, had now risen to my throat, until I felt as if I would choke on it.

Holmes sang out again, "Watson!"

The Phantom of Farewell Street

He sounded close now. Perhaps he could see us. That thought also choked me.

"Watson!" His cry came to my ear again, and panic, once more, replaced hope. His shout had a question in it. He had not seen us, and with each moment, I knew I was being hauled higher into the air, away from his searching eye.

And then, as luck would have it, my fingers felt a cord. A single strand, sticking out, just as the binds at my feet had had. I gave a pull. The knot slipped. My hands were free!

I swung into action at once. Moving my hands from my back to my front, I threw back the covering about my head. To my amazement, I found myself some fifteen feet above the ground. My captor, with one hand and both feet and me over his shoulder, was scaling the side of the Chapel, at the bell tower. It was unbelievable! But, as unbelievable as it was, and as startled as I was, I did not hesitate. Throwing the blanket to the ground, my intention was to grasp the lout about the throat and force him to release me. Instead, as he realized my new condition, he turned to look at me.

He was dressed all in black in a cloak or a cape, made from what seemed an almost velvet material. It did not shine at all and, in fact, seemed to absorb reflection so as to make the wearer nearly invisible in the dark of night. He wore a wide brimmed, black, felt hat that covered his head and most of his features, so that if he were to stand before you, with his back to you, it would be difficult to distinguish anything about his height or size, or gender, for that matter. But, what surprised me most, was what I saw as his head turned toward me. For there, under that hat, instead of a face, was a flat black mask, which covered all but his eyes. Even his neck was covered. We clung there, to the side of that building, for what must have been seconds, but seemed like days, staring at each other, astonished. The strength of the man must have been incredible, for even though it was obvious that my new situation had caught him unaware, he never faltered or wavered in his position on the wall. To this day, I am not sure how he managed it. He held on tight to both the wall and I, eyes wide with apprehension beneath the mask, knowing that with my arms free, I had the upper hand.

I moved quickly once my awareness returned. Releasing the throat that I had twisted to gain, I moved my right hand to the bottom of the mask, which hid his face. I do not believe he realized what I was about to do and, in fact, I must admit I believe he began to say something to me but, before his first utterance, I jerked my hand skyward sending both his mask and his hat to the earth below.

"Aauuugh," was the sound he made as he ducked his head down to his chest so that I might not see. Once again, I have to state, that throughout the ordeal, he never lost his grip or his composure on the wall. He held on firm and tight without a quiver, as a spider might, finding a perch where there was none. I do believe he could have continued his climb with me struggling in his grasp, had he a mind to, but the moment was lost and he knew it. Instead, in a slow and determined manner, he turned his face to mine.

Once again, I gasped as he swung his head around to meet my gaze, for here, for a second time, I was eye to eye with the same tortured, orange face I had seen in that carriage on Mary Street a few days before. The darkness of the night only served to enhance the horrific value of his features. The orange hue of his skin seemed to shine in the night, while the scars and ruts which coursed throughout his face, drawing back his mouth and his eyes, looked darker and deeper than they ever could in reality. His mouth, as before, was drawn up in a sardonic smile, as if he could not alter the look if he wished. We only stared into each other's eyes for a moment, but in that moment the feeling came over me that this was a forlorn and tormented man, tremendously sad despite the cackling and giggles he displayed from time to time.

My heart was in my throat from the start he gave me at the sight of him, but I recovered quickly and was about to speak to him; to explain who I was and that he need not fear us, when Holmes voice rang out once again.

"Watson," he cried ever nearer. "Watson, old boy, where are you?"

I spun my head to see his light coming fast in our direction. When I turned back, I found myself slipping gently from my captors grasp. Before I could speak, I was dropped to the ground in a way which let my feet hit first, breaking the fall and leaving me none the worse for wear.

Whether it was the sound or the movement that attracted him, Holmes was next to me in a moment.

"Watson, are you alright? Tell me what happened. Spare no detail…"

Holmes voice trailed off as I shot a look back up at the wall where I had just been. It was bare. The assailant must have scurried to the roof and then gone up and over it in a flash. He was nowhere to be seen.

"Watson! Watson, snap out of it!"

"I'm quite alright Holmes," I replied. "Just a bit shaken."

"Well, what happened, old boy? Tell me everything."

In less than a minute, I had relayed the entire episode. I knew so little; there wasn't much to tell. I did speak to the uncanny strength and the dexterity which the man possessed, and of his striking appearance.

"He also seems quite forlorn, Holmes," I ended.

"And how did you determine that?" he returned.

"By his overall manner, Holmes, and the melancholy look in his eyes, not to mention the weight of shame he shows. He is utterly embarrassed by his appearance to the point, unless I miss my guess, where he is actually afraid to be seen by others. And the odd thing is, that I got the feeling that his fear, in these cases, is not for himself. He seems genuinely afraid for those who view his visage. As if he pities us some how, for having seen him."

"You have gleaned all that information from your two, brief encounters, have you," Holmes commented with an inquisitive, rather than the condescending tone, which the written word implies.

He thought for a moment and then continued. "You know my methods, Watson. Intuition must be limited or non-existent in the face of fact and reason, and while I'll not discount your feelings, (and he emphasized the word 'feelings'), you must realize how little weight they may be allowed to carry in this investigation."

Rebuffed again. As long as I am associated with this man, I do not believe I will ever be fully comfortable with this, even though I realize that he means me no ill-will by it, and is merely stating what is obvious to him.

"He wants to speak to you, Holmes," I put in as a way of skirting the issue. "He thinks that I am you."

"Now we are getting somewhere." He returned with that sparkle in his eyes once again. "This makes perfect sense. It was you, after all, who answered the door when he called the other day. He has never seen my picture, apparently, and must have read or heard that we were here from that 'Vargas' business earlier this year. Aha, Watson, the pieces are beginning to fit!"

"Talk to me he shall! Come along, Watson. We'll find this Phantom's lair!"

With this statement, we set off to search for the Phantom's abode. As luck would have it, almost immediately upon Holmes' exclamation of intent, the clouds drew back revealing a clear sky and oval moon. Even dim light where there has been none is like sight to a blind man, and even though shadows were heavy, and the eerie feeling one gets in a cemetery at night returned, we found our way much easier as we circled the Chapel to gain entrance.

"Certainly you don't think that he lives here, Holmes," I put in as we walked.

"Indeed I do, Watson," he came back. "This is his home and his playground. He hides here, and even when he is seen, he is not found out. Would you like to venture a guess as to how he accomplishes that feat? How he, 'flies about and leaves no trace?'"

I stated that I would not.

"He leaps from gravestone to gravestone," he continued. "From thirty feet away, it appears that he is flying. He never leaves a track because his feet never touch the ground. If you check the top of the stones, you can see traces of his footfalls. Where lichen exists, it is disturbed and where it does not exist, the stone is marred. If there was an investigation of his amblings, he would retreat to the tower until things blew over. No sign of him would ever be found. With the climbing abilities you have described, measured against the lack of necessity to enter such a place, it seems the only logical choice."

"I would imagine he maintains the bell himself, keeping it in order so that no one need investigate any flaw in its performance. It is, therefore, the perfect perch. Aha, here is a door."

We had found a side entrance, not wanting to enter through the double, main doors, which were directly below the tower. The lock that barred our way was of the common, but sturdy variety, and Holmes made short work of it.

"You must know the criminal," Holmes once told me. "And what better way to know him, than to know how he does, what he does."

Holmes could "pick" almost any lock. He had taught himself long ago, and told me he would have done a treatise on it, were it not that it would be like giving aide to the enemy.

At any rate, in less time than it has taken me to explain the feat, we were inside the Chapel.

It was a relatively large funeral Chapel of the non-descript variety. "Christian" would be its best delineation, but it was obvious that most any denomination would be comfortable in the surroundings offered. We moved quickly to the Sanctuary, which was just below the tower. From where we were, looking up, the ceiling of the Chapel and the floor of the bell-tower compartment, were one in the same and this floor/ceiling had a trap door entrance some fifteen feet above us with a resting post next to it, so that a ladder might be leaned there. The ladder itself was not openly displayed, but within minutes, I had located it behind the choir pew.

Up we went and found the trap door extremely difficult to open, but with a few persuasive raps from a stool we had found by the alter, coupled with a prying pressure applied at the corners with the aide of my formidable walking stick, before long we were standing in the bell-tower compartment, where the bell hung awaiting those solemn occasions when it was employed.

I must admit that it shone brightly, even in the dim light of that night, in that room, bearing witness to the ambitious maintenance regimen imposed upon it by the very force we sought.

"It has been many a day since anyone has had to brave that ladder to service this chime," Holmes announced as he scanned the scene. "Our friend is very tidy."

And indeed, he was, for the room was spotless. It was apparent, at a glance, that someone had been living here, and that it was he who had jammed the trap door in an attempt at keeping anyone from entering unannounced or otherwise. Although the area was small, it had been managed well, with a sleeping mat against the north wall, a small crate serving as a table, replete with dish and cup, and another small crate employed as a lamp stand and holding numerous books. Yes, it was sparsely kept, but it was clean and quite livable. What he did in the wintertime was in question, for this abode was more of a widow's watch than a room. But for a summertime haunt, it seemed the perfect setting for the Spartan spirit.

In the center of the place was, of course, the bell; not huge by any means, but large enough to come into play as we checked for clues. More than once, I must admit, it took a glancing blow from me as I fumbled about, and once it almost rang, had I not possessed the agility to turn and hold it firm. It was a nuisance. Holmes did not seem to have this problem though, as he flitted about, turning this way and that, checking for indications of how we should find our man.

"He has a fair taste in authors," Holmes exclaimed as he rummaged through the crate of books. "Shakespeare, Leroux, Keats, Shelly and this fellow," he continued as he tossed me a small, bound text.

He had lit the lamp on the book crate and so I was obliged to maneuver my way around the bell once more to gain that spot. And when I got there, I saw that what I carried was a copy of my own renderings. It was a small copy of "The Crooked Man," which I penned some years ago.

"My word," I exclaimed to myself as I checked the publisher. "What else have we got here?"

Turning to the crate and holding the lantern out, I could easily view the texts neatly arranged there. The authors whom Holmes had mentioned were there of course, but I also noticed a Bible and a few newspapers, both local and continental.

"Did you notice this, Holmes," I said to no reply. Sherlock Holmes, of course, sees everything. "These papers from London are interesting."

"I have a question, Watson," he came back. "Other than their origin, what is common to every paper from London?"

My cursory examination brought nothing to bear, but before I could begin to delve deeply into the question and its answer, Holmes piped in.

"They all contain articles on John Merrick, Watson."

"John Merrick," I questioned.

"The Elephant Man," he returned. "The disfigured chap who passed on some years ago. He was quite popular in some circles."

"Oh yes, I remember," and I did. A terrible deformity on someone said to be a marvelous person. "Tragic."

"Yes," Holmes replied. "It seems our friend is quite curious about such people. Hugo Leroux and some of the others, all wrote about unfortunates."

"Well, we are done here," he continued. "We will have no interview tonight. We may as well retire to our rooms."

And so, we left that roost the way we had come and returned to Clarke Street. But as we passed through and out of the cemetery that evening, I never lost the feeling that we were not alone.

The next day showed itself to be glorious and warm. Holmes insisted on spending his time in study, which left me to my own devices. Immediately, I set my sights on Bridge Street and the home of my daughter, and her daughter, Anna Louise. By lunchtime, we were at the "Blue Rocks," a shoreline park, basking in the sun and thoroughly enjoying ourselves. A light breeze blew in from the sea, cooling the day and causing gentle waves to lap against both rock and shore in a light rhythm, beating out the quiet time. A picnic had been prepared, and as we dined on sandwiches and lemonade, Susan denoted points of interest within sight.

We could see Goat Island, Hog Island and Jamestown, which occupied Conanicut Island on Narragansett Bay. There were any number of sailing and steam vessels making their way to and from and around these small ports, and what struck me was, that while activity flourished, tranquility was at the day's heart. It was indeed, glorious, and one of my fondest memories.

Anna Louise was that day, and is forever, the love of my life. Even at that early age, there was the very fire of life in those crystal blue eyes. Her smile could light the room, and though not yet one month old, she smiled often. Indeed, the difficulty that I had that day was to pay attention to my own daughter, as she attempted to familiarize me with my surroundings. Although my interest was high and her remarks compelling, my gaze would often find itself resting on Anna Louise as she slept or wiggled or gurgled her own language and blew bubbles in her carriage.

Is it not curious how one can be so taken by another of such a tender age? I mean, it is not as if they can hold you in conversation, or attract you with their grace and agility. They are, in fact, awkward, helpless creatures, without the knowledge to consciously affect themselves, or anything for that matter, except perhaps the heart. And yet, a certain style shows through, doesn't it. A zeal and a spark for life; an enthusiasm, which indicates, at least to my mind, that this is someone special; grand in her own way and full of what life is all about.

I must admit that I have been reminded many times, by many people including Holmes, that all babies everywhere, induce such feelings in all people, everywhere. But these attempts at rationalization have little effect on me. For what I saw that day and still see, and has born itself out, time and again in the years that have followed, is a decency and good natured approach to life, which has never faltered, never wavered and never dulled, and has never been seen, by this author, in any other. My Anna Louise, was that day, and is to this day, unique in her way, in her style and in all our lives. She has proven the skeptics wrong, much to my delight.

My thoughts, once again, were interrupted by my daughter, whose insistence awakened me. "Look father, look," she exclaimed as she pointed to the bay north of the "Isle of Goats," as I had begun to call it. "That is 'The Gallant!'"

Before I begin the description of what I saw, let me regress for a moment to mention that, looking back, I find it an easy explanation why my Anna Louise was so special. She was, after all, the offspring of a woman who must have been just as spectacular in her early years as Anna Louise is now. It shows, even in the slight passage presented. My problem, and the regret of my life, is that I was obviously too busy or preoccupied to notice it at the time. My loss, and sorrow in that loss, is complete. And why God has given me a second blessing in Anna Louise is a mystery not even Sherlock Holmes would be able to solve. My gratitude is beyond description.

What I saw when I looked beyond the "Isle of Goats," was a sailing craft cutting through the waters of that calm bay with such speed and agility as to nearly defy description. You would think that she had engines turning full blast in order to gain such momentum. It was readily apparent that the wind was not blowing at the velocity that I witnessed. Or was it? It was at this point, while gazing at the vessel, that the realization came to light that I had no idea. Could a yacht of this or any other class, while cutting across the wayward, skimming and using them rather than becoming imbedded in their throws, actually surpass the knots accredited to that breeze? I resolved myself to ask Holmes upon our next meeting.

Recognizing the quizzical look, which must have danced across my features as my mind meandered about these thoughts, but completely missing the point of my visage, Susan broke in.

"It is the 'Admiral's Chalice,' winner, father, of four years ago. She is said to be preparing for the next defense."

"Ah, so..," I returned, drifting off in order that she not know of my ignorance of the technicalities of sailing, or of the contest she had named.

In no time at all, it seemed, 'The Gallant' had made a turn, heading further out of the bay and our sight.

The remainder of the time that day was spent in idle chatter about England and love and family, and we remained enthralled at the Blue Rocks until the dinner hour. As always, I was invited to dine with Susan and family, and learned as we strolled back to her home, that Philips, whom they had seen quite often since the Vargas business, was scheduled to attend.

"Why don't you send 'round for Mr. Holmes," Susan suggested as we walked. "I'm sure Philips will be happy to fetch him with his carriage."

"What a wonderful idea," I returned, and that is just how it happened.

It was like old times, bantering around the table, eating like kings and laughing heartily that night. Once again, Holmes was not the center of attention, which he seemed to appreciate no end. Once again, Ed and Philips told the most outrageous stories of the times of their lives, and the tales that were told on the streets of the city. Once again, we were like an extended family, and once again, I must credit my Susan for that feeling.

"And what are your feelings on this Phantom fellow," Holmes piped in when the conversation got around to local legends.

"A ghost," Philips said.

"It's a ghoul," Edward said with a twinkle in his eye. "He feeds on the corpses out there," and his voice got low. "That's why the living need not fear. At least that's what they say," and he began to laugh a fiendish laugh that turned into a giggle and ended in a chuckle all around.

"I don't think it's all that funny," Susan broke in, catching herself. "I think, no matter what is going on out there, it is a sad state of affairs. I would imagine that whoever or whatever it is in that graveyard is living a terribly lonely existence. That in itself is cause for remorse, and I think that you gentlemen, who spend your days making light of things such as this, would do well to consider how you might feel in like circumstance. This fellow, apparition or not, is in hiding much of the time, with death all around him. That is no picnic for anything living, I would say."

"Or dead," Philips added.

"Or undead," Edward topped in with, before smiling sheepishly at his wife.

At these last remarks, we all turned our attention to Susan, who looked altogether as though she were about to reach her boiling point, but Holmes chimed in and defused the situation with a question.

"Then you all do believe that there is something to this."

"On the serious side, Mr. Holmes, I do believe there is something to all this," Ed put in before the others could speak. "I know some of them that have come forward with the stories, and I must tell you, they're a sober bunch. Although I ain't never seen a thing out there by Farewell Street, I believe my friends and neighbors when they say that they have."

" I know that there's something to it too, Mr. Holmes," Philips followed. "I can feel it in my bones and can see it in the way Thor acts when we pass by there at night." (Thor is Philips carriage horse.)

"I agree with you," Holmes continued. "Watson and I have made certain discoveries, which indicate not only the existence of the Phantom, but also that he is intelligent, inventive and physically fit to the extreme. Our attempts to interview the man have failed thus far, but I think the time is coming when we shall meet."

"He'll be in your net soon then, Mr. Holmes," Philips remarked.

"Not at all, my friend," Holmes replied with a chuckle. "The fact is, we may very well be in his."

This comment got Holmes an odd look all around and before anyone could say anything, he followed up with, "and no, I don't think he committed murder."

At this, we all looked curiously at each other, but smiles soon replaced the curiosity as we realized that, once again, Sherlock Holmes had anticipated us, and the conversation soon drifted back to things mundane and trivial.

Watson's Sampler:
The Lost Casebook of Sherlock Holmes

The evening drew on, and although my enjoyment increased with each passing moment, (as, it seems, did everyone else's), Holmes mentioned that we must rise early in the morning to retrieve an answer to a wire he had sent the day before. We therefore needed to depart for our rooms soon, in order to get an early start the next day.

Philips, as was his custom, offered his services both that evening and in the morning that followed, which Holmes graciously accepted without hesitation. And so, after prolonged goodbyes and a quick story or two more, the three of us climbed aboard Philips' carriage for the short ride home.

Now while Susan's house is but a stone's throw from our rooms, and either one or both of us have walked the short distance any number of times, whenever Philips joined us for a visit, we always availed ourselves of his offer of a ride. We had all become very fond of Philips in the time that Holmes and I spent in Newport. And since, with the advent of the horseless carriage, Holmes saw that the days of transporting consumers and consumed by horse were numbered, we always accepted his offers for rides, knowing full well that we would employ him within the next few days and thus keep him afloat a while longer.

As I said, the evening had drawn on, but there was still a good amount of traffic in the streets, and as Philips' steed clopped out his easy rhythm on the cobblestones, I doffed my hat repeatedly to drivers, riders and pedestrians along the way. Upper Thames Street is both busy and quiet in the evening. It is not until you reach the wharf district of this seaside town that the noise level and bustle of the place spills out onto the streets like waves against the shore. But since our route turned off from this changeable road at "The Parade," all expectations were that we would not be jostled in the process. But, as with so many ill-advised, forgone conclusions, this was not to be.

The night was clear, cool and sweet as we progressed along our way. Philips' horse slowed to a walk, as he always did when not being coaxed, and we all relaxed distractedly as gaslights drifted by, and people, out for a stroll, spoke and waved hello. The moon was full and shining, leaving little need for artificial illumination, and as we neared "The Parade," you could easily note the flurry in the center of town. It was quiet though, as I stated before, and almost formal in its movement, as the traffic waltzed to and fro through the maze of streets in the area. There was symmetry to it, an order and gentility, which bespoke the possibility that, at long last, perhaps civility had seeped its way into the fabric of this land, and a new, systematic age was about to burst forth.

I had no sooner felt the warmth of these optimistic thoughts pass through me, than the roof came crashing in on my dreams. Without warning, Philips stood upon his perch above us, and pointing to "The Touro House," a hotel which bordered "The Parade," on the south side, he shouted, "Look, it's the demon himself!"

Both Holmes and I jumped a bit at this pronouncement, which was stated so vehemently that even the company of pedestrians about us turned to stare, first at Philips and then toward the hotel.

Silence lay on the entire scene like a blanket of snow, and with the exception of Philips, who skipped down to the ground and scurried off in some direction, we all stood transfixed, agape at the rooftops.

For there, with the half risen moon above his right shoulder, standing erect, with his arms folded upon his chest, cape billowing to his left, hat tipped tightly on his hideous, amber hued head, grinning with that frozen smile, which leant to the uneasy feeling that you got in your stomach when you saw him, was the being we had named, "The Phantom of Farewell Street." A laugh escaped him, which began as a high-pitched cackle, but quickly lowered to a guttural, hollow roar.

He stood there in defiance of us all as Philips outcry and his own reverberating bellow sent a stir through nearly everyone gathered in and about the square, until all were turned to his direction, murmuring and pointing. The agitation in the street below seemed to have little effect on our rooftop stalker's disposition, for he shifted not from his site as Holmes attempted to quiet the crowd. In fact, it was not until Philips returned from his harried excursion with a constable in tow, that we saw a change in the dark figure above.

"Stop in the name of the law," the constable sang out, in his official roar, even as Holmes dashed to his side to quell his outrage.

"Come down from there this instant," I heard him shout before Holmes had the chance to intervene.

All of this, as well, seemed to have no effect on the Phantom, and it wasn't until I noticed the constable's hand move toward his holstered firearm, that I saw the dark figure shift.

In the fairly well lit square, with the full benefit of the moon behind him, he was an easy target for my eye, even though his dark attire and cape seemed to absorb, rather than reflect the light, making the night itself his ally. He glided with the dexterity and grace that I have witnessed in few men, (although I must say that Holmes might be his equal). He moved to my right, toward the corner of the rooftop, apparently leaving himself no retreat. He was an artist of flight, fairly dancing his way toward the brink at a high rate of speed. His eyes never left the constable and Holmes, who were now in a heated discussion, apparently about how to proceed. He drove nearly to the edge in this curious attitude, and I could not for the life of me envision how he could avoid a catastrophic leap to the pavement below.

The scene itself was so intense and climactic in nature that both Holmes and the constable deserted their bickering to watch the end of the drama with the same strange fascination that held the rest of us. His steps had brought him to the edge. He never slowed for a moment. He leapt when he reached the end, extending far out over the street, gaining maximum extension, which every onlooker knew would never be enough to reach the next roof. He was going to fall.

A gasp rang out from the crowd and hung in the air like the scent of the sea. The moment, caught in time, was as if the world had stopped for an instant, and then he began to fall.

I must admit that as with all, I had been dazzled by the specter and his energetic performance. So dazzled, in fact, that I don't believe that anyone noticed the thin line stretched between the two buildings, where our caped friend seemed to be suspended in time. Along with, and attached to that thin line was a more substantial bit of weaving, which extended half way across the gap, just below and a bit behind the outstretched hand of the man, enabling him, as he fell, to grasp that line of substance and hold it fast.

He must have planted it there in case of such an eventuality as this, for as he caught the rope in his second hand, the weight of him not only pulled it tight, but began to drag it down, snapping the lesser cord and allowing the man to now swing toward the ground rather than falling flat.

A new gasp went up from the crowd as the Phantom began his pendulum plummet. Affixed as he was, like a plum bob, he sped in his arc break-neck, swinging low to the ground as if he would hit hard nonetheless. But, as he swooped toward the pavement, I saw his legs begin to move in a running fashion and when his feet touched the ground, he was already in full stride. Logic would seem to dictate that, in this situation, a person would release his hold and continue running up Touro Street as a matter of course. And that is, in fact, what most of us thought, for the onlookers, on the upper end of Touro Street began to scream and scramble in anticipation of just that eventuality. To say the least, it was a scene of mayhem the likes of which I had not seen in many a year. Horses reared and wagons tipped, delivering their cargo to earth as pedestrians cried out, racing to one side or the other in an attempt to escape whatever fate they were anticipating at the hands of this fiend hurtling himself toward them. The contents of everything imaginable spilled itself across the road and sideways, as those in his path literally abandoned all, in their attempts at flight. This all happened so fast, that there was no way for any other spectator to intervene and thus we all stuck fast to our spots, mesmerized by the pandemonium of the moment.

It was then that I spied a young woman faint, hands clasped to her breast, directly in front of where the Phantom would land. Her young man, who had turned to run, realizing that he had lost her beside him, turned back and stood stalwart at her side, ready to face the onslaught sure to come. I remember that I felt both pride and dread for him as he braced himself against the coming clash. There was fear in his eyes to be sure, but it was evident that he was not about to give ground or leave his flustered lady.

As he staunchly stood, awaiting the fight, I began to move his way, knowing that I could never gain enough ground to assist him at the first, but hoping that if he could hold on for a few moments, I might make up the distance between us and lend a hand.

The moment had arrived. All points were about to converge. I pressed myself hard to gain the speed needed to cross the square and reach the lad. At the moment, when all lines were to intersect, I looked up to see the event that never happened.

What did happen was, that the Phantom never released the rope. As he neared the pavement, his legs began to churn until he was at full flight when his first foot touched the ground. But, instead of using that momentum to propel himself along Touro Street, he held fast to the rope and used the momentum to propel himself upward again. Once that rope became tight to its anchoring pin on the roof, the ensuing force of the fall and the full out running motion of the Phantom, lifted him off the ground in pendulum motion and up the wall where he disappeared into an open window in "The Touro House," set in his travel path. As his cape slipped into the blackened room, I saw the young "Galahad" directly below him, frozen to the spot where their encounter would have taken place.

The Phantom was gone in an instant. The rope he had used now hung limply above the sidewalk where, seconds before, he had skipped along. The night was silent once again.

Both Holmes and the officer had stopped their jostling of each other to watch the scene unfold before them. Now that things were comparatively back in order, they released each other. Both Holmes and Philips regained the carriage before I arrived, and the constable ran to the building, wildly blowing his whistle before gaining entrance at the ground floor.

"Should we take up the chase," I asked as I sat.

"Not at all," Holmes replied off handedly. "There is no reason for such exertion. Our would-be quarry has flown the scene at any rate. Our best course of action would be a leisurely ride. The long way home perhaps."

"Phillips, old boy."

"Yes, Mr. Holmes," was the reply from our visibly shaken driver.

"Would you care to make a few of your American dollars?"

"Always up for that, sir."

"Well, how about a short ride down Thames Street before we retire?"

"Very good, sir," he replied.

What was now transpiring at "The Parade," was a renewed excitement. The fleeing masses, seeing that their perceived assailant had himself fled, now turned on their heels and became a mob, apparently bent on avenging the injustice that fear had created. As the first police officer entered the building, and the other constables in earshot of his whistle took up the chase, the multitude in and around the square began to clamber toward the door in a boisterous procession. To give credit to those souls not enticed into action by the turn of events, I must state that not everyone leapt at the chance and became as a pack of dogs after a single cat. Many either stood to chat or continued on as they were before the incident. To their credit, not everyone became a hunter. On the other hand, enough did join the fray to reinvigorate the confusion and tumult, which had until then, died down momentarily.

We left the scene in much the same condition that it had become when Philips first sounded the alert. In other words, pandemonium reigned anew.

We started off at a gentle pace as we had before, but instead of turning up the hill toward home, we continued straight down Thames Street.

"I thought you were in a hurry to get to bed," I interjected once we were going.

"Watson," he said in a low tone, placing his extended index finger against his pursed lips as he paused, "it is a curious thing in life, and one that should be known by all, though I've never heard it verbalized, that everything changes everything," and a brief smile danced across his lips before he returned his finger to them.

"Take, for instance, this scene we have just observed," he began again. "While it did not entirely change my plans, it did alter them considerably."

"But how so, Holmes," I asked.

He looked off dreamily as he spoke and said. "We are dealing with a very clever man here Watson. Very clever indeed," and he tapped his lower teeth with his pipe stem, which he had produced from thin air it seemed, like a magician. A smile crossed his lips as he turned to let his view precede us toward lower Thames Street, and he did not speak again, leaving my question dangling like a loose tooth.

Thames Street, especially in summer, is one of the busiest thoroughfares in all of Newport County. A host of individuals scurry to and fro completing whatever urgent business takes them to their heels at all hours of the day here, but especially in the evening, when the tavern doors open and the restaurants ply their trade, the throng thickens and the pace slows although everyone seems to be in a hurry. Congestion is the order of the evening here. It was into this bustle that we found ourselves once Holmes had decided to continue onward and not turn to our rooms. The horses hooves clopped lightly on the cobblestones, which I have heard, have been there since colonial times. Once we went on past "The Parade" and away from the mayhem and excitement of the previous ten minutes, the scene changed considerably.

Once again, people walked along the sideways on either side of the carriage talking, laughing and generally enjoying themselves, oblivious to what had transpired moments before. Now and again someone would dart in front of our brougham, squealing and giggling and trying to disrupt the horse, but all seemed to be in good fun and Holmes and I sat back enjoying the ride.

"So, Holmes," I ventured, after a few blocks. "What do you make of this fellow?"

"Well, you may be sure of one thing, old boy," he came back with cool assurance, "he's no criminal."

"May I ask you how you came to that conclusion?"

"Watson, were you not with me this evening, and did you not see the elaborate preparations taken and the intricate implementation of them by our friend?"

"Well, of course I did Holmes. I was right here with you."

"Why do you think that we were witness to this display?"

"Well, Holmes, give me a moment."

We passed a local Cabaret with music and laughter spilling out onto the street like the warm glow that emanated from all the storefronts and Restaurants on Thames Street. My eye wandered toward that door as I attempted to examine the facts as Holmes might, piecing together the puzzle set before me. As it always seemed, I could come up with very little, but determined as always to have a go at solving these riddles, I took a stab at explaining what we had seen.

"It is my opinion, Holmes, that we might never have seen any of this, had not Philips spotted the man in the first place. The antics displayed thereafter, were none other than the result of being found out."

"Correct, Watson. Correct indeed," he returned with actual glee in his voice. "To the point where you abandon your theory, you are correct indeed," and he smiled with a knowing giggle. "I, on the other hand, have seen something more in these 'antics,' as you put it. For instance, have there ever been any reported 'sightings' of this man throughout the town before? Has he been seen in any place other than the graveyard?"

"Not that I know of," I replied.

"Correct! And yet Philips was able to see him on that rooftop without the slightest trouble."

"But can't we write that off to luck, Holmes?"

"I think not, old boy," he replied. "To my understanding of this man, from what we've experienced of him, for the most part he is not seen unless he wishes to be seen," and he drew on his pipe. "As with his elaborate escape, he obviously constructed the means to that getaway well before our arrival on the scene."

"But, I have further conjecture, Watson. Unless I miss my guess, which I have not, I would say that our good Phantom arranged the things he did, the way he did, in an attempt to gain the interview with us that he so obviously desires. When Philips reacted so erratically, as he did, I am sure that our friend had to shift to plan number two, which was to flee the scene, albeit in dramatic fashion."

"But, if your theory is correct Holmes; why all the flair? Why expend so much energy?"

"I am sure we will learn that when we do meet, Watson, which may be sooner than you think." Then, turning his attention to Philips, he said, "we may start for home now, my good man," and he tapped the back of Philips' seat with his stick.

We swung up Mill Street toward Spring Street. To our left, Trinity Church Tower loomed above the shorter, stouter homes and shops of the city, its spire lit from within, like a beacon to those wayward ships seeking safe haven. As it seemed with everything in Newport, there was a quiet, gentle elegance about the place, which bespoke the quality to be found in this little city. A nice place to retire, I thought as we rode along slowly.

Left again on Spring Street, which reminded me more of London than any other area in the colonies with its residences and the occasional shop packed in close, yet handsomely so. Spring Street is narrow and long, and empties out into the center of the city at "The Parade," where both the Court House and the former State House are located. In no time, we reached the corner of Spring and Touro, where "The Parade" begins, just two city blocks up from the fracas, which started us on this large, square journey around town. We were, in actuality, half way up Touro hill, looking down two blocks to where we had begun. We were also one block from Clarke Street, where our rooms reside.

Even then, there was activity at the building by the Thames Street turn. A policeman was at attention at the door where the crowd had rushed in. People were being escorted from the place apparently based on their official or residential status. The police wagon was parked outside, seemingly in the event of either public resistance or a capture. In fact, the casual observer, happening by at this particular time and unaware of previous events, would fairly conclude that a raid of some sort was taking place. That was the look of the scene.

Philips reined up so that we might view the spectacle from a distance, and to be at the ready, should we want, once again, to join the fray. But Holmes bade him continue on to our rooms, which he did without opposition.

"Holmes, what is the meaning of it all," I asked as we climbed the stairs after sending Philips on his way. "You seem to be in possession of knowledge that has escaped the rest of us, and with all due respect, I cannot see where keeping us, and especially me in the dark, can be of much good."

He stopped on the step and turned to me with a half smile.

"You are correct on all counts, Watson, and were it not that answers are to be forthcoming momentarily, I myself would reveal all that I know."

"That is a strange turn of phrase," I commented as he turned and continued up and to our door. "What on earth do you mean?"

He answered not, but made a sign that I should keep quiet, then turned the key and entered our abode.

I must confess a sense of dread swept over me as I crossed the threshold. Holmes' actions had set me on alarm and then the stealth with which he entered our own rooms and the blackness which reigned within, set fear in motion within me. I could see nothing in my own apartment. It was as if every shade had been drawn against the advent of any single beam of light. So utter was the darkness that I lost track of Holmes as soon as he entered before me, and had it not been for the slight hall illumination, casting its glow on the floor of the place, I could easily have been fooled into thinking that Holmes had stepped off a ledge and was now plummeting to oblivion in some dark abyss. My first instinct was to head straightway for the light fixture on the wall, but before I could even strike a match, Holmes spoke.

"Do you prefer this blackness sir, or are we a liberty to pierce the dark?"

There was a slight, high-pitched giggle to my left and back, to the furthest recess of the room. I turned to face the noise but could see nothing in the still, black air. The thought ran through my mind that our unwanted guest could, even at this very moment, be charging at us in the night, and we would never know. He had not answered yet, and once more, my mind raced to think that if, by some magic of the devil, he could see in this shadow, he might well be moving tactically, so that an attack would come from our most vulnerable side. I braced myself against such an onslaught, ready to release all the fury of righteousness I possessed toward any foe that I encountered, when he spoke.

His voice was very low and gravelly, not at all like the giggle I had heard just moments before. It was so different, in fact, that I remember thinking that perhaps two intruders had invaded our domicile. That thought deserted my head readily though, when the same slight giggle escaped him at the end of his pronouncement.

"This is your place, Mr. Holmes. You may light it as you wish, although you may not want to see what the illumination brings to bear," (and the muffled giggle).

"The eyes receive evidence, my friend," Holmes returned, "and evidence is only to be feared by the guilty."

"Then strike your light," the voice returned with determination.

A match flared and a flame sprang into existence as Holmes lit a candle on the central table. It is amazing how the slightest glow in utter darkness will spread throughout and show much more than one might think it worthy. So it was with this small blaze.

It was true that every shade had been drawn in our place, so that no one could see in or out. As I surveyed the area, it was also evident that not a single article, other than the shades, had been disturbed in the slightest. As my eyes grew more accustomed to the dim glow of the room, I searched out our guest in the corner where his voice had emanated, and realized that while I had glanced that way before, I must have missed his presence standing there, for he was dressed entirely in black and had lifted his cape in a manner that covered his face. And since his face was the only thing not already sheathed in black, he had effectively disappeared in the dimness.

"There is no need to fear," Holmes said, which made me wonder to whom he spoke. "My friend Watson is a physician, and I believe you have made his acquaintance twice in the past. I, on the other hand, have not had the good fortune." And with that, Holmes stretched out his hand and approached the dark figure.

"Prepare yourself," I heard in that same low, hiss of a voice. "You have not seen the likes of me."

The Phantom of Farewell Street

It is strange how a moment's hesitation may seem longer than it is, for the man did not reveal himself immediately, but waited that moment for us to prepare. But when he did move his arm, he seemed to raise it slightly before thrusting it downward with an actor's flair, revealing the visage I have attempted to describe previously and will now begin anew.

Since we were not now in the throws of competition, as it were, and the person before me could be viewed in steady light without the jostle of the contest, he could be studied, (although I find that an unnecessarily harsh term), more readily and in finer detail.

The man stood straight as an arrow, shoulders square, arms at his sides, head cocked up, chin out, glaring at us over his cheek bones. His skin, or at least that film which was covering his bones, was amber in color, orange to be more exact, and in this light, it seemed almost to glow. It was a fearsome look he gave us, crazed and monstrous as a soulless beast gone mad with anger or pain. He wore a top hat and as the flames in Holmes' taper grew stronger and more was revealed, I could see that he was dressed in formal attire, as if headed for the "Monster's Ball" once his visit with us was through. He did not move, but stood there waiting for our initial reaction to pass. A reaction, which I am pleased to report, never came. There was no gasp from this crowd.

Holmes, who had extended his hand only moments before, now took another step toward the fellow.

"It is a pleasure," he said, hand still at the ready, anticipating a return. "You are Sebastian Lockhart, are you not?"

At this pronouncement, the reaction so fervently sought by our guest, became his own. He was visibly shaken by the question. His entire demeanor shifted from the confident, posturing stature of a man in control to the uneasy attitude of a man caught off guard. He turned his full attention toward Holmes and had the look, even through his disfigured features, of someone baffled and unable to speak.

Either for effect, or to give the fellow a chance to gather himself, Holmes paused a few moments before continuing. When it was evident that no sound would issue from that tortured face, he broke the silence while removing his hand from consideration for a shake.

"I am Sherlock Holmes," he began. "Your interest in this interview has not escaped me, and may only be eclipsed by my own."

Our friend was still not ready to speak. He stood there, mouth agape, and actually took a half step forward, toward Holmes, but he made not a sound, though his mouth was moving slightly.

Holmes, seeing that the man was obviously in shock, continued without prompting so as not to cause him any further pain.

"You will find, sir, that I do my homework very well. In your case, I suspected that you were the famous 'Phantom' as soon as I read about the tragedy that befell you in, 'The Newport Herald.' The initials 'S and L' on the knob of your walking stick confirmed the rest."

Watson's Sampler:
The Lost Casebook of Sherlock Holmes

Mr. Lockhart turned his head to look at the stick, which he held outward and under his arm. Clearly enough, even in this dim light, the silver knob, with its pronouncement "S & L" could be seen, if you cared to look. His eyes moved back to Holmes, who once again shot out his hand for a shake. Slowly, this time, Sebastian Lockhart returned the gesture and the introduction was complete.

"Strike the lights," Holmes said to me as he shook the hand vigorously while directing Lockhart to a chair at the central table. By the time I had lit the remaining lamps, they were already settled and awaiting me. I took a chair as well and made ready to jot any notes that may be necessary.

Mr. Lockhart, at last, had found his tongue.

"It is truly amazing, Mr. Holmes. There are few who know my identity at all, and no one whom I, myself have not told. Your simple deduction, in the light of what little you have seen, is truly astounding and has left me quite at a loss."

"Let me assure you, my friend," Holmes began again, "that my findings and my methods are elemental at best. Anyone with a knack for observation coupled with the knowledge I have acquired, would have come to the same conclusion without delay."

"I am not so sure of that," he returned, with the same tortured voice I had heard before. "I have made it my business to hide my fate from the world, until my present state of affairs took this turn for the worse. Now, it seems, I am forced to reveal myself in order to let my innocence be known."

"Pray, tell us all," Holmes chimed in, his nose perched on his index fingers and his chin perched on his thumbs. "And spare no details. For my associate, Dr. Watson," (and we exchanged nods), "knows little of this affair."

At this time, Sebastian Lockhart seemed to begin to attempt to calm himself. He relaxed in his chair a mite and sighed heavily while he dressed down from his outer garments. Removing his gloves revealed that the amber hue, which encompassed his face, remained consistent throughout, at least to these appendages. The scarring was terrible. I felt very badly for the man, for while all of my instincts as a physician cried out to help, my knowledge of the medical profession confirmed that there was absolutely nothing that could be done. Whatever had befallen this poor unfortunate was obviously irreversible and untreatable. The only thing one could deem as fortunate was that he was in no apparent physical pain, and it was also apparent from his antics that his wounds posed no restraint upon him. Nonetheless, even with the expressional limitations evident upon his facial appearance, an overall melancholy came to the fore throughout.

He glanced once more at both of us, as if to set us, and himself one last time before he began. When he did begin, his tone was low and steady, as if he had prepared this speech many a time, plodding one word after the other, until the story's journey was ended. And while he lost control of himself, and fluttered here and there at the extremities of his tale, he got through it admirably, (if I might be so bold), for it was harrowing indeed.

It went as follows:

"I am a sailor by trade, having learned from my father and his brother off these very shores, for as long as I can remember. We began as fishers, but as I grew older, I realized that before we made our way to George's Banks, we would put in at one of the islands or at a port on the Cape and unload small quantities of freights, which this one or that would commission my father to deliver. It seemed to start as a minor diversion, but before long I noticed that we were making more and more stops, and fishing less and less. One thing led to another and the business grew to the point where my father was obliged to purchase a second boat, to meet demands, and then a third and a forth, until he had a small fleet of seven boats, either delivering goods or fishing the shoals throughout southern New England. It was a glorious time, sir. At one point, while purchasing boats for the various purposes we had grown into, a small sail boat was thrown in with the bargain."

"I became a sailor at thirteen. By the time I was fifteen, I was taking special deliveries and rush orders to Boston, Block Island, Groton and everywhere in between. At sixteen I was racing at the amateur level, and winning. It was perhaps the happiest time of my life and our future looked bright."

"But, at eighteen, one of my father's boats went down off Conanicus Island with all hands, and I was plunged into my first great nightmare. My father and uncle were both on that vessel. I was left an orphan in a moment with no one to turn to and nowhere to go. My only salvation was that their death dropped the business into my hands and that business was booming."

"Do not misunderstand Mr. Holmes; it was a dreadful time for me, but perseverance is often the key to survival at sea, and applying those same principles to my personal and professional life, even at that age, kept me afloat while the ravages of grief passed. I actually feel that it was the hard work which saved me. With little training in management and schedules, not only for picking up and delivering freight but for dispatching fishers and completing billing schedules, payroll schedules, bank accounts, storage and all that goes with all of that, I was busy night and day for months. But by the time I could raise my head above the stacks of paper on my desk and overcome my own inadequacies, I could see that the company, which now was my company, had realized profits beyond any expectations I might ever have had. At that moment, my admiration for my father grew tenfold. To have created a business with the power and prestige that I now commanded, from the insecurity and limitations of a single boat, could only have been accomplished by talent, hard work and sacrifice. Since I had now been introduced to both the hard work and the sacrifice, I could well appreciate and respect what my father must have gone through in building the business."

"All went well for two years. With the schedules we had in place, being both those that my father had established and the new, amended versions I created while fumbling around, the business ran smoothly enough to bring in a steady profit month to month."

"Being single and now an orphan with no personal responsibility other than myself, the money I received each month was more than adequate for my needs, so I lived well and saved much. Before long I purchased the latest sailing vessel, which I made my home and office."

"I began to dabble in sail boat design. Not on any grand scale mind you, it was just a hobby. I had even created working models of new designs in the 'Admiral's Chalice' version boats, experimenting here and there with changes intended to increase speed and maneuverability."

"I tell you, Mr. Holmes, it seemed that this field of endeavor was where my talents were best displayed. Word of the designs spread, and interest in them piqued as the adaptations and adjustments I made to the basic flow of the vessels began to show in the glide, pitch and draft of my models."

"Then disaster struck my life once again, Mr. Holmes, in the most heinous fashion."

"Block Island lays quietly off this very coast. My company has held the commission for some time to transport building supplies to the community in residence there. It is a routine run made by one of the larger boats in the group on a weekly basis. Some time back," and he giggled that high, shrill, little giggle of his for the first time since he began this discourse, "the captain of that boat took ill on the very day she was to make that routine journey. It was determined that he would not soon be well, some infection or another, and I was informed late in the afternoon that the trip had been cancelled. Now, gentlemen, while I am not a rigid man, I do know the importance of schedules and appointed times. Word had not been sent to those awaiting the wares stowed in our hull. Our boat was scheduled to be in New Bedford the next day to retrieve a new shipment bound for Boston, and the skipper of the vessel had been prescribed a three-day bed rest, in order to rid himself of disease. Thus, the way seemed clear to me. Without much delay, I took control of the boat, gathered the crew and embarked on the short journey. My feeling was that we could leave Newport harbor at seven pm, gain Block Island shore before midnight, unload, spend the night at a lodging ashore and be fresh to depart for New Bedford sound next morning. I knew that lodging ashore would be costly, but my crew of four was giving up a night with their families, so I felt it was the best I could do."

"Everything began as planned. We started off a little after seven. It was a dark night, overcast but neither windy nor raining. I knew the route by heart, as did all of my men, for we had made this short voyage many times. In our hold, we carried all manner of varnish and paint. Rooming houses are the latest thing in the construction craze on that small island. With Newport's yachting populous growing every year, Block Island has become the perfect recreational destination for locals and vacationers alike. Hospitality is therefore booming at this time on that island."

"The air was still and the water calm as we made our way passing those few tardy pleasure craft who return home to safe harbor in Newport after a day of fun on local waters. We were making good time and nearly halfway there when the final lights of the final boats faded from our view and the town lights from the Island could be seen in the distance. Ahh, it was peaceful and quiet, and I am sure that we all would have been lulled and rocked to sleep had we been on open seas with no destination at hand. I remember how I smiled to myself as I steered our course, as a tribute to my own cleverness at pulling this together, turning minor tragedy to victory."

"It was then that things went terribly wrong."

"Mr. Holmes, you are a man who has crossed the ocean and lived on an island yourself. I do not know if you have ever been away from the salt air for any period of time, but if you have, you know that the smell and taste of the sea is like no other savor on earth. It lives within you and cannot be mistaken for any other aroma."

The Phantom of Farewell Street

"In the fragrance of the night air, which wafted up from the bay and is perfume to the sailor, a faint but acrid ingredient reached my senses. So foreign was the scent from the calm of the bouquet encompassing me that I started the moment it was present. There was smoke about."

"A quick scan of the surface revealed no vessel in view. No stoker of flames nearby to emit the plumes of exhaust that contaminate the purity of the ocean breeze."

"Now, gentlemen, I want you to know that I can't state strongly enough the danger and helplessness created by fire at sea. In harbor, in sight of land and help, nothing is more frightening and potentially deadly to the sailor as fire is. My mind came alive at the first suggestion of the fumes. One of the mates ran to me from the port rail, before I could even sound the alarm. His eyes told me of his anxiety before he was able to speak. We had a problem and we both knew it."

"'Make ready the life raft,' I called as I headed for the hatch above the cargo hold. 'Just in case,' I followed with, to try and keep him calm."

"As I stepped to the hatch, another ship's mate went past me to starboard, also heading aft to where the raft was. I could see the fear in his eyes as well, and knew that he was of like mind with me and the other."

"Now don't get me wrong, gentlemen, when I speak of fear and anxiety aboard ship. For while the sane man is always a bit anxious at sea, it is not a bad thing," and he giggled. "Anxiety gives the edge that is needed for long hours and dangerous work, and if you loose that edge, you may very well loose your life."

"That said, you will recall that I now had two of my four man crew in sight and prepared for any eventuality. I was at the hatch and preparing to lift it when the third crewman, who was manning the bow, came up."

"'Need any help sir,' he said as calm as you please."

"'Just checking on Jake,' I said back to him, 'you'd better get aft with the rest until I sound the all clear.'"

"Off he went, still calm as can be. His name is Will and he has always been hard to excite. He's a good man in a bad situation, but we didn't have a bad situation yet. Not as far as I knew, anyway."

"Having my crew together in one place was my main concern at this point. If I needed help later, I'd know where to get it, but we had only smelled smoke so far. We hadn't seen anything wrong."

"Jake was the only member of the crew not accounted for. He had been stationed in the hold with the cargo for our trip to the island. His assignment was to be sure that nothing shifted or spilled in transit. It was an important job, but a rather easy one on this boat, because everything was double lashed and secured with extra care, being that we were carrying a liquid cargo."

"I looked aft to check the men. They were there, awaiting whatever I might tell them to do. The lifeboat was down from its perch and we were all ready to abandon ship, if it were necessary. I looked back from them to the hatch lid, which is set on the raised edges of the entryway. All was quiet and peaceful without a sign of danger anywhere, just the faintest wisp of oily smoke passing by our nostrils on the breeze."

"I lifted the lid."

181

"Flames burst upon me from below, sending me sprawling backward on the deck and sending the lid toppling over, so that the hatch itself was now free of obstruction. In the next few moments, things happened in rapid succession."

"I knew that I had sustained no injury. I gave a quick look back to my men who were concerned and advancing toward me. I held up my hand while I righted myself as a sign that I was all right, and to tell them to hold their positions. We all realized at this point that the boat was forfeit. No fire of that intensity could be controlled in time to save her and, considering the cargo, insuring our safety was the only priority. Three of the four crewmen were prepared to abandon, but Jake was still below."

"I had to try to get him."

"'Lower that boat,' I yelled to them, as I turned back to the hatch."

"As you probably already know, a fire which has been covered and smothered for a time will flare up once revealed to the open air often times will recede once the initial influx of oxygen balances itself. This is what must have happened below decks because as quickly as the flames erupted, they subsided. It was clear that while this fire was serious, it had not gathered enough strength to maintain a hard burn. It was also clear that the highly flammable cargo, which we carried, had not become involved as yet. There was still time. My course was clear. If Jake had not already succumbed to the ravages of the smoke and fire, I might have enough time to find and remove him before the cargo ignited."

"I knew that it was risky, but gentlemen, we had never lost a man to disaster since I had taken over the company and I didn't intend to now."

"Without further delay, I jumped over the hatch lip, fully expecting to land on the hull floor, but to my surprise, the steps, which led into the hold, were intact. Smoke was billowing through the deck opening, but it was wood smoke from what I could determine nasally. I made my way to the hull floor. The location of the fire was apparently toward the bow, and with the now opened hatch serving as a vent, most of the smoke was channeling its way out of that portal, which gradually served to clear the air within the hold."

"I did not have to go far in order to locate my crewman. He was, in fact, lying in a heap directly beneath the steps I had taken. He was unconscious when I found him, with a gash on his brow, which told me that in all likelihood, he had knocked himself out by running into the very stair where I stood, undoubtedly while scurrying around to sound the alarm. He lay there, on his back, and even as I bent to help him, he began moaning and coughing and coming to."

"The air was thick with smoke and getting black as pitch as I hoisted him up and we moved to the stair. I could feel him regaining his strength with each step, as we mounted the incline to freedom. I had Jake positioned in front of me as we ascended, and his head and shoulders had already cleared the hatchway entrance at deck level when the explosion occurred."

"We had been drifting for the past few minutes since we reacted to the smell of smoke and in that time, we may have struck off course to the point where a rogue swell had swept across our port side and tipped the craft to starboard. While the shift caused by the wave was not strong or abrupt enough to dislodge two old seadogs such as Jake and myself from the stair, I could hear the tins filled with paint and stain and thinner begin to shift below as the tethers, which secured them to the hull, must have been weakened by the fire. I heard a crash, and tried to turn to view the damage when the blast occurred. And gentlemen, what a blast it was. The force of it propelled me into Jake, and at the same time, propelled both of us out of the hatch like packing from a cannon."

"It is at this point, gentlemen, that things became very cloudy. I must have wandered in and out of consciousness for the next few hours. What I do remember is, that the detonation sent me sailing through the air. I was completely ablaze. When the chemicals we were transporting ignited, creating the concussion and resultant fire, it had splashed me thoroughly, lighting my entire body on fire. I was covered, gentlemen, and terrified, and flying through the air. I remember landing on the deck of the boat. Strangely enough, there was not much pain. Perhaps I was in shock. But I do remember that before I could react to my then, present situation, another explosion erupted amidships, which sent me sailing once again. This time I landed in the water. Fortunately, the sea dowsed the fire immediately, unfortunately, as you can see, the damage was already done."

"It seems that I floated semi-conscious for hours. At some point, I must have found the hatch lid, for I remember waking briefly to find myself atop it in the chop. What had become of my mates, I knew not. All I could hope was that they were safe, since the cargo and its transport were a total loss. How long I drifted, I do not know, but when I finally came too, I found myself in a Hospital in Boston. And when I regained myself enough to communicate, they told me that a fishing boat had found me miles off the coast, and had brought me in. I had been in that Hospital for three weeks, they said, in and out of delirium. My face, of course, and much of my body, had been scarred and stained as you see it. Within days, I removed the bandages and fled. I was able to procure some clothing and a hooded cape while leaving the Hospital, but gentlemen; my condition had left me in such a physical and mental state that I literally walked most of the way back to Newport," and he giggled despite himself.

"It was as if I were a criminal. I was not safe, and those unfortunate enough to view my countenance fled in horror, which was most distressful."

He had lowered his head as he spoke these words and I remember thinking how unfair it all was. I was also of the mind that he might begin to weep, and leaned forward to pat his back to comfort him.

I was unable to fulfill this purpose however, for as I moved to him, he raised his head with a flurry and began his narrative anew.

"It was, therefore, of the utmost importance that I avoid the public at all costs. My design was to get back to Newport where, at least the lay of the land was familiar, and therefore my secretive movements would be easier. But gentlemen, it was necessary for me to travel much of the distance between Boston and my home on foot, with but a brief respite when I hid myself on a freight train between two stops on the line."

"It would have been humorous, had it not been so tragic, gentlemen," and he giggled to himself again. "I had finally gotten myself comfortable in one of the half-filled cars, when the train began to slow to a stop. I would estimate that the time span, which elapsed between the start and the stop positions of the train, could only have been about twenty minutes or so. Why our trip was cut so short, I do not know.

Perhaps we were stopping to pick up more freight, or perhaps someone had seen me climb aboard, but neither explanation matters now."

"We were stopped for but a moment, but as I cowered in the corner of that car, thinking that at any second I might be discovered or arrested or worse, that moment seemed an eternity."

"But then, without warning, the train began to move again. I was apparently saved from the humiliation I feared, and I once again relaxed. Searching the freight car turned up little that I could scavenge, but there was hay on the floor and with it I fashioned a makeshift bed in the far corner. My plan was to rest through the night and the ride, and begin anew, after the nap, hoping to be near Providence or even closer to Newport when I left the train."

"I must have been wearier than I realized, for I was asleep before I knew it, and a dreamless sleep it was. How long I lay there, I know not, although logic dictates that not much time elapsed before I was by a sharp kick to my back. I must have been sleeping on my side with my face to the wall, for whoever the man was, he delivered a thunderous blow to my back at my left shoulder, which sent me crashing into the sidewall of the car in a ferocious manner. Dazed, in pain and disoriented, I tried to gain my feet, but before I could right myself, I heard a gruff voice say, 'that's right, get up you bum,' and another blow struck me down from the rear again."

"I tell you now, gentlemen, that I do not know what came over me. Whether pain, or fear, or anger, or a combination of them all, the energy that I felt course through my body at that instant, was like nothing I had ever felt before. Maybe it was because I had survived so long at sea. Maybe it was because I was angry and frustrated from the hand that fate had dealt me. Maybe it was Divine intervention for a man who had lost so much. But in that moment, gentlemen, when my senses came alive and my body began to react, a change came over me that has never left, and has given me strength and abilities like none I have ever known."

"Before I knew it, and before another blow could be struck, I was on the side wall of the car. These freight cars are built with open spaces between the wallboards to save both weight and money, and I leapt there from the floor positioning myself parallel to the floor, about four feet up."

"I heard my opponent mutter something to himself or others not yet seen as I hung there like a spider."

"With another kick, I launched myself to the roof of the box, grabbing the open slats with my hands and picking my feet up to the ceiling, sticking them through the slat holes as well, so that I could maneuver like a fly and get the better of the man."

"I could tell by his movements, that he had not seen this last maneuver, and had absolutely no idea where I had gone. I remained still and quiet as he attempted to search me out in the gloom of the car. It is true that he had a small lantern, which projected a meager diameter of light as he aimed it here and there in his search, but he seemed not to grasp the idea that I might be above him. It took little effort to position myself to his back, gaining the advantage of surprise."

"Gentlemen, once again I must comment on the ease with which my body moved and responded to all of my mental commands. It both amazed and exhilarated me then, as it has since."

"So there I am, positioned above my adversary. I think he may have been a railway employee, hired to keep tramps from procuring free rides. His posture and attitude as he searched the boxcar, indicated that he was not just another traveler looking to steal from me. A thief or a tramp would have fled by then."

"Deduction," Holmes whispered to me with a smile.

Sebastian continued. "I must admit gentlemen, that my anger had gotten the better of me. As with my other senses and abilities, my emotions are now also more intense than they were, and I find that I must keep them reigned tightly at all times," and he giggled again more heartily this time, and with less inhibition. In fact, it took him a moment to compose himself after the outburst, but once quieted, he continued.

"So there I was above him, ready to pounce, anger kindled but, I came up with an alternative plan which I felt would be humorous, so I dropped down behind him and planted my foot on the seat of his pants. Gentlemen, you would have laughed to see it. He was bent slightly, trying to get the better view of the corner where he thought I had leapt earlier. When I laid the sole leather to him, he sprang up, arching his back from the power of the blow. I believe he was actually on tiptoe for a moment. The man must have stood well over six feet tall and weighed over two hundred and fifty pounds, but in that position, he looked like a giant ballerina in mid stride. It was hilarious, to say the least."

"He gained himself in a flash, and let out such a roar of anger that I actually feared for my life momentarily. Fists clenched, jaw set and teeth locked in a hideous grin of ferocity, the man from the railroad spun to face me full on. I am sure that he was prepared for murder. His eyes shown brightly, even in the gloom of the car, and as a beam from the lantern which he held, rose from my feet to my chest, I set myself for the confrontation that was sure to come."

"But then it happened, gentlemen. I admit that I had forgotten myself in the skirmish. Perhaps my anger, or the exhilaration that I felt from the movement had momentarily distracted me from the facts, but as the beam hit my face, this face, filled with the agitation I had been feeling, I saw all the color drain from the man in a second. His eyes actually began to roll back in his head until there was little left but the white. For a moment, I feared for his life. But, as quickly as the color fled his face, the anger dried within me, until I was left with only pity in my heart for this poor unfortunate, and shame for myself."

"He began to swoon, but I was able to leap forward and maneuver him into a sitting position. By now the train was moving at a fair clip, but as soon as he was 'situated', (and he giggled), I jumped from the car, into the night."

"Gentlemen, you can only imagine the range of emotions I felt as I huddled in the woods, in the night, after leaving that train. It was a profound feeling of exhilaration, mingled with fear and dread. Exhilaration because of the new strength and agility I had found within myself during this episode, accompanied by the fear and dread of the horror and reaction I cause to those unfortunate enough to view this visage. Increased power for good, and evil, gentlemen. The polarity is overwhelming."

"I vowed that evening, to avoid the outside world with all my energy, and to live life as a hermit, as much as possible. My fortune, or what remained of it, was in the banks and boats of Newport and so, I set off the next morning, being careful not to be noticed again, and made my way back to the city where I grew up."

"Once back in town, by cover of night, I entered the vessel I had called home and retrieved as many of my belongings as I could carry unnoticed and, taking all of the money on board, headed for the graveyard. At the time, I was amazed that everything was where it should be. It wasn't until later that I found, that because I had been listed as missing at the courts, and because there was no next of kin, my property was left undisturbed until a disposition could be decided. Since I knew where extra keys were hidden for my boats, I was left unmolested to steal my own possessions."

"It was well past midnight, that first night, when I left the docks to make my way up Thames Street to Farewell, and off to the cemetery."

"Now, my choice of the cemetery..."

"Is obvious," Holmes broke in. "Solitude for you, foreboding for the populace; the perfect combination for your needs."

"And I knew the place, sir," Sebastian returned. "When my relatives were laid to rest, in order to get away from everyone, I discovered the Chapel tower where you discovered my lair. I spent much of the day of my father's funeral in that loft. My friends were unable to locate me until I returned to them at the grave. I revisited that place on a number of occasions when I wanted to be alone or pray. As you said, it was a perfect place."

"And so, back to that night," Holmes injected impatiently.

"Sir," Sebastian returned in a somber tone.

"Well, you haven't taken us on this walk from the docks to the cemetery for no reason, have you? Something must have happened along the way. What was it?"

Holmes, as always, was headstrong to get to the point. He always seemed to be in a, 'without further ado,' mood, and this was no exception.

"Of course, you are correct, Mr. Holmes," Sebastian replied in a lesser tone. "Something did happen along that way, that night."

"My trip from the docks to the graveyard was not without incident, for as I made my way along Thames Street, hurrying with arms full, I failed to hear a young man approaching from a side street. He, as I discovered that morning, was a baker's apprentice, who also had his vision impaired by a stack of boxes that he carried."

"We met violently at the corner. I am afraid that I must not have gotten the better of things, as my head must have struck the curb at my fall. I awoke in the bakery to the most wonderful aroma of fresh bread baking. I was startled, to say the least, and sprang to my feet, prepared to flee or stand my ground according to the dictates of the moment. But, to my surprise, this young man stood there calmly, in front of the oven, baking his bread. At the sound of my clumsy rising, he turned to me, and with a voice betraying neither malice nor fear, he said, 'Aha, I see you're up. None the worse for wear, I hope. You've got a nasty bump there." And then he smiled.

"Gentlemen, I could have wept. Do you know how wonderful it was to have someone acknowledge me as a person, without fear or loathing? In that moment, I was human again and not the monster I had felt I'd become. For, mark my words, though I had only recently been scarred, my attitudes and emotions had already become bigoted toward people. It amazes me to this day, how quickly my outlook could have changed, but it had. My few short incidents with people had burned a scar in my soul deeper than any on my body, but those few kind words from that young stranger, melted my fear and returned me to humanity. He was and is to this day, a wonderful person."

"We had fresh bread and coffee. It was glorious. In my agitated state, I had not realized how long it had been since I'd eaten. I'm afraid I gorged myself somewhat. When, at last, I had finished, he smiled at me from his ovens and said, 'I can see that you are in trouble, my friend. I would like you to know that I am here to help, if you will allow it.'"

"Gentlemen, once again I have to tell you what it meant to me to have someone care. It was nearly overwhelming, and yet I tried to keep my feelings concealed, so not to impose myself on this young man."

"To keep things brief; I spent the next half hour or so telling my new found friend what I have told you thus far. His name is Albert Hanson and as I said, he is a baker's apprentice. It was his job to open the shop in the early hours and bake the morning bread, so that it would be fresh made for the restaurants and households in the neighborhood. He has been my eyes and ears in this community, and has become an invaluable friend. I do not know how I could have survived without him. He is a Godsend…"

It was at this point in the narrative that there was a firm rap at the door. Holmes gave our guest a knowing look that all but said, "be quiet and be still," and then he glided over to the door soundless, to have a listen. No sooner was he there than there was a louder, more urgent rap, followed by Peterson's voice saying, "come along, Mr. Holmes, open up. We've seen your light on from the street and we know you're in there."

"One moment, Peterson," Holmes replied, and we both looked to our guest and found the chair on which he sat, deserted, and the side window open to the night.

A wry smile skipped across Holmes' face as he unlocked the door and allowed Peterson to enter.

"Come in, my good man," he said.

"Mr. Holmes," Peterson said in a stern manner, "I know you're up to something. Isn't it a bit late for you gentlemen to be awake, fully clothed, with the lights burning?"

I popped in at this point with, "Is there a law…," but Holmes cut me off by stating, "We were entertaining."

"And where is your guest," Peterson returned with that same stern air, while his gaze fell about the room.

"Alas, he felt the necessity to depart," Holmes said, still smiling.

Peterson was not amused. "Mr. Holmes," he continued, "my hope is that you will not hide any information from me. I am well aware of the part you played in tonight's confusion at 'The Parade.' If something happened after that incident that pertains to any investigation in progress, I need you to tell me the details at this time."

"There isn't really much to tell," Holmes returned. "I mean, if you really want to know about this evening's fracas, I would say that my driver was the one who caused the commotion."

"Your driver," Peterson blurted.

"Yes, my driver, Philips. Had he not made such a fuss, none of the ensuing hysteria would have occurred."

"But what of the Phantom," Peterson ventured with the same flustered air.

"Well, with the exception of being the focal point of the evenings disturbances, and perhaps a minor trespass, the Phantom, as you call him, had very little to do with anything. The tumult was caused by fear rather than actual danger. And while this, 'Phantom,' may be a bit melodramatic and thus construed as malicious, the assumption is well, nigh false."

"Is that so," Peterson said. "And is this knowledge first hand?"

"Yes, in fact, it is," Holmes continued. "He was our guest, here, this evening."

Peterson looked from Holmes to me and back again. "You had this man in your custody, and you let him go?"

"In truth sir, he never was in, 'my custody,' but as I said, he was my guest, and as for his departure, the impetus was your vigorous knock at our door and the equally vigorous announcement as to who you are, which set him at his heels. Until your intrusion, he was sitting in this chair."

"Mr. Holmes, Doctor," Peterson continued, "you above all should realize how desperately we want to speak to this individual about the graveyard matter. I must ask you to divulge everything you know about this 'Phantom' fellow."

"That, I am not sure we can do at this time," Holmes responded, "for I am afraid that you sent him on his way before he could reveal much."

And before Peterson could initiate any further protestation, Holmes added, "but, in the spirit of trying to be helpful, it is my opinion that this man would not intentionally injure anyone."

"Well, Mr. Holmes, that may be your opinion, but it does not alter the fact that he is wanted for questioning."

"But, Peterson, the bird has flown and I know not where. Be patient, my friend, for I feel that all will be revealed soon."

"Patience," Peterson returned, "is a luxury of the unemployed. As for me, I have superiors and the public to answer to."

"Do you not also need accuracy with your quick resolution," Holmes countered.

"Of course, sir, but..."

"Then I suggest," Holmes broke in, "that we employ patience. All answers may be forthcoming."

"Does that mean that you've found a link between the crime and the Phantom," Peterson enquired in a less abrasive tone.

"A connection; yes. But perhaps not the connection you would infer."

"Murder, is what I infer, Mr. Holmes."

"I realize that, Peterson, and that is not what I think the connection is. A murderer never goes to the extremes that this man has in order to contact one of the investigators of the crime. This alone tells me that the man is guilty of nothing."

"Then what is the connection, Mr. Holmes?"

"Patience, Peterson. Employ patience, and as the flower blooms in the light of day, so shall this puzzle unfold before us. Now, if you don't mind, the hour is late and there is much to do tomorrow."

Peterson stood staring. At one point, he seemed to be about to speak, but in that same moment, he wagged his head and started for the door.

"We'll speak tomorrow, gentlemen," he said as he turned the knob.

"I'm sure we will," Holmes returned.

And he was gone.

After a quick turn around our rooms, checking every window and adjacent roof, Holmes turned to me.

"Let us retire to bed, Watson. Our day begins early in the morning."

I made my way to bed, remembering how Holmes had remarked about rising early to receive a reply to a wire he had sent some time before. But it seemed that my head had barely touched the pillow when Holmes roused me once again.

"Come along, Watson," he said as he hurried from my room to the parlor. "Our work has begun."

The sun had not yet risen as I clambered out of bed to follow him.

"I do not believe that the telegraph office is open at this hour, Holmes," I exclaimed as I laced my shoes.

"Telegraph office? Haven't you been paying attention, Watson? We are off to the bakery to visit our Mr. Hanson before sunrise."

"But what of the telegram," I protested.

"The telegram is of little consequence now. Hanson is the key to the matter, Watson. Hanson is the key."

We made our way into the early morning hours, traveling the four blocks to the spot where Sebastian had said that he and Albert Hanson had met.

I remember, looking back, that the thought crossed my mind of how strange life really is, and how all of these occurrences and odd meetings could have taken place as close to our abode as they had, without either Holmes or myself having the slightest hint of an idea that anything was amiss. It is indeed difficult to comprehend that some psychic link does not exist between an investigator, (even one independent of the circumstances), and an incident which might come into play one day, in some later inquiry. An eerie feeling pervades ones system on these occasions as it does when one, say, misses passage on a train that meets with calamity, or sleeps the night away while someone is murdered close by. And the question comes to mind, "why didn't I sense that these things were happening?"

To that question there is, of course, no answer. But it does puzzle me each time it happens, which, in my life, has been more often than one would expect.

By the time I had finished my mental meander we were standing at the very corner that Sebastian had described in his narrative. There was absolutely no traffic on the street, save a lonely milk wagon slowly making his way toward the homes in that district known, in Newport, as "the Point."

As we eyed the area for the baker, I remarked, "What shall we do now," to Holmes, who had remained silent throughout our walk.

"We shall follow our noses," was his reply and he breathed in deeply with his nostrils.

I also followed in turn, and as the first whiffs entered my senses, the sweet, warm, full-bodied aroma of baking bread burst upon me like your first sip of hot cocoa on a brisk winter's day. I must admit that my mouth began to water slightly at the introduction of this grand sensation.

Before I could speak again, Holmes was moving. The bakery lay up Thames Street and around the bend, in an alleyway, just out of sight. It must also have been the bakery, which my daughter used, for the proximity to her house was correct. This was yet another instance where she and I were so close to each other, and yet so far apart.

We marched right to the place with Holmes in the lead. A try at the door found it to be locked. It was still very early in the morning and obvious that the store was not yet prepared for customers.

Holmes knocked. There was no response, and peering through the window revealed no activity within, although much of the place was hidden from our view.

Holmes knocked again with more vigor. From the rear of the shop, a door swung our way and a face spied out. His look changed abruptly when he saw the two of us standing there. The door shut quickly, and opened again, just as quickly, to reveal a young man of no more than eighteen years, walking toward us, wiping his hand on a towel of some sort.

"We are not open as yet," he said when he reached the spot where he felt we could hear.

"Albert Hanson," Holmes asked through the door.

"Yes, sir," Hanson replied with a question in his tone.

"We need to speak with you about a matter of grave importance. My name is Sherlock Holmes and this is Dr. John Watson."

With that pronouncement, Albert Hanson renewed the wiping of his hands and moved, again, toward the door. The bolt was released, and we were ushered inside.

"How do you do, gentlemen," he said. "I've heard of you. Come on into the back. We can talk there while I continue my work."

We moved into the rear of the shop where the ovens were. The rich fragrance, which had wafted so lazily throughout the neighborhood, was stronger and not quite so pleasant here for the strength. We were escorted to a small table in the corner, and before we were settled, two cups of coffee appeared.

We exchanged niceties while Hanson checked his dough, but as soon as he seemed secure in the knowledge that all was well, Holmes began his questions.

"We have heard some rather nice things about you from Mr. Sebastian," he began. "Would you be so kind as to relate your version of your first encounter to us?"

Hanson looked puzzled. "You have seen Sebastian," he asked.

"Yes," Holmes returned, "he visited us in our rooms just last evening."

"That's odd," Hanson continued, "I was not aware that he has begun making social calls."

"I do not know that you would term it a 'social call.' It was more of a personal business meeting."

"And how is he," Hanson continued unflustered. "It has been a time since I have seen him."

"I should imagine three days," Holmes said. "Since the night of the graveyard death, I would say."

"Yes, exactly Mr. Holmes, just as you say. I have been unable to locate him since that very night. Could it be that he was involved with that unfortunate man's death?"

"One reason we are here is to answer that very question."

"But I know nothing of the matter," Hanson replied.

"I am aware of that," said Holmes, "but you may have information that will help our investigation nonetheless."

"Whatever do you mean," Hanson replied, indignant.

"First of all, Mr. Hanson," Holmes returned with a smile, "realize one thing. I am convinced that Sebastian was not a willing participant in any of this. That also means that you are an innocent as well."

"What I am trying to find is the truth; who did this thing and why. I believe that you have information which would assist me in finding that truth. The very reason that you are unaware that you might know something of value further proves your innocence, and if you will cooperate, you might set us on the road to what really happened the other night."

Hanson studied us for a moment as if sizing us up, as well as the situation.

I gave him a nod and an assuring expression to indicate that we were truly looking out for Sebastian's best interests, as well as his own.

In a moment or two, his face began to clear, as the worry furrows dissolved into the smooth calm of a man without stress. He took a deep breath and said, "How may I help you, gentlemen?"

"All that we need to know is, what has transpired between Sebastian and yourself since you made each other's acquaintance?"

"Well, sir," Hanson began, "there is nothing of much importance. We met in an inauspicious way, at the corner over there," and he pointed. "I could tell he was a fellow in trouble right off, but there was goodness in his manner and a graceful style about him that was genuine."

"Did his appearance shock you," I put in.

"No, sir, not really," he replied. "I noticed, of course, but I'm a grown man and not so easily frightened."

I smiled back at this "grown man," who was, in actuality, no more than a teenager, and was about to commend him on his good sense, when Holmes broke in.

"Continue with your narrative, my good man," he said without any inflection.

"Well," he began again, "we bump into each other out there, and everything he's carrying goes everywhere. So, without taking any notice of anything else, I start picking stuff up as I apologize. But he's backing away, trying to hide his face with his arm. Like I said, I hadn't noticed, but as I came around with his stuff, I could see that portion of his head not hidden, and I knew that he had trouble. When I went to hand him his things, he giggled this high-pitched giggle, and backed away further. It was then that he tripped over one of his own things and falling back, struck his head and went out cold. I then made three trips here, to the shop, carrying him in first, then his things and finally my boxes. He remained unconscious, in the very chair you are in Doctor, until my first batch was nearly baked. When he awoke, I introduced myself."

"I'll tell you plain, gentlemen, I did not react to his appearance because I felt no reaction. A man looks like what a man looks like, and that should be the end of it. Any judgment, on the basis of appearance, would be sinful, to my way of thinking."

"At any rate, I think that the fact that I didn't react to the sight of him, calmed him somehow. He accepted my offer of coffee and a friendship was struck then and there. The rest is history. He stays with me at my place now and then, when the weather is bad, but for much of the time, I do not know where he is."

"That is not entirely true, is it Mr. Hanson," Holmes interrupted. "You know of the steeple hideaway, do you not?"

After a moment's pause Hanson said, "yes, I do, but I was unaware that you knew of it."

"I assure you Mr. Hanson, there is much that we know," Holmes continued, "and while I realize that you feel that you are helping your friend by keeping things from us, you will do him no service by continuing this tactic."

"We are here to help, sir," he added forcefully. "Cooperation is the key to our success. Now continue, and leave out nothing, if you please."

"Well, gentlemen," the man began again, "I hope you can understand why I would attempt and will continue to attempt to protect my friend. He is unusual, to say the least, and there are many who would find fault with him out of hand. Therefore, gentlemen, I will not give him up upon request of you or anyone else."

"Believe me," I piped in, "when I state in all earnestness, that we mean neither he nor yourself any harm."

"Believe me," he returned in turn, "when I state that I am inclined to believe you. Your reputation has always been exemplary, as far as I know, but it is not you whom I fear. You will admit, that when you say that you are investigating the graveyard death, what you mean is that you are helping the police."

"We are," I answered.

"Well, can you assure me that their discretion is of the quality of your own?"

"No, we cannot," Holmes broke in, "and you make a valid point, except that there is something you might not understand. Since our meeting with Mr. Sebastian, I now consider myself his representative in matters concerning his interests. That means that I am now not at liberty to divulge information about him to the police or anyone for that matter."

Hanson's demeanor eased somewhat at this pronouncement. He had been busily flitting about from table to oven and oven to water basin, creating concoctions which looked as delicious as they smelled. Cinnamon seemed to be the sweetener of choice as cinnamon bread and cinnamon buns were removed from a hot central oven and placed on a table before us for frosting. Holmes took a respite from his questioning to allow

Mr. Hanson time to complete his tasks, which gave us all a moment to step back and mull over what had transpired thus far.

When, at last, the buns were frosted and the bread was set out to cool, and a new round of delights were snuggled within the ovens, Hanson turned and presented us each with the most delectable glazed cinnamon roll I believe I have ever tasted. His smile beamed as my eyes rolled back in my head at the very outset of its consumption. The experience was exquisite.

With the pride in his work satisfied and his suspicions eased, Albert Hanson pulled up a chair himself and sat with us while drinking a large cup of fresh, brewed coffee.

"My story is as simple as this," he began. "I met Sebastian in the manner I have described and became his liaison with the outside world. We decided, almost immediately, that one of the areas where I could be most useful was in the matter of his belongings. Within the next few days, I visited his boat in the evenings to procure those items he felt were essential."

"Can you enumerate," Holmes asked.

"Papers and clothing mostly," Hanson returned, "and books, he is an avid reader."

"But, to continue, things went well enough I suppose, until the third evening, when I noticed a light within the cabin of the boat. The lock had been forced and broken, and coming upon the scene I feared the worst."

"That night I did not enter the boat, for I could see clearly from the dock. There, within the vessel, was a man searching about. From the first, I did not think this man was a thief because of the care he took while hunting. But, he was looking for something, and while my first instinct was to confront him, I realized that my desires may not coincide necessarily with my friend's, and since any clumsy attempt on my part to hinder this fellow might lead ultimately to Sebastian's exposure, I decided to retire and seek his council first."

"A wise decision," Holmes piped in, "for I am certain that there was nothing of value left, since you both had been there before."

"Quite right, sir." Hanson replied. "I was after clothing that evening, having removed the remainder of the money along with the books and papers on the previous trips."

"At any rate, I returned home and told Sebastian of this new excitement. Immediately he asked for a description of the man. As soon as I recounted his features, he exclaimed that it must be Thomas Glum, his employee and member of his crew on the night which left him marked."

"He was quite excited, gentlemen. He said that this helped confirm his belief that they had all made it to shore safely and survived the tragedy. He giggled repeatedly that evening."

At this point, Hanson paused to take a sip of coffee and to check his wares in the ovens. Holmes steepled his two index fingers beneath his nose watching him lazily. Holmes was not fond of interruptions when studying an ongoing narrative, and although we were both aware that we were infringing upon this man's livelihood, Holmes remained impatient. With a sigh, he absentmindedly looked down and reached for his cinnamon bun, which he nibbled in that same nonchalant manner, until the taste hit his tongue. I'll never forget how I couldn't stop smiling at the expression which rose upon his face when the combination of cinnamon, frosting and baked dough awakened his senses. He stared at the bun in such a curious manner that it was obvious that he had never tasted anything like this before. It was well known that Holmes did not favor sweets, considering them a distraction to the labor of ingesting energy, which he considered eating to be. He ate well, don't get me wrong, for he knew the benefits of a healthful diet, but food was for replenishment rather than refreshment, and sweets were an extravagance not necessary to that end. Holmes, therefore, rarely indulged. At least until now.

His eyes widened with the anticipation of his next bite. His interest was so centered on this new sensation he had found, that I don't think he even noticed me studying him. How amusing it was to watch this master of self-control, lose himself in something as common as a breakfast roll. Not to say that those particular rolls were not wonderful, for they were, which is evidenced by the distraction to which they led Holmes, but for Holmes to be derailed by breakfast food was uniquely unique.

After a second bite, which was far more generous than the first, I noticed that he watched the pastry in his hand, all the way to its rest on the napkin provided, before he regained himself and returned his keen eye to our host and storyteller.

"Thomas Glum," Hanson continued, "was not only Sebastian's employee, but an acquaintance. Not a friend, in the classic sense, but more than just employer, employee. Thomas has a family, you see, and so, while they didn't chum around together, they liked and respected each other. Sebastian stated his trust in this fellow and reiterated repeatedly that if it were Tom in the cabin, his motives must be honorable."

"It was with this knowledge and a faith in Sebastian equal to his faith in Tom that I returned to the boat that very night and spoke to Thomas Glum at length about his captain's circumstance and current situation. He was quite relieved, I must say, to find that Sebastian was alive. He immediately requested an audience, which I later arranged."

"He then took the time to recount to me the details of what was even then transpiring with regard to the business and his reasons for being at the boat. As it turned out, the courts had been pressed into service since Sebastian's whereabouts were unknown and the worst was thought, and had temporarily turned over his holdings to a local lawyer involved with many of the seafaring businesses in the area. You see gentlemen, many an arrangement had already been made and scheduled before the accident, and while the loss may have been tragic or at least was thought to be, the businesses in question and the people concerned demanded services or refunds. Glum was, in fact, there that evening, searching out the funds and manifests resultant of those contracts."

"I, of course, informed him that Sebastian, himself had those papers and funds from his and my previous excursions to that very cabin."

"We then arranged a meeting between he and Sebastian to happen two days hence in the cemetery."

"Why the cemetery," Holmes asked.

"Sebastian always felt safer there. Few people about, stories of 'the phantom' and all, privacy... That is why I did not suggest that they meet at my home. Too much exposure, if you will."

"The meeting did take place then," Holmes queried.

"For all I know it did, sir." Hanson came back. "I have seen neither of them since."

"But you realize that the meeting took place on the very night in which a man died in that graveyard," I said.

"Yes I do, but that does not dissuade me from believing that the arranged meeting between those two did not take place prior to the death."

"Don't you think that it is all quite coincidental," Holmes put in.

"Coincidence or no, sir," Hanson returned, "I believe in my friend. He would not willingly harm anyone. If this man stumbled on the meeting, and consequently died of fright, it is unfortunate, but that does not indicate foul play, at least to my mind."

"I tend to agree," Holmes responded, "but there are many questions left yet unanswered. Tell me. Do you expect to be speaking to Sebastian in the near future?"

"Indications are that I will not, Mr. Holmes. I have searched for him at the cemetery without success and he has not been to my rooms since the incident. My feeling is that he does not want me involved, and is avoiding me to that purpose. And if this is so, I am afraid that I will not be able to assist you in finding him. He has many hideouts, and as you already know, he is a very clever man. He will not be found unless he desires to be found."

"Once again, we are in agreement," Holmes said, as he began to fuss with his coat. "I am afraid we have occupied enough of your work day, Mr. Hanson. We're off. I will be in touch."

And with that, he raised himself from his chair and marched out of the door, leaving me at a loss as to what to do. As quickly as I could, I gathered my things together and bidding Mr. Hanson "adieu," scurried after my friend.

Fortunately, Holmes was not far off. He awaited me on the next corner, where it was, I am sure, that he realized what he had done.

For a man so intently focused on the problem at hand, Sherlock Holmes was forever a bungler where courtesy was concerned. And while it is true that leeway must be allowed in the gifted and exceptional, those readers familiar with my accounts will concur, that Holmes pressed this leniency to the limit repeatedly.

As I said, he awaited me at the corner, and as I took up my post at his side, he gave me a look that, while it was in no way sheepish, was indicative of the fact that he knew that he had done it again.

As was his habit, he almost immediately engaged me in conversation in an effort to distract me from any preemptive attempt at rebuke.

"Watson," he began, "while here in America, I have heard an expression repeatedly, which I find peculiar. The expression goes that a person knows this or that, 'like the back of his hand.' Such as, 'I know this city like the back of my hand.' My question is, and what seems peculiar is, that it is a rare bird indeed who actually does know the back of his hand."

I looked at him oddly.

"How many wrinkles does any knuckle have on the back of their hand, Watson?"

I ventured a peek.

"My point exactly," he exclaimed. "If you do not know the number of the wrinkles on any knuckle on the back of either hand, how am I to suppose that you know anything at all about the back of your hand? And if you don't know anything at all about the back of your hand, how can you relate it to knowing anything at all about anything at all?" And he smiled.

I must admit that I smiled as well, which, of course, was the object of the exercise.

"Well then," I said, once the moment passed, "what are we about today?"

"I have a few enquiries," he returned, "and I have an assignment for you, if you will, Watson."

"At your service, sir."

"I want you to hunt up this Mr. Glum, Watson. I would suggest that you begin at the courts. The lawyer in charge of Sebastian's affairs will undoubtedly know where he is. We need as much information as possible about what took place that night, or did not take place, as the case may be. I will meet you for luncheon in our rooms."

The courthouse did not begin its business until 9:00 am. After Holmes had announced our plans, we walked back to Clarke Street to find Phillips awaiting us with his carriage.

"Are you ready Mr. Holmes," he said as we approached.

"I am indeed," Holmes returned as he stepped inside. "Watson," he turned to me, "you have your assignment. I will expect a complete report upon my return."

Before I could make a remark or bid him farewell, he had closed the carriage door and Philips had stirred the horse. They left me standing in front of our abode as quickly as that, and while I was not prepared for this course, these turns were not out of the ordinary, so I simply turned on my heel, went upstairs, brewed some coffee and awaited the courts schedule.

I must say that America's system of juris prudence is no less cumbersome than England's. The clerk's office seemed over run with duties to the point where I was almost embarrassed to ask that they add to their hardships by summoning up the information I needed. The clerk's assistant, whom they assigned to me, gave me a stare as I explained what I required and the approximate timetable through which these events had occurred. It was not until I mentioned that to my knowledge this was public information that he scurried off to the stacks to retrieve the names of the parties involved in the case. It took him but minutes to comply with my request, once he set his mind to it, and it occurred to me, as it has many times, that if mankind just got on with things, instead of agonizing over cost and efficiency, the results would almost always be more cost effective and efficient.

Once again reassured of my logician's prowess and with the possession of the means to complete the task at hand, I left the courts for the offices of one Thomas Rathkamp, Attorney at Law.

Arriving at the office on Bull Street, near City Hall, I was shown into a small chamber after being delivered a stern warning from the receptionist that my meeting with Mr. Rathkamp must be brief because he had an appointment at court. I was also reminded that I did not have an appointment, in a way that I feel could only have been meant to explain the lack of courtesy I was experiencing.

Within a minute of my ushering, a short, rotund, but not altogether unpleasant looking fellow entered the room with his hat in his hand and his light coat over his arm.

"How may I help you, sir," he addressed me.

"My name is Dr. John Watson," I began, but was cut off in mid sentence.

"I know who you are, sir, and you will have to excuse me for my abruptness, but I am running late and expected at court. Ask your questions, for I must leave."

I thought to myself, "a long way to go to save time."

"I represent Mr. Sebastian," I began again. "He was to meet Mr. Glum three nights ago, and I wish to speak with him about that meeting. Do you know where I might find the man?"

"He is in Boston," the attorney replied. "He has been there for four days, on company business."

I must admit that I was not prepared for this explanation and was taken back by the pronouncement. And it seems that my hesitation was not lost on my inhospitable host as well, for at the momentary loss of communication, he began to don his cloak and move toward the door.

"But what of the meeting," I blurted, as I regained myself.

"It never took place," he said as he reached for the handle.

"Then what happened," I asked as I reached for the same handle and held it fast.

After looking my hand for a few seconds, his eyes came up to meet mine.

"I went there in his stead," he said.

"And…," I said, egging him on.

After another moment, he said, "and no one ever showed up. I remained on the spot for at least an hour, but no one ever approached me."

"Are you sure you were in the right place," I offered.

"Of course I was, sir. I have lived in this community all my life. I know this city throughout and I know that cemetery."

"Like the back of your hand," I ventured.

"Exactly," he returned emphatically. "Now, if you don't mind, I am late because of you."

And with that, he removed my hand from the door handle, and out he went.

You will no doubt understand why a smile crossed my lips amid the puzzlement caused by Rathkamp's statement. My first instinct was to follow him and accost him on the street with more questions, but the dictates of common courtesy required that I leave him to his business. And thus, I set about on my own, which was to return to Clarke Street and await Holmes with my report.

Since I had left my hat and stick near the receptionist's desk, I did not exit through the door that Rathkamp had used, for it led directly to the street. But rather, I turned to the other door at the front of the building, and was about to leave when a bell sounded six times. Turning at the clang, I noticed a clock on the back table, which read eleven o'clock. Checking my pocket watch, I found it to be indeed, eleven in the a.m.

Stepping through to the outer office, I retrieved my hat and stick, bid adieu to the young lady I had spoken with earlier, mentioned that I thought that her employer's clock was broken, and exited the building.

Watson's Sampler:
The Lost Casebook of Sherlock Holmes

Knowing that I had time to spare before my luncheon with Holmes, I spent the next two hours wandering the streets of this fair city. My first thoughts had been to pay a visit to my daughter, but knowing that I would have been hard pressed not to tarry too long, I abandoned the idea in favor of a stroll. People's well being, if not their lives were at stake after all, which made my appearance at home far too important to risk on an enthralled dawdle. I spent my hours by making an enlarged circle, begun by heading for the beach area and then detouring through a path the locals called Cliff Walk, finally cutting back through to Bellevue Avenue for the trip home. All in all, it was a refreshing and invigorating morning, and although I arrived at my door a few minutes late for lunch, Holmes was later still, which seemed always to be the custom.

When, at last, he did burst in, (for he always did seem to burst in upon a room with a flurry of energy), he removed his coat, rang for our repast and sat as close to me as he could, in a manner I can only describe as eager anticipation.

I, on the other hand, was reading when he arrived, and made a point of finishing the page before I turned to him.

"What have you learned, Watson," he said when our eyes met. He actually rubbed his hands together as he spoke. "What have you learned from our Barrister?"

"How do you know that I did not speak to Glum," I asked.

"It is obvious from your shoes and trouser legs that you have been walking a great deal this morning, and unless you trampled about while interviewing our friend, you would not have enough time to see the Lawyer, interview Glum and still walk a few miles. Since Glum was your second appointment, it seems apparent that you were unable to see him."

I was about to break in on this monologue when Holmes raised a hand to stop me.

"It is also fairly obvious that you do have some news for me. The fact that you finished your reading before beginning your narrative is sign enough. If you had no information, it would have been easy enough to tell me so quickly, and return to your article."

I had to admit that he was correct. As always seemed to be the case, once spoken, his conclusions were obvious and elementary.

"Now, what is your news," he asked as he pulled up a seat. "Tell me everything and leave nothing out."

At this request, I recounted the entirety of my morning's events to him without omitting a single detail. Throughout the discourse, which did not take much time, he remained attentive, never asking a single question. I completed my remarks and his demeanor never changed. He seemed to be taking it all in passively enough without comment. Once done, I enquired if Holmes found anything irregular in the account.

"Well," he returned, "there are a few irregularities of which I will want to speak to Glum and Rathkamp. For instance, it seems odd to me that Glum should be on company business, when the future of the company may depend on his meeting with Sebastian."

"And, what of Rathkamp? Why would Sebastian fail to keep the appointment he had requested? Was it that he did not recognize the lawyer? Could Sebastian have seen Rathkamp without Rathkamp noticing him? We both saw the meeting place. Even a clever fellow like Sebastian would be hard pressed to go unnoticed there. In other words, Watson, yes, there are irregularities."

"Such as Rathkamp's clock," I said half to myself and under my breath.

"Rathkamp's clock," he returned.

"Oh, yes, Rathkamp's clock," I answered. "I didn't realize you were listening. All I meant was that the clock in Rathkamp's office is malfunctioning. Irregular, if you will."

"Whatever do you mean, Watson," he asked.

"Well," I returned, "as I was leaving the office, the clock struck six. That is all. It was eleven in the morning, and the clock struck six."

Holmes was quiet for a moment as if in thought. Then, with a look of added interest in his eye and a waving of his finger, he asked, "did the clock toll six with evenly spaced claps, such as dong, dong, dong and so on? Or, was it more like three repeatings of two claps each; like dong-dong, dong-dong, dong-dong?"

I agreed that what I had heard was the latter expression of the time.

"Then what he has, must surely be a ship's clock," he said with a laugh. "He should be interested in the sea after all, living here, in the city by the sea and representing companies such as Sebastian's."

"It all works out rather nicely, doesn't it? By the way, old fellow, was there an inscription on the clock?"

"I only heard it Holmes. I didn't hunt it down and look at it."

"That is our loss, Watson. More attention to detail would suit you in the future."

To this remark, I made no reply. Holmes often spoke to everyone, including me, in this manner, demeaning our keenness of eye when scrutinizing a scene or situation. To my way of thinking, it is not always desirable to be so alert. His talent for detail is excellent for his pursuit and calling in life, but to feel that others should be as precise, and to remark upon it, has always left me a bit cold. For, in the long run, are we not all, to some degree, incarcerated by our own natures and given to them, not by design, but by essence? Sure enough, I may learn to sharpen my senses to the minor details of a moment, and I have to some degree, but to train myself in the aspects of minutia to the sharpened edge that Sherlock Holmes has, would require a fundamental change in me which, to my mind, would be quite impossible and in the least, dangerous to attempt. I could no more become that kind of nit picking, camel-straining person, than Holmes could become cavalier.

And it is upon this point that the foundation of our disagreement rests, although I fear that Holmes is unaware of our rift. You see, his nature will not permit him to examine, or even notice, any other aspect of abstract thought but his own. That is his jailer, and the reason why I let his remark pass.

"What is our next course of action, Holmes," I replied instead.

"Well," he began with a twinkle in his eye, "I have news."

"While you were engaging the Barrister and strolling the countryside, I revisited our client's abode in the tower. You will recall the numerous British news letters he had piled there?"

I agreed that I did.

"Well, I reread them in this better light. You see, I have often thought that we overlooked something because of the lack of illumination and time available to us that night. After meeting and finally speaking with Sebastian, this idea grew, because his demeanor, his posture, his proactive inclinations were inconsistent with someone who might spend time studying an unfortunate such as John Merrick. So, I reread those papers, and do you know what I've discovered? There is another regularity within them. Another story line, which plays itself out within the confines of those columns. It is the story of the Harrington Boatworks of Bristol, England, and its desire to mount a challenge for 'The Admiral's Chalice,' next year, off these very Newport shores."

"The Admiral's Chalice," I blustered, without too much thought.

"Yes, 'The Admiral's Chalice,'" he returned, "it is the thread that connects it all, Watson."

"You will recall that I have been studying local customs for some time while you have been busy with your domestic duties as father and grandfather. Well, in those studies, I found that, 'The Admiral's Chalice,' has taken on the characteristics, you could say the trappings of a religion, in some quarters. Especially those quarters which receive money."

"For example, Watson, are you aware that as many as seventy thousand people may fill this city on any given year when there is a challenge for the 'Chalice?' Are you also aware that the City of Newport, Rhode Island is known worldwide, not only among the racing community, but also within much of the general population, because of this race? The scope of the knowledge of this single yachting event is amazing in comparison to any other and with good reason. To this date, the Americans have yet to loose. They have held the 'Chalice' since they defeated our own Scotland, off our own shores in the first race some seventy-five years ago. They have defended the 'Chalice' twenty times since, and have never relinquished their grasp upon it. Fortunes have risen and fallen for want of this trophy, and as desperate as those who wish to wrest it from those who have it, the keepers of the 'Chalice' will stop at nothing to retain it. High stakes are at play."

"But what has this to do with Sebastian," I asked.

"He is a boat designer, Watson. Can you not remember the simplest detail?"

I had to admit that I hadn't remembered.

"It is that talent which has him involved, and I fear, that talent which has him in harms way."

Philips had just turned the corner to Clarke Street as we emerged from our quarters.

"Where are we going, Holmes," I asked.

"We are going to pay Mr. Hanson another visit," he returned. "We must get a message to Sebastian."

Why we had hired a carriage to go the four or five blocks to Hanson's workplace, I did not know. But we were there in less time than it would have taken us to walk, so I had no complaint. We reigned up in front of the bakery to find Hanson just leaving.

"Hello, Albert," Philips sang out as he saw the young man.

"Hello to you, Mr. Phillips," Hanson returned cheerily.

"Hop in," Philips said. "I'll give you a ride home while you talk with Mr. Holmes."

"Mr. Holmes," Hanson came back questioningly, until Holmes swung the door of the carriage open to reveal our presence within.

"Mr. Holmes," he repeated more steadfastly as he ducked his head and entered the brougham. "Short time, no see," he continued, good naturedly, as we pulled away from the curbstone. "And hello to you Doctor."

I returned his salutation, but Holmes pressed right to work.

"Have you heard from our friend," he began.

"I have not", was the reply.

"And your feeling is that he won't contact you?"

"I do not think that he will contact either of us, for fear of entangling me or revealing himself. I am sure that he feels that you are much too close to the police."

"I tend to agree," Holmes said thoughtfully. "But I need to see him, and he needs to see us, Albert. I am fearful for his life."

"His life Sir," Albert returned. "Who would want to harm Mr. Sebastian?"

"The same people who killed the man in the cemetery, -or sent him there to be killed."

We both gasped a bit.

"Albert, do you have any of Sebastian's papers at you residence?"

"Yes, a few, Sir."

"Good! I need to check them. Also, have you ever heard Sebastian mention the Harrington Boatworks of Bristol, England?"

"You mean Bristol, Rhode Island, don't you Sir," Albert returned.

"Bristol, Rhode Island," I repeated.

"Yes, Sir, Doctor. There's a Harrington Boatworks in Bristol, not far from the ferry landing. Mr. Sebastian has mentioned it on occasion. He had been working on a boat design with those fellows."

"Do you hear that, Watson," Holmes broke in. "It all begins to fall into place."

It was but a short ride to Hanson's rooms on Mann Avenue, near the center of the city. Here he lived on the third floor of a three story building, which had obviously been a family home at some point but was now reduced to an apartment facility. We walked the stairs and entered the abode with Philips in tow, for he was an acquaintance of our Mr. Hanson and was invited in by him.

The rooms were three in number plus toilet and were comfortable looking, if not elegant. We were offered refreshments, but declined, although I do think that Philips would have enjoyed the merest repast and seemed ready to leap at the suggestion. Holmes, though, was decidedly against any dalliance and made it clear that to his way of thinking, conditions were coming to a head, and that Sebastian's safety might be at risk.

At this pronouncement, Hanson went straight to the cupboard and retrieved a large portfolio filled with pictures of boats, marked up with calculations and dimensions, business logos and schedules, writings of various subject matter and correspondence.

To everyone's surprise but my own, Holmes took these documents and went to work straight-away on the floor, spreading out each leaf and design to study them intently, and compare them one to the other. Once he had finished arranging and rearranging the papers, they covered the floor like a carpet. It was then that he literally dove into his work, studying with glass in hand each piece of the written, printed or drawn account.

It has always amazed me just how neat Holmes can be within the confines of the disorder he creates in the occupation of his talents. For, although he had created a dispersal, which had exiled Hanson, Philips and myself to the far reaches of the perimeter of the room, with little chance of moving lest we disturb a page and ruin a clue; Holmes, on the other hand, bounded about the place like an acrobat, never touching a scrap or disrupting the symmetry of the place, although there were scant inches between the sheets. And, as was his custom, as he danced so merrily among the leaves, he uttered squeaks and grunts and hums, which indicated to no one, the condition of his affection toward each note.

Philips had witnessed a display like this once or twice before, although void of the prancing which Holmes exhibited in this particular instance, and he nodded knowingly at Hanson, who stared agape at both of us for explanation.

For my part, I raised a reassuring hand to the befuddled man in an effort to dispel his trepidation and restore confidence in him that while he was indeed witnessing the unusual in human behavior, I, in my vast knowledge of the working of this particular specimen of eccentricity, was not aghast, but rather used to it.

I was also, for my part, aware that an effort in which Holmes expended this much energy, would conclude swiftly with an explanation for all, which would hopefully help us see what Holmes saw. And Holmes, for his part, did not disappoint. With an, "Aha," so loud that it gave poor Albert a start, Holmes snatched a piece of correspondence from the floor with all the flourish of an editor screaming, "stop the presses," and vaulted to our sides.

"I have seen enough," he declared. "Hanson," he said as if he were a top sergeant giving orders, "if you would be so kind as to return these pieces to their folder and then, take this sheet to Officer Peterson of the Police Homicide Squad. Have him check this man against what he has learned of the victim at the cemetery. I am sure that with a little diligence, he will find that this is the dead man." Holmes then handed Albert a paper which was clearly some sort of correspondence received by Sebastian from the man in question.

"I then want you to take the day and do all that you can to locate Sebastian. Tell him that it is of the utmost importance that I see him this very night at my rooms. Assure him also, that he has nothing to fear, and that we are well on our way to proving his innocence. Are you able to do these things for us, Albert?"

"I'll do my best, Mr. Holmes," was the reply.

"That's all we may ask," Holmes finished.

"And, what of us," I asked, knowing full well that there must be immediate plans for the rest of us, since we weren't delivering this vital information ourselves.

"We are going to visit the Barrister, Watson."

"The Barrister," I repeated.

"Yes," he returned, "indeed! It is quite obvious that he is deeply enmeshed in this business and is no doubt aware that we have found him out."

"The Barrister," I repeated again.

"Yes, Watson, the Barrister! He has given himself away with that rather hastily concocted story about attempting to meet with Sebastian himself. It must have given him quite a turn when you appeared at his door with your questions this morning. His awkward fabrication suggests a naivety in the possibility that his part in the drama might be discovered, but I am afraid that he is no longer naive and will establish clearer alibis and employ more clever tactics, if given time to develop them. That is why we must go now, before his wheels are set in motion."

We left Hanson's apartment and proceeded directly to court. As you will remember, Rathkamp had indicated an appointment there, which concluded our interview of the morning, and Holmes was of the opinion that this appointment was no ruse.

"I would say that he was probably happy to have such a sufficient and convenient excuse to leave you in the lurch," Holmes announced as we sped down Broadway toward the Municipal Courthouse. "He lied so badly that he must have welcomed the reprieve."

Our enquiries at court resulted in our gaining the knowledge that Rathkamp had completed his business and returned to his office. It being but a few blocks to that destination, we released Philips, directing him to remain available, taking no other fares. His instructions were to grain and water his horse and meet us at our rooms within the hour.

"Are we in for a bit of a chase," he asked before we parted, his eyes gleaming with excitement.

"I do not know," Holmes replied. "It very much depends on our officer of the court, but since preparedness is the mark of success, and I always intend to be successful, we'll need you and your steed fed and at the ready."

At that he left us and we walked briskly to Rathkamp's suite. Mid afternoon had arrived and the streets were busy with commercial and pedestrian traffic. The day was warm and full of life as the citizens of Newport darted across their broad main roads in pursuit of their own devices.

"What did you find," I asked Holmes just before we scurried and traversed one of these very same roads, just ahead of a wagon carrying casks of some sort.

"I found our victim, Watson. He is one Henry McClarin of Dublin, and he designs boats."

"But what on earth has that got to do with…"

Holmes put up his hand so that I would quiet. Ahead of us, on the opposite side of the street, stood Rathkamp's office. In front of that office, on the walkway, two men were in heated discussion. Although they were just out of earshot, we could tell by their animated gestures that their exchange was not of a social nature. I, of course, recognized Rathkamp at once as the more stylish of the two; the other man resembling the mode of a laborer. Their meeting was either short in duration, or they had been at it for some time, for it ended abruptly, as we watched, with the working man walking off, after collecting a small package from the lawyer.

Holmes was intrigued by their entire display, not moving from our vantage point until the laborer was out of sight. He also turned away once when Rathkamp chanced to glance our way, blocking his view of me at the same moment.

When all was quiet, and normality had returned, we continued to Rathkamp's office and let ourselves into the outer room.

"I would speak to Mr. Rathkamp," Holmes announced to the dour secretary.

"Do you have an appointment, sir," she returned.

"No, I do not," Holmes continued quietly enough until he got to the phrase, "but I think he will want to see me. Tell him Sherlock Holmes is here."

"There is no need to shout, sir," she came back sternly. "I am afraid that Mr. Rathkamp is a very busy man and has no time today…"

The door to the inner office opened and out stepped Rathkamp with a broad smile.

"Mr. Sherlock Holmes," he began. "My, my, it is a pleasure to meet you. Won't you come in?"

As we passed into the inner office, I heard him say to the secretary, "it's all right Mildred, this should not take long," and he closed the door behind him.

"How may I help you, gentlemen," he asked as he motioned to the chairs that we did not take.

"I have but one question, sir," Holmes stated. "What was your role in the death of Henry McClarin?"

"Excuse me, sir," Rathkamp replied angrily. "What are you accusing me of? You have no right to come to my office and ask me a question like that! Get out of here!"

I have to admit that I was just as surprised at Holmes' outburst as was Rathkamp. He had given me no warning, and as we were ushered out by the now, ill tempered attorney, he neither resisted nor spoke a word of explanation. We were back at the walkway in a moment's time where I, for one, stood staring at Holmes in befuddlement.

"What was that about, Holmes," I began when no hint of an explanation seemed forthcoming.

"That, my dear fellow, is what cattlemen like to refer to as a prod. Come along. We'll wait in our rooms for the results to attend us."

We made our way back home with Sherlock Holmes stepping out at such an exaggerated pace, that although the difference in our stride is minimal; I had all I could do to keep up. This forced march did not end until we were safely inside our abode on Clarke Street where, once inside, the fervor of the moment seemed to pass. It was not until this time that I could muster the wherewithal to demand an explanation.

"Holmes," I repeated, "what was that all about?"

"I am merely trying to set things in motion, Watson," was his reply. "Sit yourself, and follow this."

I sat at the corner table, taking the note pad which I kept there.

"In the first place, Glum was to meet Sebastian. This did not happen because Rathkamp sent him to Boston. Now, Rathkamp was to meet Sebastian. This, also, did not happen, and although Rathkamp claims that he was on the scene and at the correct time, I find that difficult to believe."

"Now, we know that McClarin was on the spot during the night and that whatever transpired caused McClarin's death."

"McClarin and Sebastian know each other. Their correspondence confirms this. Sebastian was also in contact with Harrington Boatworks of both Bristol, Rhode Island

and Bristol, England. It would not surprise me in the least that McClarin is also associated with Harrington Boatworks."

"It is also fairly apparent that Rathkamp is also associated with the Boatworks as well. That clock you heard in his office confirmed it. I noticed that a plaque denoting the Harrington name was attached to that very clock."

"When we approached Rathkamp's office, he was involved in an animated conversation with a man out on the walk. Why couldn't they speak inside? Because of Rathkamp's secretary. Had this man been a client, their discussion would have been protected and they would have had nothing to say that couldn't have been said in front of witnesses. They spoke outside because they are in cahoots, needing the subject matter of their discussion to remain secret."

"It was that observance of that conversation and the corroboration of the clock, which led me to the accusation."

"He will react now, Watson. He will either flee or stand and fight, but he will react to this accusation. Mark my words, he will react, and that will be his undoing. Were he innocent, he would do nothing, knowing that time would bear him out. But this man is not innocent and therefore he will react."

"Now I suggest that we sit tight and await news from our young Mr. Hanson."

And with that he walked to the window, opened it, lit his pipe, pulled up a chair so that he might watch the comings and goings of those about us and sat down, looking much like a Siamese cat surveying his realm.

I, on the other hand, after reviewing his announcement in my mind and in my notes, began the arduous course of trying to understand what had just been explained. For, as has happened so many times before, (and I believe my audience will bear me out), the intricacies and convolutions of the mind of Sherlock Holmes are of such a complex sophistication, that even once explained, they may take hours to process into normalcy and thus fully appreciate. I find myself in this predicament frequently, and although I invariably reach the same conclusions as my mentor in this process, I find that I must constantly rehash his analysis to do so. And, so it was again that a reexamination of the facts before me was the prudent course, which I attacked with diligence.

Not that the study took too long, mind you. Once seen through and discerned chronologically, the facts fell into place like a child's puzzle, and the conclusions were as clear as spring water.

There were questions though. And, as I have often viewed my role, in part, as one who broaches all manner of inquiry in the pursuit of the truth, I began to formulate and jot these questions as much for the benefit of this manuscript as for the case itself. But, no sooner had I begun this particular task, than Holmes was up from his perch and moving toward the door.

"Philips," he said as he passed me, and he had opened the door before our chauffer could knock.

"Where are we bound," Philips exclaimed without missing a beat.

It has always struck me that many of the Americans we met during our stay in the colonies assimilated Holmes quirky, unpredictable behavior into their own and therefore generally failed to be startled by his actions, once they knew him. I, and many of my fellow Brits on the other hand, are continually being caught off guard by his little surprises, such as opening a door before it is knocked. The conclusion I have come to from these observances is, that there is a cultural difference between our peoples. The British are certainly more steadfast in their thinking and actions, whereas the Americans tend to be more flamboyant, accommodating rather than contending with change. Perhaps that is, in part, how they defeated us so many years ago. But I digress.

Holmes answer to Philips was, "to Hanson's," and we were off, down the stairs and into the carriage, clopping along the Newport streets once again.

"Shall I ask why we are returning to where we have just been," I ventured.

"Because, my dear fellow, it occurred to me as I sat upon my roost, that our young Mr. Hanson may be in some danger."

"How do you say, Holmes?"

"It is this way, Watson. If there is a conspiracy here in the matter of our Mr. McClarin, and if the conspirators now know that they are suspected, they will undoubtedly try to sever their links with the incident in question."

"Namely Hanson and Sebastian," I said, completing the thought. "But isn't Hanson still on our errand?"

"He may be," Holmes returned, "but since there are three of us, and since we know where he abides, my plan is to drop you there, in the event that he returns, and to continue on myself to search him out."

"I do not consider that he is in much danger now," he continued. "These scoundrels seem to employ the cover of darkness for their dirty work. But to be safe, we must collect our friend and put both he and Sebastian in our charge until justice is served."

As he finished these remarks, Philips reined up in front of Hanson's home to find the young man climbing his outer stair.

"Mr. Holmes," he said, "why are you here?"

"We are here for your benefit," Holmes returned. "Why would you ask such a question?"

Hanson's expression fell immediately upon hearing these words.

"What is it," Holmes asked in reaction to this change.

"Mr. Holmes," Hanson continued, "perhaps we should go inside."

Once settled in Hanson's sitting room, Holmes, Philips and I listened to Hanson's report.

"Gentlemen," he began. "Much has happened since you dropped me. First of all, I went directly to the police and although Officer Peterson was not there, I left your message at the desk."

"Then I thought I would return here to gather my thoughts and look over the evidence you have laid out, in hopes that I might find some clue as to Sebastian's whereabouts."

"Smart thinking," I put in.

"Thank you," he returned. "Except that when I got here, there was a Mr. Mathews waiting for me, or rather, I caught him leaving. He was dressed in course clothes, you know. Like a laborer or dock worker, but he was well spoken and pleasant."

"When I asked him what his business was, he said that Mr. Sherlock Holmes had sent him round."

At this point I turned to Holmes to check his expression. He did not betray the least little note of surprise. I was about to ask the obvious question, when Hanson began to speak again.

"I told him that I had delivered the message as instructed, but that I hadn't begun to search for Sebastian as yet."

"He thought for a moment and then he told me that you, Mr. Holmes, had said that if I did find Sebastian, he should meet you and Dr. Watson at the end of Narragansett Avenue, at the Cliff Walk. He said that you would be twenty paces down to the right of the end of the road. He said it wasn't safe to go to your rooms."

"What time were we to meet," Holmes asked.

"Seven-thirty," Hanson replied.

A quick click of my watch showed the time to be five-forty.

"And did you search out Sebastian," I asked.

"Watson, are we not in the same room," Holmes interrupted. "It is fairly obvious that Sebastian was here when Hanson finally made it up the stair."

We all stopped and stared at Holmes.

"There is no time for explanation," he continued. "Suffice it to say that there are pieces of the puzzle I constructed," and he pointed to the tidy mess he had made of the floor, "and some of them are missing. Pieces that Sebastian has used to fill in his own blanks, and undoubtedly arrived at the same conclusion that I have. The path is clear, once seen."

We did not stop our stare, and would not have, I fear, had Holmes not continued on to the next step.

"You passed on the information to this man, didn't you Hanson."

"I had no reason not to," He returned. "Why would anyone come to me, claiming to be your confederate, if it were not so? Who knows that we even know each other?"

"Rathkamp for one," Holmes answered. "We must have been followed somehow. Blast my incompetence!"

"These are clever people. I fear we are all in peril."

Holmes then broke off from this discourse to think for a moment and consult his time piece.

"We do have time though, and knowledge on our side. Hanson, why were you outside just now when we drove up?"

"I had just returned from the police, sir. Another unsuccessful trip, I might add. Peterson was not there."

"And earlier," Holmes continued, "Sebastian had left your rooms as soon as he heard the news, correct?"

"Yes, sir. He took those articles you mentioned and he left immediately. He did say that he would make you're appointment, though."

"Of course he did," Holmes said, drifting off in thought as he spoke. "Hanson, I want you to come with us. We will drop you off at our rooms. You'll be safe there and you'll be able to meet with the police when they arrive."

"When they arrive, sir?"

"Yes, of course, when they arrive. Peterson will surely be by as soon as he receives the information you left him and corroborates the evidence. He would not be able to stay away, even if he wanted to."

"But now, let me see," Holmes continued, "Sebastian's clothes. Did I not see some of them in this closet?"

Holmes moved swiftly across the room to the closet, which he threw open to reveal a few articles of clothing plus a long cape and the hat that Sebastian had been wearing at our first encounter. Holmes removed these two articles and closed the door.

"These will come in handy," he said as he removed the veil from the hat before plopping it on his head. "Philips, we are leaving."

Once seated in Philips' brougham, I noted the time, which was just past six p.m. We went directly to Clarke Street where we deposited Hanson, with instructions to send Peterson along for the seven-thirty meeting.

"Do not forget your Webly," Holmes admonished.

I must admit that I hadn't been carrying it and probably wouldn't have retrieved it, had he not said something. I went immediately to my room and got it.

By six-thirty-five, Holmes and I were back in Philips carriage, beginning our ride to Narragansett Avenue

Late September is a glorious time of year in New England. The days are long, but not too long. The atmosphere is warm, but not oppressive, and the nights are cool. The summer season has not lost its grasp on the land, and yet a hint of autumn injects itself here and there, with just enough sharpness to hearken up images of falling leaves of gold and red and orange. I have been many places in my life and seen many things, but looking back from my vantage point now, I realize that no more wondrous assortment of coloration exists in all of Christendom, than those adorning the trees of the most public of streets in the autumn in New England. All the worth of the world could no replicate the majesty of a single stroll down one of the common thoroughfares in any of its fair towns or cities, or country lanes for that matter. No artist could capture the grandeur of the crispness and smell of the air, and the way the breeze lends motion to the scene. These enhancements of experience would be lost in oil and canvas. Of all seasons on earth, including springtime in Paris, autumn in New England is the most exquisite.

I had not yet completed my musings when Philips reined up near the end of Narragansett Avenue. I had been lost so completely in the mood, that it wasn't until we stopped, that I realized that I had traveled to this exact spot earlier in the day, during my stroll after the interview with Rathkamp. The ocean lay ahead of us in the distance, at the base of the cliffs, of which the path that paralleled the sea was named.

"Cliff Walk," I said to myself, under my breath, as I checked my pocket watch and gave it a quick wind.

"We are a might early, aren't we Holmes?"

"We are, by design," he returned. "Since it is fairly obvious that I must explain everything, here is my thinking. This Mathews person has called for a meeting here at seven-thirty. We have every reason to believe that this meeting is intended to do Sebastian some harm. I therefore submit that the intimates of this evil intent might very easily be here early, in order to set their trap, so to speak. Our greatest ally is fore knowledge. If you have not noticed, Watson, Sebastian and I are of approximately the same height and stature, and another ally to our cause is the fact that Sebastian almost invariably keeps himself covered against the misadventures produced by innocents encountering his features. Therefore, with the help of the articles I procured from Hanson's, I intend to take Sebastian's place on the "Walk," and, with your assistance and the enforcement powers of your Webly, we shall settle with these blackguards once and for all."

With this Holmes donned the cape and hat and stepped from the carriage. It was nearly ten past seven, and evening had already begun to settle in upon our scene. Long shadows were giving way to a general gloom, as Holmes began his march to the top of Cliff Walk. Before he had left Philips and I, he gave instructions that I was to follow him as soon as he made the turn at the "Walk." His feeling was, that if the villains were lying in wait, they would be so distracted by their realization that Sebastian, (in the form of Holmes), had shown early, that they would not notice me turning the same corner a few minutes later. From the corner it would be possible for me to see all that transpired on the path and the proximity would lend me opportunity to intervene at a moments notice. Philips, also, would be able to see me from the top of the small rise in the street, with his horse and carriage at the ready, should I leave that post.

All was set in motion. Holmes made the turn as planned and I started after him. Philips held steady on the road, awaiting the outcome of our little plot. A light breeze pushed a mist up from the sea, which hit the cliff face and shot skyward, lending a chill to the air. With Holmes out of sight, I walked at an even pace toward that misty veil, confident that our plan would work and we would put an end to this nasty business. I must have touched the pocket where I kept my pistol at least three times during that one-hundred yard walk. You can never be too sure about such things.

Except for Holmes, Philips and myself, the place looked deserted. What once was a thriving thoroughfare earlier in the day, had become a place of solitude, as if the populace could sense the sinister quality of the air and refrained from venturing forth, for fear that some ill occurrence would befall them. But this did not necessarily mean that we were alone. For, although the seaward side of the "Walk," was open, except for a very short hedge, the land opposite the sea was filled with trees and bushes, brambles and rocks and all manner of places to remain watchful but unseen. The rising fog and the lowered sun also served to conceal any treacherous foe, who might seize upon an unprotected moment for detrimental acts. The wind had picked up its pace as well, as I walked those few yards, so that by the time I had reached my destination, the resonance from both sea and air had risen to a level which made me fearful that any cry of warning to Holmes, or rebuke to an attacker, would be carried off like a child's kite in such conditions.

Nonetheless, I continued on at the proper stride, not hurrying as my heart urged, until I had reached my post at the corner of the way.

There was Holmes at the appointed spot, facing the sea, but standing back a bit, so that the wind did not catch his brim and reveal him to be any other than Sebastian himself. I must say that in that light, in that place, with all the turmoil that the deterioration of the elements had set astir, I would have been hard pressed to say that it was Holmes instead of Sebastian who stood upon that precipice. And I marveled at the bravery of the man, who, with faith only in my protection, put himself in harm's way, intent only in saving another.

I drew my pistol from my pocket. If a confrontation was about to take place, any wasted time spent fumbling about might prove deadly.

The wind began to howl and I could see from my place above the waves that the storm, which was coming ashore bag and baggage, (and dropped by often on these shores), was about to make a grand entrance once again.

Time was moving on and yet nothing had happened. Sebastian, himself would be here soon, I knew it, and seeing Holmes and myself, might quicken his pace and bring him into danger. I reached for my watch once again. It must be seven-thirty by now. The time piece proved me wrong. We were early yet, and while the minute hand had made progress, its destination was still some way off. I ventured a look back toward Philips and his steed. There he was, ever vigilant, though unschooled in the perils Holmes and I had often faced. I noted to myself that I must commend him on his bravery at my earliest convenience, for he has never failed us in all we've asked of him since our arrival in Newport and seemed ever ready to take our part throughout. Stout fellow, that Philips.

I turned back to see Holmes, as I was thinking these thoughts. There he stood unmolested, looking out to sea as though he had not a care in the world, completely ignoring the growing gale.

I decided to check my fob once more, but just as I glanced down to grasp it, movement caught my eye. It was a flash of speed, the action of which happened before I had time to react. In the gloom of the storm, in the dark of the night, a figure had darted out from the underbrush at Holmes' back. It slipped right up to him from its place of concealment and before either he or I had time to counter, it pushed Holmes headlong over the hedge and over the cliff. Holmes did not even make a sound. He was there and then he was gone in a moment, with this new, smaller figure standing in his place. I must admit that for the fraction of a second, I was stunned. The figure of the man came into view as I regained my senses and that figure stood where Holmes had stood, peering over the cliff after him in a manner which told of a ruthless soul, more curious than concerned. Self once regained, it took no consideration for me to raise my Webly and fire a round at this scoundrel, whose visage was darker than the night.

But, alas, the blast of air that rocked the surf and climbed the crag also effected my shot, for as I know my aim was true, the bullet went wide of its mark, setting the villain to his heels and back, out of sight.

It took but a moment for me to find the spot where Holmes had stood before the plunge, but from that vantage point, I could see nothing, for as the cliff-face did jut out somewhat at this site, it must have hollowed just below, leaving reconnaissance of what lie beneath you, at its base, impossible.

"Holmes," I cried in desperation, knowing not whether he was alive or dead, available or swept away. No answer returned.

"Holmes," I cried again more vehemently, as I scurried too and fro along the path, looking for my companion and for any access to whatever lay beneath this ledge. I was frantic. Surely I had taken much too long to do anything that would be beneficial to my associate, if indeed he could have gained benefit from any action at all.

210

"Holmes," I cried one last time, desperate, casting off all hope of recovery in the realization that in my helplessness, I had failed my one, best friend.

"Holmes." The word escaped my mouth, not as a call, but as a plea of some sort...

"Watson."

Both name and voice familiar, my heart leapt within me at the sound of it.

"Holmes," I cried again, with determination.

"Watson," came the return. "I am here, over the cliff face."

I scrambled to the spot above where I felt Holmes' voice had come, but I could see nothing from where I stood.

"Watson," he said again, and he was close, perhaps just over the side.

I stepped beyond the small hedge, which was border to the path, and although there was no room between hedge and cliff face, I found myself leaning out, over the bluff, straining to catch a glimpse of my friend. There, below me on the shallowest of ledges, clung Sherlock Holmes, by one hand. I could see from where I stood, that the configuration of the crag was in a state where the years of battering from sea and surf had indented the face wall to the extent that an overhang reminiscent of a cave mouth had been created. It was at the top of this cave mouth that Sherlock Holmes clung for his life, some seventy-five feet above the jagged rocks below.

He had but one hand hold, and while it seemed strong and unlikely to give way, there was nowhere else for Holmes to reach and make an attempt at climbing out. He was stuck, and he was at least fifteen feet below me.

My heart began to race, but there was no time to loose. Holmes was, most assuredly strong, but he had his limits, and I felt that I had already wasted too much time in locating him. The only thought that flashed through me at that moment was, "where was Philips?"

Be that as it may, I soon became frantic. There was no more time to loose. Looking back, I, to this day, cannot grasp whether my actions were voluntary or involuntary, but before I knew it, I was over the side with as much agility as I could muster, clinging to anything that presented itself and stretching for all my worth toward the dangling detective. Even with my best effort, the gap between us was insurmountably large, and as I lingered there unable to move closer, and with no time to find another way, our eyes met and for that second our gaze disclosed the sadness in our hearts. We were about to part, and with no time to halt this farewell, I read the same sorrow in Holmes eye that I, myself felt. Not fear nor panic, no trepidation as to what lie ahead, none of that for Sherlock Holmes. His look was melancholy, more mournful of the death of our friendship than of any fate which might befall him. He was a hero and a friend 'til the end.

It was at this moment that I slipped. Not a big slip, mind you, but a slip none the less. I slid some twelve inches from my perch. It startled me though, and I remember looking up at my hand hold to see what had given.

It was then, that I fell!

And as I fell, my descent took me directly toward Holmes, sliding feet first. I cannot say whether he was as astounded as I at this turn of events, but I can say that we were about to meet again, disastrously, on our way to the abyss, if something did not alter our fortunes immediately.

I do not know whether he let go or I kicked him inadvertently, but, again, what I do know is that within a flash, his hand was no longer attached to the crag from which it had clung. Without hesitation or the knowledge of, "why," I shot out my hand to his as he fell, and were it luck or intervention, I hit his wrist with my outstretched hand and closed fast upon it. My other hand was dragging along behind it, raking the cliff face to such a measure as to break off two of my finger nails. This was, perhaps, the most desperate moment of my life and somehow, in that desperation, I found a certain strength, albeit short lived.

In the next moment we found ourselves still both alive, but in a worse circumstance than before. I had Holmes tightly around the wrist, which he reciprocated, giving us an interlocking bond. My other hand, on the other hand, now resided where his other hand had once been, on the shallowest jut of the crag.

We were doomed on the spot. I could not lift Holmes, and in his weakened condition from hanging in solitude for so long, he could not climb over me. To make matters worse, if he could have scrambled up my torso, there was still nowhere for him to ascend further. I occupied the only hand hold.

Once again we looked at each other morosely, knowing our fate and our inability to alter it.

"Let me go," Holmes said at last and he released my wrist.

"I will not," I returned sternly and with as much gumption as I could muster.

"We will die, Watson," he said as he ventured to look at the rocks which waited below.

"Then we will die together," I returned.

His head spun back toward me and our eyes met. Never before had I seen the look that lay upon his face that night. He was touched by my remark and it took him off guard; a position of which he was unfamiliar. I do believe he was about to make some clumsy utterance, but I stepped in ahead with, "we'll meet God together, arm in arm."

My hand and arms were becoming weary and I could feel them start to slip. I doubled my efforts, but to no avail as I felt the strength deserting me like hot air from a pierced balloon.

We only had a moment left, and as I searched and caught his eye one last time I said, "See you on the other side, Holmes."

And then, he was gone! Sherlock Holmes was gone. Snatched up and away like a bowler in the March wind. He was gone and out of my hand before I knew it. So vigorous was the force which catapulted him from my grasp that I swung there on the brink like the pendulum of a clock. I had no idea what to make of the situation. He had not fallen, of that much I was certain, but where had he gone and what was I to do now. Should I renew my efforts at the cliff? The release of his weight had altered my own prospects considerably. Perhaps, without the encumbrance, I could climb up and save myself.

Not wishing to waste any time, I made a lunge with my free hand and attempted to grab the cliff face but, alas, as I have stated, there were no hand holds save the one I had already secured. My next thought was to change hands on that knob, so that I might gain a few seconds of cling time before the inevitability of gravity took hold.

Whether that maneuver would have been successful or not I will never know, for in the next moment I, too, was being carried away like so many leaves before the wind.

To say that I was in shock would be understating the situation. I was blind with astonishment. One moment I was on the brink of collapse, the next, I was standing next to Holmes on the Cliff Walk path once again.

I am sure that I stammered out some sort of expletive, to which Holmes, who had obviously taken the few moments allowed him by my rescue, to regain his sanity, exclaimed, "Ta-Da," as he pointed to our deliverer.

There, standing near me, all in black, back to my front, but impossible not to recognize once he turned at Holmes proclamation, was none other than Sebastian himself. He giggled as he spun, and although his features had been devastated to the point where he always seemed to have a macabre smile, at that moment, that smile, seemed genuine, without any hint of the malevolence it usually, albeit mistakenly, projected.

He had a length of rope in his hand, which was obviously secured to some anchor out of view, and using his unique abilities, had swung out and caught us up as a trapeze artist might catch a flyer. I learned later that he had also arrived early for the appointment, and seeing what had transpired with Holmes and myself, had secured the use of the lash from his own carriage and affected our rescue.

I almost reflexively extended my hand and had every intention of pulling the man into a full embrace, for as astonished as I was at the moment, my gratitude would dictate nothing less. But, as I moved, he stepped aside and peered over my shoulder. Something had caught his eye, and noticing his distraction, both Holmes and I spun to determine the object of interest.

There, not one-hundred feet from us, at the very corner where I had kept my vigil a short time before, was the figure of a man watching our little drama as it had played out before him.

The weather conditions had not improved and with darkness now upon us, the form at the corner was unrecognizable except for his height and general stature, which were held in silhouette from a yonder street lamp that, while unseen, cast its affect upon our peeper. We, as well, must have been nearly invisible to him, for while it was apparent that his attention was directed toward us, he did not readily move when Sebastian burst past both Holmes and myself in pursuit of the man.

"Sebastian," I called after him, (for what reason I have yet to understand, for my cry only served to falter his footsteps), giving our mysterious spectator the moment he needed to fly away down the street. Sebastian, for his part, stopped and turned to me, only to realize, (apparently from the look on my face), that I had nothing of relevance to offer the situation and had thus misspoken.

"Get him," I blundered out as he, once again, took up the chase.

Holmes and myself, both startled and weak from our previous escapade, brought up the rear. Yes, but while it was true that we had been shaken by the experience, we had by no means been overthrown. We were both up to the task at hand and while we rounded the corner a few steps behind our agile friend, we were, nevertheless, in time to witness the next act in the drama.

For here is how the scene played out:

The street light, which had enabled our recognition of the silhouette moments before, now illuminated the street between ourselves and where Philips carriage stood. There, next to Phillips carriage, facing the opposite direction and therefore facing away from us, was a coach, the driver of which held poor Philips at bay with a pistol in his hand. The man, whom we had seen in silhouette, was making a mad dash for the coach, waving his arms and calling out to the man with the pistol as Sebastian closed the distance between them at every bound. Had the first man not had such a lead, I can state with all confidence that Sebastian would have overtaken him in no time at all, but since he was already half way to the coach before we had rounded the turn, his effort was doomed to fall short. This fact did not distract Sebastian though, for although both Holmes and I slowed our pace at the folly of the attempt, Sebastian kept full on, not missing a beat. The criminal also did not skip a beat, and although at one point he dared steal a glimpse over his shoulder, which would have slowed any man, the sight of Sebastian at his heels, fierce look in his eye, cape billowing behind him, made the culprit all the swifter for fear. He screamed to the coachman who, holding the gun on Philips, seemed in a quandary as to what to do.

What he did do was turn and fire a shot in the direction of Sebastian, which made everyone start, save the target of the discharge. He then hopped to his seat, gathered his reins and waved to his confederate to hurry along so that they might make their escape. The man in flight made it to the coach, and although he had but a little time to spare, he was able to jump aboard and have his man begin the gallop well in advance of Sebastian reaching the spot. Not that any of this slowed Sebastian's approach. For, even as the four-wheeler pulled off and gained a good pace, Sebastian kept on coming, full out, passing Philips and the spot where the coach had stood in full stride, without any let up at all.

Philips, for all this time, still stood on his perch with his hands raised, watching the procession pass. It was not until they all were by him, (and he had to turn somewhat to watch), that he regained his presence of mind and looked to us, where we stood as audience to it all. A moment later, he stirred up his horse and came to pick us up.

But as we waited on Philips, our attention was still set on the action further down the road. For here were our two felons, one inside the coach screaming in his fear as he saw Sebastian approach, and the other outside, on top, whipping at his horse in a frenzied attempt to extract greater effort from the beast.

For the life of me, I must admit that I have never known another man with the physical abilities of Sebastian Lockhart. Even the word, "amazing," would not do him justice. For, here, on that street, was a horse and coach, well nigh to full speed, with a man at the rear window, shrieking in panic, eyes wide with anguish and terror, relegated to sit and watch while this man of frightful appearance overtook them. With a great leap, that could only have sent shock waves through the villain within, Sebastian gained the rear bar and rail of the coach. I can not imagine the scoundrel's anxiety at the sight of that amber face, draped in black, surrounded by the oncoming storm and night, drawing closer and closer to this, his only means of escape, and then gaining it, like a seagull on a clam with nothing left to do but get inside and devour the contents.

At that moment of both triumph for Sebastian and horror for his prey, Holmes and I glanced at each other, but not with the enthusiasm that victory often shows. In fact, I was aware at once that Holmes felt the same sorrow and pity that I did, concerning the entire scene. For there was no triumph here, only fear and loathing. Sebastian was indeed the hero of the moment, but at a price perhaps too dear to pay.

We were cut short in our thoughts by the arrival of Philips, who reined up before us in anticipation of initiating our own chase. We climbed aboard, and as Philips struck his whip, we saw the coach before us, Sebastian still holding fast to the rail, vanish around the corner to a side street at full gallop.

We took up the hunt immediately. Philips horse was of a stout heart and although it had been used primarily as a walking, carriage steed in the past, with the advent of its master's acquaintance with Sherlock Holmes, he was elevated to a more vigorous role of recent times and had become stronger, if not more fleet of foot. At the sound of the whip, he readily accelerated until he was at full capacity in no time. We remained in this condition until we rounded the same corner where we had last seen the coach. But as we rounded that corner, it was apparent that our efforts at overtaking the four-wheeler would be futile, for it was not in sight, and there were now numerous avenues on our left hand side, any one of which might have been employed in either escaping us, or dislodging their unwanted passenger, or both.

Philips reined up at first, then bolted down the first left for a few steps, but as I stated, the futility of the exercise was apparent and the decision was made all around to return to the main thoroughfare and find our way home to await news.

As Philips retraced our steps back to Annandale Road, I could see the disappointment in Holmes' eyes. We had been so close to capturing these would be murderers, that to miss them was a harsh blow. Not that we were without hope. Sebastian was still at their throats and even if he weren't successful at bringing them to ground, we did now, have stronger leads and indications that others were to blame for the death of Henry McClairin in the cemetery.

I was about to remind Holmes of that very thing, as we made our turn, but before a word could be uttered, a distinct and now familiar giggle introduced itself into our somber scene. I turned to look at Holmes, who did not meet my eye, for he had turned completely around in the carriage to see if the sound had originated from behind our conveyance. A quick glance of my own part showed no one to be there, but as we both eyed each other on our way back to front, the wagon was rocked by the introduction of a large weight depositing itself in the rear seat of the vehicle. We spun round to find Sebastian sitting there.

"What on earth," I blurted at the sight of him.

He returned my exclamation with another giggle.

"What has happened," Holmes asked sternly, but not angrily. "Where have the rascals flown?"

"Up that way and around the bend," returned Sebastian, a bit resignedly, pointing in the direction we had just come from. "They are out of reach by now."

"But what has happened," I asked. "You had them so squarely in your sights."

Watson's Sampler:
The Lost Casebook of Sherlock Holmes

"That is true, Doctor," he said. "I had them, there is no doubt of it. They were mine to control as surely as I am sitting here this moment, but I could not bring myself to plague them any further. Gentlemen, I have never seen anyone so afraid in all my life. The man within the coach screamed at the sight of me, flinging himself to the furthest corner of the interior. His face was twisted and tormented beyond description and he never once looked to put up any resistance. He was consumed with dread at the very sight of me."

"Knowing that this man was subdued by his own mind, I climbed to the top of the coach to see if I could make the driver rein up. I tell you, gentlemen, we were traveling at such a break neck speed that I, myself feared for all our lives as we rounded the bend onto this road. Once on top, I could see the coachman whipping his steed for all he was worth. We were bouncing and rocking so much that I could not make headway toward him, but was forced to hold onto the rails for my life. It was then that he chanced to spin and face me, reins in one hand, pistol in the other. I was frozen to the spot, gentlemen. One pull of the trigger at such a range, even at the speed and clamor with which we found ourselves, and I was sure to be hit and probably killed instantly."

But he never pulled the trigger. When our eyes met, a start flew through him, as if he, himself had been shot. His very visage changed from one of fierce resolve to horror in that moment.

Sebastian broke off his discourse and sat there panting for a moment, gathering himself for his next statement. Our carriage kept on at a slow pace down Annandale Road toward the city center. I believe that Philips had slowed the pace in order to better hear. We had not given chase, although we now knew in which direction our foes had fled, because Holmes had held up his hand at Sebastian's pronouncement, to indicate to Philips to stay the course and continue home. We would be there soon enough.

"Are you alright, old man," I asked as a friend and a physician, seeing him in obvious distress.

"As you must be aware, I am not 'alright,' Doctor. I am a monster."

"When the driver saw me and looked me in the eye, his expression and pallor changed immediately. He dropped his pistol in the process, but I dare say that in his shock and amazement at the sight of my face, he never even knew it. It was he, now, who was frozen in his place, unable to look away or even utter a cry, for fear had consumed him. We were traveling at such a rate that all of our lives were now in danger and yet, he did not react to our circumstance, did not notice the physical danger, did not move to save us, (although he had the power to), for he was petrified. Petrified at the sight of me."

At this point Sebastian lowered his head, but anticipating our thoughts, that we would surely come to his aid with what he felt were hollow rejoinings of sympathy, he lifted his head, eyes wet with tears, and continued his narrative.

"I am afraid that I, too, held his gaze longer than I should, for I was as amazed at his countenance as he was of mine. My trance was fleeting though, for I could not bear the pain that the sight of me caused in these men."

"As it happened, we were passing under a tree limb at that moment and as it was well within my grasp, I took the opportunity and rid them of me. I am no coward, gentlemen, and so I cannot sit by idly while others, no matter how low, are terrorized.

The fact that I was, and am, the cause and origin of this terror, has no bearing on my sympathies. I watched the coachman regain control of himself and his carriage, once I was safely clear of him, or should I say, 'he, clear of me.' The rest you know."

"I dropped by at my earliest convenience," and at this statement, he giggled again.

The remainder of the carriage ride back to Clarke Street was spent in relative silence. Holmes did go into a short discourse on how this incident and the evidence he had been compiling proved conclusively that Sebastian could, in no sense, be construed to have had any premeditation in the death at the graveyard. There was nothing to worry about. His exoneration would happen as soon as Holmes had time to speak to Officer Peterson.

"That cannot happen soon enough," I put in, in an effort to alleviate the melancholy attitude surrounding us all, but it was to no avail, for as I said, we spent much of the remaining ride in silence.

Night had fallen on the city of Newport, Rhode Island, but if you have read this narrative to this point, you will know that nightfall does not necessarily mean a cessation of activity in that community. Although we had just come from the darkened serenity of a district where evening brought an end to much of the clamor of the day, as we grew nearer to the center of this minor metropolis, the bustle began anew.

Annandale Road, on which we traveled, empties out onto Bath Street, which in turn empties onto Bellevue Avenue, a major thoroughfare. Carriages, wagons, motor cars and all manner of wheeled and pedestrian traffic gather on these streets at almost any hour, for either business or leisure. Shops are often open here well into the evening and restaurants serving every savory delight yet known; ply their wares on the suspecting throng. If I have not mentioned it before, Newport, Rhode Island is the playground of the wealthy and powerful in America, and in much of that town, the evidence of the relationship with affluence is commonplace. Our way was therefore hindered, not only by the crowd, but by our singular passenger who was nervous about being seen, as people would have been, had they seen him. In other words, we were soon forced to take an alternate route home, avoiding the hubbub which the main roads generated.

Now, it wasn't so much that Sebastian, or any of us for that matter, felt that he would be recognized, because as always, he was well prepared and concealed thoroughly even though Philips carriage was open. It was the state of emotional anxiety that Sebastian now found himself, which sent us to hiding. He hid himself as never before, keeping his head down continually while sitting in the rear most corner of the seat. As we traveled on, his condition seemed to become worse to the point that by the time we arrived at Clarke Street, he would not let us look at him or speak to him, hiding his face in his hands continually.

But to put that matter aside for a moment, as I said, we arrived at Clarke Street and found a police carriage awaiting us in front of our boarding house. Sebastian groaned grievously at the sight of it, which sent Holmes into a flurry of activity. He grabbed Sebastian by the shoulders and snapped him to attention with a single shake.

"Listen, old man," he said. "We are at the beginning of the end of this nasty business. Pull yourself together and quickly. You are far too intelligent to be acting this way, and I think you know it. If life has dealt you a difficult blow, then that's the way it is. But life has not ended, sir, and as each of us in our own way must choose, each day, to stand and fight or flee, you also must make that choice. You may run off now to your life of gloom and shadows if you wish. Heaven knows, with your physical abilities, we three here would be hard pressed to stop you at any rate. But it is your mental abilities that I appeal to now."

"That you are innocent of any wrongdoing we both are aware. But being innocent is not, in itself, enough at times. At times you must proclaim your innocence and be judged nonetheless, and that time has come for you, my friend. Stand with me! Step out into the light with courage and let them see who you are. Let the chips fall, as all men must, and we will stand with you."

"Here, here," I said with conviction while Philips nodded in agreement.

You could see that Sebastian remained guarded as he looked from one of us to the other, but his jaw began to set and his shoulders squared as we waited those moments. Philips had reined up across the street from our rooms and as we prepared to depart the carriage, it was clear that while Sebastian was in no way convinced that this was the proper course of action, the courage, which he had always displayed at our every meeting, had taken control once again and directed him to do what he knew we felt was right. I extended my hand, which he took with a firm grasp, and I shook it vigorously. He was as good a man as I have known.

In our room, Peterson paced as Hanson sat ringing his hands. He stood up excitedly as we entered with Holmes in the lead.

"Peterson," Holmes began, "you have missed our rendezvous."

"Yes, and I am sorry Mr. Holmes," Peterson returned, "but we arrived here so late that we would never have made it in time. I sent the motor car along on the chance that you needed their assistance and decided to stay with Mr. Hanson here, to get further details."

"And has he been forthcoming," Holmes asked with a smile.

"As much as can be expected, Sir, but he claims, and it seems to be true, that he is nearly as in the dark as I am. Perhaps you will enlighten us."

It was then that Peterson noticed Sebastian who had entered the room last, after myself and Philips.

"Hello," he said. "Who have we here?"

"Ah," said Holmes. "Officer Peterson, let me introduce Mr. Sebastian Lockhart, also known as 'The Phantom of Farewell Street.'"

Peterson looked back and forth between Holmes and Sebastian, mouth wide with wonder. Sebastian had fumbled down his veil so that his features were obscured somewhat, and yet the amber hue of his epidermis could not be concealed fully. To my surprise, Peterson made no outward, astonished gesture at the sight of him, although his appearance was only partially hidden. As I said, he merely bobbed back and forth between the two men in wonder, not uttering a sound.

Before Peterson could regain himself, there was a knock at the door. I stepped to and opened it to find the same young, uniformed chap who had appeared at that same door at the beginning of this adventure. He stood there once again with his hat in his hand.

"Is Lieutenant Peterson within," he asked.

"What is it," Peterson broke in, pushing through.

The young officer straightened a bit. "You're needed downtown Sir," he began. "We have a man in custody, screaming that the Phantom is on a murderous spree."

"The Phantom," returned Peterson with a glance at our shrouded guest.

"Yes, sir," he continued, "they have turned themselves in. They claim that they tried to do him in this very night, but by some supernatural event, he has not only survived, but is, even now, vigorously attempting to slay them. They have turned themselves in and are seeking protective custody."

Peterson, once again, glared at Sebastian, (who had now his own wondrous bob between Holmes and Peterson), but before he had time to clamp on the irons, Holmes stepped in with a hand up.

"Perhaps we should all avail ourselves of the pleasure of the constabulary and its hospitality," he exclaimed placing each of his now outstretched hands on the shoulders of Peterson and Sebastian. "I am of a mind that we might clear up this little mess this very night."

"Will you vouch for this fellow," Peterson returned with a wary eye.

"But of course," Holmes replied with a pat on Peterson's shoulder. "At any rate, sir, it may have been the Phantom who these blokes were after, but it was I who they attacked."

To this Peterson exclaimed, "What," but Holmes only laughed as he guided the two men out of our door to the waiting carriages below.

During our short trip to the center of the Thames Street district where Police Headquarters is located, Holmes recounted our evening's exploits amid the comforts of Philips carriage. Directly upon arriving at the station, Peterson, Holmes and I went straightway to the room where the two hysterics were still chanting about monsters and ghouls in the night, to two eager uniforms whose attention they commanded all too easily.

Hanson, Philips and Sebastian had been ushered into another room by the young constable who appeared at our door, and although the post was sparsely populated due to the hour and the nature of their business, the whispers sent up at the appearance of, "The Phantom," were audible throughout. It was not until Peterson closed the door behind him, that the low impact clamor of our arrival was obstructed from our senses.

Peterson, who seemed forever to have little patience with any tomfoolery, ordered both infatuated patrolmen outside without ceremony. This gruff, businesslike, well grounded attitude quelled the animation of both felons as well, and set them on a different tact.

"We have sent for our counselor," one of the pair stated off handedly, as we took our seats around the small table set in the room for just the examination we were about to perform. Peterson removed a small note pad and pencil from his pocket as he sat.

"We'll say no more until our lawyer is present," said the same young fellow, as he scrutinized both Holmes and myself with a piercing stare.

"Oh, you won't say a word," Peterson started as he pushed back his chair he had just taken and rose, looming over the men. "Well, we'll just see about that."

"If I might, Lieutenant," Holmes broke in with as much calm as Peterson had shown agitation. "I suggest that we do just as these men have suggested and await the arrival of their advocate. His presence would be required shortly at any rate, therefore why not give all concerned every consideration afforded them by law and wait for him to come to us."

Peterson seemed almost on the verge of protest, but then with a queer look at Holmes and I, took the seat he had vacated moments before and began thumping his fingers on the table in a controlled perturbation. The prisoners had a stunned look on their faces, which Holmes returned with that famous smile as if remembering the two-hundred cases solved throughout the years.

In my years with Holmes, I have come to realize that in his own way, anticipation of victory was his most fulfilling and cherished reward. It was only in the moments when, at last, the pieces fit and the end was sure, that Holmes could honestly enjoy the fruits of his labor. (Before that moment stood the anxiety, danger and uncertainty, which often haunted both he and his clients, for as confident as he was in his own ability, he was not a prophet, and on more than one occasion, while he did indeed solve the conundrum, it was not always without a price.) And to Holmes, in the deep waters where he spent much of his professional life, any price was too costly and often too deadly to be acceptable.

On the other hand, the tediousness of day to day existence dismayed the man so, that often, even after the most vigorous and rewarding cases, I would find him some time later, in such a depressed and disheveled condition, that I would literally have to companion him twenty-four hours a day to keep him from withering away or worse yet, turning to the solution for stimulation. In many of these cases, as I have documented over the years, it was only the renewed hunt which stirred him from this funk.

And so, again, let me mention that the best time in any case was those few moments of anticipation, when Sherlock Holmes knew the answer and we all awaited the explanation. It was in these times that he displayed that knowing smile, which bemused and irritated his allies and foes alike.

It was that smile which he wore as we awaited the lawyer, who we both expected to enter at any moment. It was that smile which told me, if no one else, just how much he was enjoying himself.

The test of patience had barely begun before Rathkamp burst into the room with a flurry.

"I represent these gentlemen," he exclaimed breathlessly. "Have any charges been brought?"

"Not as yet," said Peterson. "Although they have confessed to attempted murder."

"Murder," Rathkamp repeated. "I think you must be mistaken," while giving the miscreants a forbidding stare. "I demand a few minutes with these men."

Peterson nodded after a moment's thought, and we all began to file out with Holmes appearing to take up the rear. But, before we could remove ourselves, he turned to Rathkamp and said, "It is the Chalice, is it not, my dear fellow?"

Well, you would have thought that Rathkamp had been struck by a cudgel. His mouth dropped open. His skin paled considerably, to the point where I was of a mind to extend assistance. His knees buckled somewhat, and I believe he would have fainted away had he not been standing directly by a chair, which he employed immediately.

Peterson had also witnessed this blow, having heard Holmes' remark and turned to see the reaction.

We all stood gazing at the man. Rathkamp's two charges were also in a funk, apparently as unaware of what Holmes had meant by the remark as the rest of us.

"Do we still need to retire to another room," Holmes asked of the dumbstruck solicitor.

After a silence in which we all gaped at Rathkamp and he gaped at nothing in particular, he shook his head resignedly and we all filed back to our original places within the room.

"Is there some explanation for this," Peterson asked in a manner more irritated than curious. "Well," he belched, and when no reply issued from the solicitor, we all turned as one to Holmes.

"I will tell you what I know," began Holmes, "and perhaps Mr. Rathkamp will fill in any cavities appearing along the way."

The councilor said nothing, but flashed a short glance at Holmes at the mention of his name. It was apparent that he was in shock, and still reeling from my colleague's remark, would be of little help at this juncture.

"To begin at the beginning," Holmes stated without really waiting, "we have Mr. Sebastian Lockhart, a business man and transporter of goods both up and down the coastline, with a fair reputation among those who either employ his services or try to compete with them."

Holmes, at this point, stood up and began to stroll the room as a teacher might wander the classroom while in lecture.

"What some of us might not know," and he glanced at the two wide-eyed hooligans from the cliff, "is that he is also known in these parts as, 'The Phantom of Farewell Street.'"

The two looked one to the other before returning their attention to Holmes, who continued his oration without pause.

"What may not be so clear to the rest of us, is that he also designs sailing craft," and his glance now fell upon the lawyer whose head rested in his hands in resignation.

"His appearance," continued Holmes without a hitch, "is the result of injuries sustained in an accident on board one of his own vessels off these very shores."

"But let it be known, that before those events which changed Mr. Lockhart's features and his life, he had employed his spare time in developing a new design for the formula yachts which compete for 'The Admiral's Chalice.' There is documentation of this fact in the possession of Mr. Albert Hanson, who awaits us in the outer office."

There was not a sound in the room as we listened to Holmes' oration. He had paused at this point, I assume, to let those of us not familiar with the facts catch up, as it were, and digest his pronouncements so that what followed might make sense and not just become another tidbit on this lineage of knowledge, tending to confuse rather than enlighten.

It was during this pause that Peterson made a move to speak, but Holmes held up his hand in a gesture of foreknowledge saying, "much of this intelligence has come to my attention as late as this very afternoon, sir. This is, in fact, my first opportunity to give a full explanation, and aside from sending you what I could by way of Mr. Hanson, you are the first to hear this report, albeit in a crowd. I have hidden nothing from you."

Peterson, who had raised his hand somewhat, when first he thought that he might get a word in, now lowered it slowly back to the table in front of him. His look was befuddled, but his head nodded in resigned agreement, which gave Holmes his cue to continue, as if he needed one.

"This brings us to Mr. McClarin of Dublin, Ireland."

Peterson perked up at this announcement, clearly done with his pout and back in the game.

"Henry McClarin is an Irishman, not unknown in racing circles, who had made it clear in recent years that he intended to mount a challenge for 'The Admiral's Chalice' and wrest it from America, returning it to Britain, where he felt it rightfully belonged. After all, while it did originate as a British competition, you Yanks have been less than cooperative in relinquishing your hold of the thing since you got it."

"At any rate, Henry McClarin vowed publicly, in many of the British daily sheets, to mount his attempt."

"Have I missed anything so far, Mr. Rathkamp?"

Rathkamp sat in his seat as if he were made of stone. He neither spoke nor moved to look up, as Holmes eyed him inquiringly.

"I'll take that as a no," he said, before he turned from him to the rest of us.

"Now it should be noted that the yachts in question, which race for 'The Admiral's Chalice', are known as formula boats, which means that any craft conforming to the design formula presented in the bi-laws of the race, is eligible to compete."

"Sea worthiness and speed are, or course, also considerations to be weighed by the creators of such craft and are ultimately tested in the pre-race trials, which are held in the months before the event. But a box of six sides, so long as it meets the formulaic standards set forth, would have to at least, be considered, according to 'The Admiral's Chalice' bi-laws and charter, as drawn up by the founder's of the event."

"McClarin stated on more than one occasion and in more than one publication, that it was his opinion that this formula could be manipulated into a design which would revolutionize the sport, while returning the 'Chalice' to England's shores."

"I, myself, though I am no sailor, can remember reading a detailed account of this formula in the 'London Times,' no more than eighteen months ago. I must admit that I even considered trying my hand at a design, and was confident, feeling that it was a purely mathematical exercise, that I could shed light on a way to improve England's chances. Were it not for the events which led me to your land, I may have attempted it…but I stray from the narrative."

"By the way, Lieutenant, may we have the three fellows in with us now? Knowing who 'The Phantom' is, must surely belie any fear these two might have that he is out to murder them."

At this point he turned to the two would be villains, saying, "I assure you, gentlemen, that although flamboyant, Mr. Lockhart is far from a ruffian. You have nothing to fear from his presence in the room."

The two glanced at each other once again. They looked beaten and befuddled and although their earlier actions had nearly cost me my life, I couldn't help but feel a pang of sorrow as I watched them struggle with their fear.

Peterson, on the other hand, paid no mind to any of this and had already sent for the others, before those in custody could react or attempt to dissuade him.

All three were ushered in by a rather stout patrolman and stood to one side, as if awaiting further instructions. With the exception of a slight giggle from Sebastian, which made Peterson's brow furrow and made the rascal's pop to attention, all was quiet.

"Get these men something to sit on," Peterson barked to the stout patrolman who scurried through the door to complete his assignment. "We can't have them loomin' over us."

"Is there anything else you desire Mr. Holmes," he continued, half sarcastically, half sincerely.

"No, Lieutenant," Holmes returned, apparently oblivious to the inflection. "That should do nicely."

Holmes then made a few remarks in order to bring our new guests up to date in his story, and although Philips and Hanson reacted occasionally, Sebastian remained quiet and attentive. He was as still as I had ever seen him in our brief acquaintance.

"You did submit a design to McClarin, did you not Mr. Lockhart," Holmes asked, once he had completed his recount.

"Yes," was the reply delivered without further explanation.

"The good news is," Holmes continued, "that it was accepted, and plans are yet underway to create a vessel from your design."

"The Beetle Leap," Sebastian blurted.

"I beg your pardon," returned Holmes.

"The Beetle Leap," Sebastian said again. "That's the name I had chosen for the craft. 'The Beetle Leap.' Quick as a bug, she would be," and he giggled, of course.

"Aha," returned Holmes with his own chuckle. "The Beetle Leap, extraordinary."

"Could we continue," came Peterson, his impatience showing.

"Certainly, sir," returned Holmes

"And so Mr. Lockhart sent his design to Mr. McClarin, who recognized the promise in it and made initial plans to construct the boat. He had an associate with Harrington Boatworks of Bristol, England. They had constructed sailing vessels for him in the past, so he approached them with the design. They agreed with his assessment apparently, for even as Mr. Lockhart was yet in the grasp of the disaster which befell him, Mr. McClarin was immersed in his plan to traverse the Atlantic, congratulate him in person on his winning design and announce the plan to build the boat. All was set into play. As good luck would have it, Harrington Boatworks had a subsidiary in the

States as close as Bristol, Rhode Island. As bad luck would have it, that subsidiary had legal council in the name of Mr. Rathkamp here."

"Now our Mr. Rathkamp is an interesting fellow. Aren't you Mr. Rathkamp," to which Rathkamp did not reply. "Not only does he represent these fellows," (and Holmes indicated our two would be assassins), "but he also represents Harrington Boatworks, our own Mr. Lockhart and, I would venture to suggest, certain maritime business concerns and, if I am not mistaken, a certain group from Connecticut who now grace the mantel of their Club with 'The Admiral's Chalice.'"

"Am I close, Mr. Rathkamp," Holmes queried, to no response.

"Perhaps a reminder of how readily these suppositions may be verified will aid in resolving your misgivings about coming clean in this matter."

After a moment's thought, Rathkamp bobbed his head in ascent, resignedly, one last time and started at his hands on the table.

"This was not all my doing," Rathkamp began in a low monotone, nearly inaudible. "There are forces at play here, which you may not understand."

"Fear and avarice are not so difficult to comprehend dear fellow, since we all share such frailties. I assure you," said Holmes, "that they are commonplace. It is the degree that separates us between those in control and those out of it. Criminals cannot control frailties common to us all. They are weak sir, as you are weak, and therefore dangerous!"

At this remark, Rathkamp seemed to take exception, for he slammed his hands on the table before him, as one would who has taken just about enough, and rose up, as if he were about to pounce on Holmes.

Holmes, for his part, being as quick as his wit, turned to face his foe across the span, only to have the blackguard stop in mid action and return to calm.

"Not all that out of control," Peterson piped in haughtily, as the barrister returned to his seat. He continued with, "Tell me Mr. Holmes, will we be naming any accomplices today?"

"I shall not," returned Holmes, "because I have made no investigation thereof. My concern thus, has only been for Lockhart. But, it is also possible that you will not need my assistance in that regard, for as you can see plainly, Mr. Rathkamp here is not an ignorant fellow and must surely understand the benefits attained by cooperation."

Rathkamp did not move to speak. He had returned to his acquiesced posture and remained that way 'til the end. Holmes, on the other hand, remained animated, beginning where he had left off in the story.

"Word of McClarin's arrival date and intention must surely have gotten 'round to Mr. Rathkamp from one camp or another in his course of doing business with the numerous parties concerned. Whether he understood the ramifications of an actual meeting between McClarin and Sebastian can only be speculated at this point, but if he did understand them, we have a motive. This is how I see our drama played out:

Because Rathkamp represents both Harrington Boatworks and Sebastian, he gets word of McClarin's intent and perhaps, even that he has arrived from Britain. He also receives knowledge from Mr. Glum, that Sebastian is alive and disfigured, living in the graveyard and being hailed as 'The Phantom.' He also, at that time, learns that Sebastian requests a meeting. Glum's reward for delivering this information is that he is rushed away on a fool's errand with the assurance that Mr. Rathkamp will keep the appointment. Rathkamp then sends McClarin to keep the meeting, in the graveyard, probably with some explanation that indicates that Sebastian is an eccentric, and, I would say definitely with the story of 'The Phantom of Farewell Street,' replete with fantastic images described to chill the man before he got there."

"Sebastian, of course, has no knowledge of Mr. McClarin or anything about any plot hatched by Rathkamp or any other accomplice. He thinks that he is about to meet an old friend."

"McClarin keeps the appointment and is at the assigned place at the time assigned by Rathkamp, in an unfamiliar land with his imagination set churning by the tales he has been told. Sebastian, without foreknowledge of whom he is meeting, makes one of his animated entrances and literally scares his benefactor to death, unintentionally, of course. Sebastian then flees the scene and Rathkamp, or his cronies, step in and remove the man's purse and any documents connecting him to the boat yard and the yacht plans."

"It was a well conceived arrangement on Rathkamp's part. Although he may not have been sure of the outcome, to have both men in such close proximity to each other in such a secluded spot would have made it easy to accomplish any means of foul play. Without sounding too callous, may I suggest that McClarin may have well saved Sebastian's life by expiring on the scene."

"Now, to the extent that Sebastian fled in light of these events is understandable. He is sensitive to his condition and has been trying to conceal himself from the public since he returned to this city. I would imagine that expecting to see a friend, prepared for his appearance and then encountering a stranger, who dies on the spot, probably frightened the man as much as it did the victim. The difference was, and I am sure that Dr. Watson will bear me out, that our Mr. McClarin's lifestyle and therefore his health, were not conducive to surviving the jolt."

There was a moment of silence before Rathkamp exclaimed, "I had no prior knowledge of any pre-existing condition which would have caused such a catastrophic failure within the man. He was fine and fit when he left me. I was as shocked as anyone at the outcome of that meeting."

"But it is obvious that you did not explain to McClarin about the person he was meeting," Holmes ventured.

"Well," Rathkamp continued, "there may have been a few details left out. But the intention was never there to kill the man. I want that understood Detective," and he turned to Peterson. "We never intended any harm to come to him. We only thought that if he saw who he was supposed to work with, he might reconsider, or maybe return home and let us handle this affair. That was all we were trying to do. There was no intention…"

Rathkamp broke off his speech because his voice was rising and he was beginning to repeat himself.

"There may not have been intention, but that has little to do with the outcome in the eyes of the law," Holmes interjected, "as you must well be aware."

And then to Peterson, Holmes suggested, "were I you, constable, I would be interested in consulting our guest as to who the 'we' is in his last statement. You may find the answer very interesting indeed."

Watson's Sampler:
The Lost Casebook of Sherlock Holmes

"And that ends my little dissertation. No further explanation should be necessary. Sebastian Lockhart is innocent, that is obvious."

"But then where are the plans for the racing vessel, Mr. Holmes," Hanson asked.

"The originals are at your home, Mr. Hanson," Holmes returned. "I recognized them while rummaging around, and left them out in plain view on the floor. As for the copy which McClarin brought with him from Europe; I am confident that it will turn up in Rathkamp's wall safe, behind the diploma in his office. In all that has happened recently, I am sure that he has not had a proper opportunity to dispose of it."

"And now Officer Peterson, if there is nothing further, it has been an exhausting day. With your permission, my friends and I would like to retire to our own abodes and take leave of your gracious hospitality. I can assure you that we will all be available," (and he glanced at Sebastian as he said, "we"), "should you have any further questions."

Peterson, though he looked bewildered as well as depleted, stood and bowed slightly from the waist as a sign of permission to depart.

We were conducted to our rooms by police carriage with Philips following in his brougham. When we arrived everyone, save the officers, came up for a nightcap.

It may have been true that we looked exhausted as Holmes had said, but I am confident that I speak for all when I state that we were also exhilarated with the knowledge that our ordeal was now at an end and justice had been brought to bear. I poured us all a sherry as Holmes lit his pipe and opened the very window employed by Sebastian not so long ago.

No one spoke until we each had our glasses, at which time Holmes turned to face us.

"To The Beetle Leap," he announced holding his glass high.

It took a moment for the rest of us, but Sebastian chimed right in with, "to The Beetle Leap," at which point we all followed suit, raising our glasses and downing the contents. Philips even began to clap his hands at the finale of the toast, which elicited applause all 'round.

"It is done then," Sebastian said, once we settled down, and although a slight giggle escaped him, as it had so many times before, his melancholy was apparent.

And now, surrounded by his friends in the joyous occasion of victory over evil, even now, with those who I must admit, (being one of them), had all but forgotten the shock and horror experienced by the first look at that face; he sat back down, forlorn, after toasting to his and our success.

I also must admit that I, as well as our guests, caught up as we were in the moment of triumph, failed to grasp or even recognize the gravity of the situation which now befell Sebastian. We all continued on and began to sing some silly University victory song, which was popular at the time, except for Holmes who had also taken a seat. With only three voices trolling, "Hail, hail our victory stands," it was more than evident that our lauding of ourselves was not appreciated by all and it thus tailed off quickly until we three were all silent and bewildered.

Now I fear that I have many times, either wittingly or unwittingly portrayed Sherlock Holmes to be more the calculator than the sentimentalist, more the logician than the physician, more the analyst than the sympathizer, and I stand by those descriptions. Perhaps it was the intricate series of causes and effects, which piqued his interest and set his mind to work, but as we ended our carol and looked back and forth between Sebastian and Holmes for an answer to the sullen, sober look on both of them, Holmes began to elucidate the very cause of Sebastian's moroseness.

As I look back on the events from my present vantage, I am far more understanding of the situation than I was on that night. Although almost everything that happened was about Sebastian's appearance and the profound effect it had on so many, and although he was and is forever aware of that appearance and those effects; in the events that led up to the capture of Rathkamp and his cohorts, the physical exertion, the concentration, the very necessity to focus on and use the abilities he had acquired through the tragedy that left him savaged, had actually distracted him from the grief created by that appearance. In other words, it seemed that he had almost gained relief from his misery by the more terrible events which had assailed him.

Now that things were set aright, while the rest of us celebrated the end of our distress, Sebastian would now have to revisit the haunts of his new life, which obviously were more devastating than any of the dangers he had faced recently.

Call me dimwitted if you must, but as I stated, I failed to grasp the gravity of the situation and even as Holmes explained it to us, I, as well as the others, were less than appreciative of the weight of his circumstance. Perhaps it was because we had so utterly accepted him, perhaps it was because we were, "used to him," but none of us, save Holmes, could see much of a problem.

"You have friends now," we offered. "We will never abandon you."

"You may stay with me, permanently," Hanson announced.

"And I will chauffer you anywhere, at any time, free of charge," Philips added. "So long as I am not employed by Mr. Holmes at the time, that is."

At this we all laughed, but the cloud remained for Holmes and Sebastian.

And so, that concludes the case of "The Phantom of Farewell Street," but there is more to tell.

Many things came to light in the weeks which followed the capture of the group, which the public, through the local pages had grown to know as, "the graveyard thieves."

Sebastian Lockhart had taken up Albert Hanson's generous offer and had, in fact, moved in with him, but had remained within his walls throughout the few weeks mentioned. Hanson had brought us word of the situation.

Holmes had been retained by the police, at a small stipend, to assist with the wrap-up of the "graveyard," case, as a consultant. This summarily meant that Holmes was leading the team, although it was unofficial, but as we all know, when Holmes is involved, he leads.

Within the investigation, he had uncovered that there was a relatively small band of conspirators involved, headed mainly by business people in the community of Newport who did not want "The Chalice," to leave these shores and travel abroad with any foreign group who launched a successful challenge. Their motives were purely economic.

The truth was that Harrington Boatworks had not been involved whatsoever with these people, who had gone to such great lengths to secure plans for a boat, which might or might not ever have been built. Plans, I might add, which they never laid their hands on. Plans, which remained secure within the Harrington Boatworks safe throughout the ordeal, and remained there until a warrant was issued for their release. Plans that, in fact, were made public by "The Newport Herald," as part of the story presented by that paper with the full consent of one, Mr. Sebastian Lockhart.

He had diagrammed them himself, and it changed the face of formula boat racing completely.

There was a hiatus of more than ten years in that arena, while new boats were constructed and tested worldwide, resultant in a fleet of new, sleek vessels, far superior to the old design and ready for the new era brought 'round by the change.

But now to Sebastian, a hero in his own right, left a prisoner of fear and shame within the walls of his new home.

He would not leave Hanson's rooms during the daytime. As I mentioned earlier, news reached us from Hanson himself of this self imposed exile from the public thoroughfare during daylight hours.

Depressed and moody, pacing constantly in the throws of a pent up energy, which invigorated him and yet exhausted him in his attempts to control it, he had sunk into a black hole of despair since the story broke in the papers, outlining his entire history, his terrible accident and the fact that he was "The Phantom of Farewell Street." Hanson reported that he ate and slept little, would see no one, and only seemed to come fully alive at night, when he would slip out onto the roof of their building and disappear into the murky shadows only to return just before daybreak, alive with energy, and unable to rest.

Until recently, their quarters had been besieged by those in the press who wanted interviews and photographs of the notorious phantom. But, since Hanson worked at the bakery from the early morning until the early afternoon and since Sebastian kept the doors bolted and barred against entry, no questioning had taken place. Persistence, however, won out, and because of continued complaints from other tenants and threats from the landlord that Hanson's infamous friend might get them both tossed from the place, a statement, which I, myself, composed, plus the boat design and diagram were released, finally satisfying the hounds for the moment.

This, of course, did nothing to console our Mr. Lockhart or deter him from his nightly jaunts, and as Holmes concluded his involvement with the case at hand, he turned his attention to this unfortunate.

"He will not see you Mr. Holmes," came Hanson's voice behind a locked door one early evening. "He will see no one but me, I'm afraid."

We had stopped by on the chance of speaking with the man. As a physician, upon hearing the reports from Albert, it was clear that the situation left unchecked would lead to mental as well as physical deterioration of an extent beyond reclamation. Something must be done to stop this downward trend and Holmes had a plan. Sebastian's cooperation was essential, of course, and thus Holmes knew that we must confront him face to face with our proposal. A message sent and received through Hanson would not do. We had to speak with him ourselves.

That is why I was surprised to hear Holmes comply with Sebastian's stated wish to be left alone that evening, but when I pressed the issue, he simply waved me off with his hand, stating that we would see him the next night without fail.

The next evening, after a full day where both Holmes and I visited with my family until dinner was at an end, I set out my clothing in readiness for our evenings embark to the Hanson homestead.

"I do not think that particular suit will do tonight," Holmes said as he glanced at my wardrobe. "There is moisture and a chill in the air."

"But surely, we will only be exposed temporarily," I returned, noting that the ride to Hanson's took no time at all.

"But we are not going to Hanson's," he came back. "Please wear something more suitable to the elements."

And to be sure, it was true. For once the sun had relinquished its grasp and allowed evening to take hold in full force, we set out on our way, walking briskly through the square, only to jog left at Farewell Street. It was not long before we arrived at the very cemetery where this entire adventure had begun. As we passed through the gates and headed for the Chapel, the nature of the unbeknown appointment our Sebastian had with us, became clear. Holmes intended to meet him in what Sebastian now, obviously felt was his own element.

We made our way through the graveyard to the Chapel door. A mist had apparently formed off shore, creeping by us in the night and as we walked silently past the stones which seemed more scattered than arranged this time. A slight chill crept up my spine. I attempted to mention this fact to Holmes but he shushed me directly, so that I knew that stealth was now the measure of the evening.

I am happy to report that we reached the Chapel without incident and went directly to the tower, which we ascended, gaining entrance to the belfry as we had before. The night was becoming cool, just as Holmes had suggested, and as I peered out from my vantage point, I could see the change occur as well as feel it. The haze, which remained low to the ground encroached from the south and was passing by the Chapel like a ghostly wave from the ocean, coming ashore, leaving gravestones, trees, walls and fences standing tall against its depth, while leaving the ground, the grass and the lanes submerged and out of view. Eerier still was the silence which befell the place as this apparition of moisture passed hushing both cricket and bird who, until that point, had kept us company with their occasional outbursts of chatter. It was as if nothing moved on the planet. As if this mist were the hand of God, causing stillness where it fell, bringing all of life to full attention. I have to tell you that I was shaken somewhat by all of this, for I found myself, as well as Holmes, standing motionless, like statues on a ledge, joining in with all around us in silent reverie. But, I regained my faculties quickly, not being easily awed for spending so much time in pursuit of adventure with the master detective. And so, having realized my position and now knowing that I was indeed in control of the moment, I attempted to light a cigar, thus reestablishing my mastery of myself and my environment. Like the night itself, which cannot be denied, a gentle but emphatic force closed upon the hand about to strike the match. My head spun round to find Holmes grasping that hand, his index finger to his pursed lips to signal the need for quiet. As has happened many times, his signal for quiet bewildered me. It seemed obvious from the landscape and the lack of resonance that we were quite alone and would remain in that state indefinitely. I cast a queried eye toward him, but his face was steel and his hand now moved from his lips to his front where he made another gesture to be still where I was.

I complied, of course, bowing to years of experience with this fellow whose lack of imagination has nearly always been his greatest asset in times like these. If he indicated that it was time to be still, it was. No specters had crept into his mind and panicked him. No flight of fancy had distracted him from his course. Something was afoot and he was keenly aware of it.

My thoughts were brought to an abrupt end, as suddenly on the parapet, we were in the company of another. As if he had dropped in like a spider from the sky with a web slung high in the trees, he was next to us, silently standing. I can not to this day tell you if I was even aware of him until Holmes struck a match to reveal him to us, and us to him. Both he and I jumped within ourselves at the bearing of that flame. He wheeled around to face us, and those eyes filled with fierce anger and surprised dread, flashed and met my gaze.

It was Sebastian, of course, but in many ways it was not him as well. He stared at us for a moment, and in that moment the thought crossed my mind that he might attack. But instead, he let out a low groan, which almost turned into a growl before he leapt from the stand and disappeared below us in the night.

Both Holmes and I turned to look at each other, and although Holmes is widely known as an unmoved logician, I have yet to see in him again, a countenance so full of sorrow.

Was Sebastian now lost? Had his plight and situation finally overtaken his good nature and turned him into that thing he had not been before? Would he now truly embrace and become "The Phantom of Farewell Street?"

Before either of us could speak these words, he was beside us again.

"What," he hissed with the air of a wounded animal, more dangerous than weak.

I must admit to you that my hand instinctively went to my coat pocket where I keep my Webly but, of course, I had not brought it with me. I mention this, not to indicate any intention of shooting the man, but to give the reader a better understanding of just how angry, hurt and desperate he looked. I would have put little past him in this state and had my pistol been in place, I might have drawn it as a deterrent against extremes.

Holmes, on the other hand, remained calm, regaining his composure as soon as Sebastian approached.

"I need your assistance," he said in a steady, polite manner.

"Assistance," returned the other, who was visibly disarmed by the request. "What assistance could you need from me? And why have you come at me in this manner, setting traps in the night..."

"You would not see us," Holmes answered, cutting him off before his anger intensified. "And I also wanted you to know that I am not a man who is easily denied."

You could see ferocity well up within Sebastian, but before it crested, Holmes held up his hand and said, "I must apologize. All too often my ego gets the best of me and I am indelicate. I am here because, as I said, Dr. Watson and I need your assistance in a matter of the utmost gravity. We felt that in light of our recent collaborations you might be willing to lend a hand."

While it is true that our friend's face lost little in the way of intensity during Holmes comments, I could see a flicker of curiosity play across his features, which inevitably tended to soften them.

"What matter is this," he said with a stern seriousness.

"We have a friend who has been wrongfully accused, found guilty by his accusers and is about to be sentenced to the most inhuman punishment ever conceived. Without our assistance, I am afraid he may not survive."

"And you feel that I might be of assistance somehow?"

"Yes," returned Holmes. "In fact, only you can save this man."

"What are you talking about," Sebastian replied, as he turned from us and took two steps toward the edge. "I know no one in jeopardy."

"Oh, but you do," returned Holmes. "And I think we can help him."

"Then who is he," Sebastian barked as he turned to us exasperated.

"You know quite well that it is you," Holmes answered.

"You cannot help me," Sebastian said, and you could tell, at least for the moment, that the fight had left him. He turned away from us once again, putting his hands to his face in silent dismay. Holmes words were as true as could be, for you could see in Sebastian's demeanor that he had accused, convicted and sentenced himself to this life he now led; this life without social interaction, more like an animal than a man.

"To continue this way will kill you," Holmes put forth and the words rang true. "I think I have a way out."

"You do," I asked out of nowhere, not realizing that I would speak before I actually did.

"Yes, I do," said Holmes with a smile in my direction. "Our friend Sebastian Lockhart must meet the public!"

Both Sebastian and I were dumbstruck momentarily, as this thought bounced about in our minds.

"Are you insane," Sebastian bellowed at the return of his senses.

"Not at all," Holmes replied with a smile at both of us. "You, Sebastian, have to face up to the fact that you have to face up to the public," and he giggled that eerie, high pitched giggle we had heard issue from Sebastian so many times during our adventure, but not since.

"I...I...I...cannot," the man stammered back at Holmes.

"Yes you can, and you will," was the reply he received. "You are a fighting man, Lockhart, there is no doubt of it, and haunting this cemetery is not fighting, but giving in. You do not 'give in' well. It is obvious. Even now, standing here, arguing with me, your sanity returns. You are a much saner man now than the man we met here just minutes ago."

"Here, here," I said, inadvertently again.

"You will meet the public and set your life aright! Face your enemy and make him yours. I will arrange it."

Sebastian did not speak. He looked at us with a queried eye, but you could see that, while fear presided over his thoughts, he trusted Holmes thoroughly.

I, as well, was skeptical, but the truths that Holmes had set before us were certainly well founded. Sebastian could not continue on his present course, stalking through the night for exercise and holing up in the daytime at Hanson's. He was more of a human than that. Self exile within reach of society would inevitably create catastrophe one day. The pattern of behavior must be stopped.

I struck a match and lit my cigar as a wave of calm washed over me, realizing these facts. Leaning back, I saw that this simple gesture of normalcy broke the spell of silence brought about by Holmes final remark and the three of us relaxed ourselves.

Sebastian still did not speak, but he did move to the steeple rail and sat upon it with his arms folded, gazing at us and the graveyard, in thought.

Holmes lit his pipe also, looking out upon the fog shrouded scene, quietly reviewing his own thoughts.

In that moment we were three friends enjoying the night, comfortable in our own company. As I look back to then, it seems to me that far too often we take for granted the little things in life that come so easily to most in polite society. The laughter of friends, the warmth of a fire, the communion of thoughts and wishes shared by a couple or a group, a walk in the park, or a night at the theater are all so casually accepted as common place, rather than being seen as the blessing they are. To Sebastian Lockhart, on that night, in that graveyard, the tranquility of quietly resting with two others, once strangers, now friends, was a glorious occasion, which he had not experienced in too long a time. We stayed there until dawn.

There is a game played in these United States, which has often been described as having marked similarities to Rounder's. Far be it from me to disagree with the experts, but I find little in common between the two and my fear is that this boring, uncomfortable, diminutive game may not survive the rigors of society and vanish from the landscape without ever being truly considered a sport. I must mention, however, that the name of the game is baseball and I bring it up here, within these pages so that when there is no longer any baseball in America, you will know that there once was, and that when there was baseball, it was played in a stadium.

"Cardine's Field," in the heart of an area of Newport known as "the basin," was, for all practical purposes, the first baseball stadium in America. It was large and wide, with something known as an "infield," and something known as an "outfield," and seating for hundreds in "the stands," and thousands, if you employed the park surrounded by these "stands."

It was at "Cardine's Field," that Sherlock Holmes introduced Sebastian Lockhart to the city of Newport.

The Phantom of Farewell Street

There had been an announcement in the papers naming Lockhart as the Phantom and naming Sherlock Holmes as the Master of Ceremonies at, what had only been described as a coming out party.

Lieutenant Peterson had arranged for the location, and the public was invited. The announcement stated that Holmes and I would speak and answer questions about our exploits, but the most important purpose of the meeting was to welcome Sebastian Lockhart to the community.

I must admit, it was a brilliant idea. Yes, it was a bit of a circus, but in what might seem a curious way, it was exactly what we wanted. The event was held on Saturday afternoon and it seemed as if the entire city had turned out. The newspapers had run a picture of Sebastian, which only served to fuel the fire. People from all over Aquidneck Island wanted to get a look at him.

Sebastian, for his part, was very apprehensive about the whole thing, but although he required encouragement from us all, (including my daughter and her family, who were introduced to him in an effort to ease the process), you could see his excitement at the prospect of being free from his self imposed exile from society.

"This will not be easy," Holmes reminded him often. "But I think, in your heart, you know you are up to the task."

"Be prepared," he continued. "Everyone will stare. Some will be repulsed, some will be sympathetic, but all will be curious, at least at first."

"In time you will be accepted by some but not all. Your appearance will dissuade the shallow and fearful. This is your cross to bear. You must be more patient with ignorance than most of us. You must let the foolish be foolish. As God does," he added.

"On the other hand, in many ways you will return to normalcy. For the most part, your fortune is intact and your business permits have not expired. Dr. Watson and I have arranged for you to meet with your old crew, most of whom still worked your boats while you were away. You may begin conducting business almost immediately."

"And don't forget that prize winning design. That boat still needs to be built and raced. Many builders have contacted Peterson in search of you. The fear in Newport is, that until this new class vessel is fabricated and challenges for "The Chalice," the race, the prestige and the profits gleaned from the event will be lost to the city. In many ways, you are their hope."

And so it was that the affair at Cardine's Field took place to an audience, which spilled out into the streets of the city, causing such congestion that traffic had to be rerouted to avail the basin district.

Holmes and I warmed the crowd with our tales of adventure and daring while Sebastian, in the company of my family and his friends, awaited their cue in a small tent erected for that very purpose.

And when things quieted and the time seemed right, Holmes began to tell the tale of "The Phantom of Farewell Street," which consisted of the repeated bravery and heroism of Sebastian Lockhart; how he saved his crew on the night he was disfigured and how he saved us from the ravages of a fall from Cliff Walk. In all, it was stirring tribute, both complimentary and graphic in content. The audience was reminded repeatedly that Sebastian was disfigured, and they were also reminded of the remarkable physical prowess the man seemed to have gained from the accident. But most of all, they were reminded repeatedly of his hearty and gentle nature which, although it could have been, was never diminished throughout his ordeal.

And then the moment came when Sebastian was announced. I remember it distinctly. We were standing on a small stage erected for the occasion so that we might be above the crowd somewhat. All was quiet from the audience as Holmes announced, "And here, fair people, I give you Sebastian Lockhart!"

I do not know what had been transpiring between Sebastian's small contingent of friends and himself, but at the sound of Holmes' introduction, Sebastian Lockhart literally burst forth from the tent and leapt upon the stage. Although it was raised some five feet from the ground, he leapt upon it so that he was standing, straight up, at Holmes' side when he landed. And he giggled. That same hideous, amusing, little giggle he had let out so many times before. It emerged from his throat again. Apparently his nerves had got the best of him in all the excitement of the moment and he took the stage like an acrobat completing his routine.

Reaction from the crowd was immediate. There was an audible gasp and perhaps even a shriek or two. A large space between the stage and the assemblage grew in moments as the spectators backed away, putting distance between themselves and us. Some actually attempted to flee the scene, but with so many in the confined space, there was nowhere to go.

Holmes, of course, raised his hands and asked for calm immediately. And, I should mention that many people were startled more than frightened, but it was a tumultuous scene for a moment.

But then a strange thing happened. Just as the throng seemed to catch itself and begin coming closer to the stage to get a second look. And those callous, angry individuals, who always seem to be about, began barking slogans of ridicule and jeering at Sebastian for his appearance; Peterson, of all people, took the stage and put his arm around the man.

"This is a good man," he bellowed, "and I am proud to know him."

To this day I do not know what prompted Peterson to behave as he did. He and Sebastian were not that well acquainted. Perhaps it was Holmes' words that struck a cord. Perhaps it was the police training which gave rise to the understanding of how to control a crowd. Perhaps it was just the decency of the fellow. But in any case, the effect was sure. The crowd quieted immediately. The jeering stopped and order was regained.

Then something else happened. Albert Hanson took the stage. He walked over to Sebastian and quietly stood next to him. Then without warning, Philips was up there. Then my daughter and her husband appeared with baby Anna Louise, who my daughter handed to Sebastian to hold. Then, from here and there in the crowd, Sebastian's crew members and employees, all took the stage and stood there near him quietly. Policemen also entered our cluster and stood there looking out. Others, people I did not know, who had perhaps done business with Sebastian in the past, came up, trying to get close enough to shake his hand and wish him well. All in all, the stage was soon too small for the numbers, so that I found myself and others having to step off to make way for the throng.

It was about this time that Holmes made an announcement that there would be a reception line forming to the right for anyone wishing to meet himself or Sebastian.

We were there until evening, and although many chose not to stay for whatever reason, many more did stay, making courage the master of prejudice and fear, all around.

EPILOGUE

In the weeks and months that followed, Sherlock Holmes and I saw less and less of Sebastian Lockhart. He was alive again and busier than ever. Nearly everyone who worked with him in the past eventually returned.

Rathkamp, for all the distress he had caused early on, had, in fact, managed the business dealings of Sebastian's shipping pursuits rather well. His fortunes, once regained, had actually grown. And now, Sebastian, being a minor celebrity of sorts, was finding it necessary to expand to accommodate his orders.

He was also working hard on developing his boat to contend for "The Chalice." Many local shipyards made contact, wishing to be the first to fashion the vessel based on his design. Offers poured in. It was even rumored, although never confirmed, that the Connecticut yachting firm which now held the award had ventured a proposal. But, in the end, Sebastian had gone with a local group and they were engaged in creating the next challenger.

As for Holmes and I, our lives returned to the peace we had known before the events that introduced us to, "The Phantom of Farewell Street," but with a better appreciation of how connected we all really are to one another. Even Holmes, with his scientific approach to everything, even life itself, seemed more open and available.

"We are unaware of the power of good and evil that we take with us as we go through life," he said soon after these events. "The most trivial sign or gesture might speak volumes to a person berated. We must remember at all times that everything, in effect, does change everything, making sensitivity key in every social encounter."

And, as always, Holmes was as good as his word. He became close to my daughter's family, even going so far as to rock baby Anna Louise to sleep on many occasion.

All in all we became one, big, happy family with Philips and Hanson joining our disjointed crew. And Holmes and I decided to stay on for some time in America, semi-retired observers, watching a family and a Country grow.

THE END

AFTERWARD
TO THESE STORIES

In the introduction to this book I stated not only that "truth is, in fact, at times, stranger than fiction," but that I was going to show you that it was within the introduction.

The actual truth is that I lied.

The truth is made up of verifiable facts, and facts are like tools; you use them to build a story, so that when you are finished, that story is, at least, factually true. It's verifiable and sound.

Fiction is not made up of verifiable facts and is therefore not true. Fiction is like a toy. You play with it.

Facts, therefore, equal work; fiction equals play.

This book is a work of fiction, and I mention this now, at the end, after playing, so that no one will get the mistaken idea that I believe in any of the fantastic things I have written about. I wrote about them, not because I believe that they exist, but because they are fun to write about.

I needed to make that clear. I hope I have. And I hope you have enjoyed these stories.

Watson's Sampler:
The Lost Casebook of Sherlock Holmes